The only child of a schoolteacher and a circus clown, Christina Jones has been writing all her life. As well as writing novels, Christina contributes short stories and articles to many national magazines and newspapers. Her first novel, *Going the Distance*, was chosen for WH Smith's Fresh Talent promotion, and her last, *Nothing to Lose*, was short-listed for the Thumping Good Read Award, with film and television rights sold.

After years of travelling, Christina now lives in Oxfordshire with her husband Rob and a houseful of rescued cats.

Find out more about Christina and her books by visiting her website:

www.christinajones.co.uk

Tickled Pink

Christina Jones

HarperCollins*Publishers*

HarperCollins*Publishers*
77–85 Fulham Palace Road,
Hammersmith, London W6 8JB

www.fireandwater.com

A paperback original 2002
1 3 5 7 9 8 6 4 2

A catalogue record for this book
is available from the British Library

ISBN 0 00 712686 7

Typeset in Sabon by Palimpsest Book Production Limited,
Polmont, Stirlingshire

Printed and bound in Great Britain by
Clays Ltd, St Ives plc

Tickled Pink is about friendship and laughter, loyalty and love, and is dedicated to two people who have given me more of these than anyone has a right to expect.

Pat Powell
(31.12.67 – 30.6.01)
my best friend for ever

and

Hilary Johnson
without whom none of it would have happened

The names of the major characters in this novel have been shamelessly plundered from my friends. I owe a huge debt of gratitude to the following for allowing me to pinch their nearest and dearest: Bridget Billany for Ellis; Norrie Allan for Norrie; Lesley and Phillipa Cookman for Posy; Emma Fabian for Lola and Mimi; and Lorraine Osborne for Flynn Malone.

I also want to thank Rob and Laura, Hilary Johnson, Sarah Molloy and Mags Wheeler, and all my friends – in and out of the RNA – who so tirelessly supported me with so much kindness while I was writing this book under the most difficult of circumstances.

You're all stars. I couldn't have done it without you.

Chapter One

Watching Ritchie Dalgetty marry Sonia Tozer in Steeple Fritton's parish church was absolutely the worst thing that Posy had ever done. Sitting halfway down the nave, on the bridegroom's side of the aisle, naturally, she witnessed the man who had been hers since childhood plight his troth to another.

Once the register had been signed – Posy hoped upon hope that it was in blood dripping from one of Sonia's more vital arteries – the happy couple emerged from the vestry, followed sullenly by five frightening prepubescent bridesmaids in candyfloss pink nylon.

After pausing for a victorious moment on the chancel steps, the entourage then swept back up the aisle to the heart-rending cries of Whitney Houston swearing that she would always lurve yoooouuuu.

For Posy and the churchful of guests, this came as something of a melodic relief after an interminable descant version of 'A Whiter Shade of Pale' from the First Lesser Fritton Brownies.

Posy, who had been staring hard at her dusty hassock

with its lopsided embroidery throughout the whole service, clenched her teeth even more fiercely as Ritchie and Sonia passed the end of her pew, and prayed for an omnipotent lightning strike.

None came. God, it appeared, wasn't listening to dumped fiancées.

Instead, the bells pealed their triumphal celebration and the congregation poured joyously out into the frosty January sunshine. Cameras rattled, cigarettes were lit, and women in hats and unfamiliar high heels shrieked at each other, their breath flowing out in smoky plumes. Disbelieving and totally stunned, Posy shivered in the brightness and just wanted to crawl away into the graveyard and join the slumbering incumbents beneath their mossy headstones.

Sonia, all floating swan's-down and stephanotis, beamed at everyone. Ritchie beamed at Sonia. Posy, who knew she'd never beam again, pulled her conker-brown hat low over her eyes so that no one would see if she cried.

'Lovely wedding,' Vi Bickeridge from Steeple Fritton's corner shop bellowed in Posy's ear. 'And you'd never guess she were almost six months gone, would you? Don't show at all, do she? Mind, them skinny ones usually carries well. I remember –'

Posy gave a noncommittal please-please-leave-me-alone snort, and slithered away across the frosty hummocks of the unmarked graves.

How could Ritchie have done this to her? How could he? How could he have cheated on her? How could he have created an accidental baby with the pale-eyed, adenoidal Sonia?

Although, Posy reckoned, as it was rumoured throughout Steeple Fritton that Sonia nee Tozer wore thongs and very little else, that may account for something. But how could Ritchie have married her, and then added insult to injury by allowing Posy to watch the ritual culmination of his folly?

Of course, she didn't have to be there. She shouldn't have come. Everyone told her she shouldn't have come. No one believed that she would go.

Until the last minute, she hadn't actually believed it herself.

Her entire family had been shocked rigid that she'd planned to be at the wedding. She'd never tell any of them that she'd fondly believed that Ritchie, turning from his seat in the front pew, and spotting her there in her natty burnt orange suit and the floppy brown hat, might just realize his mistake and at the eleventh hour put *The Graduate* into reverse, and cancel the whole thing.

But he hadn't. And now simpering Sonia was Mrs Dalgetty: the name Posy had scrawled on everything she'd possessed since first clapping eyes on Ritchie in the playground of Steeple Fritton Mixed Infants twenty years earlier.

Twenty years! An entire lifetime wasted! Ferociously, Posy ground the toe of her matching burnt orange boot into the shingle path. The air was thick with the fragrance of low-hanging smoke and the chill of a winter afternoon, and a clash of expensive scents which wafted and entwined and enticed, making her feel sick.

'You coming in the car with me, Glad, Rose and Tatty for the do?' Never one to take push off for an answer,

Vi Bickeridge had yomped across the graveyard to seek her out. 'They've got salmon roulette for a starter.'

There was no way on earth that Posy was going to sit at a trestle table in the village hall – the very place where she and Ritchie had exchanged their first kiss at a youth club Christmas party – and watch murderously as the new Mr and Mrs Dalgetty took the floor to the strains of 'Three Times A Lady'.

'Er, no, probably not. I've, um, got to help Mum and Dad.'

Vi Bickeridge pulled her shaggy eyebrows together in disbelief. 'They won't need you this afternoon. They're hardly rushed off their feet, are they? No one wants B&Bs no more. Not when they can have five-star country house stuff with sauna and gym and a golf course just down the road at Colworth Manor. Sunny Dene'll probably go bust afore too long.'

'Tell me something I don't know,' Posy muttered. 'It's all I ever hear at home. And why won't anyone look at me?'

The entire village population was milling around in the churchyard, trying to keep warm, and all seemed unable to meet her eyes. Even people like Rose Lusty, Glad Blissit and Tatty Spry – people she'd known all her life – seemed to find reading the headstones suddenly irresistible.

Posy gazed at the sea of familiar faces all hellbent on drinking themselves silly at the expense of someone else. How many of them, she wondered, had slipped her surreptitious glances throughout the ceremony to see how much she really minded Sonia stepping into her white satin shoes?

'They won't look at you because, although they feels

sorry for you, they all knows you shouldn't be here. Damn daft idea of yours if you asks me. Oh, bless them!' Vi Bickeridge clapped her hands in delight as a swoosh of children – most of them Tatty Spry's – in the latest Tesco designer gear started to clamber on to the crumbling catacomb of Sir Arthur Fritton, village founder and one-time Lord of the Manor. 'They soon gets bored, don't they? I wonder what sort of mum young Sonia will make, eh?'

Longing to snatch off her hat, kick off her silly high-heeled boots, and run as far from Steeple Fritton's church-yard as possible, Posy gave a sad shrug. Children . . . She and Ritchie had planned on four. Sonia and Ritchie definitely couldn't have planned on any. The thongs obviously had a lot to answer for.

The protracted photographic session seemed to be coming to an end just before everyone succumbed to frostbite. Having twice managed to avoid the photo-grapher's urging that she should join in on the 'friends of the happy couple' set piece, Posy watched as everyone surged towards the gates.

'Come on!' Vi Bickeridge had got her second wind. 'Don't want to miss the confetti throwing, do we?'

Unable to shake off the manacle grip of someone who had spent the last forty years unscrewing the tops from recalcitrant Kilner jars in the corner shop, Posy found herself amongst a crush of overexcited villagers all clustered round the white Mercedes.

'Why, in God's name, do Ritchie and Sonia need a car to drive them the couple of hundred yards through the village to the reception?'

'Because,' Vi Bickeridge hissed from the side of her

mouth as she ferreted in her handbag for her cut-price confetti, 'they're not having their do in the village hall. They've booked the banqueting hall at Colworth Manor, with the ballroom for afters.'

Colworth Manor? Posy sighed angrily. Why was she surprised? Why should she even care? When she had planned her wedding to Ritchie, here at this church on such a glorious winter's day, she'd imagined that they'd walk to the village hall, all country-simple, followed by the congregation in a sort of rustic Thomas Hardy configuration.

She'd be carrying a tumbled sheaf of holly and ivy, and have winter roses in her hair. Ritchie would be wearing an artistically crumpled linen suit with a freshly picked sprig of mistletoe in the buttonhole, and the tiny brides-maids would be skipping along in seasonal dresses of crimson and green . . .

She stared into the dark and flower-filled recesses of the Mercedes, her eyes drawn helplessly towards the happy couple like a Paul McKenna victim. Ritchie was grinning inanely at no one, still starchily unrecognizable in top hat and tails, while Sonia had the victorious bared-teeth grin of brides the world over.

Posy felt the knot of pain rise from under her ribs and hover somewhere in her throat. At any moment she'd burst into tears and ruin the whole cool 'I don't give a damn' façade.

She blinked and swallowed, and at that moment Ritchie turned his head and looked at her for the first time. His eyes, deeper blue now in the darkness of the limousine, met hers and asked a million questions. Feeling the shiver of pain and revulsion and – sod it, yes

– badly timed but unmistakable stirring attraction, Posy jerked her head away just as a shower of confetti rained down on her, mercifully blurring the awful vision.

Spitting out bits of pastel tissue paper, Posy freed herself from Vi Bickeridge's grasp at last and sprinted away from the church. Hurling her hat in a cartwheel of pique into the nearest field and longing to do the same with the boots and the stupid clingy suit, she didn't stop running until she'd reached the crossroads which dissected Steeple Fritton's two commons.

The village dozed drowsily, silently, snugly, beneath the weak January sun. For once, the white lanes were deserted, the cottage windows closed and soundless. Everyone was joining in the celebrations. Everyone except Vi Bickeridge's Clive who'd been ordered to keep the store open for the sale of headache tablets and Alka Seltzer, and Posy's own parents who had never shut up shop even on Christmas Day. Just in case.

Her mum and dad and Dom, her younger brother, had been uniformly outraged on her behalf when Ritchie's duplicity had been discovered. It had only added to their incredulity when she'd told them she was going to the wedding. Her best friends in the village, Amanda and Nikki, had told her she was barking.

Not knowing her reasons, and loudly voicing fears that she'd interrupt the service at the 'does anyone here know of any reason why . . .', they'd all advised her not to go within a mile of the event. And of course, Posy thought, sinking down on the bench by the war memorial, they'd been right.

Now she'd have to live the rest of her life in Steeple Fritton, with her Ritchie, who she sadly realized she'd love forever, and the bug-eyed Sonia happily ensconced in one of the Bunny Burrow starter homes. She'd have to bump into them at every claustrophobic village occasion, and probably even be expected – within weeks – to coo at the bat-eared, cloven-hoofed baby in its tartan Mothercare sling.

No, she bloody wouldn't! She stood up angrily, shivering, brushing bits of grit from the seat of her girlie tight skirt. Steeple Fritton wasn't big enough for her and damn Sonia nee Tozer. One of them was going to have to leave. And quickly.

It took less than five minutes to stomp the distance between the war memorial and Sunny Dene. Posy paused for a moment and gazed at the sprawling three-storey, much-built-on cottage with pure pleasure. Overgrown with ivy, jostled by flowers in the summer and shaded by a horse chestnut tree, it was straight from the front of a chocolate box. The back garden, of course, was straight from the front of a Hornby Double O catalogue, given over as it was in its entirety to her dad's model railway layout.

Sunny Dene may be odd, but it was the only home she'd known – and now, because of Sonia Tozer and her thongs, she'd have to leave it for ever.

Posy scrunched up the drive and thundered through the open door beside the faded lettering that told the world that Norrie and Dilys Nightingale offered a home-from-home welcome, comfy beds and a full English breakfast. Dinner optional. Rates on application.

The dogs, Trevor and Kenneth, loped joyously towards her, their claws scrabbling on the flagstones.

'Oh, why can't men be more like dogs.' Posy breathed

in the warmth of home and fondled their silky heads. She smiled as they both attempted to chew the toes of her orange boots. 'You know exactly where you are with dogs.'

Clattering across the spotless flagged hallway with its 1930s furniture and huge vases of mop-headed chrysan-themums and with Trevor and Kenneth dancing attend-ance, she pushed open the kitchen door.

'Is it all over? Oh, shit, Pose, you look awful. Do you want to talk about it?' Dom, her eighteen-year-old brother, was sitting at the kitchen table, and peered short-sightedly up from the intricate innards of a 1950s Hornby locomotive. It was really difficult to tell where the miniature railway engine ended and Dom started. For something so tiny, the oil and grease were all-encompassing. 'Shall I get you a coffee?'

'Yes. Cheers. No. Yes. Thanks.' Posy kicked off the boots. Trevor and Kenneth immediately dragged them under the table. 'Are Mum and Dad around?'

'Taking the opportunity to snooze by the fire as the village has turned into the *Marie Celeste*,' Dom put his specs back on, poured black coffee into a Tweenies mug and added several spoonfuls of sugar. 'Shall I shout for them?'

Posy shook her head. 'No. Not yet. In fact, not at all. I don't want an inquest.' The coffee was hot and strong and burned her tongue. She liked it. It resited the rawness away from her heart.

'Was it really scabby?' Dom picked up a pair of tweezers.

'Very. And don't say I told you so – I know I shouldn't have gone.'

Dom disappeared into the mechanical entrails again, using a magnifying glass to carry out the repair with surgical precision. 'No, you shouldn't. Not unless you were going to black both their eyes just before the photographs.'

'I wouldn't have been able to reach. They're both descended from giraffes.'

And that was another thing that was so galling: they'd looked so right together. Ritchie and Sonia: tall and elegant. Posy gritted her teeth in mute anguish against the grainy rim of the mug. She, being not a lot over five-foot-four, had always bobbed along beside Ritchie like a Yorkshire terrier frantically trying to match strides with a greyhound. Not only had she been saddled with the name of a Noel Streatfeild heroine, but with her cloud of dark curls and bird-delicate frame, she actually looked like one.

Which was pretty appalling for someone whose only other life ambition, apart from becoming Mrs Ritchie Dalgetty, had been to become the motorcycling champion of the world.

'I'm going to leave.'

Dom's eyes widened. 'Leave? Leave where?'

'Here.'

'Home, you mean? The village? Sunny Dene?'

'All of them, yes. I should have done it months ago. When, well, you know . . .'

Dom nodded kindly. He knew. The whole village knew. 'But where will you go? Down to Auntie Cath's for a while, or something?'

'Miles away. Forever. This isn't something that can be sorted by me spending a couple of weeks with various

10

relatives. This is crunch time. I've got to do something on my own.'

'But the business. The B&B . . . I mean, you can't do anything else, can you?'

Posy paused on the coffee dregs. No, she couldn't, but it was pretty galling to be told so. Especially now. She could make a bed to her mother's exacting standards in three minutes flat; she could cook and serve a dozen fried breakfasts in her sleep; and if they were going to get into listing life-skills, she could also ride a motorbike, strip it down and fine-tune it with the best of them, and even shared some of her father's and Dom's knowledge on the repair and upkeep of all things steam-driven.

But she couldn't do anything else.

'I'll easily find another hotel job, and that'll solve the accommodation problem, and if I go somewhere huge, like a city or something, there'll be loads of choices.'

'Think it over,' Dom perched on the edge of the kitchen table. 'Don't do anything hasty. You've never lived anywhere else. You'd have no friends, no one who knows you –'

'Exactly,' Posy slammed the empty mug on to the table making bits of the Hornby jump in alarm. 'No one to keep asking me if I'm okay, or peering at me to see if I mind, or desperate to tell me the minute Sonia goes into labour or –'

'Point taken. Don't shout. So, what are you going to do? Look down the sits vac? Stick a pin in the map and send away for hotel details?'

'I'm going to pack. Now. And say goodbye to Mum and Dad and then just go.'

'Jesus Christ!' Dom slid from the table. 'You can't just ride off into the sunset!'

'Watch me,' Posy said darkly, knocking over the greater part of a dismembered layout of Crewe Station circa 1942. 'Just bloody watch me.'

Chapter Two

Running away from home wasn't as easy as all that, of course.

Having no transport other than a BMW 1100 touring motorcycle – an ex-motorway patrolling beast once owned by the local constabulary, bought by Posy at auction, and immediately re-sprayed peacock blue and sugar pink – taking all her worldly possessions was proving to be a non-starter. She gazed around her tiny bedroom and wondered again just what she should leave behind.

The photographs of Ritchie had long gone, ritually incinerated around the time that Sonia had announced her pregnancy to a stunned Steeple Fritton; her wardrobe consisted solely of jeans and vests and Dom's cast-off jumpers; her bookcase was a shrine to Carl Fogarty, Joey Dunlop and Barry Sheene; her make-up bag was far slimmer than her mother's.

There was still far too much to cram into two panniers and a top box.

Trevor and Kenneth, sitting side by side on her bed,

watching every move with worried brown eyes, thumped their tails disconsolately. Posy tried not to look at them. Leaving Steeple Fritton and all her family and friends would be bad enough – a life without Trevor and Kenneth was practically unthinkable.

'Dom's just told me!' Dilys Nightingale, plump and brightly-coloured like a beach ball, hurled open Posy's bedroom door without her customary knock. 'You're not serious, are you?'

Posy paused in rolling up her favourite pair of Levis. 'Deadly. And Dom shouldn't have said anything.'

Dilys pursed glossy tangerine lips. 'He's worried. He said you weren't going to Auntie Cath's.'

Everyone in the Nightingale family hightailed it to Auntie Cath's in times of strife.

'I'm not. I'm going to, to, oh . . .' Posy screwed her eyes shut. Where in the world was a suitable place to be running away to? Not London. Steeple Fritton to London in one hit would be far too much of a culture shock. No one would believe her. She opened her eyes again. 'Swindon.'

'Swindon? Why on earth would you want to go to Swindon?'

Posy, who had clutched the town out of the air, really didn't have a clue. 'Oh, well, because it's developing quickly, so there should be plenty of work and hotels and guest houses and things . . . And because it's almost a city, so I'll be anonymous. And because it's not that far away from here, so that you can visit and –'

She stopped. Even to her, the reasons sounded pretty pathetic.

Dilys blinked greengage eyelids and nodded gently.

'Yes, well, why don't you sleep on it, love? You'll probably feel differently in the morning. Sometimes it's braver to stay put than to run away.'

'I'm not brave and I'm not running away.' Posy squeezed a multicoloured stripy jumper into a tight ball. 'I'm getting a new life. And sleeping on it won't help. I haven't slept for months. I'm going. Tonight. Because if I don't, then I probably never will and I'll always be unhappy . . .'

'But *Swindon*?'

Deliberately ignoring her mother's anxious face, Posy dithered for a second over a navy blue sweater with a lot of unravelled sleeve, then discarded it. Why not Swindon? Swindon was less than a hundred miles north-west of Steeple Fritton as the crow flew – and probably only an hour away if she and the BMW took the motorway route. Why not Swindon? Why not anywhere that didn't have memories of Ritchie's infidelity and her broken heart imprinted on every corner?

'Because I'm bound to find a job and . . . and no one there will look at me and think I'm a fool.'

Dilys Nightingale gathered Posy in her arms as Trevor and Kenneth tried to muscle in on the act. 'I do understand why you want to go, but it's going to be a whole lot different out there on your own. You've always lived at Sunny Dene, in the village, where you know everyone –'

'Which is exactly what Dom said and exactly why I have to go.' Posy sniffed into her mother's shoulder. The blouse was rainbow striped and smelled of familiar things like cooking and miniature railway engine oil. 'I'll be okay. I've got enough money to see me through for a

15

month at least. And, and if I can't find a job or anything within that time then I'll come back, but at least I'll have tried, won't I?'

Dilys held her at arm's length. 'We'll miss you though. Especially with Dom going back to university in a couple of weeks. The place will be so empty. Both of you gone at the same time and so soon after Christmas.'

Posy groaned at the threat of maternal emotional blackmail. 'I'll miss you, too. But I'm twenty-five and I haven't got a life any more.'

'Yes you have,' Dilys said fiercely. 'Of course you have. Your life's here. There's more to life than Ritchie Dalgetty.'

'Not to mine there isn't.'

'Oh, Posy . . .' Dilys blinked the greengage lids furiously. 'But you really don't have to go immediately. They, er, Ritchie and Sonia, they'll be away on their honeymoon for a fortnight.'

'*My* honeymoon.' Posy felt the tears prickle in her nose and sniffed them back. '*Our* honeymoon. Ritchie and I had . . . had . . . oh, you know, we had, Mum. Planned it. Always. Two weeks in Paris! Sonia shouldn't be going to damn Paris!'

'Hopefully she'll drop off the top of the Eiffel Tower on the first night,' Dilys said vigorously. 'And that treacherous bastard with her. But at least reconsider leaving tonight. It's already dark. You won't be able to find anywhere to stay –'

'There'll be hotels, like I told Dom,' Posy said with more conviction than she felt. 'And guest houses and millions of places all desperate for my expertise. It'll be fine.'

Dilys gave her the sort of look that mothers always give when they're sure it'll be anything but fine. 'And it'll be even finer tomorrow morning. Everything looks better in daylight. If you stay tonight I'll cook something special.'

Posy sighed. Her mother's culinary something specials would make angels weep. It'd probably be the last decent meal she'd have for months. It was an unfair bribe. 'Okay, you win. But I'll still be leaving Steeple Fritton at the crack of dawn tomorrow.'

Trevor and Kenneth buried their noses in their paws and howled.

And she had. At first light, Trevor and Kenneth had slunk into the conservatory at the sight of all the luggage and had refused to speak to her at all. Her parents and Dom had managed to speak, but made it plain by their woebegone expressions that she was doing The Wrong Thing. Her best friends, Amanda and Nikki, from whom she'd never been separated since starting infants school, wept, and even Vi Bickeridge, who had turned up out of the blue for the departure, told her helpfully that she was off on a fool's errand.

Ignoring them all, Posy had roared away from Sunny Dene and Steeple Fritton and everything she loved and knew she'd never be happy again.

Now, almost two hours later, on a dark and dreary January Sunday morning, sitting astride the BMW motorcycle in the car park of a service station on the westbound M4, Posy took stock. Steeple Fritton was behind her and Swindon awaited, and as long as she didn't think about Ritchie and Sonia, she'd be fine.

Irritatingly, somewhere across the constant six-lane thrum of traffic, church bells were ringing. As church bells would be forever synonymous with weddings, and weddings with treachery and deceit, she closed both her mind and her ears. Weddings were to be no-go areas in her new life. She'd never marry now. She'd probably become some aged crone, still taking the *Motor Cycle News* in her nineties, wearing leathers on her withered legs and boring people rigid with details of how to differentiate between Hornbys and Bachmann Branch Lines.

Fortified by The Tasty Bite's mega-trukka-breakfast and three cups of coffee, Posy clutched her crash helmet beneath one arm, ignored the bells, and studied the map. It seemed pretty straightforward. If she left the motorway at Junction 15, Swindon was impossible to miss. There was then nothing between her and the new life she craved but a short stretch of main road.

Well, nothing but the little ring of roundabouts, looking like an amber necklace on the map, which might prove a bit tricky, but she was sure she could cope with them when the time came.

Kick-starting the BMW into life, she tucked her curls into her crash helmet, ignoring the lusty shouts from a group of lorry drivers who had just ambled out of The Tasty Bite. As she swooped towards the slip road, Posy wondered for the umpteenth time why a smallish woman in black leather on a biggish bike, always seemed to bring out the worst in men.

Half an hour later she had more than a few sexist remarks to worry about. The map's little amber necklace of roundabouts, so pretty on Ordnance Survey, now had her totally foxed.

18

She'd never seen so many mini-roundabouts in one place. And each time she'd circumnavigated half a dozen of them, another clutch appeared. Giddily, she was pretty sure that she and the BMW had done the same set at least three times.

Flicking up a gear, Posy indicated left for the ninth time, and roared away from the circular confusion towards a straight bit of road. It had houses, and a sort of dual carriageway, and didn't look like any of the other bits of road she'd already covered. Feeling sure that this way must eventually lead to Swindon's town centre, Posy pushed on. And on. And on.

'Bloody hell!' She mumbled the curse into the folds of her insulating scarf. The houses and the dual carriageway had petered out with no warning. Now all she was left with was a lot of undulating green hills to either side, a single-track road ahead, and the sprawl of Swindon vanishing behind her in the wing mirrors.

Knowing that she'd have to find somewhere to turn round and try again, she slowed down to the annoyance of a line of traffic behind her. The BMW, being chunky, was too wide for the following cars to overtake safely, and the road too narrow for her to turn. Posy accelerated, hoping that a handy farm track would appear to her left. It didn't. Instead, the road grew more rural, the skeletal trees more dense, and the tantalizing back view glimpse of Swindon had disappeared completely.

However, there was faint hope on the horizon: a rickety signpost indicated that there was a turn-off a little way ahead on the left-hand side. Indicating, loving as always the thrust of power, Posy prepared to glide the BMW into the turning and retrace her steps.

19

Instantly, almost before it happened, Posy was aware of something not being quite right with the bike. As she nosed into the side road the acceleration dropped, she could feel the loss of power, and knew the motorbike was going to falter to a halt. With one gentle apologetic splutter, it did.

'Sod, damn, sod.'

A blocked carburettor was all she needed.

Posy swung her leg across the saddle, and heaved the BMW on to its stand. It was her own fault. She'd filled up with petrol after The Tasty Bite's breakfast, and should have run through all the other checks then instead of trying not to listen to the church bells and daydreaming. Snatching off her helmet, and removing her gloves and scarf, she scrambled for the tool roll. Casting aside her entire wardrobe, and various other paraphernalia of her previous existence, and dumping the whole lot on the scrubby roadside verge, she selected a suitable spanner.

Clearing the carb was a routine task, if messy, and one she'd done plenty of times before. And because of Sod's Law, usually in far less pleasant conditions than these – at least it wasn't dark, or raining, or icy, or on a busy road. Chucking her jacket on to the top box, she yanked up the sleeves of her sweater and went in for the kill.

Posy had almost completed the job when she realized she was being watched. Knowing it would be someone filled to the brim with testosterone, bursting to tell her exactly how it should be done, she didn't even bother to look up.

'I've managed, thank you. It may not be the way you'd do it, but then you're not –'

She stopped. There was a lot of heavy breathing. Oh,

great. Miles from anywhere and she'd met up with the local pervert out for his Sunday stroll. Clutching the largest spanner as a handy weapon, she took a deep breath and turned her head.

A pair of liquid brown eyes stared inquisitively at her. A pink tongue lolled over liver-freckled jowls. Muddy paws were planted four-square on the verge while a plumy tail wagged happily. Posy looked at the dog and wanted to cry. She'd never see Trevor and Kenneth again . . .

Damn Ritchie to hell. She scrubbed her fists into her eyes then remembered the oil and grease and stopped. Damn Ritchie and the whey-faced Sonia to eternal bloody hellfire! She snorted angrily. It was better to blame Ritchie and Sonia for this sudden flood of emotion. It was their fault after all.

She wasn't homesick! Homesick? At her age? Other women had left home years earlier: other women had sailed single-handed round the world, or backpacked across Asia, or, or – well, hundreds of brave solo things. Other women of her age didn't suddenly want to burst into tears because they were missing their parents and their brother and their dogs and the cosiness and familiarity of Steeple Fritton.

The dog, possibly a terrier crossed with something improbably large and shaggy, licked her nose sympathetically which made Posy even more emotional.

'She won't hurt you! She's friendly!' An elderly man in a beige anorak was powering across the scrubby grass towards her. 'Sit, Persephone!'

The dog, looking cheerfully over its shoulder at its owner, sat.

Posy sniffed. 'Persephone?'

'The wife's idea. No children, you know. Couldn't. A bit of a baby-substitute thing. Loves mythology. Had to be Persephone. Didn't work so well for her with Fido or Rover. Had Medusa and Circe previously.' He coughed. 'And that's probably far more than you need to know about it.'

'Ours are called Trevor and Kenneth, after news-readers. Maybe all dog owners are slightly doolally.' Posy managed a wobbly smile as she stood up and Persephone snuffled at the crash helmet, gloves and jacket in delight, inspecting everything as Posy repacked the tool roll.

'Very possibly.' Persephone's owner shuffled his feet. 'Where's your young man, then?'

'Uh?' Posy blinked.

She was pretty sure that Persephone's owner didn't want to know the truth. Well, neither did she. Probably somewhere in the clutches of Sonia nee Tozer perform-ing amazingly athletic sexual manoeuvres as we speak, wasn't something you'd share with a total stranger.

'Which young man?'

'The driver of the motorcycle.'

'That's me.' Posy fastened the Velcro on the tool roll.

'Really? Do you mean to say that a little thing like you . . . ?'

Posy sighed. 'It's a very easy bike to handle once you're used to it. Heavy but manoeuvrable. Size, in this case, doesn't matter.'

'Ah, right. Good Lord. And all fixed now, are you? Can't say I'd have been much help. A complete mystery to me, mechanics. The wife deals with that sort of thing.'

'I'm fine, thanks.' Posy locked the pannier, then wiped her oily hands on a piece of rag. 'If a bit messy. It's a routine job and better done here than on the main road. However, I have got one problem.'

'Oh, yes?' Sparse eyebrows raised towards a receding hairline.

'I've lost Swindon.'

'There's a lot of people whose life's ambition is to lose Swindon, my dear.'

Posy didn't laugh. It was no laughing matter. 'I wondered if you could give me some directions that don't involve that roundabout system.'

Persephone's owner sucked his gums, then let out a little whistle. 'You've got me there. Not one of my fortes, directions. The wife does the driving, you see. Them roundabouts can be a bit of a mystery for the unwary, though.'

'So I gathered. But there must be some way round them.'

'Tell you what, I live just along the road here, only a few minutes' walk. The wife will be sure to know of some short cut and you can wash your hands at the same time. No, leave the motorcycle. It'll be quite safe. We don't get a lot of passing traffic down here.'

Making sure that everything that was lockable had been, and carrying her leather jacket, crash helmet and gloves, Posy fell into step with the dog and her owner. The road flowed through the scrubby grassland like a meandering stream – just like home.

Persephone suddenly bounded ahead, disappeared through open double gates and scrunched away along a curving shingle drive.

'Here we are,' Posy's rescuer said happily. 'This is us.'

'Oh, it's lovely! It's almost like my, er, my parents' place . . .' She suddenly felt desperately homesick again and swallowed the lump in her throat. It was far, far too soon in her bid for independence to be feeling like this. 'Are you sure your wife won't mind me barging in?'

'I won't mind at all.' The front door had been opened by an elderly woman with a mass of permed grey curls. She gathered Persephone to her with much cooing, then raised her head and looked at Posy with concern. 'Have you come a cropper or something?'

'No, nothing like that. I'm fine. My motorbike broke down. I'm actually looking for Swindon and I got lost up the road. The roundabouts threw me a bit.'

'Ah, they're good at that.' The woman extended her hand, ferreting it in under the leather jacket and crash helmet to find Posy's. 'Come along in and get cleaned up, oh, and warm. Your hands are frozen.'

'Thank you. Your husband said you'd probably be able to give me directions, a short cut to Swindon?'

The woman nodded. 'Can do. Will do. Come along in and have a cup of tea while I scribble something down. The Sunday roast is well under way, so there's plenty of time for a cuppa. You pop through here into the kitchen to clean up, and I'll put the kettle on.'

Posy did as she was told. The scent of roasting lamb and rosemary swirled round her, making her more violently homesick than ever. At about this time the kitchen at Sunny Dene would be smelling much the same, as

24

her mother prepared lunch for her dad and Dom and anyone else who happened to drop by. Any B&Bers who were staying at Sunny Dene on the Sabbath were always assured of a full roast.

She swallowed again and ran water into the sink. Persephone watched her carefully as she tried not to get grease all over the draining board. Dilys always had a fit if the draining board at Sunny Dene showed even the faintest trace of motorbike or railway engine.

Posy's hostess turned from filling a cavernous teapot. 'Won't be a sec. Like to leave it to brew. Can't be doing with tea bags. You just have a cuppa while I draw you a map, then you can be on your way. Though why anyone'd want to go to Swindon if they didn't have to, I have no idea. Do you have to go there? For work or something?'

Posy leaned her elbows on the scrubbed wooden draining board, letting the suds slither up her arms, and shook her head. 'No, well, not really. But I am looking for a job and somewhere to live and Swindon seemed like a good idea. At least, it did yesterday.'

The woman hauled a massive brown teapot on to the table and unhooked a couple of flowery cups and saucers. Having thrown biscuits on to the tiled floor for Persephone, she pulled out two chairs. 'Why don't you sit down here and tell me all about it . . .'

And that was how it happened really, Posy thought, as a couple of hours later, and after a Sunday roast that had been almost as perfect as her mother's, she and the BMW roared back towards Steeple Fritton.

Swindon's magic roundabouts had changed her life.

Getting lost and feeling homesick and meeting Persephone and her owners and well, everything, had convinced her that running away was possibly not the brightest idea she'd ever had. That and the fact that there was apparently a huge employment crisis in Swindon.

According to Persephone's owner, all the telecom and internet companies had taken a proper pasting in the global trading downturn, and there were now fifty applicants for any one vacancy. Posy had also gathered that hotel live-in posts were like gold dust with year-long waiting lists; shop jobs, ditto.

Neither would she be able, it appeared, at the grand old age of twenty-five, to compete with the influx of pert seventeen-year-olds made redundant by the call-centres, all of whom understood the words on the latest Slipknot album and were prepared to flash their navel rings and work for less than the minimum wage.

'If I was you,' Persephone's owner had advised after hearing the whole sorry tale, 'I'd go home and hold your head high. Cock a snook at your ex and his new wife and show the whole damn world that you don't give a fig.'

'Yes, but I do.'

'Of course you do, but they don't have to know that do they? Now, if they comes back from their honeymoon and find that you've skedaddled, they'll know that you care like mad and they'll have won. It's your home, dear, and your B&B is your livelihood and the village is your life. I'd go back there, make a success of whatever it is you want to do, and make them do the grovelling. You shouldn't run away. After all, there's more to life than men.'

'That's what my mother said.'

'Bright woman, then, your mother. Look dear, if I'd ever been blessed with a daughter and she found herself in this very predicament, I'd tell her to be brave, never let anyone see how she really felt, get on with her life, and sod the lot of them.'

'Sod the lot of them' had become a sort of mantra all the way home to Steeple Fritton. Posy found it gave her courage, and she was well aware that she needed all the courage she could get. If she'd thought that running away was a hard thing to do, then coming back to live in the village with a broken heart and never show it, was surely going to be a total impossibility.

'Oh, God,' she muttered into the folds of her scarf as the BMW throbbed towards the Lesser Fritton, Fritton Magna, and Steeple Fritton signpost. 'How on earth am I going to be able to cope with the rest of my life? What am I going to do to show Ritchie and Sonia and everyone else that I truly don't give a damn?'

As she cruised the BMW through Steeple Fritton's Sunday afternoon lanes, there was fortunately no one around to notice that Posy Nightingale's running away from home had lasted less than twelve hours.

The village was already swathed in mist from the previous night's frost and the day's perpetual dampness, making it fuzzy and soft-focused. With its crisscrossing pathways through the scrubby grass, and its glossy tangled mounds of brambles, and its hidden alleyways of drooping hazel trees leading to who knew where, it was gloriously peaceful. And, without Ritchie in her life, forever lonely.

And lonely Sunday afternoons had to be the peak time for depression, surely? Especially winter Sunday afternoons in the fading light. Everyone had someone to be with, something to do, on a Sunday. And if you didn't, then the isolation was magnified a million times.

Get a grip, Posy thought crossly. One session of tearful self-indulgence is quite enough for one day. Now, you've come back to start your new life, so pull yourself together and damn well get on with it.

Parking the BMW and her crash helmet beside the war memorial – she had no desire to return to Sunny Dene immediately in case anyone laughed – she decided to wander round the village and compose her reasons for returning in her head. It had been so easy pouring it all out to a total stranger, things had become much clearer. But she still had her pride – and a lot of family 'I told you so's' were not what she needed right now.

The Sunday-silent village was like a film set. A perfect English rural scene suspended in aspic. White cottages and mellow brick houses complemented a short row of bow-fronted shops. The tiny creeper-covered pub, The Crooked Sixpence, squatted in an oasis of golden gravel, with shingle paths and dusty single-track roads shooting away from it like a starburst. There was no noise, no traffic, no people in sight.

Steeple Fritton looked as deserted as a Take That memorabilia shop.

Posy wasn't fooled. She knew that on the other side of the village, past the church and the new Bunny Burrow housing estate, there would be chilly children shrieking in the recreation ground, cold teenagers eyeing each other up in the bus shelter, a posse of elderly men wearing scarves and gloves sitting on the bench by the village hall, and noise and life and rural chaos.

Later, she'd seek out Amanda and Nikki and join in the Steeple Fritton buzz – but at the moment, this solitude suited her perfectly.

'Bugger me! Vi Bickeridge said you'd left home this morning!'

The sound of another human voice booming through the silence made Posy jump.

'Up here!' The voice echoed from the cottage garden to her left. 'Haven't you gone yet?'

Looking left and upwards, Posy smiled in spite of herself. It was all a bit *Alice in Wonderland* except that Glad Blissit, muffled in a brown cloth coat tied at the waist with string, a woollen headscarf knotted under the chin, a pair of zip-up bootees, and standing precariously on top of a stepladder, was no Cheshire Cat.

'Been and gone and come back again.'

Glad Blissit, clutching secateurs in one hand and a clump of ivy in the other, wobbled rather frighteningly. 'Good Lord, Posy Nightingale! Ain't you kids got no staying power?'

Still cricking her neck, Posy shrugged. 'I changed my mind. Women's prerogative and all that.'

Gladys, who was well into her seventies, had scrambled down the stepladder with remarkable agility and was now regarding Posy with a pair of fierce blue eyes. 'What sort of daft stunt is that, then? We can't have a decent chinwag about you decamping if you've damn well come back straight away, can we?'

' "We" being you and Rose Lusty and Tatty Spry, I suppose?'

'Ah – and Vi Bickeridge and the Pinks. Darn you, young Posy! Now what are we going to talk about?'

'Sorry,' Posy said, not sounding it. 'Anyway, you can tell the coven that I refuse to run away. Ritchie, um, Ritchie and Sonia don't bother me at all. I've decided to carry on as before. That'll give you all something to cackle about. After all, this is my home and Sunny Dene needs me and –'

'Sunny Dene!' Gladys rocked on her zip-up bootees. 'Sunny Dene don't need you to make its beds and butter its toast. No one stays at Sunny Dene any more, do they? Not like in the old days.' She suddenly screwed her head round towards the cottage and raised her voice. 'Ellis! There's someone here I want you to meet! Posy Nightingale. She's a runaway jilted bride!'

'No, I'm not! I'm –'

An upstairs window flew open before Posy's further protestations could be heard, and *Alice in Wonderland* turned into *Cold Comfort Farm* at a stroke.

Chapter Three

Seth Starkadder, naked at least to the waist, leaned recklessly – considering the plummeting temperatures – and gloriously from the upstairs window. 'Sorry, Gran. I was in the shower. Didn't quite hear you . . .' He looked down at Posy and seduced her with a smile. 'Oh, hi.'

'Er, hello.' Posy cricked her neck even further and gazed at this vision of youthful male loveliness, who, like Ritchie, deserved ritual disembowelling simply because he was a man.

'A runaway bride, are you?' The Seth Starkadder lookalike continued to grin down at her. 'If you're at a loose end then, maybe you'd like to show me the sights of Steeple Fritton?'

'My ends are all nicely tied, thank you, and it's getting dark, so I'll decline the sightseeing tour if it's all the same to you.'

'Shame.'

Gladys waved the secateurs in a threatening arc towards the upstairs window. 'Ellis! You get some clothes on this minute! And you're to leave this piece alone, she's been through enough – and you know what you're like with floozies!'

'I'm not a floozy –' Posy began, as Ellis obediently and rather boringly she felt, hauled his nakedness inside the upstairs window.

'They'm all floozies once he gets hold of 'em,' Gladys frowned, ripping at an ivy root. 'So, what you doing back here, then?'

Posy explained about the roundabouts and the problems with the motorbike and the meeting with Persephone's family and the lack of jobs in Swindon. And the homesickness. Especially the homesickness. There was no point in lying to Glad – the Steeple Fritton coven would soon ferret out the truth anyway. They always did.

Glad smiled gummily. 'I reckons you're doing the right thing. Brave of you, though, to make a fresh start here where you belong. Put it all behind you and don't let anyone see that you gives a damn. I felt right sorry for you yesterday at the church. Nasty thing to happen to a nice young girl like you. Mind, the reception was a real humdinger. They had to carry Clive Bickeridge home well before seven.'

Posy winced. She really didn't want to hear about the wedding reception – not unless the happy couple had been struck down by botulism before the cake-cutting.

Seth Starkadder could be heard singing lustily through the upstairs window.

'Er – I didn't know you had a grandson.'

'He's my Alfie's youngest. You remember Alfie? Married Diane Skrimmett from Lesser Fritton, or maybe that was way before your time. They lives up in the wilds of Scotland. Young Ellis finished university last summer, had a bit of trouble, and needs somewhere to stay for a bit, to keep him out of a bit more trouble, if you get my drift.'

Not really, Posy thought, and not caring.

'You and him should have a bit in common, he's near on your age, twenty-four last birthday. I always send a postal order. He didn't go to college straight away, see. Bit of trouble, again. But like I said, you don't want to get tangled up with him love-wise. Charms the birds from the trees, but he's a havoc-maker, just like his granddad.'

His granddad? Jim Blissit? Three teeth and a wall eye?

'My Jim, God rest his soul, was a fine figure of a man in his prime,' Gladys said archly, obviously reading Posy's mind.

'I'm sure he was.' Posy tried not to laugh. 'And I won't ever be getting tangled up with Ellis or any other man. They're all the same.'

'Ah, they are, right enough. Thank the Lord.' And hunching herself even further into the brown coat, Glad turned her back on Posy and concentrated again on her unseasonable gardening.

As this seemed to signify the end of the conversation, and as the evening was making rapid inroads on the afternoon, Posy trudged off in the direction of the Bickeridges' corner shop. It wouldn't be open on a Sunday, but it would delay going home for a little bit longer. Delay admitting that she'd been wrong and her family had been right, and that the only way to lay the ghost of Ritchie and Sonia was to meet it head on.

With its two commons, Steeple Fritton was shaped

much like a penny-farthing bicycle, Posy had decided in childhood. The front wheel was the huge circular groundswell of the original village itself, with Sunny Dene and the recreation ground and the war memorial and the Cressbeds council estate and a few cottages and the village hall, joined by the curving lane to the rear wheel rest of the village which seemed to rather reluctantly circumnavigate the second, smaller green.

The Crooked Sixpence, with its wide gravelled forecourt and darkened windows, looked as if it was glowering at her from beneath shaggy eyebrows, so unkempt was the thatch. Fritton church, complete with eponymous steeple, was now silent and shadowy after yesterday's act of calumny, and the glorious cottages and houses surrounding the smaller green – which, in high summer, had ducks and reeded ponds and the thwack of leather on willow and the merry cries of apple-cheeked children – all appeared uninhabited.

Steeple Fritton's parade of shops had probably been built at the turn of the twentieth century, and must have come into their own during the thirties and forties. As well as the Bickeridges', there was Rose Lusty's hairdresser's – an aggressively bright pink place dedicated to tight perms, skinny rollers and hood-dryers – and Tatty Spry's alternative therapy parlour. The fourth shop had been empty since a raid by the fraud squad about twenty years earlier.

Everyone in the village caught the infrequent buses into Reading or Newbury for proper shopping.

Pausing in front of the row of shops, Posy sighed. Once, many moons ago, she and Ritchie had talked about buying this fourth shop after their marriage, and about working together, being together every day. They were going to turn it into a sort of permanent village bring-and-buy. A junk shop, bric-a-brac, antique shop, anything really to keep them together. It had been a lovely dream.

She turned away from the dark, sad, lifeless windows. Every stone, every blade of grass, every inch of the village would always remind her of Ritchie. Staying put was the right thing to do, she knew that, but when would her heart take instructions from her brain? How long was it all going to take?

'Is it as bad as it looks?'

Posy jumped as the voice echoed in her ear. She didn't need to turn round. She could see Ellis standing behind her, dressed now in jeans and a dark jumper and a thick denim jacket, reflected in the Bickeridges' shop window. She really, really didn't want to talk to him. Not today. Not ever.

'What? Steeple Fritton? It's just a typical Sunday, that's all, but as you won't be around for long I shouldn't let it worry you.'

She hoped this sounded haughtily dismissive. The last thing she wanted was some man, especially one who thought he was God's gift as Ellis obviously did, picking up on the lone-woman-broken-heart vibes and thinking he was needed.

'Hey!' Ellis held up his hands. 'Don't go all carnivorous on me. And I'll be here for a few months at least.'

Oh, great. Posy shrugged. 'Really? I can't imagine why. There's not a lot of work and the house prices are sky-high.'

She certainly wasn't going to tell him about the Bunny

Burrow starter homes estate or the rural district council's scabbing of the countryside with a small and ugly, but vital, industrial complex on the Fritton Magna road. She didn't want to encourage him in any way.

Ellis smiled cheerfully. 'Not a problem for me. I'll be living with Gran and she's got all sorts of jobs lined up to keep me out of trouble. Then I intend to start my own business.' He looked at the picture-perfect small common. 'Is this the posh end of the market? Is this where the landed gentry live?'

Posy nodded. 'Although most of the locals have been priced out. Oh, you'll find some die-hards still here, but most of these houses belong to incomers, and some to people from London. The ones who appear every so often with their green wellies and silly hats and think they're real country folk. Still, at least when they're down they fill up The Crooked Sixpence on a Saturday night.'

'But it's the weekend now and there's no one around.'

'Such ignorance of the true workings of a country village! The incomers don't mix, and the weekenders will all be snoozing over their Sunday supplements after yomping across the countryside this morning leaving a trail of devastation in their wake. Then they have a brief lunch-time drink at The Crooked Sixpence, defrost a carton of Coronation Chicken, and relax before heading back to London. They don't actually come out to play.'

Ellis nodded towards the shops. 'Why aren't these open, then? The weekenders must have loads of cash to spend?'

'Probably – but not here. They bring everything with

them. They don't want to mingle with the yokels, you see. And this . . .' she indicated the Bickeridges' shop, 'is actually dead busy, especially on Thursdays when the post office opens.'

'One day a week? What do they do for the rest of the time?'

'Wait, of course. At least we've got a post office, which is more than can be said for Lesser Fritton or Fritton Magna.' Posy wanted to laugh at the appalled look on his face. 'Oh, we're the height of sophistication here. We've got your gran and the rest of her coven to thank for keeping it open. They organized protests at the proposed closure, brought in a few professional grey rabble-rousers, even made the local telly.'

Ellis raised his eyebrows. 'Fascinating. Thursdays, you said? I'll mark it in my diary. Wouldn't want to miss it.'

He was amusing, and gorgeous, and had no trace of a Scottish accent and Posy wanted him to go away.

'Why don't you sound like Billy Connolly?'

'Because I've been sent away to schools all over England. Never stayed anywhere for long. Any regional accent got lost years ago. And even though I only arrived last night I'll probably have your lovely Berkshire burr by the end of the week.'

Posy flushed. 'I'm not a bumpkin.'

'I'm sure you're not, but your accent is dead sexy even if you're pretty spiky. Where are you going to take me next on the guided tour?'

'Nowhere at all.'

'Pity. Although I wasn't following you, honest. I did catch the "sod off" inflection earlier.'

'Good.'

'And I do love the leathers. Are you into kinky stuff?'

'I ride a motorbike.'

Ellis grinned. 'Wow, all my fantasies are coming true! So, are you a jilted bride, like Gran said?'

'No, of course not. But doubtless you'll hear the whole sad story about a zillion times. My ex-fiancé married someone else here yesterday.'

'Oh, right. Shit. Christ – I went to the wedding reception with Gran last night. Good piss-up.' Ellis grinned at her again through the black reflective windows without sympathy. 'He was a mad bastard to dump you for her, then. She was nowhere near as pretty as you.'

'Thanks – I think she's rather gross, too. They deserve one another.' She was pleased that he hadn't offered false commiserations. He'd probably change his mind if he knew about the thongs.

'Why did he? Marry her instead of you?'

'Because she's pregnant and I'm not.'

'Bloody hell. That's a crap situation. She didn't look pregnant.'

'No, I know. But she is.' Posy really wanted to go now. To get back to Sunny Dene and start planning her new existence. To see her parents and Dom and the dogs. To stop this conversation before it lead to something awful, like tears. 'Sorry, can't stay any longer. I, er, hope you'll enjoy being here and find something to do.'

'I've told you, I've already got plans for plenty of somethings to do.' The smile was of carbon-melting quality. 'Actually, Gran reckons I'm going to be Steeple Fritton's answer to Robin of Locksley, but I prefer to think of myself as a highwayman.'

Posy wanted to laugh. Obviously the Blissit madness was inherited. Either way, Ellis had just admitted to criminal leanings, which probably accounted for 'the bit of trouble' mentioned earlier. Maybe she shouldn't have told him about all the big houses standing empty on the green.

'Lovely. I'm sure there'll be a lot of call for stand and deliver around here.'

'More than you'd think, apparently. I hope you soon find something wonderful to do with the rest of your life, too.'

'Don't be so damn patronizing.'

'I wasn't,' he looked hurt. 'I meant it. You deserve to be happy. Everyone deserves that.'

She moved away from the shop front. 'You sound like a hippie tree-hugger. And I'm sure the rest of my life will be nicely occupied, thank you.'

Not wanting to step backwards, because Ellis was still standing behind her, she shuffled sideways along the row. By the time she'd reached the empty shop again, windows blackened and inches deep in flyposters, she started to walk more normally. Ellis was standing in the same place, watching her.

Oh, go away, Posy thought irritably. Clear off and leave me alone.

'Ellis! Sweetie! Sorry I'm late!'

Posy jerked her head round at the sudden shrill trill of girlish enthusiasm. She hadn't heard anyone approach, or seen them cross the green which was reflected in all its lonely glory in the shop fronts. And no wonder.

Tatty Spry, an early Cher-like mass of raven ringlets and ankle-length layers of velvet and lace, had undulated silkily out of her shop door, leaving the multicoloured glass bead curtain jangling behind her like a noisy rainbow.

'It's okay, darling.' Ellis's reply was muffled as he had immediately buried his face in the ringlets. 'You know I'd wait forever for you.'

With a derisive snort, Posy stomped away. Neither Ellis nor the ringlets-and-lace Tatty took the slightest notice of her leaving.

When the hell had that happened? Ellis had only arrived in the village the day before? When had he and Tatty got it together? Oh, yes of course . . . last night at Ritchie and Sonia's wedding reception.

Why this should make her even more angry, Posy had no idea, but she stalked furiously round the rest of the village, hating all men with a vengeance, and rehearsing her 'I've come home because I wanted to, not because I was homesick and I know exactly what I'm going to do with the rest of my life' speech in her head, and trying to make it sound convincing.

After half an hour, it was cold and dark and striding round Steeple Fritton being angry seemed a pretty daft thing to be doing, so Posy decided to collect the abandoned BMW and face her parents at Sunny Dene. As she passed Glad Blissit's cottage, the upstairs window was still slightly open and shared chuckles of throaty, smoky laughter rolled out and floated teasingly on the spiky-cold January air. Obviously Ellis hadn't wasted any time at all in finding something to do with the rest of his life.

Well, then, neither would she.

*   *   *

Posy unlatched Sunny Dene's front door, feeling strangely nervous. Trevor and Kenneth, claws clicking in perfect time, leapt towards her across the flags. Deciding that they recognized her scent and approved, they licked her in rapturous welcome, then bounded away towards the dining room, the ecstatically lolling tongues and wagging tails indicating that she should follow them.

'Boys! Boys!' Dilys admonished lovingly from the kitchen doorway. 'Hold your horses – Oh, hello, Posy dear. You're just in time.'

'Am I? Good. Er, what for?'

'High tea, dear.' Dilys wobbled towards the dining room carrying a loaded cake stand and a packet of doilies. 'Your dad's through here with some new guests, they've been told all about you. Come along in and say hello.'

'Yes, okay, but Mum . . .'

'What dear?'

'I'm back.'

'Yes, I know. We knew you would be. Five people phoned and said your motorbike was parked up by the war memorial. We'd expected you sooner.'

Posy, shaking her head and trying to be rational – after all, she'd only left that morning, so it was hardly cause for the Prodigal's Return type of reception, was it? – followed her mother's ample and vividly-coloured rear across the hall.

In the dining room, Sunny Dene's two new visitors were tucking into the sort of spread only ever seen in 1950s films. Posy, who was still stuffed from Persephone's owners' lunch, hoped she wasn't supposed to join in.

41

Mr Dale and Mr Burridge, as they were introduced to her by Norrie, shook her hand gravely and called her a pretty little thing. Neither of them looked like they would see seventy-five again, and after extolling the virtues of Sunny Dene, explained to Posy that they were 'travellers in ladies wear'.

Trying hard to dismiss the mental picture of geriatric hippie transvestites, Posy smiled nicely at both of them, accepted a cup of tea and an iced fancy from Norrie, and settled down in a corner of the dining room.

Trevor and Kenneth, having sniffed Posy again and discovered that she wasn't eating anything exciting, immediately turned unfaithful and were being fed titbits of anchovies on toast by Mr Dale and Mr Burridge, while doing the out-of-sync tail-wagging routine.

'Lovely to see you've come to your senses,' Norrie hugged her as he passed. 'Running away wasn't going to be the answer, but you had to find that out for yourself. We'll have a chat about it later, shall we?'

Posy nodded and hugged him back, feeling ridiculously emotional. 'Thanks, Dad, that'd be great. So, where did these two come from?'

'Turned up at lunch time. Discovered Colworth Manor, their usual watering hole, had been taken over by a lot of very loud middle managers on a bonding exercise or something. They found it not to their taste.' Norrie lowered his voice as if imparting classified information. 'Mr D and Mr B are a bit of an anachronism. Of the old school.'

Mr D and Mr B, Norrie continued sotto voce, if they liked it, had said they would be stopping at Sunny Dene on a regular basis, and wouldn't that be lovely?

Swallowing a piece of angelica, Posy nodded. Her parents needed all the business they could get.

Norrie swept some sparse strands of hair across his shining pate. They hovered in place for a moment before sliding sideways. He tucked them behind his ears, making him look like Ermintrude. 'Are you really all right now, love?'

'Well, *all right* might be a bit optimistic. But at least I've come to a decision. I'm going to –'

There was a clatter as Mr D dropped his scone jam side down and Trevor hoovered it up before anyone else could reach it. Kenneth and Mr B both looked a bit miffed.

As Norrie disappeared to fetch a damp cloth and refill the teapot, and Mr D and Mr B, ignoring the mess on the carpet, were otherwise occupied swapping obviously hilarious road-stories with one another, Posy sidled up to her mother.

'I went for a walk round the village just now, to clear my head, and I was talking to Glad Blissit and her, um, grandson.'

Dilys's orange curls leapt about of their own accord. 'That turn-coating old witch went to the bloody wedding reception just because she was getting Babycham at someone else's expense. And from what I've heard, young Ellis is a havoc-maker.'

Posy's ears pricked up almost as much as Trevor's and Kenneth's. 'That's what Glad said. She also said he's been sent here to keep him out of trouble but –'

'You don't want to take no notice of Glad Blissit, you know she's as mad as a coot. Should have been drowned at birth. And apparently Ellis should have been castrated

43

at puberty, as poor dim Tatty Spry will soon discover.' Dilys turned her attention to Mr D and Mr B with a broad smile. 'Now, boys, anything more you'd like?'

The boys, Mr D and Mr B and Trevor and Kenneth, all nodded appreciatively.

It took ages for Dilys to restock their plates, and refresh their napkins and straighten their doilies. Posy watched all the fussing with growing impatience. Tatty Spry? What did her mother know about Ellis and Tatty Spry? The village bush telegraph must have had smoke coming out of its ears.

'Yes, well,' Posy said, as Dilys was about to whisk off into the kitchen again, 'I met Ellis again by the shops and Tatty came out to meet him and they went back to Glad's cottage.'

'Confirms what Rose Lusty told me on the phone just now.' There was a vigorous nodding of the orange curls. 'Tatty and young Ellis were superglued together all night at Colworth Manor, apparently. Daft bat. Can't imagine what she thinks she's playing at setting her cap at him, but Rose Lusty says that –' she paused to flick crumbs into a napkin.

Posy felt as though she'd missed a vital episode of her favourite soap opera – and she'd only been away from Steeple Fritton for a day. 'Go on, then, what did Rose say?'

'That Tatty wants a playmate for Zebedee.'

The soap turned into *The Times* Cryptic. 'Zebedee?'

'Tatty's youngest. Do try to keep up, love. You know what she's like for kiddies, wants another before it's too late. Rose reckons Tatty has singled Ellis out as good breeding stock.'

'Surely not?'

'Stands to reason. Although what good it'll do her, God knows. None of her other men have stuck around have they? All them fatherless kiddies and now she wants to add to the brood.'

Is that what Tatty Spry and Ellis had been doing in Glad's upstairs bedroom just now then? Creating a playmate for Zebedee? Posy managed not to laugh. Just. She reached towards the cake stand. Poor little thing. Knowing Tatty it'd probably get called Horatio. Horatio Blissit! Or Horatio Spry – not much to choose there, really.

Posy was munching her way through a cream horn without realizing it. 'Ellis is much younger than Tatty, though.'

'According to Rose, who got it from Glad last night after seven or eight Babychams, Ellis prefers older women. He's had a bit of trouble in that area before. One of the reasons he's here. To keep him out of harm's way. Fat chance with Tatty Spry on the prowl. Tatty must be heading towards forty and this is probably her last chance of batting on that particular wicket. Now, anyone for another iced fancy?'

Posy, from force of habit, started collecting the tea things on to a tray. Mr Dale and Mr Burridge watched her with open approbation. Probably, Posy thought, because it was the first time they'd been waited on by someone dressed as a whiplash queen.

Backing into the kitchen with her loaded tray, Posy pondered on her parents' laissez faire attitude. Had they known she'd come back of her own accord? Had they realized with some God-given parental insight that if they'd made a huge fuss they might have driven her away from Steeple Fritton forever? Whatever it was, she was really, really glad to be home.

She looked at her father sitting at the kitchen table, a double-entry account ledger and a calculator beside him. 'I didn't realize you were doing the books. Isn't that Dom's job usually?'

Norrie nodded. 'Yes, but he'll be going back to college soon so I thought I ought to get to grips with it. Anyway, not even someone with Dom's miracle mathematical brain could make good business sense of this.'

Posy clattered the tray on to the draining board. 'Are things really bad, then?'

Norrie heaved a huge sigh. 'About as bad as they can get, love. About as bad as they can get. Especially since that Daisy MacClean's made such a success of Colworth Manor. To be honest, if business doesn't improve soon, I'm not even sure if we're going to survive.'

Chapter Four

On that same Sunday, in the small Sussex town of Swansbury, Lola Wentworth stared miserably at the pale and lovely loneliness of her almost-sea-view apartment.

There really wasn't much to show for twenty-eight years of being a faithful mistress, she thought. Her lifetime of devotion and discretion had brought her this luxury flat full of hand-crafted furniture, a wardrobe of classic Jacques Vert outfits, a hatchback updated each year, savings of a little over five thousand pounds in her building society account, and yesterday an unexpected letter from Nigel's solicitor making an appointment for the following afternoon.

She leaned her back against the white railings of her first-floor balcony and lifted her face to the winter sun. It failed to warm her skin, just as the mug of black coffee cradled in her hands failed to warm her body. Her life was perpetually, chillingly, cold.

Below, she could hear the Sunday morning noises: children playing along the estuary path, couples calling to each other as they cracked ice on the seemingly obligatory water features in the tiny communal gardens, a radio softly playing snatches of Strauss. Ordinary, every-day noises which hurt beyond bearing. Other people living and loving with no thought that it would one day end. The human tragedy ignored.

The day stretched ahead in bleak nothingness. How she hated these sterile Sundays when everyone in the world seemed to have someone with whom to share their time; when being without Nigel hurt almost beyond bearing.

Tomorrow, at work, it would be better, and yesterday had been almost fun.

Yesterday she'd filled the day with shopping for things she didn't need in Brighton, lunching with married girlfriends, going to the cinema in the evening with the young couple in the apartment downstairs who were determined that she shouldn't spend every evening alone. Tomorrow she'd go to work at Marionette Biscuits, and be surrounded by people, and have busy familiar things occupying her mind.

Without Nigel, today and every Sunday for the rest of her life she'd know only aching desolation.

At the age of twenty, Lola had joined Marionette Biscuits as a typist. By her twenty-first birthday she was PA and Other Woman to Nigel Marion, the Managing Director. Nigel, tall, classically handsome, distinguished, and awe-inspiringly brilliant, had swept her off her feet. It had always been love. For both of them. Nigel, nineteen years her senior, had been everything she'd ever wanted in a man – apart from being married of course.

For twenty-eight years they'd worked together, managed

to escape together during sales conferences and trade fairs, and spent all night, one precious night a week when Nigel was allegedly working away, at this flat on Swansbury Water.

Nigel had never promised to leave his wife, but Lola had always hoped that one day he would. Now, he had left both of them forever.

Lola blinked as the low January sun reflected from the white quarry tiles of the balcony. It had been nearly a year since Nigel's death and the tears still appeared unexpectedly. Dashing them away, she knew she had to find something to do to pass the hours until she could return to bed. Anything to take away the endless emptiness. There were only so many times she could tidy the flat, or rearrange the flowers, or walk the solitary walk along the estuary path and look at the sea and think of Nigel and cry.

Wearily, she unpeeled herself from the balcony railings, drifted listlessly into the kitchen and placed her coffee mug in the dishwasher. It was the only thing in there, and looked small, lost and alone. She slammed the door shut and picked up the telephone.

'Jenny, it's Lola. I wondered if you were doing anything this afternoon? Oh, right. No, no, of course I understand. No, I'm fine . . .'

She punched out another number.

'Sheila? Is Mike playing golf today? I wondered if you'd like to – oh, no, well, of course . . . What? No, it was nothing. Yes, next week sometime. I'll ring you . . .'

The third number rang and rang. There was no reply. Her married girlfriends had been wonderful in their efforts to make sure she wasn't left in isolation for too long, but they had their husbands, their children, to consider. They had normal family lives which couldn't be put on hold every time she felt the desperation of her loss.

Hurling the phone into the pile of cream and gold cushions on the sofa, Lola poured a huge gin and tonic, picked up the Sunday supplements, and headed for the bedroom.

The following afternoon, having crossed Swansbury's busy High Street, Lola approached the granite portals of Everton and Simpkins, Solicitors, with a feeling of some trepidation.

'Ms Wentworth for Mr Everton,' she announced herself to the receptionist. 'We have an appointment at three.'

'He's expecting you. I'll let him know you're here.'

Lola waited, savouring the warmth as the intercom call was made, and eventually Toby Everton appeared in the doorway. They shook hands and made murmuring introductory noises.

Lola was pretty sure that Toby Everton wouldn't have remembered her from Nigel's funeral. She'd kept a very low profile, sitting at the back of the crematorium, stifling her sobs, then slipping away before the huge swell of mourners had shuffled out into the gentle rain to admire the floral tributes.

Her grieving, by necessity, had been done very much in private. The privilege of the public outpouring of grief had fallen, naturally, to Barbara. Barbara and Nigel had been unhappily married for more than forty years when the cardiac arrest had cut the union mercifully short in the middle of a Rotary Club Dinner Dance.

Whether anyone else from Marionette Biscuits knew or cared that it was Lola's heart that had been broken, was immaterial. Barbara was Mrs Biscuit, and as such, received the sympathy vote.

'Thank you for coming along at such short notice.' In his beige office, Toby Everton indicated a beige chair placed dead centre between two yucca plants. 'Can I get you a drink? Tea?'

Lola shook her head. She just wanted to get this meeting over with. Nigel had never discussed his will with her, and she'd assumed the bequests had been made public months ago. Maybe there had been a codicil, something private, just for her. Not that she wanted nor needed Nigel's money. She lived in the flat which Nigel had bought outright, was still working full-time at Marionette Biscuits, and the building society savings plus her private pension plan would eventually see her through her old age.

A small keepsake, though, something personal of Nigel's, would be a different matter altogether. Maybe he'd left her his watch, or his collection of framed cricketing hero cigarette cards, or his Gilbert and Sullivan CDs. To have any of those things which had been so much a part of the man she would love forever, would be wonderful.

Their affair had never been financial; a future apart never discussed. It had simply never occurred to Lola that death would manage to achieve in a matter of minutes what Barbara had failed to manage in a lifetime.

'Very well,' Toby Everton made a pyramid of his fingers. 'I have worked, as I'm sure you'll be aware, for the Marion family for some time. Nigel's death was a blow to us all. The affairs of the estate were convoluted, and probate being granted has taken some time. There is no easy way of saying this, Ms Wentworth, so I won't prolong it. I have been asked to approach you by Mrs Barbara Marion, Nigel's widow, regarding your position.'

Lola shivered. Her face, however, used to wearing a mask of indifference, gave nothing away. 'Really? And which position would that be?'

Toby gave a wry smile. 'I don't think that Nigel was quite as discreet as he believed he was. Your, um, relationship has been common knowledge to Mrs Marion and her children for some considerable time.'

Lola felt the shock jolt through her as though someone had just wired the uncomfortable beige chair to the mains. Sensing the tears welling inside her nose again, she swallowed quickly, still managing to keep the mask in place. Weeping in private was one thing, but she'd vowed there would never be tears in public.

'I'm sorry. I'm not sure what you mean.'

'Ms Wentworth, we both know what I mean. You and Nigel were having an affair for almost thirty years. It suited Barbara not to make a fuss. After all, she had the status of being the legal spouse, and all the benefits thereby accrued, and wanted to retain them. However, things have now very obviously changed. It is my duty to inform you that your position at Marionette Biscuits is to be terminated forthwith –'

'No!' Lola rocked forward on the chair, almost colliding with one of the yucca plants. 'She can't do that! She can't sack me!'

'I'm afraid she can. Mrs Marion has inherited all the Marionette Biscuits factories under the terms of the will, and, having been granted probate, intends to dispose of them immediately. She has already found a buyer for the Swansbury premises and land. The new owners will not be continuing with biscuit production. A skeleton staff will stay on until the handover, but you will not be required.'

Lola's head swam dizzily throughout this legalese. Only one thing was clear. She no longer had a job. No job . . . Without Nigel life had been unbearably lonely, but at least going into the office each day, to the place they'd shared for so long, made him closer somehow, and his loss slightly easier to bear. But now – not working at Marionette Biscuits? Not working at all?

She was only forty-nine! What on earth was she going to do with the rest of her life? No Nigel, no job . . . She might as well have died with him . . . In those lonely dark hours while being visited by the four-in-the-morning horrors, she often wished she had. There was nothing left for her without him.

She groped in her handbag for a tissue, ducking her crumpled face away from Toby Everton's professional gaze. This was too awful to take in. All the pain of losing Nigel swamped her again, and she suddenly missed him so much that she couldn't breathe.

Sucking in steadying gulps of air, she raised her head. 'I, er, don't know what to say. I would have thought that this, um, wasn't a matter for a solicitor . . .' she stopped, fumbling for thoughts, stumbling over words. 'What I mean is, surely if the factory is being sold, I would just be informed of my redundancy along with the other employees, wouldn't I?'

'But you're not like the other employees, are you, Ms Wentworth?' Toby Everton rolled smoothly on, obviously used to dealing with tearful clients and making no comment. 'You are very, very different.'

Lola felt the misery trickle down her spine. She had never been ashamed of being the other woman in Nigel's life. She'd been a good mistress, fitting her own life around his, always understanding when the family's demands had to come first. She'd spent solo Christmases and birthdays for as long as she could remember, and had never, ever once phoned Nigel at home, or begged for more of his time, or embarrassed him in any way.

Their time together had been blissful, and Lola had always been more than happy to settle for those precious shared moments. At work they had been professional and were sure that successive Marionette Biscuits employees were unaware of their private status. However, it seemed that Barbara had known all the time, and for whatever reason had decided to keep her own counsel – until now.

Lola leaned forward, pulling her green wool dress down until it almost covered her knees. Her clothes were always uncluttered, her hair was bobbed and blonde, her body slender and toned. She'd had plenty of free time and money to make sure her physical standards never slipped. Suddenly it was desperately important that Toby Everton didn't think she was all the things she knew she'd been called – slapper, a bit on the side, a heartless tart, a husband-stealer.

'I loved Nigel deeply. He loved me. We fell in love. That's all. I never wanted to hurt Bar— Mrs Marion.'

Toby nodded, his eyes gentle. 'I know, Ms Wentworth. I was Nigel's friend as well as his solicitor. You made him very happy. He adored you. I'm in no position to judge on moral issues, nor would I want to. What I do have to do is present you with the legal facts.'

Lola stared over Toby Everton's head and watched the white January sky reflect across Swansbury's rooftops. When she'd regained control, she looked at him again. 'Very well. Thank you. I understand that my job has gone, which is something of a shock. At my age I'm probably unemployable, but no doubt I can retrain. Or work from home or –'

'This is the difficult part,' Toby fiddled with his tie. 'With regard to your accommodation. There are complications on this issue, too.'

'Complications? I'm sorry, I must be very dense, but I don't understand –'

Toby Everton's voice was quiet, as if by lowering the cadence he could soften the blow. 'Ms Wentworth, I'm afraid you no longer have a home.'

Lola felt loneliness and despair swamp her. All the private tears suddenly threatened to become very public. Her voice wobbled. 'I may not have got a job, Mr Everton, but I certainly have a home. Of course I have. I've got the flat, at Swansbury Water, one of the apartments by the river –'

'Your name is not on the deeds.'

'No, I know, although I'm sure Nigel did offer. It was his property. But I've always lived there. We'd, that is, I'd, always imagined that one day, we'd live there together. Openly.' She sighed. 'I didn't want the flat to be in my name, like a gift. Foolish, I know. But it was really important that I didn't take more from Nigel than I could give back, you see. I lived in his flat because the arrangement suited us both. We'd always said we'd change the ownership details one day . . .' Lola sat back rigidly in the chair, the realization slowly dawning. 'You mean it's Barbara's flat now?'

'Yes.'

'And that means –'

'Unfortunately, Ms Wentworth, it means that the Marion family want, and can legally have because you aren't even an official tenant, immediate vacant possession.'

This time Lola didn't even try to hide the tears.

Toby poured her a glass of water. 'Do you have savings? Somewhere else you can go?'

Ignoring the glass, Lola clawed at mental lifelines and immediately discarded them. There was nothing. Only the pathetic building society account. Oh, why hadn't she been more prudent with her money? – and the pension plan which wouldn't kick in for another eleven years. There was nothing else. She was jobless and homeless and broke. And worse, far worse, was that every link with Nigel was being severed at a stroke. Barbara Marion had taken her revenge.

Standing shakily outside Everton and Simpkins offices, vaguely aware of the swish of traffic a few inches in front of her, Lola tried to clear her brain. Tried to think of what she should do next. What, if anything, she could do to salvage the situation.

She couldn't go back to the Marionette office, that

was certain. The news of the closure would have been broken by now. She couldn't bear to see the faces of the colleagues she'd shared her working life with for so long, looking shell-shocked and shattered as the realization of the redundancies sank in. There wasn't even any point in clearing her desk. There was nothing there that she'd need in the future.

The future? What future? What future was there for a homeless woman of nearly fifty who knew of nothing but the sales and marketing and promotion of fancy biscuits?

She stepped into the road, and was immediately accosted by the blaring of a dozen horns. Leaping back on to the pavement, she glared at the drivers. She really didn't care if she was run over – as long as they made a decent job of it. Finished her off. She wouldn't want to spend months being hospitalized, then discharged to – where? – a hostel for the unloved and unwanted?

Despite everything, Lola smiled to herself at the notion. She had never truly looked on the half-empty-glass side of life, not even after Nigel's death. She wasn't suicidal – just grieving. And shocked. And desperately lonely. Crossing the road more carefully, she acknowledged to herself that many people, not knowing the circumstances, would say that she'd got her just deserts. That any woman who knowingly stole another woman's husband deserved to be humiliated and left with nothing.

Only she hadn't stolen Nigel, had she? Merely shared a small and wonderful part of his life. He'd remained with Barbara because of the children, and then later when they'd grown up because he felt guilty, and all Lola had done was snatch blissful moments to make him happy. As he'd made her. And now, she thought, miserably clambering into the hatchback in the riverside car park, she'd never be happy again.

She drove through Swansbury and back to the flat on autopilot, giving herself a stern mental talking-to. Her happiness wasn't an issue here, she decided, as she unlocked her front door, probably for the last time. Happiness was pure self-indulgence – and something that she'd think about later – like Scarlett O'Hara. Right now the only thing on the agenda must be damage limitation and survival.

The sight of the flat now, under the awful new circumstances, brought the grief rushing back in. Every item of furniture, every small ornament, had a Nigel-memory poignantly attached. Was she supposed to leave everything behind for Nigel's family? Did Barbara not only have a right to the apartment, but also to the squashy sofas and the reclining chairs and the beautiful Indian coffee tables?

Still numbed, Lola pulled her suitcases from the wardrobe, poured a treble gin with a splash of tonic, and picked up the phone.

Two hours later, Jenny, Sheila and Mo, her married girlfriends, sat in the middle of the mayhem. They'd rushed to her aid as soon as they could. Their loyalty had made her cry again. They'd formed a sort of rescue chain, taking it in turns to pack her possessions, refill her glass and pass the Kleenex box.

'Isn't there any way you can fight this?' Jenny sat on one of the bulging suitcases. 'You know, go for a stay of execution or something?'

Lola shook her head. 'Toby Everton said not. There's no point. I have no legal rights at all. I'd have had more rights if I'd been a squatter. The flat is part of the estate and the entire estate went to Barbara.'

Sheila frowned. 'So where will you go? Oh, I know we've all offered you a bed short-term, but I mean . . . Haven't you got any family at all?'

Lola nursed her gin and stared out of the open glass doors, across the balcony, and watched the low January sun dripping silver stars into the estuary. An only child, her parents had died years ago. There'd been a couple of elderly aunts, both now in nursing homes, and her Cousin Mimi whom she hated.

'I've got a cousin in Somerset, but there's no way that she'd help. She made her feelings very clear about me and Nigel years ago. I think her own husband has played away on and off throughout their marriage. She was never going to look kindly on me being the Other Woman.'

Jenny, Sheila and Mo said nothing. Lola knew that they had a certain sympathy with Cousin Mimi's point of view. She honestly couldn't blame them.

'Why don't you ring her anyway?' Mo suggested. 'Sod the facts, just say you've got some time off, you're going to be in her neck of the woods, want to visit to make amends. You know the sort of thing.'

'She'll pretend to be a Latvian au pair or something as soon as she knows it's me. She won't want me within corrupting distance of her Howard.' Lola sighed. 'In fact I'm pretty sure she thinks it's like a disease. That I'm genetically programmed to pinch married men.'

'Try it,' Jenny scrambled from the suitcase and handed

59

her the phone. 'It'll be better than nothing. Two weeks in Somerset will give you time to think. Time to plan . . .'

Lola took the phone but didn't punch out Mimi's number. She didn't want Jenny and Sheila and Mo to see her humiliated further. 'I'll do it later. When she's had supper and is feeling more mellow. Now, is there any more gin?'

Cousin Mimi was anything but mellow, even after supper. Her voice, squawking like a wet hen down the telephone line, made Lola hold the receiver away from her ear and wince. Jenny, Sheila and Mo had returned to their families, insisting that Lola told them the minute she knew where and when she was going. It had taken several more gin and tonics before she'd been brave enough to contact Mimi. Now she wished she hadn't bothered.

After five minutes of pure vitriol spouted re men who cheated on their wives, tarts who pinched other women's men, the government's lax approach to morality, and the state of the adulterous nation in general, Mimi finally ran out of steam.

'So,' Lola said, 'I take it that you don't want me to visit.'

'Well, if you're in the area, I suppose you could pop in . . .'

'It would only be for a couple of weeks . . .'

'A couple of weeks! You mean you'd want to sleep here?'

'That was the general idea, yes. And I promise I won't wander about the house in provocative underwear or try to lure Howard into the spare bedroom with promises of tantric passion.'

'Howard isn't here.' Mimi's voice was icy. 'He's away for a month. Trouble in Geneva.'

Lola smiled to herself. Over the years there had conveniently been trouble in some distant enclave that couldn't be sorted without Howard's personal and lengthy intervention. 'Oh, right, so in that case you'll be glad of some company, won't you?'

Mimi's pause wasn't flattering. 'Well, I suppose so. Just as long as you pay the going rate. We're a tourist spot, you know. We're on the Super Somerset list.'

'I'm more than willing to pay my way, Mimi. And January is hardly high season, is it? I'll see you sometime tomorrow.'

'*Tomorrow?*'

'Tomorrow,' Lola said firmly. 'I'll leave here after breakfast. And I'll take you out to dinner tomorrow night. Thanks for asking me.'

She put the phone down, and gazed at the denuded apartment. Her suitcases were packed, the few personal items which she'd added over the years, were wrapped and sealed in two cardboard boxes. Everything else she'd left for the Marion family.

Lifting her favourite photograph of Nigel from the mantelpiece, Lola kissed it, then holding it tightly against her, slowly walked into the bedroom – hers and Nigel's bedroom – for the very last time.

Chapter Five

The two weeks spent with Mimi had been an unmitigated disaster. Lola had never been so glad to see the back of Somerset in her life. However, it had given her a little time to adjust to the shock of being jobless and homeless, and had, in retrospect and however awful, been better than being lonely in Swansbury.

Not that she'd have the indulgence of being lonely in Swansbury any longer. The apartment would be up for sale by now, or even worse, be inhabited by Barbara Marion or one of the Marion offspring as a weekend retreat. Feeling the cold grief start to clutch in her throat, Lola steered her thoughts away from Nigel and their one-time home and concentrated on her driving.

The fortnight in Somerset would have been even more therapeutic if she'd been able to talk over her sadness with Mimi, she realized as she left Bath behind and headed towards the motorway. But Mimi had been too full of Howard's suspected infidelity, this time in Geneva, and how women like Lola should be tarred and feathered and railroaded out of town.

Listening to Mimi's constant self-centred bitchy whine, Lola had decided that she couldn't blame Howard for playing away, and had also come to the conclusion that if more wives behaved like mistresses, then there would probably be a lot more happy marriages and far fewer divorces.

Not that she'd shared this nugget with her cousin, naturally. It would have been rude in the extreme, and Mimi's grudging hospitality had at least served a purpose, but now the grieving and eventual healing would be down to her alone. Like everything else. Like the rest of her life. Alone.

It would be a challenge, at least. Something to get her teeth into. Worrying about survival was a whole new area for the four o'clock horrors to run riot in. The only immediate problem now, of course, she thought as she joined the stream of vehicles on the motorway, was where the hell was this lone existence going to be? Where on earth was she supposed to go next to face this challenge?

The M4's Tuesday afternoon traffic was steady; three lanes of tin boxes beetling off to various destinations. Lola, cruising along the inside lane because there was no point in driving quickly to nowhere, wondered if any of them were as rootless as she.

She'd find somewhere cheap to stay tonight, then think about it all again in the morning. Prioritize, that was the thing to do. She'd always been good at prioritizing at Marionette Biscuits. Nigel had said so ... She swallowed and blinked and again quickly changed tack. Prioritize ... Okay ... Do it. Now. Think ...

What did she really need? Easy: money and a roof over her head. A job and a home.

What if, she wondered idly, listening to Radio Two and sailing past the entrance to a service station, she could solve both her problems in one fell swoop?

What if – just supposing – she found herself a job that also provided accommodation?

The idea was suddenly so exciting that she found herself singing along to Smokie's 'Living Next Door to Alice' without realizing that she'd even remembered the words. For the first time since Nigel's death, Lola felt the numb hopelessness slightly thawing. Her spirits, while not exactly rising, had at least perked up.

The idea, just a glimmer, was already spreading tentacles. Her brain was racing. Yes, it was a possibility – and one so simple that she couldn't imagine why she hadn't thought of it before.

Hotels . . . Hotels were bound to have lots of live-in jobs, weren't they? She could buy a *Daltons Weekly* and a copy of *The Lady* and find a live-in job anywhere – anywhere at all. Hotels, or private houses, or pubs, or restaurants, or maybe nursing homes even . . .

Naturally there would be no references from Marionette Biscuits, and her age was definitely against her, so she could hardly expect to walk into a management position in her new job, but she could surely do something in return for bed and board? Cook? Clean? Care? Oh yes, she'd been good at caring . . .

There surely would be umpteen live-in places where her age would be a definite advantage, and her housekeeping skills appreciated? Somewhere where she could lose herself and her past and channel all her loving into looking after other people – other people who would relish her company as Nigel had done, but differently, of course. There would never be another emotional entanglement. Having loved as deeply as she and Nigel had done, she knew she'd never fall in love again. But *caring* . . .

As with all sudden, exciting and brilliant ideas, Lola now itched to put it into immediate action. Cursing for not stopping off at the service station, booking herself in for a night or two at the Travel Lodge which was all she could afford, and buying a paper to search through the small ads, she drummed her fingers on the steering wheel – this time to the beat of The Sweet – and wondered if she should leave the motorway at the next exit. Or should she stay on until Reading? No, a million doubts could creep in between here and Reading. She'd leave at the next junction and take her chances.

She could pick up a *Daltons Weekly* and the most recent edition of *The Lady* in the next town, find a room for the night, ring round any suitable vacancies, and start her new life within what – probably not more than a day or two?

Yes! Yes! Yes! Lola pressed her foot down, and headed almost happily towards the next slip road.

Stirwell Newtown was pretty unprepossessing. Small and grey, it appeared to have fallen into disrepair around the time that breeze block architecture was all the rage. As far as Lola could make out, the double-yellow-lined high street offered just one depressed row of single-storey shops. On closer inspection she noticed that most of them were either boarded up or had metal bars on the windows: obviously to deter looters or to stop the staff escaping.

Lola shivered. At least she wouldn't be starting her new life here. All she needed from Stirwell Newtown was a couple of magazines, maybe a café where she could grab a coffee, then she'd rejoin the motorway, find somewhere to stay in Reading overnight, and plan her next move.

As well as lacking hospitality, Stirwell Newtown also seemed pretty short on car parks. Probably, Lola decided, having driven round a bleak and miserable one-way system twice, because no one in their right mind would ever want to stop here.

Eventually finding an un-yellow-lined gap between The Marrakech Kebab House which was closed and the 8 'til Late which wasn't, Lola parked alongside an industrial sized wheelie bin and a Fiesta on bricks. Nervously, she glanced around for potential joyriders, and not spotting any made sure the hatchback was securely locked, and hurried into the convenience shop.

Cornucopia wasn't the word. The high shelves and narrow aisles were stacked with every commodity known to man. A group of rather dispirited-looking and overweight women in leggings and leather jackets were milling round the sweets and crisps with their noisy offspring, while even more of the same were queuing at the tiny post office counter. Lola groaned. It was obviously child benefits day – and the 8 'til Late had one harassed assistant who seemed to be dividing his time unequally between the shop and the post office.

Bursting with impatience now that she had a plan in mind, she forced her way through a gridlock of buggies and shopping trolleys towards the newsstand. There were no copies of *The Lady* on display, so picking up the last *Daltons Weekly*, Lola joined the queue and listened to several older customers cheerfully discussing whether tins of chicken jalfrezi would be an adequate substitute for steak and kidney pudding for the old man's tea.

In her past life, Lola would have listened and smiled and stored up the conversation to repeat to Nigel that evening. Since his death, one of the hardest things to bear had been the lack of someone to talk to, to share these nonsensical snippets with. In those first few desolate weeks, she'd wondered if she would ever be normal again. But now, this live-in plan, this grain of an idea, had somehow managed to make the numb, gin-filled days of early mourning seem distant, almost as though they had happened to someone else.

In this hot and overcrowded convenience store, she realized that she was possibly going to survive. Nigel, she knew, would have been proud of her.

By the time she'd reached sight of the counter, she was aware that she was the subject of some speculation by the leggings brigade. With their uniform bleached hair and dark roots and their down-turned mouths, they were staring covetously at her black silk trousers and red cashmere jacket, rather like an avid lepidopterist might gaze greedily on a Queen Alexandra's Birdwing.

Lola avoided their eyes. She understood how they felt. She watched happy couples with the same naked jealousy.

Fifteen minutes later, clutching her *Daltons Weekly*, Lola emerged triumphant from the 8 'til Late. To her relief the hatchback was still where she'd left it – only now it was surrounded by people.

Had there been an accident? No, thank God, there was no sign of a crumpled body, no ambulance, only a sort of low-loader lorry pulling up to the wheelie bin. The jostling crowd took no notice of her at all. Shivering suddenly, sure that she had just intercepted Stirwell Newtown's junior mafia attempting to break into her car, Lola pushed her way through the throng.

'Excuse me! Is there a problem here?'

'Oooh, lah-di-dah!' A bearded youth in a fluorescent orange jacket pulled a face. 'Yeah there is, if this is your car.'

'It's my car. And what's the problem?' Fear made Lola's voice rise imperiously.

The bearded youth looked scornful. 'Don't you come over all Princess Anne with me, love. Can't you read?'

Realizing that there were three fluorescent orange jackets amongst the clutch of anoraks and shell suits, Lola's heart plummeted. Traffic wardens! There were no double-yellows. She'd checked. She hadn't seen any no parking signs . . . Bugger! A parking ticket was all she needed. She had so little money . . .

'Sorry? Are you telling me –' She edged closer and looked at her car. 'Oh my God!!!'

Her hatchback had been wheel clamped.

The leggings brigade, joined by the elderly Chicken Jalfrezis, had now drifted from the 8 'til Late and had swelled the ranks of the interested spectators. Lola, panic rising in her throat, shook her head. 'There must be some mistake.'

'No mistake, love.' The second of the fluorescent

jackets jabbed towards a notice pasted to the wheelie bin. 'Wheel clamping zone. Vehicles illegally parked will be clamped and towed away. Retrieval £500. Which bit of that don't you understand?'

Five hundred pounds! Lola pressed her lips together to stop the scream escaping, then opened them slowly, trying to sound friendly. 'No, I mean, I'm here now, so all you have to do is unclamp it and I'll just drive off and –'

'What you'll just have to do,' the third fluorescent joined in on cue, 'is get your arse down to the compound with your five hundred smackers.' He looked over his shoulder and nodded towards the driver of the lorry. 'Take her away, Sam!'

Lola watched in horror as some sort of grappling hook was attached to the hatchback's rear bumper and the lorry started to winch the car towards the road.

'All my stuff's in there!' She grabbed the nearest fluorescent arm. 'Everything! You can't take my belongings!'

'You can get 'em when you collect the car, love. You pays your five hundred quid, we unlocks the clamp, and you get everything back.'

Lola hurled herself towards the car. 'I want my suitcases! You've got no right to do this! No right at all!'

'We've got every right, sweetheart. You parks in the wrong place and along we comes and we clamps your car. Easy enough to understand, I'd say.'

The winch was winding up with fearsome clanking noises, hauling the hatchback on to its front wheels. Frantically, Lola tried again to leap for a door handle.

A shell-suited arm pulled her back. 'Leave it, love. It ain't worth it.'

'But my things! Everything! My car!' Lola blinked back angry tears. 'They can't take it.'

'Bloody fascists,' the owner of the shell suit agreed. 'Sets 'emselves up. They're not from the council, you know, they're private cowboys. Sits round the corner, waiting for someone who don't know their game and bingo. Just like taking sweets from a baby.'

The crowd was swelling by the minute. It was probably the most excitement Stirwell Newtown had seen in years. A couple of the leggings and dark roots contingent had joined the shell suit and were now haranguing the lorry driver.

'Let her get her stuff out, you big bully!'

'You're scum, you are!'

The shell suit nodded her frizzy perm in Lola's face. 'Tell you what, love. You'd be better getting off down to the compound, dishing out your dosh, getting your car back and forgetting this. They don't take prisoners, these boys.'

Lola sketched a smile. The advice was probably well-meant even though it was nothing that she wanted to hear. There was no point in fighting the battle here. It was awful, but she'd cope. She'd have to cope. She couldn't afford to pay five hundred pounds, but there was no choice. Without the car there could be no live-in dream. No future.

She clutched at the arm of the nearest clamper. 'The, um, compound. Where is it exactly?'

'Stirwell Oldtown. Five miles down the road.'

'And how do I get there?'

'That's your problem, love. Mind, my brother runs the only taxi service in Stirwell, so I usually gives him the business ... Oh, and another thing, when you're booking your cab you'd better make sure you've got enough cash.'

Lola blinked. Cash? She hadn't got more than fifteen pounds in her purse – probably all of which would go on the taxi fare. 'I've got a cheque book and –'

'Bet you ain't got a cheque card what'll guarantee five hundred quid, though, have you, love? We only takes cash. No cash, no car. Oh, looks like we're away! See ya!'

The three fluorescent clampers leapt into the lorry cab, and Lola watched the nightmarish scene in mute fury as her hatchback disappeared into the cold grey gloom.

The show over, the crowd drifted away. Even her rescuer in the shell suit and bad perm had vanished. Letting out a shuddering breath, Lola wondered if she'd wake up in a minute and find this was yet another awful dream. Alone in a strange town, her car and all her worldly possessions whisked away, and no chance of ever seeing them again.

The sense of loss and bewilderment swept over her, and she dashed at the tears with the corner of the *Daltons Weekly*. All the euphoria of earlier had seeped away. If only she hadn't had the stupid live-in brainwave! If only she'd kept going on the motorway! If only –

'Here!' A taxi drew up alongside, and a replica of one of the fluorescents leaned from the window. 'Understand from our Pete that you wants a lift to the old compound, right? And that you'll be stopping off at a couple of hole in the walls, right? Better hop in, sweetheart . . .'

Against her better judgement, Lola hopped. What a scam! Keeping it in the family with a vengeance. Too weary and worried to care, she sank back in the unpleasant plastic seats and allowed the unsavoury Pete's unsavoury brother to whisk her away.

The clamping compound was, as Lola had feared, miles from anywhere. Well, miles from anywhere except a run-down high-rise estate and a landfill site. Towering wire fences surrounded row upon row of cars, some of which looked as though they'd been in situ for years.

Having parted with thirteen pounds to the taxi driver who had driven off with a triumphant blare of 1980s air-horns, Lola staggered across the cracked and broken concrete towards a lone Portakabin.

Inside, it was fuggy with cigarette smoke and stale air, and lit with one bare light bulb. The man behind the desk was unkempt, unshaven, and possibly unwashed.

'I've come to collect my car.'

'Got the cash, have you?'

'Yes.' She'd had to make visits to two cashpoints and drawn half from her bank account and half from the building society. The taxi driver had added on waiting time.

'Name. Address. Registration number. Ownership details. All on this form.' The man behind the desk pushed a piece of paper and a ballpoint pen towards her. 'If it all tallies with Swansea, you pay the cash over and you get your car and a receipt. Okay?'

Lola nodded, her hand shaking as she filled in the details, including Swansbury as her address. She didn't think 'no fixed abode' would further her cause. Fear was rapidly being overtaken by anger. She'd been conned and there wasn't a damn thing she could do about it. All she wanted was to reclaim the car and get as far away from this godforsaken place as quickly as possible.

She pushed the form and pen back across the desk.

'Okay. We'll just check this out. A coupla phone calls. Hang on.'

The man shuffled out of sight behind a screen and Lola hung. And hung.

Fifteen minutes later he reappeared. 'Bit of a problem here. Don't all tally.'

Anger was definitely in the ascendancy now. 'Crap! I might look like a cabbage but I'm not that green! Just let me have my car back. I've got the money. I've –'

'It's not your car, though, love, is it?' The man tapped the biro against his nicotine-stained teeth and stared again at the piece of paper in his hand. 'Not unless your name is Nigel Marion, which –' he let his gaze roll insolently up and down her body, 'I'd say it isn't.'

Oh, shit. Lola closed her eyes. Nigel had, he'd said, on the advice of the Marionette accountant, always registered her cars in his name – for the company tax concession. Bugger, bugger, bugger . . .

'I can explain.'

'Sorry, love. No point. We runs a legal business here and we always checks out the ownership details against the DVLA's computer. You don't own the car and until Mr Nigel Marion comes to bail it out, then here it stays.'

'He can't. He's dead.' Tears burned her eyes. This was too terrible for words. 'It's my car. I'm the registered keeper. Look, I've got the documents . . .'

'Keeper ain't the same as the owner and we can only

73

release to the owner. And if this guy has croaked, then tough tit . . . The car stays here until someone comes to prove they're next of kin and therefore rightful owner, which I guess you ain't.'

'It's my car! Mine!'

'No it ain't. Here, I've got yer bits and bobs out, we don't want them.' He yanked Lola's retrieved luggage up on to the counter. 'Sign for this lot and then bugger off. And when you can prove that you have a right to the car you can pay your dosh and drive it away. Until then, naff off!'

Shaking with fury, Lola signed the form, grabbed her bags with difficulty, and stumbled from the Portakabin.

Having staggered back across the uneven concrete loaded like a packhorse, she dumped the three suitcases and two cardboard boxes – everything she'd taken from the Swansbury flat – on the grey and weedy pavement outside the high-wire compound. What the hell was she going to do now?

There was no way she could expect anyone from the Marion family to help her out. Barbara, when notified, would no doubt grab the hatchback to add to Nigel's estate. Oh, why had she and Nigel never sorted things out legally? Why had he died before changing his will? Why had she not insisted that the things that mattered should be her responsibility?

Of course she knew the answers. Because neither of them had expected Nigel to die and leave all the ends untied. Lola groaned in abject misery. If Cousin Mimi and her married girlfriends in Swansbury were right and being a mistress was a sin – then she was certainly being made to atone for it now.

The late January afternoon was closing in. The grey skies seemed to have liquefied and melted over the tops of the tower blocks obscuring several floors. Shivering inside her silk and cashmere, Lola sat on the largest of the cardboard boxes, looked at the *Daltons Weekly* still tucked hopefully under her arm, and buried her head in her hands.

'You going to Reading?'

A truncated single-decker bus had thrummed to a halt alongside her. The woman behind the wheel was beaming.

Lola looked up blankly. God knows how long she'd been sitting there lost in her desolation. She certainly hadn't heard the bus arrive. 'Oh, um, yes . . .'

Well, why not? What did it matter where she went? Nothing mattered any more.

'Get yerself and yer stuff on board then,' the driver advised cheerfully. 'Only this ain't a recognized stop, but then again you don't look like the usual passenger we gets around here.'

Lola bumped and bundled the suitcases and boxes on to the bus, paid the fare to Reading and sat down heavily. There were only three other passengers, and they all regarded Lola with interest. She avoided their eyes. Probably they were all homicidal maniacs; she always seemed to attract them whenever she used public transport.

The bus chuntered its way through both the Stirwells and out into the countryside. Lola, her eyes still averted, watched the dark scenery reflected in the windows and felt as though she'd now reached rock bottom. With no transport to add to no home and no job, and just the five hundred pounds she'd taken to bail out the car, and all her possessions in cardboard boxes, she might as well join Reading's street people sooner rather than later.

Two passengers got off the bus and three more got on. The route to Reading seemed lengthy and tortuous. Lola didn't care. It was warm and she was in no hurry.

'You wouldn't be looking for somewhere to stay, I suppose?' A voice spoke in her ear. 'Only with all that baggage you look like you're off somewhere nice. And I wondered, if you hadn't arranged anything and you were going to Reading on spec, so to speak, you might like to come and stay with me.'

Lola's heart sank. One of the homicidal maniacs had swapped seats and was now sitting behind her. And it was getting really dark outside – and she'd have to strike up a conversation in case they turned nasty.

'Oh, er, well, no, it's very kind of you, but I've got all my plans made and people waiting for me and everything . . .' Lola slowly turned her head and looked at the woman behind her. 'Oh . . .'

The passenger didn't look like a homicidal maniac. In fact she looked cosy and cheerful and kind. But it was the riot of colour surrounding her that Lola noticed most. A halo of fat orange curls, orange lips and fingernails, rosy apples of rouge, bright green eyelids, and a hairy coat of rainbow shades.

And a smile. A huge warm, welcoming, friendly smile.

'I'm not mad,' the woman said briskly. 'No, don't deny it, that's what you were thinking, dear, wasn't it? I'm not a mind-reader, either. I could see it in your eyes. I'm Dilys Nightingale and I run a B&B in Steeple Fritton a couple of stops along the road, here –' She fished into her handbag and produced a card. 'I just wondered if you were looking for a place to stay.'

Lola stared down at the proffered picture of an exquisite white gabled cottage, with various extended bits poking out at odd angles, and at the flowers in the garden, and the overhanging horse chestnut tree. A sign saying Sunny Dene was in the foreground and there were two dogs sitting by the gate.

It looked like home. And she was tired and miserable and very, very lonely.

'Well, I don't have to go to Reading immediately. But it would only be for one night of course.'

'Bless you. Whatever. I'll get my daughter to rustle you up an evening meal when we get in.'

'That'd be lovely,' Lola said weakly. 'I haven't eaten all day.'

'Good thing then, my blasted car packing up this morning, else I wouldn't have been on this bus and we'd have missed each other.' Dilys's orange lips were smiling happily. 'You look like you could do with a good meal and a decent night's sleep. Had a bad day?'

'The worst,' Lola found herself returning the smile.

'Man trouble, no doubt. Feel free to talk about it if you want to, otherwise don't worry. I'm not nosy.' Dilys settled back in her seat. 'My daughter, Posy, has had more man trouble than you can shake a stick at. There's nothing you can tell me about men that'll shock me.'

Lola nodded. She didn't want to talk about anything with Dilys, especially about her daughter's man trouble. She just wanted to eat and sleep and find something suitable in *Daltons Weekly* and run away. Again.

The bus started to slow down and Dilys leaned forward again. 'Here we are. Steeple Fritton. I'll help you with your bags and stuff. Soon be home now, dear. Oh, and I'd better warn you, you may have a bit of bother with Trevor and Kenneth – mind they sleep in with Posy most nights, or sometimes they take it in turns. If you don't want them in your bedroom just tell them to go. Posy's quite happy to have them both.'

Jesus Christ, Lola thought as she swayed to the front of the bus, I've just agreed to spend the night in a brothel.

Chapter Six

Posy slid her feet from the pegs, relaxing her grip on the motorbike's handlebars. The never-ending sea of vehicles ahead had once more ground to a halt. Packed three-abreast, there wasn't even a suitable gap into which she could swoop the BMW and head for freedom. Frustratingly, every set of Reading's murky rush hour traffic lights seemed to be on red tonight.

Another fruitless day, she thought, inching forward as the traffic in front of her stuttered towards the next obstacle. Nearly three weeks since she'd discovered just how bad business was at Sunny Dene, and still she'd managed to do nothing about it.

She'd taken various casual temporary jobs which had lasted a matter of days and paid peanuts – but nothing the agencies offered her had been temp to perm – and without that vital perm bit, any regular income so much needed to shore up the B&B, was out of the question.

She'd had no idea that Sunny Dene was teetering on the verge of bankruptcy, and had promised to find herself some outside work, quickly. She'd assured her

parents that it would be all part of her new life –
managing to bring in some extra money and still help
out at the B&B.

She'd be so exhausted each night that there'd be no
time to dwell on her broken heart.

And to make matters worse, Dom had left for university – which saved on food but made Sunny Dene seem
even more deserted – and the new Mr and Mrs Ritchie
Dalgetty were back from Paris and once again resident
in Steeple Fritton.

Irritably, Posy scuffed at the ground with the toe of
her boot but fortunately, before her thoughts could once
more travel the Ritchie-Sonia wax effigy path, the traffic
queue began to totter from the town centre towards the
ring road. Posy revved up, indicated right, confidently
overtook all the four-wheeled vehicles, and roared away
from the town.

At least she could maintain a steady speed on the
almost clear roads. There was a hint of snow on the
brisk north wind in the gathering February dusk and
she was starving, too. Another day at interviews for
jobs she couldn't do had meant there had been no
time to eat, so it'd be great to get back to Sunny
Dene.

If only Ritchie and Sonia had tumbled from the top
of the Eiffel Tower, life would be perfect.

Posy sighed into the folds of her scarf as she swerved
the BMW towards the linking villages of Lesser Fritton
and Fritton Magna. Ritchie and Sonia were now joined
at the hip in their Bunny Burrow starter home and had
been seen in The Crooked Sixpence, as, apparently, had
Ellis Blissit. Amanda and Nikki had been very good

about keeping her updated. Their mobile phones had been on red alert for days.

Actually, she quite fancied a visit to the pub tonight – just to be sociable, of course. Nothing at all to do with the fact that she might just bump into Ellis. Beautiful, black-haired and black-eyed he may be, but he was still a man, and she was never, ever going to have anything to do with men again . . .

But, she had to admit, Ellis had livened up the village gossip no end. According to Glad and Rose Lusty and Vi Bickeridge, Ellis had left a trail of shattered hearts and paternity suits behind him. Holing him up in Steeple Fritton was supposed to have been a cure-all – but the affair with Tatty was, apparently, still raging.

Ellis Blissit, Posy had decided, was no better than Ritchie. Faithless, sex-crazed, irresponsible . . .

She laughed at herself. She was already starting to sound exactly like Dilys.

She'd reached the B&B almost without realizing it, and freewheeled the motorbike into Sunny Dene's garage. Lights spilled from the windows, making warm and welcome pathways through the chilly mist which rose from the common. It was such a pity, Posy thought, that Dilys and Norrie didn't have the houseful of guests they deserved. Mr D and Mr B had become regular visitors, but Sunny Dene needed far, far more than that.

Trevor and Kenneth scuttled across the flagged hall-way as she opened the door, burrowing their noses into her pockets, sniffing out the chocolate drops which had quickly become a homecoming routine. She dropped her crash helmet and gloves on to the hallstand and ripped open the packet.

'You spoil them,' Norrie said, passing through the hallway towards the dining room, wearing a pinny and carrying a steaming vegetable dish.

'And you don't, I suppose?' Posy grinned as the chocolate drop packet was emptied with the speed of light. She looked at the dish. 'Oh, sod it, it was supposed to be my turn to cook dinner. I didn't realize I was that late.'

'We've got a lady in,' Norrie lowered his voice. 'Your mother found her on the bus. Man trouble, she reckons. She'll tell you all about it. She's in the kitchen changing a washer.'

Posy's spirits soared. Whoopee – another paying guest. Someone else to help with Sunny Dene's financial burden. And possibly someone who could become a friend. And another one with man troubles. They could go to the pub and drink Tequila – well, not that The Crooked Sixpence stretched to anything as exotic as Tequila, of course, but maybe a Babycham or three – and get maudlin and drown each other's sorrows.

She practically skipped into the kitchen.

Most of Dilys was out of sight beneath the sink. A workmanlike tool box was on the flagged floor beside her. Glorious scents wafted from the oven.

'Hi,' Posy addressed Dilys's generous bum which was encased in some shiny stretchy fabric in rainbow stripes. 'Sorry I'm late. Dad said you were in here. Problems?'

Dilys extricated herself and sat on the floor looking up at Posy. The orange hair was on end and most of today's eye shadow had melted into harsh creases. 'Not really. Damn tap washer needed changing. Did that, then thought while I was at it I'd have a go at the U-bend. Saves on the plumber's bills.'

Posy leaned against the edge of the table. 'And did you get the car sorted out this morning, too?'

Dilys shook her head. Her face moved, her hair didn't. 'Never rains but it pours, eh? Bit of a bugger, the car. Beyond me. I can usually sort out most things mechanical. Don't want to have to take it to the garage if I can help it.'

Posy understood. The labour charge alone would probably break her parents' fragile bank. It was why the whole family had learned to turn their hands to practically everything.

'I'll have a look if you like. I know it's not the same as a bike engine but the principle is similar.'

'Would you?' Dilys scrambled to her feet. 'What a star you are.'

'Don't say that yet. If you can't sort it out I doubt if I can, but I'll certainly have a go after dinner.'

'Leave it till the weekend, dear. I won't be needing it. I went into Reading on the bus and got all my bits and pieces.' Dilys removed her rubber gloves and put the plumbing gubbins back in the tool box. 'What about you, then? Had a good day?'

'Not really. Three interviews for jobs that I'm hopelessly unqualified to do and don't stand a dog's chance of getting.' Posy didn't meet Dilys's eyes. She knew that her mother was counting on some extra money very, very soon. 'With all those mobile phone tekkies now out of work, there are more electronics whizz kids looking for jobs, any jobs, than ever.'

The kitchen door opened and Norrie, flanked by

Trevor and Kenneth, reached across the cooker and dumped an almost full plate and a gravy boat. 'She's not got much of an appetite. Only picked at her first course and hardly touched her casserole. Probably won't want the rhubarb crumble.'

Posy's stomach rumbled. 'Well, you know it won't go to waste – anyway, who is she? Where did she come from? And more importantly, how long is she staying?'

'God knows,' Norrie raised his eyebrows to the non-existent hairline, extracted an individual rhubarb crumble from the cooker, and with Trevor and Kenneth dancing attendance, disappeared again.

Dilys poured two cups of tea from the flowery teapot and handed one to Posy. 'Her name's Lola.'

'And?' Posy sipped the tea. 'You've just made her sound like Lucrezia Borgia.'

'In my book Lola is a tart's name, *and* she's got all her worldly goods in a couple of suitcases and some cardboard boxes. Playing away, you mark my words, and her husband found out and, bingo, our Lola's on her bike.'

Posy spluttered with laughter. 'You don't know that.'

'No, but you're going to find out, dear, aren't you? Get yourself into the dining room and have your meal and chat to her, then report back.'

'Mum!'

Dilys fluffed at her curls. 'You find out what you can about young Lola, and I'll tell you the latest on the Ellis Blissit and Tatty Spry affair.'

Posy peeled herself away from the table. 'Okay, done.'

The dining room was, of course, deserted except for

the mysterious Lola. Posy, sitting in her usual seat by the window that looked out on to Sunny Dene's back garden of stunted apple trees, lavender beds, tumbled cottage garden borders, a half-hidden sundial and the full working model railway layout, picked up her knife and fork with a feeling of disappointment.

Lola had chosen to sit in the far corner, with her back to the rest of the room. She hadn't looked up when Posy came in, and had her head down, sipping her coffee with her shoulders hunched.

Bobbed blonde hair – classy; red sweater – expensive; black trousers – also probably expensive. Posy sighed. Lola didn't look like a Levis and T-shirt girl, then. And apart from rushing over and plonking herself down beside her and striking up an obviously unwanted conversation, Posy felt there wasn't much else she could do.

Loss of Brownie points with Dilys straight away, damn it. Not to mention no further info on Ellis and Tatty Spry. Bugger.

She wolfed down the soup and then the casserole, without the help of Trevor and Kenneth who seemed to have abandoned the dining room tonight. They'd probably picked up Lola's Greta Garbo vibes and decided to steer clear.

Norrie came in with the rhubarb crumble and coffee, made comic gestures towards Lola, and receiving negative gestures back from Posy, disappeared again.

Having scraped the last of the custard from the bowl, she collected her empties, pushed back her chair and walked across to Lola's table.

'Hi, I'm Posy . . . Oh!'

The face that turned to look at her was high-cheekboned and very beautiful, but older than she'd imagined. It was also streaked with tears.

'God, I'm sorry,' Posy backed off. 'I didn't mean to intrude. Excuse me . . .'

Feeling awful, she rushed out of the dining room, shoved the dishes into the dishwasher and clattered up the myriad skewwhiff staircases to her room.

It took her five minutes to pull off the interview trousers and neatish blouse she'd worn under her leather jacket, and pull on a pair of faded jeans and Dom's second-best rugby shirt which he'd probably have missed by now, and leap down the stairs again.

Calling out to Norrie and Dilys, telling them she was going to The Crooked Sixpence – and not getting a reply because they were obviously snuggled up with Trevor and Kenneth and deeply immersed in one of the soaps anyway – she quietly closed Sunny Dene's door.

The pub was, as always at this hour, deserted apart from the elderly Pinks, a family from the Cressbeds council estate, in the corner. She hadn't had any phone calls from Amanda and Nikki so guessed the Dalgetty coast was clear.

Ordering a glass of wine, Posy hauled herself on to one of the rickety bar stools.

Hogarth, the landlord, served the drink in a tumbler with his usual lack of civility. He rarely acknowledged his customers, never asked any questions, or in fact instigated much conversation at all. Apart from the words necessary for drink buying and the obligatory please and thank you, he and Posy had rarely held what could pass for a conversation.

Hogarth had been the landlord here for as long as Posy could remember. Sometimes he disappeared for weeks on end to see to his other businesses – what and where they were remained an unsolved mystery – and just shut the pub with no warning. It was always regarded as a mixed blessing when he returned.

Whether there was a Mrs Hogarth or not, she had no idea. No one in Steeple Fritton knew, either. And Hogarth offspring she hadn't even considered. You'd surely have to be drunk or desperate to want to procreate with The Crooked Sixpence's landlord.

But The Crooked Sixpence itself could be a lovely pub, Posy thought, if only somebody cared. It was proper olde-worlde, rather than some huge corporate brewery trying to make it look that way with acres of weathered plastic panelling and fake polystyrene beams.

There were grubby armchairs and carved settles on either side of the fireplace, but no fire – just unraked grey ashes – and the tables and chairs were good dark wood beneath their patina of grime. A glorious, but unpolished, grandmother clock idly ticked away the time. All the fixtures and fittings looked right, and the colours, at one time dark reds and golds, were authentic too. It was just all so neglected and unloved.

'Thanks,' she handed Hogarth the tumbler for a refill, knowing she should drink more slowly. She couldn't keep on spending money like this. 'Quiet in here tonight.'

Hogarth paused in unscrewing the top from the wine bottle, gawping over his shoulder. 'What?'

'Er, I said, it's quiet in here tonight.'

'It's quiet in here every bloody night –' The wine was decanted in a vicious spurt. 'And that's the way we like it, as you well know.'

'Oh, er, right, yes of course,' Posy shifted uncomfortably on her stool. 'Only I just wondered if maybe there was a reason why you've never encouraged more trade.'

'Well, don't wonder.' Hogarth hurled the glass across the bar. 'The village wants a traditional village pub and that's what I gives them. They don't want no idle chit-chat, nor jukeboxes, nor darts, snooker, fruit machines or bloody pub quizzes, nor nothing along those lines.'

'Well, yes, but . . .'

Hogarth leaned grimy elbows on the grimy bar. 'Look, I knows that you youngsters wants pubs with rock and roll, and football on the telly, and drugs and stuff coming out of your ears, but my clientele likes their pints quiet, and their pubs, too.'

'But I'm one of your clientele. And Nikki and Amanda and loads of other young people in Steeple Fritton. And we all have to go somewhere else if we want a bit of life –'

'Good bloody riddance,' Hogarth snarled. 'You youngsters spend piddle all. Serious drinking is for the grown-ups, right? And the grown-ups in the village want a proper pub. And that's what they get 'ere.'

Posy blinked. Not much chance of Hogarth turning The Crooked Sixpence into the next JD Wetherspoons, then.

One of the elderly corner customer contingent had unfurled itself, wandered to the bar, and now peered at her from beneath raggle-taggle eyebrows.

'Hello, young Posy. I 'eard you'd done a runner.'

Posy, from her perch on the stool, looked down at the wrinkled face, the tortoise neck, and the emaciated body all encased in flaky layers of olive green clothing, and sighed. 'That was weeks ago. I've been back for ages.'

'Have you? Bugger it.' The wrinkles merged together as the mouth emitted a cackle, a claw closed around a bottle of Guinness, and the heap of clothing started to shuffle back towards the corner. 'We'll have to gossip about something else now.'

'Which one was that?' Posy forgot the no-talking rule and looked hopefully towards Hogarth.

'Oh, don't ask me. Them Pink twins is indecipherable.'

Posy smiled. Years ago, when she'd first started drinking in The Crooked Sixpence, she'd made a huge mistake about the Pinks. Hogarth, in an unusually loquacious mood, had explained to a disbelieving Posy that the Pinks were talented musicians.

'Them Pinks,' he'd said, 'are dead, dead musical. Now, when they has a bit of a singsong, that's proper pub stuff. Not all this electric bollocks. Martha and Mary is real talented.'

'Martha? Mary?' Posy had blinked. The gender had completely passed her by. And musical? 'Nah! Surely not . . .'

'Martha and Mary Pink has been living on the Cressbeds Estate and drinking in this pub ever since I was a nipper,' Hogarth had said, practically garrulous. 'And their parents and grandparents afore them. The other one over there is their brother, he plays the accordion –'

'Does he? How clever. No, don't tell me.' Posy had

been entranced. 'If they're Martha and Mary, then he must be Joseph, like in the Bible.'

'He's Neddy,' Hogarth had said, waddling away from the bar. 'Like in the donkey.'

Posy still giggled at the memory but didn't have time to dwell on it as at that moment the door creaked open. The three Pinks all lifted rheumy eyes in excitement, clattering their Guinness bottles together as they lost coordination. Posy, praying that it wasn't Ritchie and Sonia, held her breath and hardly dared to look.

'Hi, Posy. It must be my lucky day. I hoped I'd find you in here, and all alone, too.'

Chapter Seven

Posy looked at Ellis Blissit and sighed with relief. 'Oh, it's you . . .'

'Not the warmest welcome I've ever had, but at least you're under ninety-seven, unlike most of the clientele.' Ellis, looking a little frayed round the edges, made his way towards her and grinned. 'What are you drinking?'

Posy peered into her glass. 'Hogarth's version of house white I think.'

'I'll get you a refill, but I'm afraid I can't stop very long.'

'No, it's all right, really. I don't want you to buy me a drink.' Posy tried not to notice his dishevelled black hair or the over-brightness of his black eyes and especially not the fact that the top two buttons of his faded 501s were undone. 'I, er, wouldn't want to keep you.'

'Perceptive as well as beautiful. Tatty couldn't get a baby-sitter so we're, um, having a night in at her place. It's half-time at the moment. Oh, hi . . .' He beamed as Hogarth rumbled towards them. 'Can I have another wine for Posy, please, and a bottle of Jack Daniel's to take out.'

Hogarth squinted suspiciously. 'Who's Jack Daniels?'

'It's a bourbon,' Ellis looked slightly thrown. 'But if you don't keep it, then Southern Comfort will do.'

Hogarth grunted. 'We ain't got nothing poncey like that. You can have stout or brown ale to take out.'

'Go for the stout,' Posy advised. 'The iron'll give you stamina.'

'Will Tatty drink stout?'

'Tatty? God, she'll drink anything that some bloke will pay for,' Posy shrieked with laughter, then stopped. 'Um, yes, I mean, I expect so.'

Hogarth plonked two bottles of stout on the bar, decanted another angry gush of wine into Posy's glass and snatched Ellis's money, leaving scorch marks on the counter top.

'Things still bad at the B&B?' Ellis asked, squeezing the change into the back pocket of the 501s and managing to display a fair expanse of tanned and muscled midriff. 'Gran said you were having a hard time.'

'The worst.' Posy sighed. 'Have you found anything yet?'

'I've started being a highwayman, which in turn should lead to the Robin Hood bit of my business.'

'Uh?' Posy blinked over the edge of her glass. 'In English?'

Ellis laughed. 'I've bought a second-hand white van. I'm going to use it as a sort of taxi-cum-bus-cum-delivery service for the village – as and when required. And I'll charge the rich ones loads and the skint ones nothing.'

'Very enterprising of you and more honest than I'd

imagined you were going to be. I'm quite impressed. If only more people thought the way you do.' Posy stared into her wine glass and wished she hadn't. There were little black things floating in it. 'Our problem at Sunny Dene is that no one comes to stay in the village any more. The place just doesn't attract outsiders, or visitors, let alone holidaymakers.'

'You should advertise.'

'Don't you think we've done all that? We've spent more on advertising than a multinational company.'

'Sorry – mind you, it applies to the whole of Steeple Fritton if you ask me. No one even passes through it, let alone stops over.'

Posy nodded. 'What we need to do is put it on the map.'

'Like Glastonbury or Cropredy?'

'Yes – well, no. Not like that exactly. Not a music festival. It's been done too many times and gets bad press, which is the last thing this village needs. But the same principle. You see, you say Glastonbury and Cropredy and everyone in the world knows what you mean. We could do that with Steeple Fritton, make it synonymous with –'

'Bad pubs and empty guest houses?'

'Ellis Blissit, don't be such a defeatist. Look, you admit that you need a life-challenge and so do I. Sunny Dene needs visitors, so does this place, not to mention the entire village. Why don't we make it happen?'

'Yeah, right. And how do you plan to do that?'

'That's it . . . That's where it starts to come unravelled.' Posy sighed. 'I have absolutely no idea.'

Ellis grinned again. 'Why don't we meet in here, say a week on Saturday, and talk about it?'

Posy eyed him warily. 'You're not asking me for a date, are you?'

'Wouldn't dare. No, I'm serious. We'll just mull over a few ideas, see what we've got to work with.' He glanced up at the sonorously ticking clock. 'Shit – I'll have to dash. Tatty'll have finished putting the kids to bed. So, I'll see you in here about seven next Saturday, okay?'

Why not? Oh, well, there were millions of reasons why not – but still . . .

Posy nodded. 'I'll be here.'

Ellis turned away from the bar, just as The Crooked Sixpence's door opened again and the Pinks fluttered into their welcome routine. Posy, who was still engaged in wondering just what Steeple Fritton could offer the world and storing up Ellis's highwayman bus service and night-in-with-Tatty stories to tell Dilys and Norrie, nearly tumbled from her bar stool.

Ritchie and Sonia, holding hands, stood in the doorway.

Whimpering, cursing herself for not having her mobile with her and therefore not being on the receiving end of Nikki and Amanda's warning call, Posy panicked. Ritchie looked totally, totally gorgeous. Her heart lurched at the sight of him, and all the old, familiar feelings rushed back unbidden.

Without thinking any further, she grabbed Ellis's shoulder. 'Could you, um, just hang on for a moment?'

Ellis flicked a glance towards the newcomers, looked back at Posy, and fortunately didn't shake off her hand. Before she realized it, he'd dumped the stout bottles on the bar and had slid his arms round her waist.

'I, um, actually meant if you could just pretend to be

with me . . .' Posy wriggled slightly, not daring to look at Ritchie and Sonia. 'You don't have to – oh!'

Ellis kissed her. It was a seriously professional kiss. It was the sort of kiss that meant business. Posy, after a half-hearted attempt to push him away, found herself kissing him back. It was a bit disturbing to find that he tasted of Tatty's patchouli and musk oil.

'Hey!' Hogarth's shout penetrated the roaring in her ears. 'You can pack that in! We don't 'ave any of that in here!'

Shakily, Posy opened her eyes and squirmed away from Ellis. He was grinning at her. Ritchie and Sonia were nowhere to be seen and the Pinks were rocking backwards and forwards in their corner, chortling with glee.

'Um, er . . .' Posy blinked in embarrassment. 'Ooops . . .'

'Ooops indeed,' Ellis said cheerfully, picking up the bottles of stout and looking over his shoulder. 'Mission accomplished, though. They've obviously decided not to stay. And I must be going, but any time you want rescuing like that just give me a yell. I think I'm going to like living here. See you next Saturday then, if not before. Bye.'

Posy was still staring at the doorway long after he'd left. Oh, God! Oh, *God*! What had she done? Her lips were tingling – and so was a whole lot more of her. Bugger!

She started to smile. It had got rid of Sonia and Ritchie though – and the Pinks would waste no time in telling everyone in Steeple Fritton and – oooh! What on earth would Tatty make of it?

She took a gulp of wine and was still smiling when

the door clicked and the Pinks started to rev up again. Praying it wasn't Ritchie and Sonia on a return visit, Posy reckoned this must be the busiest night the pub had seen in years.

Lola, a black jacket draped over the red cashmere, stood in the doorway, looked at the inside of The Crooked Sixpence, and immediately turned to leave.

The Pinks shrilled their disappointment.

'Er, Lola!' Posy quickly pulled herself together and gingerly patted the neighbouring stool. 'Over here. It's nicer than it looks.'

At least she'd stopped crying, Posy thought, as Lola picked her way across the bar like someone tiptoeing through a pig pen. Her eyes were still reddened and puffy, and the make-up she'd obviously hastily applied didn't hide the blotches. Despite all that, Posy conceded, Lola was a very beautiful woman.

'How did you know my name?' Lola looked at the bar stool and remained standing.

'Oh, er, Mum told me,' Posy muttered. 'At Sunny Dene. I'm Posy. Dilys and Norrie's daughter.'

Lola was staring at the years of ingrained dirt on the bar top with tangible horror. 'I know. Dilys told me – and so did you.'

'I wasn't sure that you'd heard me in the dining room. You seemed upset.'

'I was. I am. And I must be mad to be in here.'

'There isn't a lot of choice in Steeple Fritton, to be honest,' Posy said, as Hogarth lumbered his way towards them again. 'It's this or sitting in your room with the telly or in Sunny Dene's residents' lounge with the telly.'

She thought Lola had muttered Christ, but she couldn't be sure.

Hogarth leered at them. 'What's it to be? Another wine?'

'Gin and tonic,' Lola said quickly, 'and let me see the glass first.'

Hogarth snorted and shuffled towards the back of the bar. There was a lot of clanking and unseen sleight of hand, and eventually he returned with a fairly respectable highball glass.

'This do you, yer ladyship?'

Apparently oblivious to the sarcasm, Lola took the glass, held it up to the dim light bulb overhead, ran her finger round the rim, then nodded grudgingly. 'I don't suppose it has ever seen a dishwasher in its life, but it'll have to do.'

'Dishwasher?' Hogarth snatched it away and started assaulting the Gordon's bottle. 'What's a dishwasher?'

'He's not joking,' Posy hissed. 'Believe me. Best not to go down that route. Hogarth doesn't encourage conversation.'

The gin and tonic without the added luxuries of ice and a slice, was thumped on the bar. Lola looked as though she was about to burst into tears again. From the corner of her eye Posy could see one of the Pinks unfurling their layers of dusty rags and looking as though they were going to stumble towards the bar with cheery Steeple Fritton greetings for the newcomer. As it wasn't wearing a headscarf, Posy guessed this must be Neddy. The ancient accordion strapped to his chest was a bit of a giveaway, too.

Pretty sure that Neddy Pink would be a villager too

far for Lola in her present state, Posy urgently indicated a corner table. 'Why don't we sit over there? A bit more private.'

Apart from the Pinks and Hogarth they had the place to themselves. Privacy was not a problem. However, Lola seemed to welcome the suggestion and followed her into the dark recess.

'So,' Posy surveyed what was left of her wine. 'What brings you to Steeple Fritton?'

'Bad luck and your mother.'

'Oh, right. Are you staying long?'

Lola shook her head. 'Just tonight, thank goodness. I'm leaving for Reading in the morning.'

Posy's heart sank. One night at the B&B wasn't going to shore up the coffers at all.

'I'll give you a lift if you like,' Posy offered, remembering that Dilys said she'd picked Lola up on the bus and that therefore, assuming Ellis's Dormobile service wasn't yet functional, transport might be a problem. 'I'm off on a job hunt myself.'

'Thank you.' Lola's eyes filled with tears again. She fished a handkerchief from the pocket of her black coat. 'Oh, I'm sorry. It's just I'm not used to people being kind, and I've had one of the worst days of my life and this place is just like a bloody nightmare!'

'It gets better,' Posy said gently. 'But I know how you feel.'

'I don't think you can possibly know how I feel. I've lost everything. Absolutely everything.'

Posy stared at the dregs of the wine and waited.

'Have you any idea what it's like to have nothing?' Lola knocked back the gin in one go. 'To have nowhere

98

to call home? No job? No bloody nothing?'

Posy shook her head. 'Well, no, not exactly. But I do know what it's like to be unhappy.'

Lola sniffed, reaching again for the hankie. 'But at least you're young. You've got everything ahead of you. My life's over.'

'It can't be that bad, surely? Was it a man?'

The tears trickled unbidden down Lola's cheeks. 'He died. Last year.'

'Oh, how awful. I'm so sorry.'

Posy wanted to touch Lola's hand in a gesture of sympathy. This was far, far worse than damn Ritchie cheating on her. Lola must have been left completely destitute. There had probably been death duties, or monstrous debts, or something financially terrible – her knowledge of what happened after a partner's death was pretty much second-hand.

'And couldn't you stay in the house that you shared? Because of the memories?'

'Something like that, yes.'

Money troubles definitely, Posy thought, as well as grief. Poor, poor Lola. Deciding to throw caution to the wind and hang the expense, Posy picked up both glasses and, much to Hogarth's delight, rushed to the bar for refills. This wasn't a moment for penny-pinching.

'Thanks . . .' Lola swigged at the second G&T without even glancing at the smeared tumbler. 'It's very kind. And what about you? Same sort of thing?'

'Oh, no, nothing nearly so awful. Mine just married someone else.'

'Mine already was.'

'What?' Posy frowned.

'Married to someone else. He wasn't my husband, you see, so when he died I was left with nothing.'

Posy stared at Lola across the slightly uneven rim of the tumbler. This woman, this elegant, beautiful woman was another bloody Sonia nee Tozer! A man-stealer! And she'd been feeling sorry for her!

She sat back in her chair, wobbling slightly as not all four of its legs touched the carpet at the same time. 'Well, sorry, but don't you think his wife, um, widow, might have some sort of right to be slightly more upset than you?'

'Knowing his wife, no, not really.'

'But I know what it feels like to be made a fool of. How could you cheat on –?'

Lola stood up, pushing back her chair so quickly that it fell over. The Pinks applauded. She wrapped the black jacket tightly round her. 'Look, this really is none of your business. You can't begin to understand, and I shouldn't have said anything.'

Not even bothering to finish her drink, Lola stiffly righted the fallen chair and headed for the door. Posy glared after her. Hogarth, leaning on his elbows amongst the spillage stains, had his mouth open.

The Crooked Sixpence's dim, dark atmosphere plunged even deeper into depression as the door slammed shut behind Lola, leaving the unrelenting ticking of the grandmother clock slicing through the silent misery.

Posy stared angrily into her tumbler, once more feeling very, very alone. Oh, God – she'd insulted a Sunny Dene guest! Lola was probably on her way out of the B&B at that very moment. Dilys and Norrie would kill her. And despite the bliss of Ellis's kiss, she realized that she still wanted Ritchie so much that it hurt.

Without warning, the Pinks suddenly erupted en masse from their corner, and shuffled towards the bar. Martha and Mary creakingly regrouped as Neddy whipped out his accordion.

Before anyone could stop them, they wheezed raucously into a ripsnorting version of 'Happy Days Are Here Again'.

Chapter Eight

As the chill morning rain swirled across the common, Norrie beamed happily at Lola.

'I understand Posy has offered you a lift into Reading? The BMW is amazing, you'll love it, I'm sure. And I do hope you enjoyed your brief stay with us?'

'Oh, er, yes, very much, thank you.' Lola gathered her suitcases and cardboard boxes together under Sunny Dene's porch, and thought longingly of a smooth luxurious fast ride away from Steeple Fritton ensconced in BMW luxury. 'But I think the arrangements may have altered a bit. With Posy, that is.'

Norrie whistled the dogs to heel, unfurling his umbrella. 'Really? I'm sure she said she'd offered. I know she's going into Reading –'

'Later, I think she said. Not until this afternoon or something.' Lola smiled at Norrie, knowing that the smile didn't reach her eyes. It barely reached the corners of her mouth.

She simply had to get away before she bumped into Posy again. She knew she couldn't cope with another barrage of censure. It had been her own fault, of course: giving away too much too soon and to a complete stranger.

It was just that Posy had been friendly, and it seemed so long since she'd had a friend; and an unexpected girlie night out, albeit in that dingy pub, was one of the nicest things that had happened to her for months. How the hell was she supposed to have known that Posy was yet another member of the Wronged Women of the World club?

'You could always get a taxi,' Norrie said, barging into her thoughts, as the dogs danced impatiently round his legs. 'Mind, it'll have to be from somewhere else because we don't have a taxi service round here. And of course, Dilys's car is off the road, otherwise she'd have been pleased to oblige.'

'What about buses?'

'Not today, I'm afraid. There'll be one tomorrow about three-ish – maybe.'

Lola groaned. Having spent a sleepless night in Sunny Dene's admittedly gorgeous bedroom, and having managed to eat none of the continental breakfast she'd asked for, all she really wanted to do now was to get away from Steeple Fritton and start her new life as soon as possible. But how?

As Posy was obviously out of the question it looked like it would have to be a taxi – and she could scarcely afford the bus fare.

'Right on cue,' Norrie raised his voice as the garage doors opened and Posy peered out. 'Ms Wentworth here thought you weren't going into Reading until this afternoon.'

'Did she? I wonder why.'

'There!' Norrie rubbed his hands together and nodded at Lola. 'All sorted. You can go with Posy after all.'

Posy, looking decidedly unfriendly and very threatening in black leather, raised her eyebrows. 'If you still want a lift the offer still stands. Getting out of here is virtually impossible and as we'll never see one another again I don't suppose it will matter too much.'

Norrie looked puzzled as Posy ducked back into the garage. Lola sighed again, swallowed the 'Not on your bloody life' that was bubbling to her lips, and called after her. 'Yes, well, under the circumstances, thank you, I'd be very grateful, and . . . Good God! I'm not getting on that thing! I've never ridden a motorbike in my life!'

Posy hauled the monstrous peacock blue and vibrant pink machine on to its stand.

'Seems like a good time to start, then, if you want to get to Reading this morning, that is.'

'But I've got all my luggage! And it's raining! And Norrie said you had a BMW.'

'He did. I have. This is it.'

Lola stared at the motorbike and then at Posy with growing irritation. Oh, this was the final straw.

Posy had now clambered astride the bike and tipped back her visor. 'You could always leave your stuff here, come into Reading with me on the pillion, then if you find a job I'll bring you back for your luggage.'

Norrie beamed. 'Sounds a good plan to me. There, isn't that lovely to be sorted? It's been nice having you to stay, my dear. Good luck in your job hunting.' Whistling Trevor and Kenneth to heel, the trio splashed off across the common for their morning constitutional. Just before they all disappeared from view, Norrie turned and raised his hand in farewell. 'And any time you're back this way, you'll know where to come, won't you?'

'Yes, of course,' Lola waved back. 'But I hope it won't be necessary.'

'Me too.' Posy's fingers were poised on the ignition key. 'So? Are you coming with me or not?'

Lola glanced down at the knee-length pencil skirt and the kitten-heeled shoes she'd worn so that she'd look suitable for employment. The rain had already flattened her hair, and the icy wind was cutting through her stockings. 'I can't, well, not dressed like this and I haven't got a crash helmet and anyway, we'll probably be killed.'

'Suit yourself,' Posy shrugged inside her leather jacket. 'But there don't seem to be many other options. Look, I really do have to go, I've got an interview at nine.'

'Then go. Please. I'll sort something out, get a taxi and, er, about last night –'

Posy gave a squashed-up frown from inside her helmet. 'Let's not talk about it. We're never going to meet again. We'll just agree to differ on the subject, okay?'

'I just wanted you to know –' But Lola's words were drowned by the roar of the BMW's engine as Posy skimmed off the shingle drive and soared away.

She sighed again. She'd probably sighed more in the last two weeks than in the whole of her life. Posy had gone, Norrie was out of sight, Dilys was no doubt rewiring electrical appliances throughout the glories of Sunny Dene, and Steeple Fritton was deserted. As the rain and wind increased, Lola felt the loneliness roll back in.

'You looking for a lift somewhere?' A cheerful voice sliced through the sadness as a sleek white Dormobile pulled to a splashy halt outside Sunny Dene. A young man with dark hair and even darker eyes was beaming at her. 'You going to Reading?'

Lola blinked nervously. Was she desperate enough to risk her fate in the hands of a White Van Man? Deciding that she was, she nodded. 'Yes, actually, I am.'

'Well, then, actually, so are we.'

'How much is this going to cost me?'

'Depends what currency you're offering.' The Dormobile's door slid open and the driver, who looked far too young and trendy to be buried alive in Steeple Fritton, started heaving her luggage into its interior. He grinned at her. 'Nothing. It'll cost you nothing. This is my maiden voyage. All passengers travel free today.'

Peering inside, Lola was relieved to notice that the Dormobile was apparently already packed to the roof with people. And if it was dry and free . . .

'All aboard the Skylark!' A voice cackled from the front passenger seat. 'Shove up there, Tatty, and make room for the young lady.'

For a moment, Lola hesitated. Maybe this wasn't a wise move. Okay, with a busload she was less likely to be ravished by the beautiful black-eyed boy, but this could well be a day trip for Steeple Fritton's less-stable residents.

She hauled herself up on to the step, the tight skirt not aiding her progress, stared at her fellow passengers, and *knew* that it was.

Three women of mixed ages stared at her; at least half a dozen children who appeared to be in fancy dress were tethered in the back seats; and the Dormobile's radio reverberated to a cacophony of 1960s bubblegum music.

Lola had already formulated apologies for changing her mind. However, just as she attempted to take a backward step, the driver had hurled her luggage on top of the children, and was now helping her negotiate her way inside the Dormobile with a lot of quite unnecessary body contact.

Stumbling amongst an assortment of damp footwear and sitting as elegantly as possible next to the youngest of the three women who had black tendrilly hair like early-Cher and was dressed in layers of lace and velvet, Lola nodded her resigned thanks to the driver.

'No problem.' His eyes lingered on her legs and the ten denier black stockings. 'Nice to have a new, er, face.'

Grinning with what Lola considered was excess familiarity, he slid the door shut, bounded round to the driver's side and leapt in behind the wheel. Within seconds they were mobile, and leaving a cloud of spray in its wake, the Dormobile bounced merrily away from Steeple Fritton.

The elderly woman in the front seat eased herself round and beamed over a skeletal shoulder. The shoulder, Lola noticed, was of threadbare brown wool and covered in hairs, none of which matched those protruding from beneath its owner's tartan headscarf.

'I'm Glad Blissit, this –' she patted the driver on his well-muscled shoulder, 'is my grandson, Ellis, and them –' a nod in the direction of the women, 'is Tatty Spry, she's the hippie one, and Rose Lusty.'

Lola smiled nervously at everyone. The children had

fought their way out from under her suitcases and were singing along to the bubblegum music. It would, Lola thought, have been a touch more melodic if they'd all been singing the same tune.

'The kiddies belong to Tatty,' Glad said cheerfully, 'and various blokes.'

Tatty, the velvet and lace woman, looked rather proud at this scurrilous statement.

'You ain't a pop singer, I suppose?' Glad raised her voice as the Dormobile lurched round a leafy bend and the children cheered.

Lola shook her head. Oh, God – being killed on Posy's motorbike was looking really, really enticing compared to this.

The brown shoulders twitched. 'No, didn't think so. You'm a bit too long in the tooth. Film star?'

Again Lola shook her head. Next to her, Tatty laughed. Rose Lusty, the third member of the trio, who looked like Margaret Thatcher in her blue suit and matching handbag days, didn't. The bubblegum tune was insisting that 'Simon Says' and the children, despite the lack of space, were executing the arm movements dextrously immediately behind Lola's head.

Glad clicked her dentures together with an air of disappointment. 'What are you then?'

'Gran,' Ellis admonished gently. 'Don't be so nosy.' He glanced at Lola through the driving mirror, the black eyes amused. 'Gran gets *Hello* and *OK!* by subscription. It's her lifetime ambition to discover Madonna or Britney Spears living on the Cressbeds council estate.'

''S'all right for you, young Ellis. You gets out and about. We don't see no life in Steeple Fritton these days.' Glad yanked herself round again with a lot of grunting and sighing, and clouds of dust puffing up from the depths of the worn brown coat. 'So, who are you?'

'Lola Wentworth.'

'Lola? *Lola? LOLA?*' Glad rocked gleefully backwards and forwards as the children picked up the name-theme and started humming alternate snatches of Barry Manilow and the Kinks. 'You're a stripper!'

Dear Jesus! Lola exhaled. 'I am not a stripper.' She glared at the still-chanting children. 'Nor am I a showgirl or a damn lady-boy.'

Ellis gave her a look of sympathy through the mirror.

Glad clicked her teeth again. 'What are you, then? And what are you doing here?'

Getting out as fast as I can, Lola thought, watching the countryside disappear in a sheet of torrential rain as the Dormobile hit the bypass. Ellis's driving was nothing if not terrifying. There had been no careful approach from the slip road into the flow of traffic. He'd just pointed the white van towards the melee and put his foot to the floor. The children had clapped enthusiastically.

'You might as well answer her,' Ellis said, taking his eyes unnervingly from the road. 'She won't give up until she's got the full story.'

Lola worked some saliva into her mouth, amazed both that the Dormobile was still intact and that they were still alive. She had to shout above the roar of the engine and the intrusion of 'Quick Joey Small' from the stereo. It was a small mercy that the children had quickly tired of the Lola songs.

'Well, actually, there's nothing to tell. I met Dilys on the bus after a little mishap yesterday and she kindly invited me to stay overnight at the B&B – and now I'm going to look for a job in Reading.'

Even the children were silent.

'Dearie me . . .' Rose Lusty spoke for the first time. 'You haven't heard then?'

'Heard what?'

Glad swivelled round again. 'About the job situation in Reading. All them techno kiddies that used to be employed by the mobile phone and computer companies have flooded the market. You won't get nothing, specially not at your age.'

Lola flinched. The Dormobile was cheek by jowl with an articulated lorry. When the threat of imminent death had passed she shrugged. 'I don't think that'll be a problem. I'm not looking for anything technical – I thought I'd go into hotel work or caring . . .'

Glad and Rose chuckled together. Tatty Spry shook back a lot of spirally hair and freed several silver necklaces which had become entangled in her lace blouse. 'Any live-in type vacancy within a fifty-mile radius has been filled by the call-centre redundancies, I'm afraid. And there are waiting lists stretching into the next millennium. Silicon Valley might as well be renamed Death Valley. You couldn't have come to a worse area for jobs.'

Deciding that hurling herself from the Dormobile into the two lanes of fast-flowing traffic was the only solution to her mounting problems, Lola was just about to ask Ellis to stop and let her out, when he swerved off the dual carriageway, tore along a concrete road and stood on the brakes.

'Nursery! School! Now! Go!'

The children immediately stopped singing, unfastened themselves, gathered together various lunchboxes and bags and waterproof coats, and slithered across the seats like slinky puppies. Tatty Spry kissed each one vaguely and waved as they sauntered, the older ones fussing the youngest, through the school gates.

'Is it a non-uniform day?' Lola asked Rose Lusty, as she seemed the most normal of the trio, having watched the ragbag tribe disappear.

'That *is* Tatty's idea of uniform,' Rose sniffed. 'Those children go off every morning looking like a cross between gypsy violinists and the Bisto Kids.'

'They can fight like weasels, though,' Glad cackled over her shoulder. 'Just as well what with the way they're dressed and being called Marmaduke and Orlando and Zebedee and what have you. Poor little mites.'

Tatty stirred from her dreamy stupor and shook her head. 'I think you've got that wrong. They don't ever fight, Glad, dear. They're pacifists.'

'Pacifists what can pack a mighty punch then,' Glad huffed into her front-facing position. 'I've seen 'em kicking seven bells out of each other on the common.'

Lola closed her eyes. She'd wake up in a moment and everything – from the moment of Nigel's death – would turn out to be a *Dallas*-type dream. She opened her eyes and was horrified to find that it wasn't.

Ellis started the Dormobile again and headed towards the main road. 'Next stop, shops.' He grinned over his shoulder at Lola. 'Is there anywhere in particular you want to go?'

She shook her head. She really didn't have a clue. There had been vague notions of finding an information bureau which may provide her with a list of residential homes and hotels where she could perhaps find work or at least study her *Daltons Weekly* in peace. But now . . .

Ellis looked at her through the driving mirror. 'After I've dropped Gran and the others off, I'll have a think. Possibly the library would be your best bet. Or at least a good place to start.'

Lola muttered her thanks. He was a complete stranger and easily young enough to be her son: not unlike a lot of the boys who had come through the Marionette factory over the years, really. Looking all brash and modern on the outside, but kind and considerate beneath the surface. It was kind of him to try to help, even if there was absolutely no point at all.

Half an hour later, having deposited the trio of Tatty, Glad and Rose outside the shopping precinct, Ellis kept the Dormobile's engine running and pointed through the happy-shopper throng. 'The library is down there. I'd come with you but I can't park here. They're shit-hot on wheel clamping –'

Lola shuddered.

'So,' he continued, 'I'm collecting the others in about three hours. If you leave your luggage in here you could come back for it then if you've had any joy.'

'Thank you. You've been very kind.'

'No sweat. Hope you get sorted. Look, there's a spare umbrella, too. You don't want to get wet.'

And with a wink that Lola felt was totally inappropriate, Ellis roared away, leaving her to the mercies of yet another strange town.

As she stood in a state of bewilderment on the busy

pavement, Lola couldn't help wondering why Ellis had kissed his grandmother on the cheek, Rose Lusty on the hand, and Tatty Spry – who was probably old enough to be his mother – very lengthily on the mouth. She could almost swear there had been tongues involved, too. It really didn't bear thinking about.

A veil of despondency was best draped decorously over the next three hours, Lola thought as she headed wearily back to the pick-up point, being bumped and barged at every turn by inconsiderate, cold and saturated shoppers. There was possibly nothing worse than trying to start a new life in a strange town when your spirits, morale and bank balance, were all at rock bottom.

She'd tried. At least she'd tried. She'd followed up all the leads given to her by the helpful librarian, had worn down her kitten heels tearing around unfamiliar streets to various employment agencies, had registered her details with every one of them – and come up against the same appalling stumbling block.

She, Lola Wentworth, mistress of Marionette Biscuits and self-assured career woman, was homeless. And without a permanent address she had no chance of finding a job – and without a job she had even less chance of finding a home.

Ricocheting through the throng towards the Dormobile, Lola felt she'd reached her lowest ebb. Apart from the fact that for each advertised vacancy there were apparently a dozen younger and better-qualified candidates all of whom had the advantage of references, there was now the added stigma of being classed as a street person.

How naive she'd been to believe that her lack of

accommodation would be solved by finding a live-in post. Why hadn't she realized that between application and acceptance there would be a gap – and that gap would need an address . . .

Ellis was sitting in the front seat of the Dormobile adjusting the speed of the windscreen wipers. A mini Niagara Falls was bouncing off the bonnet. He opened the door for her. 'Any luck? No, obviously not. I can tell from your face. So, what are you going to do now?'

'I haven't got a bloody clue!'

'Okay, okay.' He held up his hands in supplication. 'Don't scream at me.'

'Well don't ask such fucking stupid questions!' Lola stopped, aghast. She'd sworn. Aloud. In the street. She'd never done that in her life before. Never let her standards slip so low. 'I'm so sorry.'

Ellis laughed. 'It's fine by me. At least it proves you're as human as the rest of us. I did have my doubts. Shall we get a cup of coffee? You look cold and wet and thoroughly pissed off. You need a caffeine shot and we've got a while before the coven returns.'

Blinking back tears of anger and frustration and sheer depression, Lola nodded. 'That would be very nice. Thank you. But what about the wheel clampers?'

'I can keep an eye out of the window of the caff,' Ellis indicated an adjacent brightly painted shop, its windows obliterated by hand-written marker pen menus. 'It'll be okay.'

Lola shuddered. 'It doesn't look, er, no, I'm sure it'll be fine.'

'It'll be more than fine,' Ellis slid from the Dormobile and indicated that Lola should follow him. 'I discovered

114

it a few days ago. They do the best coffee in the world. You could mortar bricks with the sludge at the bottom of the cup.'

Having never been in a greasy spoon in her life, Lola looked around with amazement. Plastered round the walls, obviously written by a small child with dyslexia, the menus extolled the virtue of cholesterol for all. The air was hot and clammy and she could almost taste the grease globules. The fumes wreathing from behind the Formica counter hit the ceiling, hovered like ectoplasm, then gushed forward joyously to envelop the diners. A lot of very large people seemed to be crammed on to very small chairs and were eating odd things like egg and chips with gravy.

However, Ellis had been right about one thing. The coffee was divine.

'Eggs, chips, beans, mushrooms, fried slice . . . ?' He looked at her. 'Anything else you fancy?'

'You're going to *eat* in here?'

'Of course. Ambrosia. Nectar. Er, oh, well, you know. What would you like?'

'Just another coffee please. And have you got time for a meal, I mean, with the wheel clampers and the cov— um, your grandmother and her friends returning?'

'I'm a very fast eater.' Ellis flashed white teeth in a dazzling smile. 'I like to do most things quickly.'

Lola had no idea why this remark should make her blush.

While Ellis demolished his mountain of food – fast, as he'd said, but not disgustingly so – it gave her the opportunity to make a decision. She'd have to return to Sunny Dene for another couple of days while she planned the rest of her life. The money would soon run out, Posy would ostracize her, and there wasn't a suitable job for miles. While it was possibly marginally more alluring than sleeping on the streets, the stay in Steeple Fritton would be very temporary indeed.

Through the steamy window she could see the raggle-taggle trio approaching, each carrying masses of bags. It seemed bizarre in the extreme that all Glad's should be labelled Next, Gap and Benetton.

'Looks like we're off again,' Ellis said, draining his coffee cup and standing up.

Lola found herself staring at his lean and toned midriff as he shrugged into his denim jacket and quickly averted her eyes. 'Thank you for the coffee. It was very kind of you. I do feel better.'

'Good,' Ellis gave her another inappropriate wink. 'Pleased to be of service. And now that you're going to be staying in Steeple Fritton for a while, why don't you join me and Posy in the pub next Saturday night? We're going to formulate a rescue package for the entire village.'

'Really?' Lola said without interest. The whole concept made her feel weary. 'No, I don't think so. After all, I won't be staying long, and Posy and I don't exactly see eye to eye.'

'Oh, great, I love a cat fight.' Ellis ushered her out into the street. The rain had turned to sleet and the wind was bitter. 'Anyway, at least think about it. Next Saturday night, seven o'clock in The Crooked Sixpence. Don't forget. We're going to change the world – or at least, Steeple Fritton.'

Lola looked in dismay at Glad, Rose and Tatty

scrambling excitedly into the Dormobile. Ohio Express were already singing 'Chewy Chewy' at the tops of their nasal voices from the stereo.

'Do we have to have that infantile music on now that the children have gone?'

Ellis grinned. 'That's nothing to do with the kids – I'm the world's number one Bubblegum fan. Stick with me, babe, you'll soon get used to it.'

Lola climbed into the Dormobile and wanted to cry.

Chapter Nine

Like liquid silk, the cold damp rain of the February evening slicked itself gently against his skin. Flynn Malone leaned against his dark red jeep and watched the lights of the Cork ferry, recently berthed in Swansea harbour, bob and sway out across the Irish Sea.

At least the weather made him feel at home: well, his most recent home in Tralee, that was. His real home, in Massachusetts, wouldn't feel like this at all. He quickly pushed away all nostalgic thoughts of Charlestown, of New England, of his parents, of his friends, and particularly of Vanessa.

He'd left Boston six months earlier, and he'd left Tralee – he glanced at his watch in the gloom – oh, almost a day ago . . . And now he was on British soil for the first time in his life.

It should have been sooner, of course. He'd planned to stay in Ireland for only a couple of weeks; but once he'd got ensconced with Uncle Michael and Auntie Maude and the zillions of Malone relatives from all over the Republic who had flocked to the Tralee bar just to meet him, it had been so hard to say good-bye.

'Excuse me, sir. Are you lost?' A very young man in a too-big navy blue uniform and shiny cap with a peak that looked like a predatory bird, peered at him. The musical voice had a singsong ring. 'Only you can't park here. This is a no parking zone, see?'

'Oh, right.'

The peaked cap tapped a clipboard. 'Are you coming or going?'

'I've no idea,' Flynn grinned then stopped. His Auntie Maude had warned him never to joke with English officialdom. He presumed Welsh officialdom was much the same thing. 'I've just disembarked from the ferry and I'm sorta taking stock. First time here, you know.'

The peaked cap nodded. The youthful face flickered slightly. Flynn suddenly realized that while his Bostonian Irish accent had been very much at home in Tralee, here it must sound as alien to the young official as the Welsh lilt did to him. Strange thing that, now he was in Britain, he guessed he'd be instantly branded a foreigner each time he opened his mouth. It was a pleasant prospect. He'd never been a foreigner before.

'Welcome to Wales, then. However, this is a restricted area and –' the young man stared more closely at Flynn. 'You have been through customs and the rest, haven't you?'

'Yeah, sure.' Flynn nodded.

There had been a bit of a delay while they'd examined his passport, his entry papers and his extended visa. He hadn't been surprised: there had been similar officialese ructions in Tralee when he'd applied to the Garda

Síochána for a longer than three month sojourn with Uncle Michael and Auntie Maude. It had made him think far more kindly about all those poor souls who tried to enter a country illegally.

He smiled, in what he hoped was a confident manner, at the face beneath the peaked cap. 'I cleared everything with no problems. Oh, right – do you want to see my papers as well?'

'No, not at all. That's not my area, see. Just need to keep this roadway free. Do you know where you're heading for?'

Easy one. 'I'm going to Fritton Magna.'

The peaked cap frowned. 'Where on God's earth is that?'

'Berkshire. Near Reading, I think.'

'You'll need to make for the M4 then, you can't miss it from here. Then stick with it all the way through Wales, across the Severn Bridge and into England. Then, still on the M4 just keep going till you hit Reading, see?'

After Ireland, it all sounded far too straightforward to be true.

Flynn grinned. 'Thanks. But it's really that simple? Just the one interstate, er, motorway? No intersections?'

'Nothing at all. Straight out of here, and the M4 is signposted. Join at Junction 42 and you can't go wrong. Ah, you've got a map. The run shouldn't be too difficult at this time of night. So, if you wouldn't mind moving along? It's just you can't park here, see?'

'No, I mean, yes, I see . . . Thanks.'

With a last lingering look at the murky outline of the docked ferry – his final link with Tralee and anyone that he knew – Flynn slid back into the jeep which his

Uncle Michael had procured for a knockdown price at the Dingle auctions.

Sketching a farewell wave to the peaked cap, he drove carefully away from the docks and headed, as he'd been told, for the M4. He'd got fairly accustomed to driving on the left-hand side of the road during his stay in Ireland. But only fairly. Fighting for, holding and then keeping the centre of the road seemed to take precedence in County Kerry.

The M4 was a constant hum of fast-flowing traffic. Keeping the jeep steadily in the left-hand lane and wincing occasionally at the amazing speed at which other vehicles flashed past, Flynn listened to the very correct voices on the radio and wondered what this Fritton Magna place would bring. It sounded like a real quaint English village, though. Exactly like something out of one of those Katie Fforde novels his mother adored.

The six months in Tralee meeting the family had flown past. He'd loved it. He'd loved serving in the bar, and the noise and the music and the general craik. He'd loved becoming part of the Malone brigade, and meeting people who he'd only heard about from his grandparents. He'd been homesick for Boston and his parents and Vanessa, of course. But then, even his parents weren't there now. God alone knew where they were at this moment. Flynn grinned to himself, hoping they were enjoying every minute of their own adventure.

Vanessa, though, would still be in Charlestown, doing what she'd always done, running Opal Joe's, living with her huge family, going out places with their mutual friends. All without him. He still missed her, but after six months he'd become used to being single again.

He guessed they'd just get used to being a world apart, would start to live new lives, but hopefully always keep in touch. Vanessa could have come with him of course; but she wouldn't leave Charlestown and he wouldn't stay.

The final night in Boston was still so vivid in his memory. Vanessa had made sure that, if it was to be the last they'd spend together, it was one he'd never forget . . .

Flynn was yanked back from this most pleasurable of recollections by the sudden appearance of the Severn Bridge. He blinked at the size of it. It was pretty awesome. Like a miniature Golden Gate. He'd been expecting something tiny and rustic and straight out of *Winnie the Pooh*.

He looked down at the black, silver-streaked water, and all around him at the pinpricks of light, then joined the queue of traffic moving slowly forward across the bridge out of Wales. So this was England? He wondered just what adventures this new country would bring.

Hours later Flynn wished he was back in Boston or Tralee or damn well anywhere that wasn't here. Sticking to the M4 had been, as predicted, easy. It had been after that, when he'd sailed off the intersection flagged for Reading, that things had started to go hopelessly wrong.

Somehow Reading had mysteriously disappeared.

The map, spread across the jeep's dashboard, indicated that Reading was a pretty big place. How the hell he could have missed it was anyone's guess. Unless, of course, he'd been in the wrong lane and either come off the motorway too early or too late – both of which would mean trying to find his way back on.

He thumped the steering wheel with his fist, cursing himself for his earlier complacency. He'd never be able to find his way back now. It was the middle of the night in the middle of nowhere; it was pouring with rain and he was very tired.

Maybe he could track down a motel or something. There were always motels back home, even in the most out-of-the-way places. It had to be the same in England, didn't it?

After what seemed like a lifetime of driving round twisting unlit narrow roads with no signposts and no people and definitely no motels, Flynn knew that unless he wanted to fall asleep at the wheel, the only sensible thing to do was pull over somewhere. Tiredness was making him confused and increasingly more irritated. If he slept in the jeep until daylight he guessed everything would surely be so much easier to find.

Slowing down, looking for a likely spot to pull in and with the windscreen wipers working overtime, the headlights skimmed over skeletal trees and looming hedgerows, then flickered across an elegant gateway. He peered at the lettering. 'Colworth Manor'. Maybe it was a hotel – and maybe it wasn't. It looked like some sort of stately home. He sure as hell didn't want to go pounding on the door begging a room for the night only to be chased away by the local landed gentry . . .

Deciding this wasn't going to be the best place to pull in and sleep either, he drove slowly on, and after several more minutes and what seemed like circuitous miles, the headlights picked out a skewwhiff signpost. Flynn peered hopefully at it. If it said 'M4 this way' he swore he'd kiss it.

It didn't. Even more wonderfully it said Steeple Fritton, Lesser Fritton and Fritton Magna.

Hallelujah!

With a renewed burst of energy, Flynn pushed the accelerator down hard and set off towards the trio of Frittons, his lethargy forgotten. He'd found, by accident, the very place he was looking for. And not just Fritton Magna, but three Fritton villages, Steeple, Lesser and Magna. How cute was that? His parents would just love it when he told them.

Everywhere was pitch black in the teeming rain. Had he passed through the villages without even noticing? Should he go back and see if Colworth Manor might just be a hotel?

He shook his head at the foolishness of the mere idea. No, surely there had to be some signs of life somewhere. All he had to do was keep going.

The road had suddenly widened slightly, and he seemed to be driving past buildings now. Was that a church? And some shops? Yes! Hallelujah! Civilization!

He slowed even more, peering from left to right, then . . . hey! Flynn grinned in delight and relief. A light glowed ahead through the impenetrable darkness: a warm, fuzzy lantern-type light which illuminated the front of a sprawling building, which in turn, as he got closer, became a mishmash of shapes and decor – white painted, grey slated, red bricked and tiled.

Flynn was too elated to give a damn about the aesthetics.

'Sunny Dene. Bed and Breakfast. Wow!'

He was out of the jeep and knocking on the door in a nanosecond.

A volley of barking from the interior didn't deter him. It sounded like two dogs. Maybe three. Dogs were cool. He loved animals.

There was the sound of footsteps and a muffled voice and the barking ceased. With a lot of rattling and key-turning, the door opened slightly.

'Hi,' Flynn grinned hugely at the plump woman in the purple and orange dressing gown with her bright ginger hair all awry, then at the two tail-waving dogs laughing up at him. 'Sorry to call so late, but I wondered if you'd have a room free . . .'

A beam melted across the plump face, and the eyes creased in delight. 'Of course we have, love. What an awful night! Is that your car? Right, you go and get your luggage and I'll get the kettle on.'

Sure he'd never get used to this obsession with tea at all hours, Flynn found himself in the cosiest little room ever. All deep chairs and fat sofas, the curtains pulled snugly against the wet night outside, it was like Hollywood's idea of an English country cottage come to life

Dilys Nightingale introduced herself and the dogs, handed him a steaming mug and settled down for a chat.

He told her how he'd taken the wrong exit from the motorway, and how he'd driven round for ages, and then found the manor house, and was just thinking about giving it all up as a bad job and sleeping in the car when he'd seen Sunny Dene's light.

'This is so kind of you, but I don't want to disturb your sleep,' Flynn sipped his tea, having said no to biscuits or a meal of any sort. 'It's the middle of the night and –'

'And we're a home from home,' Dilys wrapped her hands round her own mug. 'And with that accent, you sound as though you're a long way from yours . . .'

It was bliss to sit there in the warm, sipping the hot, sweet tea, letting the tiredness drain away and telling Dilys how he'd come to leave Boston in the first place. She was an excellent listener and somehow he found himself telling her about his parents and Vanessa, and how the two events that had simultaneously rocked his cosy security to the roots of its foundations had been more cataclysmic than a meteor strike.

The engineering firm where he'd worked all his life relocating to New Jersey and giving the workforce a mighty good pay-off, and his unknown English great-aunt, Bunty Malone, dying in her ninety-eighth year in Fritton Magna and leaving everything she owned to the various far-flung Malones, had changed simply everything.

Dilys pursed her lips in sympathy when he explained that Vanessa, who he'd been dating for almost three years, had refused to join him. She loved him, but not enough to leave her huge riotous extended family behind in Charlestown to travel to Britain. Not even for him.

He sighed, thinking back to that last night at home. How he'd walked back from Opal Joe's with Vanessa, knowing it would be for the last time.

The Charlestown streets had already looked misty and nostalgic; the cocktail of smells wreathing from the river and the railway and the docks had mingled with the ever-present New England countryside scent of rich earth and a million trees; and the rows of shingled houses with their white filigreed fences and their fading flower tubs would always be part of his happiest memories. But tomorrow, that was all they'd be. Tomorrow he'd set out on his own and leave Charlestown, Boston and the States forever.

'She must have been mad, dear,' Dilys leaned forward and refilled his mug. 'If you don't mind me saying so. I wouldn't have let you out of my sight, never in a million years.'

They grinned at each other.

Flynn explained how Great-Aunt Bunty's windfall could not have come at a better time. The sum of money left to his parents had been almost mind-blowing. Not a fortune to some people, of course, but large enough to mean they could at last achieve their life's ambition. The senior Malones had no intention at all of an early retirement, taking up bowls, and having two good vacations a year – oh, no. Flynn's parents were off on the cultural trail.

When he told her about his parents, Dilys laughed uproariously.

His parents were the only people he'd ever known who embraced the Arts in a suffocating bear hug. His father, a Charlestown traffic cop for thirty years, whistled Stockhausen or Bartók as he issued tickets; his mother, a cleaner at the local government offices, read Kafka in her tea breaks. Their unexpected inheritance meant they were going to put all their possessions into storage, and head off on a journey of arty enlightenment – doing a sort of Jack-Kerouac-in-comfort – travelling across Europe in a camper van.

Flynn, who had no desire to visit the birthplace of Pisanello or even the grave of Jim Morrison, had declined their invitation to join them.

At first he'd thought he'd take over the tenancy of the Charlestown house, and continue his life much as before, only without the slightly overawing influence of Jawlensky or Penderecki. The prospect had pleased him. He'd miss his parents, but it would be great to live alone, to be able to have his own home, to have slob-out parties and maybe ask Vanessa to move in.

For some time Flynn had been aware that at thirty-two, he really should have a place of his own. It was sheer laziness on his part that had kept him living with his parents, enjoying being looked after, and working less than ten minutes' drive away from his front door.

Then the lawyers had been in touch saying that as well as the financial inheritance for his parents, there was a special legacy for Flynn. Something Great-Aunt Bunty was sure he'd appreciate and look after and enjoy. Only snag being – he had to go to Fritton Magna to claim it.

Pretty sure that it was going to be one of those sweet little general stores you saw in the movies, and quite keen on becoming an English entrepreneur for a while and catching up with his Irish relatives at the same time, Flynn had quickly obtained a visa and bought a one-way Aer Lingus ticket from Boston to Shannon.

His parents were going to have the adventure of their lives, so why shouldn't he? It would have been so much better if Vanessa had been with him, but what the heck . . .

'And that's it really,' Flynn said, placing his mug back on the tray and leaning down to stroke the dogs who had fallen asleep on his feet. 'That's why I'm here.'

'Just like a film,' Dilys said, her eyes shining with delight. 'And Fritton Magna is only a stone's throw away so you'll be able to stay here as long as you need . . .'

'This isn't Fritton Magna, then?'

'Bless you, no. We're Steeple Fritton. Much more classy. Anyway, we'll try to cure your homesickness and make you part of the family for as long as you want. Now, before we both fall asleep down here, shall I show you to your room?'.

Chapter Ten

'Who's getting the five-star treatment?' Posy, who was dusting the really awkward bits of Sunny Dene's skew-whiff staircases – her regular Saturday morning treat – peered at her mother. 'Please don't tell me that Lady Lola Muck has ordered breakfast in bed?'

'I do wish you wouldn't call her that. She's a guest, and a very nice person who is having major personal problems. Why can't you show her some sympathy?' Dilys, carrying a tray and dressed entirely in sparkly lime green, shook her head so that the Christmas tree baubles she wore as earrings performed a little dance routine.

'Because she's another bloody Sonia Tozer-type man-stealer,' Posy growled, rubbing the banisters so hard that they rattled. 'And you've changed your tune. Let me remind you, you said Lola was a tart's name and it damn well suited her.'

Dilys pursed shiny apricot lips. 'Yes, well, I'll admit I was wrong. She won't be the first, or last, person to have been taken in by a man, dear, as you well know.

And we don't know the exact circumstances, do we? Anyway, we need all the custom we can get. If I started making people fill in a moral questionnaire every time they wanted B&B we'd be even emptier than we are.'

'Oh, of course I'm glad she's still here because of the money, but don't ever, ever expect me to like her.'

Dilys continued to edge her way up the stairs. 'No, well, I can understand that, but anyway this breakfast isn't for her.'

Posy huffed on a bit of varnished oak and rubbed angrily. Lola's prolonged stay had irritated her beyond belief. She was showing no signs of actually going anywhere – and even seemed to have given up trying to find employment. It was so galling having to smilingly serve food to someone you'd rather chuck it all over.

'Mr D and Mr B having a lie-in, then?' Mr Dale and Mr Burridge had rapidly eschewed Sunny Dene's 'two neighbouring singles with private facilities' in favour of the 'front of house double with canopied bed'. 'Snuggled up together in their scarlet silk pyjamas and sharing a buttered croissant?'

Dilys laughed. Everything on the tray wobbled alarmingly. 'Wrong again. We've got a new gentleman. Came in last night – well, early hours of this morning, actually. You were asleep. It was only Trevor and Kenneth barking that woke me up.'

Posy sat back on her haunches, allowing her mother to pass. 'And? Is he another one-night stand?'

'Probably, dear. You'll love him though. He's American.'

Definitely a one-night stand, then, Posy thought. American tourists were not big business in Steeple Fritton.

'Why on earth would an American be wandering around the village in the early hours?'

Dilys balanced the tray against an ample hip. 'Because he was going to stay in Reading overnight but he took the wrong exit from the motorway and ended up on the Lesser Fritton Road. He's apparently got business in Fritton Magna, but couldn't find anywhere else to stay.'

'What? With Colworth Manor not a stone's throw away? With the gorgeous Daisy offering personal services, three million rooms, ten million staff and a golf course in every bedroom? He didn't look very hard, then.'

Dilys shrugged. 'He thought about stopping there, but he thought it was a stately home, bless him. He'd been driving round and round the villages and was thinking of sleeping in his car, then he saw our sign.'

'Like a star in the East,' Posy muttered. 'And who the hell has business in Fritton Magna? Fritton Magna is even more comatose than we are.'

'Well let's just be thankful for small mercies. Anyway, he's glorious looking, dear. Just like that man whose films you love . . . oh, what's his name?'

'Tom Cruise? Brad Pitt?' Posy looked animated. Men of that ilk were few and far between – and never before had anyone even remotely that gorgeous graced the floral duvets of Sunny Dene.

Dilys shook her head, making the baubles fly into a frenzy. 'No, he's funny as well. You always laugh at him when he's in comedy films.'

Posy's spirits and enthusiasm plummeted. 'Tony Curtis, you mean?'

'No, not him. At least, I don't think so.' Dilys shook her head again just as Norrie appeared down in the hall below with the dogs. She leaned over the banisters. 'Norrie! What's the name of that American film star that our Posy always laughs at?'

'Tony Curtis.'

'Maybe it is him, then.'

'Oh, right . . . bugger.' Dejectedly, Posy resumed her dusting, all thoughts of snatching the tray from her mother and storming the American's bedroom abandoned. For Tom or Brad, yes – for someone even older than her father with a man-tan and toupee – forget it.

Twelve hours later, Hogarth glared across the bar of The Crooked Sixpence. 'You wants what?'

'Water and glasses.' Ellis spoke slowly. 'We're having a meeting. Everyone has water and glasses at meetings.'

'If you wants a bloody meeting you go and have it in the bloody bus shelter like everyone else.' Hogarth whipped a rancid cloth across the bar top. 'This is a pub. I dispenses alcoholic beverages and conviviality. If you wants to talk and drink water then you've come to the wrong place, right?'

For a Saturday evening, The Crooked Sixpence was quite full. The Pinks, complete with mercifully silent accordion, were in their corner, and the London-weekenders were out in force wearing Betty Jackson country casual chic. Fortunately Amanda and Nikki had reported that Ritchie and Sonia had been seen heading for the bright lights of Reading, so there would be no shocks tonight.

Posy had arrived at the pub armed with a notepad and pen and few ideas. Ellis had arrived slightly later, still tucking in his denim shirt, and smelling of Tatty Spry.

Deciding that peace negotiations were needed if the meeting was ever going to get off the ground, she pushed in front of Ellis and smiled at Hogarth. 'We'll have a bottle of white wine, then. And two glasses. Please.'

'Should have said that in the first place,' Hogarth lumbered off. 'And if you're having a meeting, I don't want no noise.'

'We'll be as quiet as the proverbials.'

'Good. And make the most of it. I've got a bit of business wants seeing to so I'll have to be shutting up shop here afore long.'

Posy groaned. 'Why can't you get a relief manager in to run it while you're away? Surely it'd make more sense than closing the only pub for miles every time you have to go away on a, um, bit of business?'

'You find me a manager of the right calibre and I might consider it,' Hogarth sniffed. 'But it'd have to be a proper person what knew how to run an establishment like this. None of your noncey poncey sorts what'd ruin the ambience. Now clear off with yer wine and have yer meeting, and no noise. Okay?'

'Okay.'

Settled with drinks and notepad and trying not to notice the excited and musty rustlings of the Pinks, Posy looked at Ellis across the table. She tried really hard not to remember that he'd kissed her. It wasn't a good way to start a business meeting – rating your fellow board members on Richter scale snogability levels.

And the Pinks had told Rose Lusty about the kiss and Rose Lusty had told Dilys and Dilys had wasted an entire

134

day telling Posy that Ellis would break her heart – sure as eggs were eggs.

Which was probably true, if she was ever going to put it to the test, which she wasn't.

'Right, so what brilliant ideas have you come up with for putting Steeple Fritton on the map?' Ellis tapped very even white teeth with a biro. 'I've been thinking that we need something that lasts for a whole week. Not just a weekend thing and not a music festival. We want people to come and to stay and to spend money while they're doing it. What do you reckon?'

'Along the right lines, but still too small scale. If we're going to survive at Sunny Dene we need people all the time. For the whole year. You know, have something going on so that people are always travelling into the village. And we want them to stay here, not just wander around for a couple of hours and then go home.'

Ellis nodded doubtfully. 'Or clear off to stay at that big hotel down the road. Yeah, but finding something to do here for a week would be stretching it, a year is going to be an impossibility.'

'Bourton-on-the-Water manages it nicely.' Posy clicked her tongue against her teeth. 'For a child, you are so negative.'

'I'm only a year younger than you –' he grinned, 'and I love older women.'

'So I've noticed and that isn't on the agenda.' Posy felt herself growing warm, which was strange as The Crooked Sixpence's fire was its usual bed of grey ash, and a keening wind was rattling at the windows. She tried, and failed, to look businesslike. 'Anyway, as you're

135

so young, maybe we can utilize your recent education. What did you study at university?'

'Mechanical engineering.'

'Really? I'd have thought you'd have been far more airy-fairy than that. And mechanical engineering isn't going to help us much is it? Not unless you can fix my mum's car and help my dad with his model railway.'

'Your dad's got a *model railway*?' Ellis's eyes widened in delight. 'In the loft or something?'

'Running round the whole of the back garden. It's a shrine to the days of steam – main lines, branch lines, sidings, stations . . .'

'There you go then. Our first visitor attraction.' Ellis refilled the wine glasses. Bits of black stuff bobbed happily on the surface. 'I'll have to come round to yours and have a look at it. I love railways. I've always wanted to do an overnight on a train, like Jack Lemmon and Tony Curtis in *Some Like It Hot*.'

Sunny Dene's own alleged Tony Curtis look-alike hadn't emerged all day. Jet-lagged, Dilys had reckoned, although the dark red jeep with the Irish registration plates seemed to indicate that he hadn't just flown in from Hollywood. Wherever he'd come from, they'd all hoped he'd sleep the clock round. It would mean he'd stay another night. And they might even squeeze a dinner in there as well.

Getting back to the matter in hand, Posy frowned across the table at Ellis. 'What? Just you and three hundred women on a sleeper train?'

'Of course. Well, bringing it more up-to-date, me and any babe band you'd care to mention. And you haven't written it down.'

136

Posy wrote down 'model railway' then shook her head. 'Half a dozen sad anoraks staring at my dad's layout for twenty minutes is hardly going to change the way we live.'

'It's a start – oh, here,' Ellis handed her the wine glass, his fingers brushing hers and lingering. 'Right, we've got the railway, so, next?'

Posy snatched the glass and her hand away. 'Well, I thought we could get Vi Bickeridge and Rose Lusty and, er, Tatty to make more of their shops, and I wondered about a weekly car boot sale on the common.'

'Yeah, fine,' Ellis nodded. 'Good idea, but there'd be nothing there for anyone except day-trippers. Although they would bring people in on a regular basis, I suppose, and your mum could offer good home cooking or country lunches or something and lure them in that way. Even a dining room full every weekend would help you, wouldn't it?'

'Yes, of course –' Posy scribbled frantically, then passed him a sheet of paper. 'Now, I thought if we just listed what we could offer ourselves, you know, write down our own particular strengths and –' she glanced up and read his mind. 'Jesus! You're so disgusting!'

Ellis laughed. 'It was just a thought . . . no? Okay, although I must say I've never had any complaints.'

Suddenly feeling very hot indeed, Posy wrote silently for a few moments. The life skills which she'd listed to Dom on Ritchie and Sonia's wedding day didn't seem to have grown at all. None of them would bring money-spending hordes into Steeple Fritton.

Comparing notes ten minutes later, they'd come up with very little. Leaving Ellis to magic up EuroDisney out of half a page of disjointed jottings, Posy went to the bar for another bottle of wine.

'What you having a meeting about?' Hogarth snarled. 'Anything interesting?'

'Er, no, not really.' Posy wished Hogarth would warn her when he was going to be chatty. It was quite scary when it happened all of a sudden. 'We're trying to think how to put Steeple Fritton on the map – bring in more people and stop Sunny Dene from going bankrupt. Er, you wouldn't like more punters, would you?'

There was an explosive roar which Posy took as a no. She scuttled back to the table and had just poured two more glasses of wine when the door creaked open and Lola, looking very glam in black trousers and with a white shirt beneath the black jacket and lots of gold chains, walked into the pub. The Pinks waved their headscarves in thrilled welcome.

With dismay, Posy realized that Lola had every intention of joining them. Ellis, testosterone flying, had already stood up and was dragging up another chair.

He grinned. 'I invited Lola to come along. Didn't think you'd mind. Three heads being better than one, you know. You two start without me. I'll just get another glass . . .'

Posy and Lola stared at one another.

'I don't think this is a good idea,' Lola eventually broke the deadlock.

'Neither do I. When exactly did Ellis invite you?'

'Last week. When he gave me a lift into Reading. I wasn't going to bother, but I thought if I spent one more night in my room I'd go mad.'

'What's wrong with your room? It's one of Sunny Dene's best.'

'It's a perfectly lovely room. I have no complaints about my room. I'm just getting rather tired of my own company.'

They lapsed into silence again. Posy was irritably aware that she again looked like a Marc Bolan clone in her jeans and leather jacket and with her dark curls spiralling all anyhow. Lola looked, as always, poised, elegant and as if she was just about to chair a proper board meeting. She really should try being a grown-up herself one day.

Ellis plonked a third glass and another bottle of dubious house white on the table. 'And what have you two come up with?'

'Nothing.'

'Okay, well let's bring Lola up-to-date . . .' He pushed the notes across the table. They got momentarily caught on the residue of someone's sweet sherry – probably spilt in 1945.

'Why?' Posy's voice sounded very loud. It even stopped the Pinks in their tracks. 'This has nothing to do with her.'

'Exactly,' Lola said. 'I have absolutely no interest in the salvation of Steeple Fritton –'

Only in other people's husbands, Posy thought, and glared at her. 'So why are you here?'

'Because I invited her,' Ellis interrupted. 'Because Lola is as rootless and directionless as we are. Because you have to make your own entertainment in a place like this and I not only thought that she would be useful, but that she might enjoy it. I'm actually quite a nice person.'

Despite her fury, Posy knew she was going to smile. Damn him. He was playing them both. She narrowed her eyes at Lola. 'And have you come up with some wonderful scheme, then? Something that will put the village on the map?'

Lola shook her head. 'Of course not. As I said, I don't intend to stay here any longer than is necessary. It's just that until I can find a live-in job then my hands appear to be tied.'

Ellis perked up at the image. Posy transferred her glare to him instead.

'Oy!' Hogarth leaned from behind the bar, making the London-weekenders jump. 'You! Hoity-toity madam!'

'Are you speaking to me?' Lola's voice was glacial.

'Yeah. If the cap fits. Did I hear you say you was looking for a job?'

'Well, yes, but –'

'You can have mine if you likes. You looks the part, see, not like them damn kids. Know anything about running a pub?'

'No, of course not.'

Posy frowned at Hogarth. 'What do mean she can have your job? Are you selling The Crooked Sixpence?'

'That I ain't. Leastways, not yet. But I've got other business interests in other places what needs my attention. I'm planning on being gone for a few months but I don't want to shut this place up while I'm away this time, and I wants someone to keep it running proper.'

It was the longest speech anyone had ever heard Hogarth make. Even the Pinks were shocked into silence. And Posy was sure she wasn't the only one who had no idea that Hogarth was Steeple Fritton's answer to Richard Branson.

'So?' Hogarth leaned his stomach over the bar towards Lola. 'You want to discuss it or what?'

Lola looked around the pub as though someone had just invited her to take up residence on a landfill site. 'Is there accommodation with the job?'

'No. There's my rooms upstairs of course, but you ain't having them.'

'There –' Ellis leaned closer to Posy and whispered, 'If she accepts the job here, she'll still be staying at Sunny Dene. Regular money. You can't complain.'

'I suppose not.'

'Well, we could discuss it,' Lola stood up. 'But it would have to be on my terms.'

Hogarth lifted the bar flap and ushered her through the debris. 'Come into my office, then. Let's put our cards on the table.' He stopped and glared at his customers. 'And if any of you wants a drink while I'm gone then it's tough doodah.'

The London-weekenders tittered. The Pinks clapped.

Posy exhaled. Life was very strange. Lola running The Crooked Sixpence? Hogarth having other enterprises? What else could be thrown at her tonight?

'This could be just what we need,' Ellis said happily. 'Get Lola in here and the pub might improve a hundred per cent.'

Posy slowly drained her wine glass. 'It'll mean a lot more than that, as long as she cooperates. The Crooked Sixpence could be instrumental in the Steeple Fritton revival plan. Think about it – darts matches, quizzes, a pub football team, theme nights, karaoke. Anything and

141

everything to bring people in from outside on a regular basis and then maybe – oh, I don't know. Barbecues and barn dances on the forecourt in the summer, and firework displays and well, loads of things –'

'Yeah!' Ellis's black eyes gleamed with enthusiasm and he started scribbling things on his sheet of paper. 'We'd have to have a marketing strategy then, so that everyone knew what was going on. And advertising. I reckon, properly handled, this could be huge . . .'

But Posy wasn't listening. It would work, she knew it. She could save Sunny Dene and forget all about Ritchie and Sonia. Well, okay, maybe not *forget* exactly, but they'd eventually be way down her list of things to fret about. The village would be humming with life and people, Sunny Dene would be in the black and Steeple Fritton would be synonymous with, with . . . oh, she wasn't sure.

But she could see it all. All sorts of events building up to . . . a day of jollity. A Steeple Fritton Day in the middle of summer . . . There could be a fairground, and competitions and music and lights and noise, and it would be like – oh, like Rio or Notting Hill. In fact, it could be exactly like Rio or Notting Hill if they had –

'A carnival!' She spoke the words as they formulated themselves in her brain. 'We'll have a Steeple Fritton Carnival! In June – with events and a huge party and with a procession through the village and floats and fancy dress and –'

'Carnival queens!' Ellis moved closer to her. 'We could have a carnival queen competition in the village hall and they'd all wear bikinis and I could be the judge!'

Posy didn't even look cross. It would be brilliant – all

retro and very villagey and totally wonderful . . . And it could be held year after year, and grow, and people would come from all over the place, and –

'Of course,' Ellis said, 'you know you'll have to get agreement on this?'

'What? From the parish council? Yeah, well they're not too scary, it's only the vicar, Clive Bickeridge and a few other old-timers. I'll deal with them.'

'No, I mean Lola. If she takes over the pub, then you'll need her to be on your side. The pub will be the hub of everything you're planning, and if you continue to rub her up the wrong way you'll have all sorts of problems. Sorry, Posy, but I think you and Lola are going to have to make friends.'

'No way.'

They glared at one another, then Ellis laughed. 'Can I hold the handbags then, while you and she slug it out?'

Posy frowned crossly. Damn Lola. Of course it would be better than Hogarth running the pub, but surely they didn't have to get on, did they? They didn't have to communicate at all? Ellis could do all that, surely? If his success with Tatty was anything to go by, Ellis was good with older women.

The door crashed open, bringing in gusts of icy cold air and spatters of sleet which stirred the dust on the door mat. The London-weekenders looked up and the Pinks, temporarily denied Guinness refills, gave a desultory cheer.

The newcomer, tall with dark tousled hair, incredible cheekbones, surprisingly slanting green eyes, and wearing denim and leather, sauntered across to the bar like a latter-day James Dean.

He smiled cheerfully at The Crooked Sixpence's open-mouthed drinkers. 'Hi, is anyone serving in here?'

The American accent sounded amazingly sexy and totally out of place. Posy, who had been rocking on the two back legs of her chair, immediately stopped and bounced forward. 'Christ! It isn't Tony Curtis!'

'What?' Ellis frowned. 'What him? No, of course it isn't Tony Curtis. God, Posy, you're as bad as Gran, thinking that one day there'll be a superstar in Steeple Fritton.'

'It's John Cusack!'

'Is it?' Ellis peered through the gloom. 'Well, yeah, it could be . . .'

'No,' Posy shook her head in agitation. 'It isn't *John Cusack*. At least, *he* isn't John Cusack. It's John Cusack who makes me laugh and *he* looks just like John Cusack and he's staying at Sunny Dene and oh, wow!'

'Sorry, you've lost me.' Ellis stood up and beamed at the man by the bar. 'The landlord is otherwise engaged and the natives are all insane, but I can help you. I'm Ellis Blissit –'

'Flynn Malone . . .' They shook hands. 'And that's real kind of you. I'll have a JD.'

'No you won't,' Ellis slid behind the bar. 'Hogarth doesn't stretch to JD. Why don't you try one of our local ales instead?'

Whether a local ale would be a reasonable substitute or not, no one ever discovered. Neddy Pink, accordion primed, scrambled through the tables and positioned himself by the bar. With a wheeze and a groan, he slammed into a rafter-raising version of 'Yankee Doodle Dandy'.

While the London-weekenders clapped their hands and slapped their thighs, Martha and Mary Pink whooped forward and with headscarves bobbing and dusty rags flying, leapt into a yee-haw square-dance routine, complete with linked-arm-twirling and Paul Revere yells.

They were just do-se do-ing to their partners like billyo, when Lola and Hogarth appeared from the back room.

'Excuse me!' Lola yelled through the mayhem. 'Would someone mind telling me just what the devil is going on in my pub?'

Chapter Eleven

A week later, Fritton Magna was almost exactly as Flynn had imagined it would be. The weather, which of course hadn't come into the mental picture at all, was an added bonus.

For three days it had snowed intermittently so that soft billows now made white mobcap toppings across the thatched cottages and low-pitched roofs, and the heaviness had bent the pine trees so that they all looked like Bostonian dowagers with stiff necks.

English snow seemed very different to the snow in Charlestown, being gentler and smaller and altogether prettier somehow, and only added to the magic of the Dickensian fantasy.

Flynn's welcome to Steeple Fritton had come as something of a shock, too.

Everyone at home had reminded him of the English reputation for being cold and aloof, and told him that it wouldn't be easy to make friends. Vanessa had said that the women in particular, were bound to be very reserved. So, he just hadn't reckoned on the warmth of his reception from everyone at Steeple Fritton, especially Posy and Lola.

He'd taken some pleasure in leaving a message on Vanessa's voice mail telling her that he was sharing a house with two totally drop-dead gorgeous women who were as friendly as hell and both already in love with him.

That last bit was a lie, of course, but what the heck – more than six months since leaving the States and he was still pretty mad at Vanessa. And they were gorgeous: Posy was like a beautiful tiny rock chick with her spiral curls and her jeans and leathers, while Lola was an elegant ice maiden – a real class act.

Chalk and cheese, and they didn't seem to like each other much, but they certainly both seemed to like him. It was very flattering.

At the B&B, Dilys and Norrie treated him as though he was their own son, the dogs were a dream, and the two old queens who stayed there made him roar with laughter at their camp tales. Even Ellis, who'd seemed to be a bit territorial round Posy and Lola, was really friendly now they'd discovered they had so much in common.

He would certainly never have had Ellis down for a fellow engineer and steam train fanatic – but they'd been like two kids in a candy store playing with Norrie's model railway layout that ran through Sunny Dene's back garden. It was the most incredible set-up that Flynn had ever seen, and to his joy, Norrie had models of all the classic British steam engines, including the Flying Scotsman, Mallard, even Pendennis Castle. And every day, until the bad weather had halted their games, he and Ellis had spent companionable hours routing the trains, devising timetables, and operating sidings and signals.

The week at Sunny Dene had flown by, and that first night at The Crooked Sixpence – he'd phoned his parents, who were in Norway doing Grieg, and told them all about the traditional folk dancing in the pub which was nothing like he'd seen in the bar in Tralee – had set the tone for his stay so far.

He couldn't remember when he'd last enjoyed himself so much.

And now, at last, he was here in Fritton Magna to meet Great-Aunt Bunty's solicitor and claim his inheritance.

They'd arranged to meet outside Fritton Magna Manor, which, in best Agatha Christie tradition, Flynn had chosen to interpret literally, and were now standing in a huddle outside a pair of towering and dilapidated wrought-iron gates while the snow hissed horizontally against their faces.

Flynn had found no shortage of tour guides for today's mission. Although Lola had declined the offer to join the party – she was apparently meeting various brewery reps in her new position of The Crooked Sixpence's temporary landlady – Posy and Ellis, muffled against the cold, had bundled happily into his jeep and they'd been speculating on the short but hazardous journey about what form his inheritance would take.

Ellis was a newcomer, like himself, so it was only Posy who knew anything at all about his Great-Aunt Bunty.

'She was well-known but very reclusive . . . I mean, we rarely saw her in Steeple Fritton. Mum and Dad knew her fairly well. She had some sort of smallholding where she ran an animal sanctuary. She never turned anything away, so it was a right old mixture. Still is, I suppose. There was quite a lot in the papers when she died. How she'd left the animal sanctuary to several like-minded friends in the village and enough money to ensure that her work carried on for about five hundred years.'

Flynn had been relieved by this. He adored animals, but running a sanctuary truly wasn't in his line of work. Anyway, he was far too soft-hearted to cope with it professionally. So, Great-Aunt Bunty hadn't left him the business, then. And she must have had pots of money . . . but it obviously wasn't cash . . . Or real estate. The idea of a general store had already been scotched by Posy.

He blew on his hands as the vicious north wind brought another snow flurry, and wished the lawyer would get a move on.

'Maybe we should wait in the car?' Ellis suggested. 'We're going to be ice blocks if we stand out here much longer.'

Flynn nodded reluctantly. It made sense – but he loved the cold wind and the snow and the way the village looked like a Christmas card. He wanted to drink it all in and keep it forever.

'Yeah, maybe, but I was just thinking, the inheritance couldn't be this, could it?' He jerked his head towards the manor. 'Great-Aunt Bunty hasn't left me a stately home?'

'Not a chance!' Posy had already dived towards the jeep, snowflakes dissolving in her dark curls. 'Fritton Magna Manor is only a shell and some speculator bought it up years ago to turn it into a health club then went bust.'

'Oh, right. I just wondered why the lawyer arranged to meet here . . .'

'Because it's the only big building in the village.' Posy stuck her head out of the jeep's window. 'We all know what Americans are like for "big". Anyway, he probably thought, being a foreigner, you'd get lost without some sort of recognizable landmark.'

Before Flynn could make some suitably crushing rejoinder about the 'smallness' of England, Posy rolled the window closed again and stuck her tongue out at him. He was pulling a face at her just as a sleek silver car purred to a halt behind them. Feeling a stirring of excitement, he gawped as the matching driver – sleek and silver-haired and wearing a sheepskin coat – extricated himself from the plush interior.

'Mr Malone?' The lawyer held out his hand. 'So sorry to have kept you waiting. The roads were a little more treacherous than I'd anticipated. You must be frozen. You should have waited in the car.'

'No problem.' Flynn shook the leather-gloved hand. 'I was enjoying the winter scenery.'

The lawyer, whose nose was turning purple, looked at him as if he were mad. 'Er, well, yes, whatever. If you'd like to follow me, we should be able to make it by car as long as it doesn't snow any harder. Mind you, how you intend to ship it back to America is beyond me. Still, no doubt we can discuss that later. Come along.'

Flynn hopped obediently into the jeep and started the engine. The lawyer's accent was quite incredible. He sounded like Prince Charles.

'So?' Posy leaned forward between him and Ellis, her damp curls brushing his face. 'Any clues?'

'None,' Flynn concentrated on getting the jeep along a track that had shrunk to six inches wide with a skating rink surface. 'Just that I might have trouble shipping it home.'

'Oh, right.' Posy sank down again. 'Maybe it's a stuffed animal then. Bunty did a lot of that sort of thing. When her favourites died she had them taxidermied and mounted in a sort of museum mausoleum, you know, like Victor the giraffe?'

Jesus Christ! Flynn nearly drove into the bank. 'You are kidding? She didn't stuff giraffes?'

'No, of course she didn't. Giraffes aren't big in Fritton Magna, just in case you're not up to speed with British flora and fauna. But there was this giraffe that died in a zoo and so they had him – oh, well, look, it probably isn't anything like that. Don't worry about it.'

Too late. Flynn was worrying. What if it was the whole damn stuffed animal museum? What if he was about to be faced with rows and rows of staring glassy eyes and poor sparse-haired creatures all standing sad and stiff-legged on plinths? How well would that go down in Charlestown?

'Your solicitor's slowing down,' Ellis said, from the passenger seat. 'Just by those barns. Maybe Posy's right, maybe it is a dead animal. Look, if it's a whole set, maybe we could lease them from you and make them a feature of the Steeple Fritton Carnival?'

'No way – we don't want a static display.' Posy leaned forward again. Her hair was still damp. 'What we'd have to do is put them on wheels, then we could give rides to the kiddies. Tatty would love that. Her brood would form a queue all on its own.'

'Bitchy!' Ellis tugged at one of Posy's curls. 'No, but seriously, we might be able to do something with them.'

'Oh, great, that gives us two attractions, then. My dad's model railway and a lot of dead animals. Notting Hill eat your heart out.'

'Will you two button it,' Flynn grinned at them both as he slid the jeep to a halt behind the lawyer's car, wondering, as he had all week, if this constant teasing meant they were a couple. 'I've heard about nothing but this darn embryo Mardi Gras from you ever since I arrived. Can't we concentrate on this for a moment?'

'Yeah, okay,' Posy was scrambling from the car. 'I suppose it does seem a bit boring to you. After all, you'll have gone back to America by June. Christ! It's cold!'

It was and would he? Have returned to the States by the time this carnival thing took off? He had no idea. He hadn't planned to go home yet . . . Maybe he'd go back to Tralee when this inheritance thing was sorted . . . Or maybe he'd stick around.

'Mr Malone!' The lawyer barked through a miniature blizzard. 'Over here!'

Yessir! Flynn thought, sliding across the powdery surface followed by Ellis and Posy. Lawyers were obviously lawyers the world over – even if they did speak like royalty.

'Now,' Great-Aunt Bunty's legal eagle surveyed him. 'I've checked out all your papers, I've authenticated your rights to ownership, so there's no more to be done on that side of the business. I must say, though, that I did have my doubts about you turning up at all.'

'I got delayed in Ireland.' Flynn felt exactly like he had with his tutor at high school when work hadn't been handed in on time. 'Sorry.'

'Yes, well, you're here now ...' The lawyer was unlocking the door to a ramshackle barn. 'I must also tell you that this barn has been willed by Miss Malone to her Animal Trust so you'll have to relocate your inheritance as soon as possible. As I said, transportation may prove a problem, but fortunately it won't be mine. Ah!' The door eventually opened and the lawyer almost lost his grip. 'Here we are.'

It was even colder inside the barn than out. There were holes in the corrugated iron roof where the snow spattered through, and icicles hung from the dusty rafters. There was nothing else inside the cavernous interior except several huge grey tarpaulins humped over what looked like a small mountain.

'It's a stuffed elephant,' Posy said from behind him. 'Bet you any money.'

Flynn looked at her in horror. 'You're kidding, aren't you? You said she didn't do wild animals.'

'She might have made an exception.'

'Must be two elephants,' Ellis added. 'Or three. Look at the size of it! Elephants *in flagrante*, maybe. Or elephants *à trois*.'

'It's not a damn elephant,' the lawyer said testily, obviously wondering why he couldn't be doing something cosy like divorces in the centrally heated fug of his office. 'It's a Lion.'

'Nah! That's never a lion,' Posy's voice echoed eerily against the corrugated roof. 'That's far too big to be a lion.'

153

For the first time, Flynn was beginning to wish he'd stayed in Boston.

The lawyer twitched at the nearest tarpaulin and referred to a sheaf of notes. 'It's a Super Lion, actually. Built by John Fowler in Leeds in the early 1930s. Still in perfect working order.'

Taking in the words, Flynn felt a tremble of anticipation deep inside. Surely not? Surely, it couldn't be . . . ?

The lawyer yanked even harder at the tarpaulin, revealing glossy maroon paintwork, brilliant sunflower yellow wheels that towered above them, a glimpse of barley sugar twists of chrome . . .

'It's a tractor,' Ellis said, with disappointment in his voice. 'A bloody big tractor, but still. There's not much we can do with a tractor.'

'It's not a tractor,' Flynn's mouth was dry. 'It's a showman's traction engine. A real, perfect, showman's engine.'

He was pulling at the tarps with the lawyer now. Excitement, disbelief . . . A Fowler Super Lion! It would need a crew of dozens and stepladders to remove all the sheeting, but the back end was revealed in all its glorious glory, and that was enough for now.

Towering twenty feet above them, even the wheels were taller than he was, it stood in dark, cold splendour.

'Christ!' Posy's grin was ear to ear. 'It *is* a traction engine! Wow! You lucky sod! It used to belong to old Googly Harris! I haven't seen it since I was a kid – must be over twenty years. He used to trundle about in it scaring the horses, but he died ages ago.'

Ellis was open-mouthed. 'Bloody hell! I've only ever

seen them at rallies and steam fairs. They're every steam fanatic's wildest fantasy and as rare as moon dust. There's no way you're taking this back to the States before the carnival, it'll be the star of the show. But –' he stopped and frowned at Flynn. 'How come your Great-Aunt Bunty had it, then?'

'It was left to Miss Malone by Mr Harris when he died some years ago,' the lawyer said. 'There was, I gathered, a long-running affection between them. She's called Queen Mab, by the way.'

Queen Mab . . . Like something out of a fairy tale . . . Not really hearing the voices and totally unaware of the biting cold, Flynn ran his hands over Queen Mab's maroon paintwork, shiny as patent leather and still so perfect that he could see Posy and Ellis reflected in it – all squat and elongated – and felt suddenly sad. These people, Bunty Malone and Googly Harris, dead now, had loved and laughed and enjoyed themselves . . . and he hadn't even known they existed.

Posy was stroking the massive red and yellow wheel spokes with loving tenderness, as though she'd been reunited with a beloved pet after a prolonged stay in kennels. 'Why did she leave it to Flynn, though? She didn't know him.'

'Miss Malone was well aware of the personalities of her scattered family members. In this case, she knew that Mr Malone here was a member of the Rough and Tumblers –'

'Really?' Posy's eyes widened. 'I shouldn't let Tatty get wind of that.'

Ellis punched her again.

'The Rough and Tumblers are a society of steam

preservationists in America,' the lawyer said patiently. 'Miss Malone knew that Flynn's work in locomotive engineering spread into his leisure interests. It was one of her great pleasures, finding out about her family when they knew nothing of her. She planned to leave them all exactly what she thought would please them most.'

There was silence in the barn. The poignancy of the words seemed to have affected Posy and Ellis too. Flynn wanted to thank Great-Aunt Bunty, he wanted to know her, and it was all too damn late.

'The best thing you can do is simply enjoy this,' the lawyer said gently. 'It's the most fitting memorial Miss Malone could have – leaving happiness.'

Flynn nodded, a lump in his throat. Great-Aunt Bunty's money had enabled his parents to see all the places they'd only dreamed about. Her legacies to the Malone clan in Tralee had ensured Uncle Michael and Aunt Maude would run the bar forever and a day, and that their various offspring would never want for a roof over their heads.

And for him – he looked again at the perfect specimen of early twentieth-century engineering looming above him – for him she'd left paradise.

Chapter Twelve

Obviously, Lola thought, becoming the landlady of The Crooked Sixpence wasn't exactly what she'd had in mind as a new career; but when you considered that the alternative was Rough Sleeper, it was a gift from the gods.

'So?' Hogarth frowned at her in the gloom of the bar. 'You're sure you know what you're doing?'

'Perfectly.'

Having spent almost a week working cheek by un-savoury jowl with Hogarth, Lola was itching for him to go, to leave her alone so that she could turn The Crooked Sixpence into a thriving hive of – what exactly? Well, a thriving hive of something. Anything. Anything at all would be an improvement in an establishment which would have made Jamaica Inn look like Egon Ronay Recommended.

She gave her professional and practised smile-of-confidence. 'You've trained me well. I've spoken to all the reps and breweries, I've been through the books, I know where everything is and who to contact, and I've got your accountant's phone number should anything untoward happen.'

Hogarth humped two dirty and scratched cardboard suitcases on to the bar. 'Fair enough. You seems like a capable wench. I'll just be glad to leave it to someone who knows what they're doing.'

Lola hoped that her face didn't twitch at the word wench. And as for knowing what she was doing ... well, she may have embroidered her responsibilities at Marionette Biscuits just a tad. The professional smile remained resolutely fixed. 'As long as you're giving me carte blanche –'

'Uh?' Hogarth had hauled one suitcase from the bar top, and paused with the second. 'I never said nothing about transport.'

'No, no, it means – oh, well, look, off you go. I'll be fine.' Lola still had to fight the urge to shove him bodily through the door. 'Honestly, I know about the rules and regulations, the banking, the reordering, the laws of the licensing trade. You go and enjoy yourself.'

'Enjoy meself?' Hogarth had his hand tantalizingly on the door latch. 'This ain't a bloody holiday I'm taking.'

'No, no, of course not,' Lola stretched her face into an even wider smile. 'You go and work yourself to a frazzle, then. And I'll see you later in the year.'

'Ah. September likely. Depends.'

Then without further preamble or any parting niceties, Hogarth, and his two 1930s suitcases, finally disappeared.

Lola exhaled and leaned against the bar, letting the smile slip away. It was still snowing intermittently, as it had been for more than a week, and the yellow ochre afternoon light filtered into the dismal pub making it look colder and dirtier than ever. Marionette Biscuits, and Swansbury, and the luxury apartment, and Nigel – oh, especially Nigel – seemed as though they belonged to another lifetime. Another person. Which she supposed they did.

There would be no going back now. Somehow she'd been dealt this hand and she'd have to play it to the best of her ability. All the old dreams for the future, the cosy, snug, happy future, living with Nigel in love and luxury, were dead. Her new future was going to be what she made it and at least she had somewhere to live and a job – both temporary, but not to be sniffed at. If only she didn't feel so damn lonely . . .

'No time for self-indulgence,' she said out loud, listening to her voice thump dully against the grimy walls. 'Not when there's work to be done and there's only me to do it.'

In the absence of anything like an apron, she tied a far-from-clean towel round her waist, covering the best part of her navy crepe trousers and some of her grey angora sweater. She'd really have to get into jeans like Posy if she was going to become a manual worker. The idea seemed ludicrous. A few weeks off her fiftieth birthday and she was contemplating wearing denim for the first time . . .

Looking round the gloomy pub she felt the stirrings of apprehension ripple beneath her ribs. Lola pushed them irritably away. This was no time for second thoughts or doubts of any indices. She was on her own in this particular venture – and in everything else for the rest of her life.

The other Sunny Dene residents had been fleetingly interested in her taking over The Crooked Sixpence. But only fleetingly. When it transpired that she couldn't give them any inside information on Hogarth's other business interests, where he was going, and if he was to be accompanied by a seventeen-year-old nymphet, what little interest there had been dwindled pretty rapidly.

They all seemed to be far more caught up in this daft carnival idea, and more recently, all agog at Flynn Malone's steam-driven inheritance. Lola had hardly bothered to listen to the excited dinner-table gossip. It didn't concern her or involve her in any way. Dilys and Norrie were kind and attentive, Flynn was polite, Mr D and Mr B treated her as one of the family, and Ellis flirted with her.

Posy still ignored her, but she wasn't surprised. Posy and she were a generation apart. What the hell could a child like Posy, who thought her heart had been broken, know about the real thing?

'Work,' Lola said to herself again, pulling on a pair of Marigolds and picking up a bucket. 'The cure for all ills . . .'

Work took about three hours and she'd only just scratched the surface. Having decided to close the pub for two days, much to the Pinks' consternation, in an attempt to at least get rid of the worst of the grime, Lola realized how futile the task was. She'd need an army of professional Mrs Mops to lick this place into shape. Still, at least the floors were gleaming now, and the cobwebs had been banished, clinging to her broom like grey candyfloss, and all the out-of-date bottles had been dumped from behind the bar, and a proper fire crackled cheerfully in the swept grate.

'Excuse me . . .'

The door opened, allowing the murky afternoon darkness to rush in and fill up the dingy corners, accompanied by a snow flurry and bitterly cold wind.

'I'm afraid we're closed,' Lola said, wiping a grubby glove across her forehead and not looking up. 'Until Wednesday. For refurbishment.'

'I know. I saw the notice. I'm here because of the other one.'

Lola pushed her hair behind her ears and looked at the tall, fair-haired man in the doorway. He was wearing a crombie overcoat and had melting snowflakes in his hair. 'Which other one? Oh, you mean the one about bar staff?'

She'd gummed the 'staff wanted – apply within' notice on the outside door shortly before Hogarth left. She'd hoped he wouldn't notice. There had been no mention of hiring staff, but Lola was pretty sure she couldn't run The Crooked Sixpence alone.

He nodded. 'Are you still looking?'

'Haven't even started, and for God's sake come in and close the door before we freeze to death.'

The man closed the door and looked round. 'You've certainly been working hard. I didn't know there was a carpet.'

'Have you done bar work before?'

He shook his head. 'No, but I'm sure I could learn really quickly. And I live in the village, and I know everyone who drinks in here.'

Lola could see the sense in this. A local who knew the

peccadilloes of the pub's regulars would be worth his weight in cheese and onion crisps. Which was another area she intended to explore. Pub grub. Hogarth, she understood, had never let so much as a packet of peanuts pass across the bar. She'd soon alter that.

'Right, so are you looking for full-time work?'

'No. I work in a department store in Reading. Manager. Upholstery.'

There was a pause and Lola wondered if he'd changed his mind, then realized that she was supposed to make some sort of comment. 'Oh, er, right . . . lovely. Well done. Um –'

'I've just got married and we're expecting our first baby and money is tight. I could do most evenings.'

Lola nodded. He was young and nice looking and spoke politely. He could be an asset – and it was rather sweet that she'd be helping out a newly-married couple with an imminent child.

'Okay, look if you come in again on Wednesday before we open and we'll run through a few things. I wouldn't want you to start for a couple of weeks at least until I gauge the trade, and the money won't be great.'

'You'll pay the going rate?'

'Yes, of course.' Lola made a mental note to discover exactly what that was before bankrupting herself. 'Could you do, say, four hours, three evenings a week, to be arranged as I said when I see how things go, but definitely Friday and Saturday?'

A smile split his face making him look about thirteen. 'That would be ace! Thanks so much. I'll see you on Wednesday, then, er, Mrs . . . ?'

'Ms Wentworth. Lola.'

'I'm Richard. Richard Dalgetty. Most people call me Ritchie.'

They shook hands rather awkwardly because of the Marigolds and Lola watched fondly as he closed the door behind him. She'd hired and fired plenty of times at Marionette Biscuits, and always prided herself on making good staffing choices. After she'd put him through his paces Ritchie Dalgetty, she was sure, would turn out to be a superb barman.

Knowing that she wouldn't be able to make much impression on the remaining grime in the darkness, and also because she was starving, Lola peeled off the gloves, unfastened the towel and reached for her coat. Tomorrow she'd start bright and early, and when the various brewery deliveries arrived, she'd start stacking the shelves, and the cellar, and really get to work on transforming The Crooked Sixpence into a pub that Steeple Fritton and the surrounding area would be proud of.

Locking the door behind her, Lola closed her eyes against the full spite of the spiky snowflakes as she slipped and slithered towards Sunny Dene in the darkness. As soon as possible she'd have to buy another car; Hogarth was paying her a satisfactory retaining salary, and profits – when any materialized – were to be shared. If all her moneymaking plans for the pub came to fruition, she might even be able to reverse the state of her ever-dwindling savings account. If everything went to plan, she might soon be able to replace the hatchback which she guessed still slumbered in the wheel clampers' compound.

She felt a tingle of warmth in her stomach – she'd

always loved a challenge. And right now life, while nowhere near perfect, was definitely beginning to look a whole lot better.

'You're doing *what*?' Posy's voice spiralled above the rest of the dining room's post-prandial conversation. 'Are you completely mad?'

Lola had been making traction engine small talk with Flynn Malone over coffee and had just started to tell him about The Crooked Sixpence. The traction engine didn't interest her particularly, but Flynn's voice would make anything sound alluring. He also seemed interested in what she was saying about the pub. It was nice to be having a proper grown-up conversation with someone.

She frowned at the interruption. 'Sorry? Are you talking to me?'

'Of course I'm talking to you.' Posy, who had been clearing the tables, was now glaring at them, balancing a dangerously-overloaded tray. 'I heard what you said.'

Lola shook her head. Apart from murmuring about the traction engine, she hadn't said anything much at all, had she? Just about her ideas for the pub. 'I have no idea what you're talking about.'

'How convenient.' Posy sighed in exasperation. 'Let me remind you, then. You were saying: one, that you'll be introducing pub meals. And two, that you've hired bar staff.'

To give him his due, Flynn studiously stirred the dregs of his coffee and said nothing.

Lola frowned a bit more. 'Yes, I am and yes, I have, so what on earth is wrong with that?'

Posy's curls danced around her head in fury. 'What's

164

wrong with it? Jesus! You have no damn idea, have you? You are so bloody self-centred! We – Sunny Dene – are trying to drag in customers just to keep our heads above bloody water! We've spent weeks planning how to get people to come in here for meals and now you're going to be offering a rival eating establishment not five minutes down the road! And – no, let me finish – and we – me Ellis, Flynn, even Dom when he's home – need all the extra money we can get! If you wanted to employ bar staff why the hell didn't you ask us first?'

Sunny Dene's dining room was silent. Mr B and Mr D gazed slack-jawed at Posy. Norrie and Dilys and the dogs did the same.

Shaken by the vitriolic outburst, Lola exhaled. 'I'm sorry, but if you'd bothered to speak to me then I may have known that our plans were clashing. As you've chosen to exclude me from practically all your conversations and never even manage to be civil to me when we're alone, you'll have to forgive me if I'm left unaware of your situation.'

'Well,' Posy swept away towards the kitchen, the tray wobbling even more dangerously as she glared over her shoulder, 'you're not left unaware of it now, are you?'

No, she wasn't. 'I can see that perhaps we do have a conflict of interests here.' Lola looked across the dining room towards Dilys. 'Maybe we could have a chat about this, Mrs Nightingale. I mean, I don't really want to step on anyone's toes.'

Dilys nodded, her orange curls bouncing in much the same fashion as Posy's. 'Yes, all right, dear. In half an hour? In the lounge? And I'm sorry about Posy. I've no idea what's got into her lately.'

Flynn put down his coffee cup and grinned across the table. 'Sparks certainly fly between you two, don't they? Oh, and if you're looking for staff, my girlfriend back home, ex-girlfriend now, I guess, ran a bar called Opal Joe's. I used to help her out and I spent six months working in my uncle's bar in Tralee. I can throw a mean cocktail together and pour Guinness like a dream.'

Pulling pints and wiping tables she might just manage to offer – but she had a feeling there wasn't going to be a huge run on cocktails in The Crooked Sixpence. The Guinness experience might come in handy, though. Hogarth had mentioned that the Pinks were congenitally linked, not only to each other, but also to the Black Stuff; a reference which had at the time completely mystified her.

Lola smiled weakly, 'I'll bear it in mind.'

Just over an hour later, after a very frank talk with Norrie and Dilys, Lola climbed the various sets of skewwhiff stairs to her room. She'd had no idea that Sunny Dene was in such a parlous financial state. It explained much of Posy's outrage. She'd have felt exactly the same. If only she could tell Posy that she understood now, and that a satisfactory deal had been struck. But, she thought, unlocking her door, because she'd admitted to being a mistress Posy simply didn't want to know.

The photograph of Nigel beamed at her from the bedside table, and Lola picked it up, and as always, kissed him. 'You don't know what trouble you've caused me,' she told him, holding him against her. 'Oh, not just losing all the Swansbury stuff – you couldn't help that. But even now, here, loving you is making my life so difficult . . .' She sniffed back a tear. 'Not that I regret a moment of it.'

'Hey, sorry. Don't want to intrude, but –'

Lola jerked her head up from the photograph, and looked at Flynn Malone who was standing in the open doorway. Feeling irritated that this, her private time with Nigel, was being invaded, she sighed. 'You're not intruding, it's my fault. If I'd wanted privacy I should have closed my door.'

'If any of us had wanted privacy we should never have holed up in this place,' Flynn grinned at her. 'Is that a picture of your dad? I miss my parents too.'

She winced. It had happened a lot while she and Nigel were together. People assuming that because of the age difference they couldn't possibly be lovers. She felt no inclination to explain to Flynn or anyone else. 'Yes, well being away from home turns you into a child again, doesn't it? The unfamiliarity and everything. Um, did you want something?'

'Apart from a bar job? Yeah, I did. I was sort of working round to it when Posy blew her stack downstairs. Ellis says that there are a lot of outbuildings at the back of the pub. I didn't know if you would be using them or not, but I need somewhere for Queen Mab to live, and wondered if I could rent one of them from you?'

'Sorry? Not quite with you. Queen Mab?'

'My showman's engine. She's got to be moved from Fritton Magna as soon as the snow has thawed. She needs a home until I've worked out what I'm doing.'

Why not? Lola thought wildly. She'd already got a pub she wasn't sure she could run, a barman who had never done the job before in his life, and a sort

167

of temporary home filled with misfits – why on earth not have a traction engine living in the shed?

'I haven't looked at the outbuildings very closely. I know one of them is used for storage and pub overspill, but if any of the others are suitable you're more than welcome. Aren't traction engines pretty huge, though?'

'Massive,' Flynn said happily. 'But Ellis says The Crooked Sixpence's outbuildings are as big as barns, so it should be perfect. Shall we go and take a look?'

Lola nodded. 'Yes, of course. I'm going to be in the pub early tomorrow morning for more cleaning, so we'll investigate then.'

'Tomorrow? That's ages away. Why not now?'

'Because it's dark and freezing and probably snowing and we won't be able to see anything and –'

'No reason at all then. Come on, get your coat. I'll be waiting downstairs.'

He was. And looking, Lola thought from the safe distance of the last-but-one-landing, very film-starrish in a long black coat with the collar turned up. Who on earth did he remind her of? Oh, yes, of course . . . John Cusack. The layers of dark hair and those incredible feline eyes . . .

Good Lord! She shook herself mentally. What on earth was the matter with her? Was she having a fit of rampaging hormones or something? About to descend into a second puberty? Only hours earlier she'd been thinking about getting a pair of jeans – it was probably high time she registered with the local doctor and reduced her HRT intake.

Concentrating on her best Mistress of Marionette Biscuits facial expression, she arrived at the foot of the stairs looking, she hoped, far less ruffled than she felt. 'I think we're mad doing this at this time of night, and you'll have to drive because I haven't got a car.'

'Drive?' Flynn raised his eyebrows. 'Who's driving? It's only a five minute walk.'

'I'm not walking anywhere in this weather!'

'Of course you are,' Flynn threw open the front door. 'You British are well known for enjoying a bracing walk. Come on . . . it'll be great.'

They stepped out of Sunny Dene and into Siberia.

Lola's breath was ripped from her lungs in an icy cloud. The wind whistled across the common and whipped spears of snow against her face while the ice tried to whisk her feet from under her.

To prevent herself from falling, she grabbed Flynn's arm in the darkness and then immediately let it go again. 'This is awful! Can't we do it tomorrow?'

'No.' His voice was raised above the storm. 'It's fun. We need fun. Everyone needs fun.'

She squinted up at him doubtfully. Fun, yes. Frostbite and hypothermia, no.

Still staggering, they rounded the corner away from the B&B and the common, and headed towards the second, smaller green and The Crooked Sixpence. More sheltered from the wind, the snow now fell downwards rather than horizontally, dark feathery flakes illuminated by the orange pools of the intermittent streetlamps. Everywhere was silent, white, beautiful.

'Wow,' Flynn said softly. 'It's just like a James Stewart movie.'

Lola tried to see icebound Steeple Fritton through his eyes and failed miserably. Surely, in James Stewart movies, everyone had ruddy cheeks and smiles – not runny noses and welded-together lips? And weren't there always Christmas trees and gaily wrapped parcels tucked under arms? And cheery neighbours shovelling snow?

'James Stewart movies don't usually take place in the back of beyond, in almost total darkness, without another living soul in sight and the sort of temperature guaranteed to kill within thirty seconds. And this is February in England, not Christmas Eve in Philadelphia, and –'

'Use your imagination,' Flynn grinned down at her. 'We're all in the same boat here.'

'Which boat?'

'The row-your-own variety. For various reasons we've all fetched up in this backwater. We're away from roots and responsibilities, and from security and a steady income. All any of us have got is the future and our imaginations. I know nothing about you, but you must be here because something went wrong in the past. Same with Ellis. Posy, I guess, is a bit different, but even she's starting over. And we're all just going to have to make the best of it.'

'Very philosophical,' Lola muttered, slithering on the snow. 'And, yes, okay, you're right. Actually, I was thinking along much the same lines earlier. We've all been dealt a pretty weird hand with Steeple Fritton as the Joker. The pub might be a temporary respite for me, but what are the rest of you going to do? Oh, and don't tell me that this damn stupid carnival idea is going to be the answer to everyone's prayers, because that really would be James Stewart movie country.'

He laughed. 'No, the carnival may not solve all the

problems, but it's a hell of a happy thing to focus on. To work on. To plan for. Because, who knows, it might, just might, make a difference.'

They'd reached The Crooked Sixpence and as they scrunched across the car park, even Lola, frozen as she was, had to admit it looked amazingly pretty under its dusting of white. The snow flurried round and round, changing colour as it eddied from the darkness into the light and back again. Blue shadows blurred any harsh edges and everywhere was as still and silent as a landscape painting.

But only for a nanosecond.

Round the corner, walking in Indian file, traipsed a raggle-taggle tribe of refugees. Dressed in layers of multicoloured fur and wearing peculiar ethnic headgear, moon boots and carrying torches, they varied in size from normal at the front to midget at the rear as they passed the pub beneath the streetlamp. And they were singing.

Loudly.

'Yummy, Yummy, Yummy'.

'What the hell is that?' Flynn was open-mouthed.

'Tatty Spry and her brood,' Lola tried not to laugh, which was fairly easy as her lips were practically frozen together. 'I had the dubious pleasure of sharing a bus trip with them once.'

'Jesus.'

'They're probably going to see Ellis.'

'Why on earth would Ellis want to entertain half of Haight-Ashbury?'

'Because,' Lola blinked snowflakes from her eyelashes, 'apparently Tatty and Ellis are romantically involved.'

'No way! I thought Ellis and Posy were sorta close?'

'Ellis and Posy?' Lola shook her head quickly. 'Oh, I don't think that Posy is Ellis's type. She's far too young and, well, boyish, with all that motorcycling stuff and the way she dresses. They're just friends, I gather. Ellis seems to prefer his women older and more feminine.'

'Like you?'

Despite the chill, Lola flushed angrily. 'Not like me at all! Like Tatty, I mean. According to the Sunny Dene gossip, Ellis and Tatty Spry are a hot item. As you've just seen, she has umpteen dysfunctional kids, and, also according to Dilys and Norrie, she takes them with her on her romantic assignations because no one in the village is daft enough to baby-sit twice.'

'My, my . . . This place is real fascinating, like living in a soap.' Flynn was smiling and looking even more catlike than ever. 'And judging by the way you're shivering, maybe we ought to drop the speculation on Ellis's love life and have a look at Queen Mab's home before we turn to ice blocks.'

Lola jangled the keys free from her pocket and picked her way carefully across the car park's treacherous surface. She wished she'd had the foresight, like Tatty, to bring a torch.

'They're all round the back, down the side of the pub, we'll have to just feel our way . . . ooops!'

Flynn caught her elbow just as she slipped sideways on a hidden rut in the dark. She smiled her thanks, then moved away from him, feeling her way along the side wall of The Crooked Sixpence.

'There, you can just about make out the sheds. The one on the end should be big enough, shouldn't it?'

'Yeah, I guess so. It looks great. But there must be another way in. I mean, that little track is hardly wide enough for humans let alone Queen Mab, and we'll never get her through this door.'

'There's a road at the back that joins the common and all the sheds have double doors on that side,' Lola said, fiddling with the cold key in the frozen lock. 'Hogarth said they used to be used for farm machinery years ago. But you'll have to trust me on that. I'm not trudging round there in the darkness. We really should have done this in daylight.'

'And missed Tatty Spry and the seven dwarfs? No way. Here, let me . . .'

He managed to force the door open and peered inside. 'Is there a light or something?'

'No idea,' Lola was chilled to the bone now. 'I've only ever been into the smallest shed when Hogarth was telling me about the draymen delivering . . . Look, I'm sorry if you think I'm being a lightweight on this expedition, but I'm going back now. It's too cold to hang about any longer.'

With a click and a whoop of triumph, Flynn found the light switch. The cavernous shed was illuminated by harsh, flickering fluorescent tubes and looked even colder inside than out.

'Ace,' he said happily. 'Just perfect. I'll get Queen Mab installed in here just as soon as the snow thaws. You can take the rental fee out of my bartender's wages.'

'What? Oh, yes, fine. Whatever . . . only please can you lock the door again because I'm really going home.'

Home? To Sunny Dene? Sunny Dene was *home*? Lola gave a little groan of realization.

173

Flynn, clearly misinterpreting the despair, looked at her with concern in the slanting eyes. 'Jeeze, I'm sorry. You really are frozen and I'm being selfish. Look, let's lock up now and go into the pub and have a brandy to celebrate the deal.'

Coming in from the cold, The Crooked Sixpence actually felt cosy for the first time in living memory. Lola made yet a further mental note to replace the overhead lighting with wall lamps and to make sure the fire in the grate never went out, but even without ambient lighting and heat she was pleased at the difference her cleaning had made.

Flynn, obviously eager to prove himself the world's best would-be barman, was busily dispensing treble brandies. She watched him, happy in this strange place, confident that he could handle his future, shape it, mould it into something that he wanted, rather than the other way round. She sat beside the grey-ashed fire and pulled her coat more closely round her. Well, if he could grab this second-best life by the throat and be excited by the possibilities, then so could she.

He handed her the balloon glass. 'Here's to survival in the depths of rural England.'

'To survival, and success,' Lola let the brandy fire liquid warmth into her veins, instantly filling her with a heady optimism she hadn't felt for months. She smiled at him. 'And to friendship.'

Flynn nodded. 'Yeah, to friendship, and to whatever else comes along.'

Chapter Thirteen

By the time the snow had thawed, and the slush had drained, and Steeple Fritton had stopped resembling a paddy field, Posy was almost twitching with impatience.

Much as she'd loved the snow, it had meant that her beloved motorbike had had to stay under wraps, that village life had ground sluggishly to a halt, and that there had been no new visitors at Sunny Dene. However, with the first signs of spring the plans for the carnival seemed to be galloping forward – at about the same pace as Sonia nee Tozer's pregnancy, Lola's refurbishment of The Crooked Sixpence, and Ellis's relationship with Tatty Spry.

Posy couldn't help feeling that she was being left behind.

It was March, and with the surge of new green life, came a feeling of intense restlessness. She'd even wondered, a bit treacherously, if Persephone's owner had given her the best advice about coming home and picking up the threads that day. What would have happened if she'd really run away, found Swindon, started a new life? Would it really have been worse than this feeling of stagnation that swamped her now?

Keeping away from Ritchie and Sonia had become a boring ritual rather than a cloak and dagger game. Even Amanda and Nikki had stopped ringing her on their mobiles every time the Dalgettys were spotted in the vicinity. She simply avoided being where they were, although the Glad, Rose and Vi coven were always on hand to fill her in on the more intimate details of their marital bliss.

Flynn was all wrapped up in Queen Mab, and Ellis was all wrapped up in Tatty, and even the pub was a no-go area now that Lola was in charge.

Standing on the edge of the common in the early morning dampness, watching Trevor and Kenneth snuffling happily through the undergrowth, Posy sighed heavily. Everyone else was busily engaged in doing something – and she was doing nothing – and the inertia was driving her mad.

'Wassup?'

Posy jerked her head round towards the road. Ellis had stopped the minibus on the bend and was leaning from the window.

'Nothing. Just thinking.'

'Dangerous at your age. Hang on . . .' Ellis swung from the Dormobile and sprinted towards her. 'I was going to come and see you at the B&B anyway. Haven't got time to talk now, got to drop the brats off at school –'

He indicated the minibus. Tatty's brood, plus various other village children who now used the minibus for the school run, all stuck their tongues out.

176

'Love 'em,' Ellis said with heavy sarcasm. 'Anyway, will you be at home later?'

She nodded. 'It's bed-changing day.'

'Christ! Your life is one big whirl of excitement, isn't it? However, I may just be able to alter all that.'

'Why? How?'

'Wait and see,' Ellis winked, kissed her cheek, and ran back to the minibus. As he pulled open the door, a blast of 'Goody Goody Gumdrops' assaulted the pastoral bliss.

Posy wandered round the edge of the common, exchanging weather forecasts with the other dog-walkers, still wondering if life was passing her by. She was pretty sure that nothing Ellis could suggest would inject her existence with any pizzazz. It was all such an aftermath now. Before, when she'd been really, really hurt by Ritchie's defection, and then angry with Lola for being a husband-stealer, and annoyed with everyone generally, it had given her a sharply spiked focus. Now, apathy had overtaken anger and her life was in the doldrums.

Even the carnival plans, which had seemed so exciting before, were threatening to evaporate into nothing more than a slightly enlarged village fête. The parish council had been far more enthusiastic about holding a weekly car boot sale on the common than a huge glittering once-a-year event. The carnival proposals had been deferred for a couple of weeks while the car boot sales were organized.

They were now up and running, and admittedly bringing in shoals of visitors every Sunday, so the previous week the parish council – those that hadn't dozed throughout the proceedings – had spent about fifteen minutes discussing the carnival. There was a great deal of lack of interest.

Eventually, because Posy had shouted and woken people up, Steeple Fritton Carnival had been fixed for early June.

'No point having it any later,' Mrs Bickeridge's Clive had said. 'Everyone goes off to Benidorm and suchlike then to make the most of the kiddies' 'olidays.'

As Posy had never noticed a huge village exodus to the Costas during the summer, she could only imagine he meant the weekenders. And surely the weekenders weren't going to make one jot of difference to the carnival anyway? And what had they got organized so far? What had actually materialized from those enthusiastic dreams of a few weeks ago?

The usual conglomeration of stalls: tombola and white elephant and bath and beauty, because the vicar said they always went down well; fancy dress for the kiddies which would probably mean Tatty's offspring turning up in their everyday clothes and walking off with the spoils; a carnival queen contest which the vicar had pooh-poohed on the grounds of political correctness but had fortunately been outvoted; Flynn's traction engine; and her dad's model railway . . .

Posy groaned and whistled the dogs. Trevor and Kenneth, who had discovered a dead hedgehog and were taking turns to roll in it, ignored her.

When she returned with two foul-smelling dogs and a worse temper than she'd set out with, Posy discovered that Sunny Dene was in a state of high excitement – and it wasn't just because it was bed-changing day.

As the roads were now clear, Flynn, Norrie, and Mr

D and Mr B had decided the conditions were perfect to remove Queen Mab from Fritton Magna and install her in The Crooked Sixpence's shed. They'd looked shocked when Posy said she didn't think she'd be joining them.

It was, Posy thought, shoving umpteen floral duvet covers into the washing machine, a true reflection on the state of her social life when a lot of old men – well, Flynn wasn't old of course, but still – seemed to think she'd be jumping through hoops to join them in trundling along the country lanes on a machine that had been obsolete for at least sixty years.

'We'll have a cup of coffee, dear,' Dilys said, 'when the men have gone.'

Oh, whoopee-do.

Sadly for Posy, Dilys, who was looking very spring-like in daffodil yellow with a lot of sunny sequins, was in one of her optimistic moods. Since Ellis and Flynn had repaired her car, and Flynn had fixed some dicky lighting in one of the en suites, and Ellis had helped Norrie clear all the weeds away from the model railway and unstick the points at the Crewe interchange, she'd rarely stopped singing their praises. Posy was pretty sure it wouldn't be long before one – or both – of them was mooted as a possible Ritchie-replacement.

Which in the normal run of things, as she and Amanda and Nikki had discussed over many a vodka and Coke, wouldn't be the sort of choice you'd hate to have to make. Both Ellis and Flynn were gorgeous, bright, funny, friendly and very, very sexy.

The drawback was that they were men.

And since Lola's irritatingly brilliant suggestion to link the food at The Crooked Sixpence with that of the B&B

– the pub was now offering Nightingale's Nibbles: light lunches, prepared, cooked and delivered by Norrie and Dilys, and there were Sunny Dene evening meal menus on all the bar tables, a ploy which had already seen the B&B's dining room almost full nearly every night this week – all was more than all right in Dilys's world.

For Posy it was nowhere near enough.

She knew that Sunny Dene still needed more money to keep it afloat, and was increasingly frustrated that no one shared her sense of urgency. Norrie, once he'd become accustomed to doing the accounts, was simply happy with breaking even – profit-making, it seemed, hadn't yet been considered.

It would be great when Dom was back for the Easter vac and could point out the financial pitfalls to their Mr Micawber-inclined father. In the meantime there was no way that she could keep on taking money *out* of the B&B, even her paltry salary as a family member, when her whole aim was to get money *in*.

She still needed to have a job both to restore her self-confidence and shore up the Sunny Dene coffers. But where on earth was she going to find one?

'Lola is doing a roaring trade at the pub seeing that she's only been open for just over a week,' Dilys said artlessly, dunking a custard cream into her coffee. 'Surprised you haven't been along to take a look-see.'

'I will when I have time, and I think "roaring trade" is relative. If you mean she's doubled the regular customers, well, six is hardly a full house, is it?'

Posy dunked her own custard cream and watched in dismay as it disintegrated into a gooey mess and sank below the surface. It was one of those days. 'I'll

have to speak to her about stuff for the carnival anyway.'

'Good idea. She can put up a poster for you.'

Posy tried not to groan. Dilys already had a hand-
written carnival poster in the hall of the B&B. There
was one pasted on Vi Bickeridge's corner shop window,
too. Another one in the pub – and that was all it would
take to pull the crowds in! Watch out Notting Hill!

'It may be a bit early for posters and we do need to
go further afield . . .'

'It's never too early, or too local, to advertise. Look
what Lola's done for our evening trade by advertising
us in the pub.'

Posy pushed away the half-drunk coffee and the packet
of custard creams. She really couldn't bear to hear again
how Lola was turning The Crooked Sixpence into the
twenty-first century equivalent of Berni Inns, or how
Ellis was diversifying his Highwayman role on a daily
basis. And now Flynn had got Queen Mab – and Sonia
nee Tozer had got Ritchie . . .

'I'm going out on the bike. If Ellis turns up tell him
I'll see him later.'

'Okay, dear, go and blow away the cobwebs. And
don't forget to pop into the pub to see Lola.'

She'd just manoeuvred the BMW on to the driveway,
and was sitting astride it, pulling on her crash helmet,
when Ellis arrived.

'When I was at uni I had a poster just like that on
my wall.'

'What, scruffy urchin on ex-police motorcycle?'

'Yeah.' He eyed the bike. 'Real turn-on. Do you want
a passenger?'

'Not really. I was going to belt around a bit and be introspective. Introspective is difficult if you're going to be trying to lick the back of my neck.'

Ellis grinned. 'You're too smart for your own good. Which is why I was going to make you that offer you won't be able to refuse.'

'Does it involve money?'

'Some. Not much at the moment, but who knows. How do you fancy being a courier?'

'You mean drug running?'

'Sadly, no. Nowhere near that amount of cash involved. I was thinking more of urgent same-day letters, small packages, stuff like that.'

'And I'd get paid for it?' Posy looked at him closely. 'Properly?'

'Yes, we'd spilt the money. I've done a leaflet drop round all the Frittons advertising the minibus service – and added a few extras. Like shopping for the week-enders. A gap in the market, you see. All those people wearily trudging out of London on a Friday night, not wanting to have to queue in Sainsbury's for their provisions or start stocking up when they get here – all they have to do is e-mail their lists through to my laptop before Friday lunch time, pay by credit card, and it'll be sitting there waiting for them when they arrive.'

Posy couldn't help smiling. Like the bus service, it was an extremely enterprising move.

'And is it working?'

Ellis nodded. 'Really well. Big runs on coronation chicken and Chilean Merlot – and milk and eggs and loo rolls and ciabatta bread, and anything that Jamie Oliver throws together. And I've kept it local. No point in taking trade away from the village, so the Bickeridges have extended their product range for me. I collect from them, deliver to the weekenders, and everyone's happy.'

Posy wondered just what Vi Bickeridge made of buffalo mozzarella and couscous.

'I'm impressed. And amazed that after hours of romping with Tatty you still have the energy. So, where does the courier bit come in?'

'I've also offered a localish same-day delivery service. I remembered that you'd told me there wasn't a post office any more in Fritton Magna or Lesser Fritton, so I've done a leaflet drop round there, too. I've been pretty overwhelmed on that front. I need to off load some of it and wondered if you and the BMW would be willing?'

'Dead willing,' Posy nodded. 'As long as it fits in round the stuff I do at Sunny Dene.'

'Count on it.' Ellis leaned over, lifted her curls, and kissed her ear. 'Are you sure you don't want a pillion passenger?'

'Quite sure,' Posy said sternly, again trying not to tingle. 'And thanks for the job.'

'I told you weeks ago we'd make a great team. If you weren't still pining for the love of your life you might just realize it.'

'No we wouldn't and no I'm not and no I won't.' Posy rammed the crash helmet over her curls. 'Now leave me alone and go and play with Tatty.'

After that, roaring around the damp and bosky Berkshire lanes on the BMW certainly made Posy feel better. At least here she was in control. At least, with the pulsing power at her fingertips, and the roar in her head, and the feeling of freedom, it gave her time to be alone and to think about the future.

Which was the problem, really: apart from Ellis's more than welcome part-time job, there wasn't a future. She had no direction any more.

Before, with Ritchie, her life had been mapped out. Okay, so it might have not seemed a particularly excitingly contoured map for motivated urban women who wanted to climb the career ladder and become chairmen of multinational companies, but it had suited her.

Was she the last woman left alive in the have-it-all society who had actually wanted to become a wife and mother first, and maybe have a job, later?

She'd been contented with her life: happily working in the B&B, enjoying her friends and her motorbike, having a good local social life, and being the fiancée of the only boyfriend she'd ever had.

Then there'd been the excitement of the wedding plans, and the knowledge that she and Ritchie would move into the attic flat of Sunny Dene after the marriage. She'd carry on working at the B&B, and Ritchie would carry on managing his furniture department in Reading until such time as they'd saved enough money to buy the closed-down shop, then they'd turn it into Steeple Fritton Bric-a-Brac, and when she'd been Mrs Dalgetty for a few months they'd start a family. And their plump and sweetly-smiling babies would come to work with her and Ritchie, and life would be idyllic.

She hadn't been aware then of how broke they were at home, of course. She'd realized that Colworth Manor had nicked a lot of business, but she'd put Dilys and

Norrie's grumbling down to just that: miffed small business having nose put out of joint by bigger one.

It seemed she'd been blissfully unaware of so many things . . .

So, it was just as well, Posy thought, pulling the BMW to a halt at the Lesser Fritton junction, that she knew all the facts now. If Flynn and Ellis and Lola could change their lives, then she could too. With renewed vigour, she revved the engine, leaned low across the handlebars and zoomed back towards the village.

Ten minutes later, sitting astride the BMW outside the parade of shops, she unfastened her helmet, shook free her curls and took stock. She was the only person who could do anything about *herself*. She could change her own life, she could improve Sunny Dene's finances and she could make the carnival happen the way she'd planned.

It was no good moping and mooching and feeling sorry for herself. She had to do something – and now – and while the idea that had sprung into her mind as she cruised round corners at a reckless speed was probably totally ridiculous, if she didn't ask, she'd never know.

Propping the motorcycle against the kerb, she marched into the Bickeridges' corner shop.

The place was packed with headscarves. The headscarves were attached to Glad Blissit, the female Pinks, and Rose Lusty. The headscarves all turned and stared at her.

'Good morning.'

'Morning, Posy,' Glad grinned with her gums. 'Bit early to be in here for your pension.'

Oh, ha-ha-ha. 'I'm in here because I want to take over

the shop on the end and I wondered if anyone knew who owned it.'

There was an awful and embarrassed silence.

Mrs Bickeridge straightened her paisley wrapover and peered from behind the post office's counter grille. 'You wants to do *what*?'

Posy repeated the apparently outrageous statement.

Vi Bickeridge turned her lips inside out. 'It's a den of iniquity that place and I've got no idea who owns it. We don't *rent*. Me and our Clive owns this place outright, and Rose owns hers, too, don't you, Rose?'

Rose Lusty, who had obviously been practising pin curls on herself if the frizz under the headscarf was anything to go by, nodded affirmation. 'Young Tatty rents hers though. You should ask her if the same person owns the end shop. Although you do know what went on there before, don't you?'

'Yes,' said Posy, who didn't have a clue.

'It's got a Bad Name.' Glad Blissit cackled. 'And just say you do take it over, what're you going to sell in it?'

'Oh, loads of things,' Posy said brightly again, not having a clue about that either.

'Nothing to undercut us I hope?' Clive Bickeridge had wormed his way out from behind the bacon slicer. 'We're all for free enterprise but we don't want no competition.'

'There'll be no competition for anyone here, I promise you.'

This was true because although she had absolutely no idea what she'd really do with the shop if she got it, she definitely knew she wouldn't be providing stamps

186

and sago, aromatherapy oils and herbal cure-alls, or making all the Steeple Fritton ladies of a certain age look as though they were wearing a startled sheep on their heads.

Posy ducked out of the post office before Martha and Mary Pink, who'd been building themselves up with rustles and squeaks, could ask any further awkward questions, and clumped along the row in her well-fortified Gaerne motorcycling boots. She felt about as dainty as a Storm Trooper.

Tatty's shop door was open to the warm spring air, and the rainbow beaded curtain rattled happily as Posy pushed her way through. It was cavernously dark, with little pinprick fairy lights twinkling in unexpected places. Thick with the perfume of spice and incense, the atmosphere was heavy and languid, and floor to ceiling shelves overloaded with boxes of who-knew-what, made the tiny shop seem even smaller.

'Anyone at home? – oh, shit!' Posy's steel toecap made contact with something soft and squashy on the floor.

Peering downwards, praying she hadn't just inadvertently trampled on Zebedee or Orlando or little Tallulah in the gloom, she grinned. Ellis's sweatshirt and 501s were left in a telltale trail in the direction of the stockroom.

Tatty, still remarkably fully clothed in layers of velvet and lace, appeared from between the strands of a second beaded curtain. 'Hi, Posy. Are you buying or just looking for Ellis?'

'Er, neither. I wanted to talk to you, but you're obviously busy so I'll, um, come back another time.'

'Not busy at all,' Tatty shook back the snaky ringlets and rattled an armful of bangles. 'Just trying out something that Ellis suggested. Do you want to come and look?'

'No! I mean, no, thanks. Like I said, I'll come back.'

But Tatty was clearly not taking not-on-your-life for an answer. Grabbing Posy's arm she pulled her through the bead curtain.

Once she'd got the rainbow glass out of her mouth, her eyes and her curls, Posy blinked. It was warm and very dark, even darker than the shop, and Tatty's offspring, wearing their usual mixed bag of styles, were seated on a neat row of tall stools staring at Ellis. Ellis was face down on a sort of leather operating table wearing nothing but his boxers.

'Jesus, Tatty –' Posy shook her head. 'What are you like? You can't let the kids *watch*!'

'Why not? It's how I learned. Watching my mother and my grandmother.'

Dear God! Posy swallowed. 'But it's not right! I mean –'

Ellis turned his head and grinned sleepily at her. 'Hi . . . are you going to join in?'

'No I'm damn well not! You're, you're weird!'

'It's a massage, Pose, that's all. It's part of Tatty's expansion, like we discussed in the pub. Remember? You said the shops should offer more, be open more, bring people in for stuff they couldn't get anywhere else. It was your idea. All those stressed weekenders with tons of money to spend and nothing to spend it on. They'll love this. A proper aromatherapy massage parlour on their doorsteps.'

188

Posy felt relieved but looked doubtful. 'Well, maybe, yes . . . but you'll have to make sure you advertise it as aromatherapy. We wouldn't want to give anyone the wrong idea about what Tatty was offering, would we? And what the hell is that smell, anyway?'

'Ylang-ylang and sandalwood,' Tatty reached for a pile of towels, rolled up her lace cuffs in a professional way, then flexed her fingers over Ellis's glorious torso. 'Supplied by my main man, Baz from Basingstoke. Very seductive. One of the more erotic blends of oils. I'm sure it'll be very popular. Ellis was a real sweetie to volunteer for a practice run. I haven't actually been a masseur for yonks.'

Posy found it faintly disturbing watching Tatty's long beringed fingers sinuously kneading Ellis's flesh. Aromatherapy massage or not, it still smacked of voyeurism, and were guinea pigs supposed to moan with ill-suppressed enjoyment?

'Er, am I allowed to talk?'

'Under normal circumstances, no,' Tatty's thumbs were circling on Ellis's back in an extremely erotic manner. 'I like my clients to be kept quiet and calm, as serene as possible, but as this is only a test run, yes sure. You said you wanted to ask me something?'

Posy dragged her eyes away. The kiddies, she noticed, didn't. 'It's about this shop. Vi Bickeridge says you lease it from someone and that that same someone might also own the empty shop. Can you give me their name?'

Tatty brushed a fall of ringlets away from her face with her forearm. 'Sure, but why would you want to know that?'

Ellis stirred drowsily and turned his head towards her.

'Hallelujah, you're really going for it. You're going to rent it, aren't you?'

'No, not necessarily. I mean, I can't afford to rent it. The whole point is to make money. I just thought, that if it belonged to someone local, I could take it off their hands and spruce it up a bit and do something with it, then it'd help in the overall campaign of putting Steeple Fritton on the map and –'

'Hogarth.' Tatty applied more oil to her hands, hitched up her ankle-length skirts and petticoats and hopped up on to the couch. The children clapped as she sat astride Ellis and concentrated on his shoulders.

Feeling supremely embarrassed, Posy frowned. '*Hogarth?* Hogarth owns these shops as well as the pub?'

'Yes. I pay him rent every six months. He owned the other one too until it got closed down.' Tatty looked at Posy from her straddled position. 'If you want to find out about leasing it, borrowing it, or anything else, you'll have to go and speak to Lola. She's taken over all of Hogarth's business interests while he's away. I'm sure she'll help you.'

Chapter Fourteen

Posy looked around The Crooked Sixpence in amazement. Not only was it busy – and at lunch time – but she could actually see through the windows. And there was a dartboard and a lovely 1950s Wurlitzer jukebox, a fruit machine – and, good heavens! – a television set anchored to the wall. And everything sparkled. Nothing crunched underfoot, the table tops gleamed, the bar surface was like a mirror, and the whole place looked welcoming and friendly.

Such a pity the landlady didn't.

Lola, very secretarial in her usual black and white with gold chains, was standing behind the bar as though she'd been born there.

They stared warily at one another for what seemed like ages.

'What can I get you?' Lola's smile reached neither her eyes nor her voice.

'Oh, um, nothing. That is, nothing to drink, thank you. I just wondered if we could talk?'

'Can't it wait until this evening at Sunny Dene? I'm

busy and – oh, excuse me . . .' Lola slid off along the bar to serve a customer.

Posy waited patiently until the operation was completed. 'No, not really. It won't take long.'

Immediately, another customer arrived, demanding food and a pint of whatever the gorgeous lady behind the bar recommended. Lola, Posy noticed with some surprise, dealt with the request with a composed flirtatiousness.

'Actually,' Lola said, expertly manipulating the beer pump labelled Old Duck Pond, 'if you really wanted to talk now, the only way I can manage is if you get behind the bar rather than in front of it.' She moved off again to the customer. 'There you are sir, and the cheesy pasta bake? A good choice. All our food is freshly prepared and delivered by the proprietors of the Sunny Dene B&B only a five minute walk away. You'll find their details and extensive evening menu on your table. If you'd like to take a seat, our waitress will bring your food over to you.'

Oh, very impressive! But – waitress? Posy looked blank. Who the hell had Lola engaged as a waitress?

'That's you,' Lola hissed. 'There was a girl coming in from Lesser Fritton but she hasn't turned up. I'm run off my feet and if you want to promote the Sunny Dene food then I'd suggest you grab a pinny.'

'No, but –'

'Posy, please.'

Please? Ms Tarty Man-Stealer was actually saying *please*?

'Okay, but only until we've talked, and I haven't got any skimpy waitressy clothes.'

'Just take your jacket off. They'll probably love the leather jeans and the boots. Pop into the back room and warm up a couple of cheesy bakes – oh, yes sir . . .' The professional smile welded itself back on the glossy lips. 'Sorry to have kept you waiting. How can I help you?'

Lola had also totally transformed The Crooked Sixpence's kitchen, Posy thought, hanging her biker jacket over a chair. Not that it was what most people would recognize as a kitchen, being the back room office where Hogarth had obviously slept, washed occasionally, and existed on a diet of baked beans straight from the tin.

However, Lola had added a compact fridge-freezer, a kettle, a toastie grill, a small dishwasher and a microwave oven. And like the rest of the pub, everything gleamed.

Having warmed through two dishes of Dilys's cheesy pasta, tied an apron round her waist, and trying hard not to clump too loudly in the motorcycling boots, Posy sashayed her way into the bar.

'Thanks, you're an angel,' Lola mouthed. 'When you've served him, can you do three shepherd's pies? Table by the door. Oh, and a lemon rice with chicken for the lady by the fireplace?'

By ten past three Posy's feet were throbbing, her jaw ached from smiling, and she'd collected over fifteen pounds in tips.

'Phew,' Lola sagged behind the bar. 'Let's get the door locked. No, don't worry about clearing the tables now. I'm desperate for a cup of tea. Do you want one?'

'Er, yes, I suppose so,' said Posy who didn't. 'And can we talk now?'

Over mugs of tea beside the fireplace, they talked. It was, Posy thought, quite grown-up considering they didn't like one another. But even though she couldn't like Lola, there was something different about her now, an air of competence and composure, that certainly warranted admiration. She glowed with achievement, with satisfaction, with happiness. Her face, Posy reckoned, was younger and illuminated from within, like someone madly in love.

'Thank you so much for helping out,' Lola stretched her elegant legs out across a red and blue and gold hearth rug which Posy had never noticed before. 'I couldn't have managed it without you. You were great. You wouldn't like to do it permanently, would you?'

'I do it permanently at Sunny Dene. No, sorry. Ungracious of me. And yes, I would.' Well, there was no point in cutting off your nose, was there? And she could fit it in with the B&B and the courier work for Ellis and the shop couldn't she?

'Wonderful! How many days could you manage?'

'I'm not sure. Definitely not every lunch time because – well, this is why I wanted to talk to you.'

'Oh? Go on then,' Lola swept the neat blonde hair behind her ears. 'It sounds intriguing.'

Posy explained about the shop and about discovering from Tatty that Hogarth owned it and that Lola was probably in charge of it now.

'Am I?' Lola raised her eyebrows. 'If I am he didn't mention it.'

'Oh, right.' Posy's spirits took a nose dive. 'It doesn't matter then. I just thought that I could take it over and do something with it, you know.'

Lola nodded. 'Sounds like a good idea. Something completely different and out of the blue. Actually, running this place has changed my life. It wasn't what I wanted, and I didn't think I'd enjoy it, but it's been totally therapeutic. I suppose we're all after the same thing really.'

Posy bit back the 'other people's husbands in your case' retort that was hurtling on to her tongue. 'Er, well, yes probably. Although survival and happiness will do me.'

'And me, although I thought I'd have to pass on the happiness after Nigel, er, well, after Nigel . . .'

Posy's I-spy-an-embryo-relationship antennae, sadly inherited from Dilys, twitched wildly. Ha! So there was a new man involved, was there? Was it Flynn? For some reason this made Posy almost as irritated as seeing Ellis with Tatty. As, because of Ritchie, she didn't want either Ellis or Flynn for herself, was she becoming all bitter and twisted? Not wanting to see anyone happy with anyone else? She sincerely hoped not – but what other explanation could there be?

She shrugged. 'Yes, look, I do understand. I am sorry. It must have been so awful for you when he died, but surely, equally so for his wife?'

'His wife was a bitch.'

'Yeah well, he would say that to you, wouldn't he? I'm sure that's what Sonia was told about me. I'm sure that's what every man looking for a bit on the side says.'

'I was not a bit on the side!'

Ooops. 'Whatever . . . No, sorry again, then. I don't know anything about the circumstances.'

'No you don't. I worked with Nigel for nearly thirty

years. I was in love with him for all that time and he loved me. It was an absolute two-way devotion. I knew his wife well through the business. She was rude, cruel and unbelievably awful, both to him and to everyone else she came in contact with.'

'Why didn't he leave her then?'

'Usual stuff – the children, the money, the mess, the inconvenience, plus the fact that he knew Barbara would make our lives hell. He'd always said he'd leave her when he retired and we'd run away and spend our golden years together. But it never happened. Although what we had was wonderful. The time we spent together, our home . . .'

'Oh, God, don't cry,' Posy leaned forward and awkwardly patted Lola's arm. 'Look, I'm sorry. Honestly. It's none of my business. And I shouldn't sit in judgement. Um, if we're going to be working together, and sharing the same house, I suppose I just ought to say sorry for flying off the handle before and being so snotty about everything.'

'It's okay, really.' Lola blinked quickly. 'You're very young and you'd been hurt. I'd have felt the same way. But yes, it'd be lovely to be, well, if not friends, at least not enemies.'

They smiled uneasily at one another. It was a truce, Posy thought, not a peace treaty, but it would do for the time being.

'I'll rummage around in the paperwork that Hogarth left,' Lola said, as they both eased themselves from the fireside chairs, 'and see if I can find anything out about the shop, shall I? What did you want to do with it?'

'No idea really, just something to help bring people

into the village, give me something to think about, make some money for Sunny Dene. I'd sort of wondered if I could link it to the carnival in some way.'

'The carnival? Like fancy dress hire, you mean? Isn't that a little short-term?'

Posy shrugged. 'I honestly hadn't thought past getting my hands on the shop. I imagined I'd have some brilliant ideas later, but if you can't contact Hogarth about it, it doesn't matter. He'd probably say no. Anyway, do you want a hand with clearing up before I go?'

Lola shook her head. 'No, you've done more than enough, thanks. I'll pay you of course – and, well, I don't suppose you'd like to work in here this evening, too, would you? Behind the bar?'

Posy grinned as she headed towards the door. She'd mooched about on the common only hours earlier thinking that she'd never find a job anywhere and now, if the shop came off, she'd got five! 'Yes, I'd love to. About seven if Mum and Dad can spare me, if not, as soon after as I can manage?'

'That sounds perfect. And Posy, I'm so pleased that we've got all that, um, other business sorted out.'

'Me too – Jesus Christ! What was that noise?'

'I've no idea ... Oh, goodness, I hope it's not a pile-up. My first aid is pretty minimal and I'm awful with blood.'

'Steeple Fritton doesn't do pile-ups. The roads are so deserted we never even have genteel bumps. Glad falls off her bike quite often though, but don't worry, there maybe a couple of grazed knees and a lot of swearing, but there won't be any blood.'

Despite the levity, Posy had pulled open the door of

The Crooked Sixpence with her heart pounding. The roar and clank and crunch certainly sounded as though something large and mechanical had just met a pretty sticky end.

'Oh my God!'

Lola peered over her shoulder. 'What? Is it complete carnage? Oh!'

Queen Mab, in all her maroon and golden glory, stood, rocking gently on the car park.

'Sorry if we startled you,' Flynn, looking more gorgeously John Cusack than ever, leaned down from his perch about twenty feet above them. 'Norrie had a bit of trouble finding the brake.'

Posy grinned up at her father. Like Flynn's, his face was blackened with oil and coal dust and sooty steam. He stood high up in the cab, partly obscured by the canopy, beaming proudly behind the steering wheel. Mr D and Mr B had driven Flynn's jeep back from Fritton Magna and had eased themselves from it and were now capering around the hissing, steaming monster like children.

A small and excited crowd was already milling into the car park in the wake of the traction engine. In Steeple Fritton, where a queue in the post office could cause a frenzy, the arrival of Queen Mab was possibly going to lead to mass hysteria.

'If I were you,' Posy said to Lola, 'I'd get the beer pumps on again. This lot look like they could do with a pint.'

'Too right,' Flynn swung himself from the cab with lithe ease and jumped down to the ground. He ruffled Posy's curls. 'You should have come with us. It was ace.'

Posy shrugged. 'Some of us have been working.'

'What? In here?' Flynn motioned towards the pub. 'But I thought you and Lola didn't hit it off?'

'We didn't. We probably still don't. Oh, it's a long story and you must be gagging for a pint.'

'Yeah. Right. I just wish that English beer didn't have to be warm. Maybe the landlady could sort out some iced beers for us aficionados.' He winked at Lola, and followed Norrie and Mr D and Mr B into the pub.

Alone, Posy gazed at Queen Mab, a feeling of childlike delight creeping through her veins, and sudden memories spilling from nowhere into her consciousness. Even now, several feet away, the heat from the boiler was like a furnace, and shimmered around the massive masterpiece of engineering like an aura.

She'd loved this traction engine when she was a child: watching mad old Googly Harris belt it through the lanes, with the enormous, silky, greasy pistons sliding back and forth, the smoke belching from the truncated stack, the deafening hiss of white-hot steam, and the rhythmic chug and clunk and rattle. The sheer awesome power of something so huge, so perfect, so alien.

Posy closed her eyes, reliving those times when to be a child in Steeple Fritton was pure perfection. When she and Amanda and Nikki and Ritchie and a whole gang of school friends, had spent summer days in the cornfields and winter nights in the bus shelter and Sunday afternoons gathered round the war memorial and none of them had ever wanted anything else.

Queen Mab had been part of that childhood idyll. Queen Mab and Bunty Malone's animal welfare home, and the recreation ground, and the youth club in the village hall and hanging round outside the row of shops in the evening after school just people-watching.

She opened her eyes again, slightly dismayed to find her vision was blurred. Surely she wasn't becoming sentimental? At her age? She wasn't old enough to be having nostalgia pangs like her mother did when watching Woodstock videos, was she? She swallowed the lump in her throat. Sadly, because Queen Mab had reawakened her slumbering senses, it appeared she was.

Googly Harris had steamed Queen Mab here to The Crooked Sixpence as well, she remembered. Dilys and Norrie had brought her and Dom along as children, all muffled in Paddington Bear-type duffel coats on winter nights, and they'd huddled in the radiant heat of several tons of luminescent orange coal roaring in a firebox the size of a small house, and eaten crisps and drunk Cherryade.

And Googly Harris, his face aglow in the dancing shadows, had had Queen Mab's dynamo running, so that the flywheel flew in a blur like a multicoloured gyroscope and the belt slapped round, faster and faster, driving hundreds of light bulbs which reflected kaleidoscope patterns in the brass and chrome and paint.

And the smell . . . Posy inhaled greedily again. The steam-driven smell was pure nostalgia . . . Heat and oil and coal, basic and primeval, warmth and power . . .

'I still can't believe it,' Flynn's voice made her spin back to the present. 'I can't believe she's all mine.'

For one strange moment Posy thought he was talking about Lola. 'Uh? When did that happen – oh, right. Queen Mab. No, she's gorgeous. Amazing. How are you ever going to ship her back to the States?'

'It can be done. Has been before. But I'm not sure that it'd be fair. After all, she was built for Berkshire showmen, and has lived here all her life. She belongs here. And to be honest, right now I'm not even sure that I want to go back to the States, either.'

The small crowd of villagers had swelled to larger proportions as word of the traction engine's arrival spread like wildfire. Flynn, balancing his pint of beer, was suddenly assailed from all sides by elderly rustics. It was like The Archers Go Mad on Twenty Questions and made interrogation about his plans for the future an impossibility, although Posy was pretty sure that Flynn's reluctance to leave England must have something to do with Lola. Which would be great news for Sunny Dene as every guest counted, but even so . . .

Norrie, Mr D and Mr B, had trooped out of the pub too, and stood nursing their pint pots, and gazing on their much-loved gargantuan baby. Like Flynn, they were all coal streaked and oil spattered, grimy and blissfully happy.

Posy smiled. It was lovely to see her dad so delighted. A steam-buff since infancy, this must be like his wildest dream come true. If only other dreams were so easy to fix . . .

'Wow!' Flynn eventually emerged from the crowd. 'Now I know what it must be like to be Madonna.'

'Funny bras and big biceps?'

'Bombarded with questions, pushed around by strangers and stared at a lot.'

'I think you'll have to get used to it. With that accent, you're a bit of a star attraction in Steeple Fritton, even without the traction engine. And I was thinking while you were being mobbed, if you're not going to be leaving for a while, we *could* use Queen Mab for the carnival. Googly Harris used to park her up here and it really drew the crowds at night . . .'

Flynn ran oily fingers through his hair, making the layers all spiky, and grinned. 'That sounds great to me. I'd like to have her in the parade, too, and then steam her up here in the evenings for people to stand around, and . . .'

'And what?'

Flynn shrugged. 'Don't know exactly. Just, that sounds sorta boring. What we need is music as well, then we could have a proper party out here, with dancing and stuff. Is there a village band or something?'

'Fortunately not,' Posy shuddered at the very thought.

'What about that funny old coot with the accordion?'

'Neddy Pink? Jesus, Flynn, we want to draw the crowds in, not send everyone fleeing for cover.'

'Yeah, okay. So, have you got a better idea?'

'Actually, I have . . . although where we're going to find what I'm looking for I have absolutely no idea. Still, leave it with me. And I was going to ask for a guided tour round Queen Mab's cab, but that'll have to wait, too. I'm on dinner duty at home and then I'm back in here tonight, behind the bar.'

'Yeah, Lola said. Amazing. I mean, I just thought you guys would never be friends.'

'Oh, we're not. But she needs workers and I need work.' Posy started to nudge her way through the throng towards her motorbike. She grinned over her shoulder at

Flynn. 'Enjoy your new role as a major tourist attraction. I'll see you later.'

He grinned back. 'Count on it.'

It was nearly half past seven before Posy returned to The Crooked Sixpence. The dining room at Sunny Dene had been abuzz with Queen Mab's arrival in her new home, and further detailed and exaggerated stories of moving the traction engine from the car park to the shed behind the pub had led to lengthy delays in clearing the tables. And two of the shepherd's pies and the lemon rice from the pub's lunch-time clientele, had turned up for dinner at the B&B too, so all the niceties had to be observed.

Then it had taken her ages to find something suitable to wear for barmaiding. She felt Lola wouldn't accept the leathers again. Eventually deciding that a pair of much-faded and shrunken jeans and a tight black T-shirt looked exactly the sort of thing they wore behind the bar of the Rovers Return, Posy had belted out of Sunny Dene.

'Sorry I'm late,' she hissed at Lola as she skittered behind the bar. 'You saw what it was like at home.'

Lola paused in decanting tomato juice and Worcestershire sauce into a glass. 'No problems. This is working out so well for all of us and I'm just delighted to have some help. My new barman was due to start tonight but he hasn't shown up, so it'll probably be frantic. Now, have you ever worked in a bar before? No? Okay, well it'll be a case of the blind leading the blind, but I'll show you what Hogarth taught me . . .'

Fifteen minutes later Posy felt she'd got the hang

of the pumps, the optics, the mixers and the archaic cash register. Whether she'd ever get the hang of draught Guinness was another matter. Still, as the female Pinks were currently involved in a melee round the dartboard and Neddy Pink was force-feeding the fruit machine, hopefully she wouldn't be put to the test just yet.

The jukebox crooned quietly, giving a background hum to the rise and fall of the conversations and laughter. Martha and Mary Pink, who had now got the hang of throwing the pointy bit at the dartboard, were becoming fiercely competitive with two boys in denim jackets and nose studs. Neddy had won the fruit machine jackpot – again. Posy leaned her elbows on the bar and smiled in disbelief. For the first time ever, The Crooked Sixpence was just like a real pub. Lola had certainly worked miracles.

'Oh, I meant to say to you earlier,' Lola said, as they passed each other in a pincer movement, 'I found these in Hogarth's desk.' She jingled a bunch of keys under Posy's nose. 'They don't fit any of the pub locks, so one of them might be for the shop. Give them a try.'

Posy closed her hand delightedly over the keys. 'Great. Thanks, yes, I will. I mean, if you don't think Hogarth will mind.'

'Who knows? But he didn't give me any instructions over anything other than the pub, no matter what Tatty Spry may have told you, so I've no axe to grind. If you can make something of the shop I'm sure he'll be delighted – oh, damn.'

'What?'

'We're out of tonic waters. Can you hold the fort

here while I go down to the cellar and fetch up another crate?'

'I'll go,' Posy offered. 'I'll need to find my way around down there. Will I need a torch?'

'There's a light switch at the top of the steps – but take it steady.'

The cellar steps were narrow and dark and cold. A single light bulb did nothing to improve the eerie ambience. Cobwebs festooned the walls and the breeze, which had been warm and playful at ground level, had turned chill and malevolent. Posy shuddered.

Several beer kegs, a myriad of twisted pipes, various racks and boxes and a lot of debris seemed to be all that the cellar contained. Obviously Lola's New Broom approach hadn't yet reached subterranean levels.

Running her fingers over stacks of small crates containing every mixer drink known to man she eventually found the tonic waters. Hauling them from the shelf, wanting to be out of this dank and dingy cavern, she tucked them under her arm and headed towards the steps. Then she stopped.

The door had creaked open over her head, and someone was walking down the steps towards her. She couldn't see a face, just the feet, and a huge misshapen male shadow thrown against the uneven grimy wall. Not Lola then.

'Hello?' A man's voice echoed down to her. 'Are you okay? Only Ms Wentworth said you'd been down here a long time and maybe you needed some help.'

The shadow joined its owner as the feet reached the cellar floor, and the man stood illuminated by the flickering light bulb.

Posy dropped the tonic waters with a splintering crash.

'Holy shit!'

'Christ!'

They stared at one another in silent and awful disbelief.

Chapter Fifteen

'What the bloody hell are you doing here?' Posy eventually broke the silence. Her voice bounced furiously from the dank walls and reverberated in the clammy air. 'Just what the hell –'

'I was told to come and find you, only I didn't know it was you, did I?' Ritchie Dalgetty blinked at her. 'I'm working behind the bar. It's my first night. Christ, Pose, I didn't know you worked here, too. Ms Wentworth didn't say your name or anything. She just said her new barmaid might need some help in the cellar –'

Did she indeed? How very convenient. 'Ms Wentworth,' Posy muttered, 'didn't think to mention your name to me, either.'

Ms Wentworth, she thought angrily, was, as she'd first assumed, a scheming, nasty, bitter, twisted, trouble-making cow.

Ritchie still looked completely bewildered. 'Look, I know it's a bit of a shock, but we'd have had to have met up and faced each other at some time. The village is so small I'm amazed we've avoided each other for as long as we have. Surely, it doesn't have to be a problem?'

'Of course it's a bloody problem! I need this job. I need the money. But I'm not going to work with you!'

'I need the money, too. We're so broke. Now that Sonia's given up work –'

'Sod Sonia! Don't you dare mention Sonia's name to me – ever!'

The cellar door squeaked open above their heads.

'Everything all right?' Lola called down. 'Only we're really busy up here, so if one of you could come and give me a hand I'd be more than grateful.'

I'll give you more than a hand, Posy thought murderously. She pulled her lips back into a smile. 'Just coming, Lola.'

'So?' Ritchie looked relieved. 'It'll be okay, will it?'

'No, it won't be bloody okay,' Posy clawed at another case of tonic waters. 'You get up there and tell precious Ms Wentworth that you've changed your mind about the job.'

'I can't. We're counting on the money. Sonia will kill me.'

'She'll kill you even more if she knows you're working with me.'

Ritchie pulled a face. 'Christ. Yeah.'

He was wearing black jeans and the blue shirt she'd given him the Christmas before last. And he'd lost weight, Posy thought. And he needed a shave, and there were dark circles under his eyes.

She hoped his look of total exhaustion was because he was working hard selling his three-piece suites and worrying about money and not that he and Sonia-of-the-thongs were having nightly sexual marathons. Not that she cared, of course.

Lola opened the cellar door again. 'Posy! What's the matter? Are you having a problem with the tonics?'

'Stay here!' Pushing past Ritchie, Posy bounded up the steps and emerged into the warmth and brightness of the bar. She beamed at Lola. 'No, look, here are the tonics. The tonics are fine. No problems at all with the tonics. I was just having problems with my ex-fiancé. The one who dumped me. The one I told you all about, remember? The one who you've just employed as a barman.'

'Shit.'

'Well, that's one way of putting it, I suppose. Now tell me you didn't know?'

'Of course I didn't know.' Lola looked shocked. 'How on earth was I supposed to know?'

'Because . . . because . . .' Posy frowned. Actually, how was Lola supposed to know? She'd never mentioned Ritchie's name to Lola, and she doubted if he'd given 'dumped Posy to marry pregnant slapper' as part of his CV at the interview either. 'Oh, Christ, I don't know. You just should.'

Hunching her shoulders, she clattered off into the bar to collect empty glasses. No one had told her to do this, but she knew they did it on the soaps. It gave the bar staff time to recover from whatever blow had just been dealt them, and to mingle with the customers and pick up juicy morsels of gossip.

She'd cleared two tables before she realized that everyone in the pub was watching her with interest. The Pinks, Glad Blissit, Rose Lusty, the Bickeridges . . . Of

209

course – they all knew, didn't they? They'd have all seen Ritchie arrive.

She was the bloody floor show!

David Whitfield was crooning from the jukebox as she snatched up the last glasses and stomped back behind the bar. 'Get rid of him.'

'David Whitfield? He was a special request from Mrs Blissit.'

'Ritchie. Sack him, or I'll leave.'

Even as she said it, Posy realized it was pretty futile. She was a two-bit barmaid in a run-down pub. She was hardly irreplaceable.

Lola shook her head. 'I want you to stay. I want him to stay. I need all the staff I can get. I'll just roster you on different nights, okay? Look Posy, I'm sorry, I honestly had no idea.'

By this time Ritchie had emerged from the cellar and was skulking at the far end of the bar. Glad and Rose Lusty were fighting each other to be served by him. Posy glared at them. Vultures!

Having beaten the local youths at darts by doctoring the flights, Neddy Pink was now rattling his Guinness glass against the beer pumps. Posy grabbed it from him and started yanking at the lever. She looked across at Lola who was doing something technical with Advocaat. 'Well, okay, maybe you didn't know that Ritchie was – oh, bugger!'

Creamy froth erupted orgasmically from the pump.

'You'n cocked that up good and proper,' Neddy Pink said helpfully, as the ooze-slick dripped over the edge of the bar. 'You'n got your thoughts on young Ritchie I'll be bound.'

'Bollocks!' Posy snapped, skidding the glass through the froth and creating a miniature snow storm. 'Get your own bloody Guinness! I've had enough!'

'Here, let me,' Flynn Malone's soothing voice said softly beside her. 'I'm great with Guinness after all those hours in Uncle Michael's bar in Tralee. There's a knack to it, look . . .'

'Thanks,' Posy wiped Guinness from her T-shirt. 'And where did you materialize from? You're not working here too, are you? If you are, we'll have more this side of the bar than the other.'

'I'd just come in for a quiet drink,' Flynn expertly flicked the Guinness pump handle back and forth, gently filling the tilted glass. 'Just as well, really. There you are, sir.'

Slurping at the creamy head with abandon, Neddy emerged with frothy gums. 'Very nice, thank you. No doubt you'll be able to teach young Posy a few more tricks.'

Flynn laughed. 'Oh, somehow I doubt that.'

Posy suddenly felt extremely warm and definitely hemmed in. Flynn on one side and Ritchie on the other. Some girls would kill for just such a dilemma.

'I'll, um, go and wipe the tables and empty the ashtrays, er, again, shall I?'

'Good idea, and you'll be all right for the rest of tonight, won't you?' Lola looked quite anxious. 'Working with, um, Ritchie?'

Posy sighed. 'Yes, I suppose so. But please make sure we never meet again.'

Wiping tables became a marathon as everyone, without exception, had their own theory to expound on the situation. Most of them, including the Pinks and the coven, seemed to find it better than *Coronation Street*. Several were sympathetic. No one thought Lola should be shot at dawn for orchestrating such a meeting.

And how did she feel? Posy paused in scrumpling up crisp packets. Okay, really. Well, she wasn't cured, that was for sure. She was still hurt and angry, and – oh, yes, – she still fancied Ritchie like mad.

Bugger.

The rest of the evening passed without further incident. Posy avoided looking at Ritchie, and Ritchie avoided her full stop. Flynn sat on one of the newly-refurbished bar stools and talked exclusively to Lola through several Jack Daniel's. The Pinks sang along to the jukebox and ricocheted bits of peanut across the room as they did so. The local youths mended the flights and played darts with Eric Bristow bravado. The bar hummed with people and laughter and lively conversation.

The Crooked Sixpence had at last come into its own.

'If you want to get away, I'll help Lola clear up,' Flynn said at eleven o'clock. 'I think you've had enough excitement for one night.'

'She's told you, has she?' Posy pulled on her leather jacket, pocketing her night's pay and Hogarth's keys. 'All about Ritchie?'

'Yeah, some of it. Maybe it's for the best. No, don't snap my head off. Look, it's done now. You've faced each other. It'll never be so hard again. You can really make a start on getting over it.'

She grinned at him. 'You're a nice man, Flynn Malone, and a whizz with Guinness. They must be missing you in Boston.'

'Maybe. Who knows? They'll have to miss me for a bit longer though because I'm not going back yet awhile.'

'Because of Queen Mab or because of Lola?'

Flynn grinned. 'Because of a lot of things. Will you be okay getting home?'

'Of course. It's only five minutes, and I'm tougher than most of the wannabe muggers round here. Goodnight – and thanks again.'

Outside, the air was crisp and cold, still wintry despite the day's pretence at spring, and Posy turned up the collar of her leather jacket. What a weird day; so many things had happened, and exhausted though she was, there'd be plenty to keep her awake tonight . . .

'Posy?'

'Were you hanging around waiting for me? Go away.' She peered at Ritchie in the darkness. 'You seem to have missed the turning for Bunny Burrow, or have you forgotten where you now live?'

He laughed. 'It's great to be friends again.'

'We're not bloody friends. We'll never be friends. We haven't been friends for ages. We were friends until we were sixteen, then sex got in the way.'

He laughed again. She wished he wouldn't. It wasn't amusing. Posy exhaled. 'Look, we've got nothing to say to one another, have we? Nothing at all.'

'Can I walk home with you?'

'No! We stopped doing that in youth club days, remember? After I'd got my first motorbike and you were the most scaredy pillion passenger in the world. Then when you bought that clapped-out van and we went everywhere in it even if it was only a couple of minutes' walk away and –' Posy stopped. Too many memories were flooding in. Things that she'd kept shut out for ages and ages. 'Just go away.'

He didn't. He continued to walk beside her. 'Yeah, they were the best times. Shit, I must have been mad to, um . . . You look really nice tonight.'

'Nice? Like rice pudding? Or a cup of tea? Or a hot bath?'

'Yeah.'

'Bugger off,' she smiled at him. The banter was easy. They'd had years of practice. 'Clear off home to your wife and imminent child.'

He said nothing in the darkness. Home-going Steeple Frittonians passed them and gave them curious stares. Posy knew it'd be all round the village by morning. Dilys and Norrie would probably have plenty to say about it.

Ritchie sighed. 'I'm sorry.'

'What?'

'I'm sorry. For, well, for all of it. I should never have . . . You didn't deserve . . .'

'Oh, for goodness' sake just make do with sorry,' Posy snapped. 'We both know what you mean. And go home, please.'

'Yeah, okay. And you're all right now? I mean, I was so surprised that you came to the wedding. I couldn't believe it when I saw you there and –'

'I was only there to see if Sonia would get struck by a thunderbolt. And to ill-wish you both all the unhappiness in the world.'

'Don't, Posy. Don't you think I haven't beaten myself up over this ever since . . . ever since . . .'

'Ever since you did what all men do and thought a bit

214

on the side was your hormonally-given right? Because as long as I didn't find out no one would get hurt? Because it didn't mean anything to you, it was just sex? I've heard it all before, remember? Six months ago when you had to tell me about it because Sonia was pregnant.' She sighed. 'There's nothing we can do about it now. And to be honest I don't even care. I stopped hating you ages ago, and apathy is a real killer.'

'Do you know what really screwed me up?' Ritchie stopped walking. 'The day after the wedding, when everyone told me that you'd left the village. I couldn't believe it. Couldn't bear to think that I'd done that to you –'

'Don't flatter yourself. I wasn't running away from you, despite what the coven may have said.' She kept walking, glad he couldn't see her face. He'd always known when she was lying. Shame really that she hadn't been equally intuitive. 'I'd been thinking about leaving for ages. I was going to work in Swindon, but . . . but the job fell through.'

'Oh, right. Sorry.'

'Will you please stop saying sorry!'

'Yeah, sorry, I mean . . . Oh, Christ!' He caught up with her again. 'Anyway, I'm glad you're still here. And you've got someone else now, haven't you? I was so jealous when I saw you together. Daft, I know. I've got no right, but –'

'I haven't got anyone – oh, yes, you mean Ellis.' Just in time she remembered the staged kissing incident in The Crooked Sixpence. 'Yes, Ellis and me are like that.' Realizing that Ritchie probably couldn't see her entwined fingers in the dark, she felt she ought to explain

215

further. 'Getting on great, you know. Having fun. No strings.'

'Good. Only Sonia said that he, Glad Blissit's grandson, was knocking off Tatty Spry.'

'Sonia's got her wires crossed. Such a pity she couldn't have managed it with her legs. Goodnight.'

The next morning, after a rather brief but unpleasant inquisitional period from Dilys during breakfast-cooking owing to Glad and Rose and Vi all having been on the phone at first light, Posy jangled Hogarth's set of keys outside the empty shop.

Trevor and Kenneth polka'd excitedly round her legs as she slotted the Yale into the lock. Surprisingly, she thought, she'd slept really well, with no dreams of Ritchie to interfere with her exhaustion. And Flynn was right – she'd faced up to the first meeting, and coped with it, and had come away feeling in control.

And, if the feelings she'd been left with weren't entirely negative, then that was understandable, wasn't it? She'd loved Ritchie for a long time, and hated him for a brief one. It was just mathematics, really. Anyway, just so long as Lola played fair with the rotas, she and Ritchie would never have to spend any time in one another's company again.

The shop door opened easily. Trevor and Kenneth were shoulder to shoulder, impatient to be the first in. Posy had imagined the shop would be padlocked and alarmed after the police raid, and would let off a screeching vibrato which would fetch Tatty and Rose and the Bickeridges running along the row. It wasn't and didn't and she stepped inside.

'Blimey!'

Owing to the inches-deep and years-old fly-posting on the windows, she'd expected the shop to be a further extension of Hogarth's pub squalor, or at least show the remnants of some previous porn baron tenant; therefore the empty shelves, bare counters and clear floor space came as something of a shock.

It was clinically tidy, only the thick layer of dust over every surface, and the festoons of cobwebs in the corners, indicating just how long the shop had been unused.

And there was no sinister air about it; all it felt was cold and unloved and lonely. But there was a faint all-pervading smell of – what? Antiseptic? Disinfectant? Something medical she was sure. Maybe it was lethal aromatherapy fumes emanating from Tatty's shop next door?

Posy found it quite emotional, walking round the eerily echoing space, thinking that if things had been different, she and Ritchie would have rented this place and really made it the bric-a-brac shop they'd dreamed of.

'Sod Ritchie!'

Her voice bounced off the cream walls. Trevor and Kenneth broke off in their snuffling through the dust for a moment to stare at her. She gathered, by the wagging of their tails, that they concurred with the sentiment.

Fleetingly she wondered about the legality of the whole shop scheme. But only for a very briefly. Who on earth was going to care? The place had been empty for almost a lifetime. Hogarth wasn't due back for months, and everyone else was doing their bit to attract visitors and money into the village, so why shouldn't she?

'What on earth are you doing?' Ellis, looking cross,

suddenly appeared in the open doorway. The dogs scampered ecstatically towards him and he bent down to return the greetings. 'Tatty said she heard noises in here and sent me to investigate.'

'Proper little hero, aren't you?'

'Oh, ha-ha. Christ, what's that smell?'

'Second-hand patchouli and ylang-ylang at a guess. And what are you doing at Tatty's first thing in the morning anyway?'

'I had a sleep-over. Mind you, the kids didn't give me much chance to lie in. I was up at half-four reading *Winnie the Pooh*.'

'Aaah, sweet. You'll make a lovely father.'

'Pul-ease! Still, at least it meant I was awake early enough to collect the mail, and now I'm just about to do the school run and then the shopping trip. You haven't forgotten the courier stuff, have you?'

'As if.'

Ellis still looked angry. 'That's okay, then. There are a few letters for today, and a package to go out to Maplesford, but it isn't urgent. Anytime in the next couple of days will do for that. It was delivered to someone in Fritton Magna by mistake so I've taken it on. It's quite big but you should be able to manage it on the bike, and if you can, then I'll be able to pass all one-off parcels on to you. But the letters still need to be out in the next hour.'

'Oh, and just when I was planning to have a lazy day, too.'

Ellis peered at her. 'Is that a glint of sarcasm showing from beneath the razor-sharp wit?'

'Sarcastic, *moi*? Listen, child. You may think you've

had a tough morning so far, but I've already cooked breakfast at Sunny Dene and walked the dogs, I'm now investigating my new shop premises, then I'll deliver the mail for you, be back at the B&B to play chambermaid, then into the pub as a lunch-time waitress, back to Sunny Dene for the dinners, into the pub for the evening barmaiding shift –'

'Is that all?'

Posy grinned. 'Great, isn't it? The way things work out? All we need to do now is get the carnival thing up and running, and we might have achieved our goal.'

'And is that what this ear-to-ear beaming is all about? Being busy, making money, and bringing visitors into Steeple Fritton?'

'Of course.'

'Nothing to do with being walked home last night by a certain ex-fiancé?'

'Is that why you're so ratty?' Posy groaned. 'God! That didn't take long, did it? Who told you?'

'Gran phoned Tatty last night. Tatty was really miffed that she hadn't been there to see it for herself.' Ellis looked serious. 'Look, I know I'm the last person to advise on moral issues, but you will be careful, won't you? You've changed so much in the few weeks since we first met. You're stronger and happier, but you could blow it all by falling for him again, especially now he's married.'

Posy hooted with laughter. 'Hark at you, Dear Deirdre! Is that honestly why you were looking so po-faced? Really? You're the last person on earth to be entitled to an opinion. Have you and Tatty created Horatio yet?'

'Uh?'

'Horatio or Hebe? The next child on Tatty's must-have list.'

Ellis wrinkled his nose. 'No. No way. Tatty and I are just having fun.'

'You might be having fun. Tatty is deadly serious. She wants another baby and a long-term father figure for the brood.'

'But, I don't want children. I don't like children and even if I did, I'm far too young to have children. And me and Tatty aren't a permanent fixture.'

Posy laughed at the anguished expression. 'Then tell Tatty that and sort out your own emotional chaos before you start lecturing me on mine. Oh, and by the way, Ritchie believed the snog in the snug incident. He thinks we're a couple. He warned me that you might hurt me.'

'Cheeky bastard!'

'Pot and kettle and both black if you ask me, but that's men for you. So, now you're here, are you going to offer to help me scrape all the crap off these windows?'

'Maybe later.'

'I'll take that as a no then, shall I?'

Ellis really did still look quite discomfited, she thought. She had a feeling it wasn't because he didn't want to become a window cleaner. Was it because Ritchie had assumed they were a couple? Or had it truly not occurred to him that fast and loose for him might be last-ditch at permanence for Tatty?

'Don't look so scared. I'm not pining for Ritchie, nor have I really got my claws into you. We were only pretending. Tatty, of course, is an entirely different matter.'

220

Posy frowned as Ellis turned tail through the doorway, the dogs bouncing in his wake knowing that they'd pick up titbits at every shop in the row. Had he really not thought about Tatty's feelings in their relationship? Was he, like all men, damn selfish and self-obsessed, and happily assuming that Tatty felt exactly as he did?

Maybe, though, she shouldn't have mentioned the Horatio or Hebe element. It was only village gossip after all . . . Oh, what the hell! Tatty was old enough and experienced enough to fight her own battles. Whether she wanted Ellis simply as a sperm donor, or as Mr Tatty Spry, it was really no one else's business.

Posy wandered about in the shop for a few more moments, trying to picture it filled with something, and with hordes of customers who were just desperate to have the very something that she was offering.

'Ferrets.'

Posy swirled round. Martha and Mary Pink, a matching pair in brown tweed coats, brown zip-up bootees, and brown woollen headscarves, were framed in the doorway.

'Goodness, you made me jump. Er, did you say ferrets?'

'Ferrets,' they nodded. 'Old Perce Betterton kept ferrets in here.'

Posy blinked. Were ferrets likely to have been the cause of the Fraud Squad raid? Porn ferrets? Drug-dealing ferrets? Money-laundering ferrets? 'Sorry?'

'Ferrets. And all manner of other stuff. Stuff, y'see. Stuff to be stuffed.'

'Nope. Still not with you, I'm afraid.'

The Pink twins shared an exasperated expression.

'Garn, Posy. Try to keep up, duck. Old Perce Betterton kept this shop afore it was closed down. He did stuffing. Some for that handsome Yankee bloke's Auntie Bunty. 'Er over at Fritton Magna with the animals . . .'

Cogs whirred, and bits dropped into place. Flynn's Great-Aunt Bunty Malone. Animal saviour. Had all her favourites stuffed and mounted . . . Oh, yuck!

'This place was a taxidermist's?'

'Nothing to do with taxis, my duck. Perce never drove in 'is life. 'E stuffed animals.'

'Yes, yes, I understand. So, why was the shop closed down? I mean, it's been empty for years, and I remember the night it was raided when I was a child. Everyone then just assumed it was being used as storage for mucky mags or something.'

Martha and Mary did a synchronized head-shake. 'Old Perce used more than formaldehyde to stuff his animals. Oh, not yon dishy Yankee bloke's Auntie's ones, duck. Bunty was well above board. But 'e 'ad a nice little sideline in moving stuff around. Money and stuff. You know, when you wasn't allowed to take more 'n fifty quid out of the country?'

'Before my time, I think.' Posy tried to imagine Perce Betterton in this little shop, removing entrails, and inserting sawdust and glassy eyes and fifty pound notes into poodles. 'Are you making this up?'

They shook their heads together, the fringes on the headscarves scattering dust motes in the morning sunshine. 'On our mother's life, Posy. Honest. In Perce's day a lot of people sailed away from Old Blighty with their nicely-preserved Fido or Tiddles who had an even more nicely-preserved little nest egg shoved up their bums.'

222

'Why didn't anyone tell me?'

'There's not many left alive that knows. We was going to tell you yesterday morning when you said you was interested in the shop but you'd cluttered off before we could say anything. And last night in the pub there was too many ears about.' They leaned closer, as one. 'We never said nothing much at the time being as Perce was a second cousin and it were a bit of a slur on the family name. Anyway, old Perce had been dead for years when the whole thing came to light, so it was best left unsaid. A Dalmatian it was, on the Harwich ferry. Burst.'

Oh dear, oh dear. 'And?'

'Filled to the gullet with fivers, duck. Not a penny of it been declared to the taxman. Led to all sorts of nasty investigations. Found this place filled with terriers and ferrets and owls and things and about half a million quid.'

'Bloody hell! And people just left their money here? Didn't try and get it back?'

'Couldn't, duck, could they? Perce dropped dead in The Crooked Sixpence. Bad pint, we allus said. Hogarth never cleaned 'is pipes. Anyway, we reckoned no one was able to get in here quick enough to get their money out, and they couldn't demand it back as they wasn't officially supposed to have it. Hogarth didn't know nothing about it, see, and no one else wanted to take the place on. 'E just shut up shop and that was it.'

'Until the Dalmatian exploded on the Harwich ferry?'

'Exactly.' The Pinks looked delighted that she'd got the picture at last. 'Then the coppers came in and took everything away, and, course Hogarth was exterminated –'

223

'Exonerated?'

'Ah, possibly that, too. Anyway, it being family, us and Neddy cleaned the place up and then Hogarth locked the doors and no one said nowt more about it. Just thought you'd like to know, duck.'

'Yes, right, thanks . . .'

'Pleasure.'

Posy watched as the Pinks wandered dustily away in their brown rags, like happy zombies, then walked back into the shop.

'Oh, shit!'

The Pinks' revelations put a whole new slant on the shop's ambience. And the origins of that smell . . .

'Excuse me!' The voice was imperious and slightly whiny.

Posy didn't even bother to turn round. 'Yes, I know. I've already been told, thank you. The place used to be a taxidermist's. I'm not too happy about it, either.'

'I'm not interested in whether you're happy or not. I'm just warning you to stay away from my husband.'

Posy turned round then. Quickly.

Sonia nee Tozer, Sonia-of-the-thongs, Sonia-bloody-man-stealing-tart-Dalgetty, stood in the doorway.

It was slightly cheering to notice that she looked absolutely, appallingly, awful. Now in her eighth month of pregnancy, she was huge and bloated. There was no pre-birth bloom, no radiance. Sonia looked grey-faced, grubby and about to burst. A bit like the Dalmatian on the Harwich ferry.

'Go away,' Posy said wearily. 'Clear off. This is my shop and I don't want you anywhere near it.'

'And I don't want you anywhere near my man.'

'*Your* man? Oh, excuse me. Haven't you got your possessive pronouns in a bit of a twist here?'

Sonia wobbled a step or two forward. 'Don't you try to come all clever with me, Posy Nightingale. Ritchie's all mine, now. If you couldn't keep hold of him, then that's tough tit. He doesn't want you, see? So, stop throwing yourself at him or you'll have me to deal with.'

'Oh, yeah. And what're you going to do? Roll on me? Get a life, Sonia. You're welcome to him.'

Flicking back her lank hair, Sonia thrust her face forward. 'He said you kept on and on at him last night to walk you home. Everyone says you were all over him in the pub. Everyone says –'

'Sonia, shut up. Shut up and bugger off. I'm not interested in what Ritchie has told you about last night. Ritchie is an ace liar, remember? Nor am I prepared to have a slanging match with you over someone as unimportant as bloody Ritchie Dalgetty. We live in the same village, we're bound to bump into each other, and I'll talk to who I want when I want. But take it from me, I certainly don't want Ritchie. Okay?'

Trevor and Kenneth returned at that point, barged through the open door, sniffed Sonia in a casual way, then bounded across to Posy. She bent down to fuss them, hoping it would give her a moment to compose herself. The last thing she wanted was for bloody Sonia to see she was shaking.

'Next time he works in the pub I'm going to be there to keep an eye on him,' Sonia said triumphantly. 'And you.'

'It'll be a waste of your time,' Posy sighed into Trevor's coat as Kenneth reassuringly licked her face. 'We won't be working the same shifts in future.'

'So you say,' Sonia turned on her heel with a sort of shuddering lumber. 'But why should I believe you? I know you'll do anything you can to get him back, but you take it from me, I'll be watching you from now on. You played with fire last night, but do it again and you'll get burned. Understand me?'

Chapter Sixteen

On the day that March gave way to April, Lola wandered round the vast shed that housed Queen Mab and wondered if Hogarth would have a fit over the way she was playing fast and loose with his properties.

The Crooked Sixpence was unrecognizable, she'd got a mammoth showman's traction engine living in his brewery storage shed, and she'd given Posy the keys to his shop, which now appeared to be in the process of a complete transformation.

Still, whatever Hogarth's eventual reaction, his departure had been the catalyst in this feeling of new hope and new beginnings, and for that reason alone she refused to feel guilty. For the first time since Nigel's death, she really believed that there may be a happy future. And having ended hostilities with Posy was wonderful, too.

She'd felt awful about employing Ritchie without realizing his relationship to Posy – but even that seemed to be okay now. They were working on different shifts, and Ritchie was always accompanied by his rather sullen and very pregnant wife who sat in a corner all evening and glowered over a solitary pineapple juice.

Just why Ritchie could have preferred the dour Sonia to the vivacious and gorgeous Posy, she had no idea. It was another one of life's mysteries: falling in love. The chemistry. The irrationality of it all. As she well knew.

Lola ran her hand along the deep red paintwork on the traction engine's boiler. She'd very much missed her previous life, her girlfriends in Swansbury, and the bustle of office life at Marionette Biscuits. And of course, Nigel. But, against all the odds, Sunny Dene, Steeple Fritton, the villagers and The Crooked Sixpence were rapidly taking the place of the former – but would there ever be anyone who could replace Nigel in her heart?

She shook her head. Replace was the wrong word. No one would ever take Nigel's place: what they'd had was far too special. She smiled at the preposterous notion. A few weeks ago and she'd have scoffed at the very idea of ever loving again. Nigel had been her one and only. But now, especially today, she felt that there might, one day, be another man, another love: different of course, but equally as amazing.

She very much missed the emotional and physical pleasures of loving and being loved. If she had to live her life for another thirty plus years, she really didn't want to live it alone.

The shed doors scraped open noisily, letting filtered sunshine spill across the cold concrete floor, interrupting her introspection.

Flynn grinned at her. 'Hey, you're in here early. You disappeared so quickly after breakfast, I thought you must be in the pub bottling up. You're keen.'

'Curious,' Lola craned her neck to look at the majestic height of Queen Mab. 'When I woke up this morning I promised myself that today I'd do things I'd never done before. As, until recently, I've never been anywhere near a traction engine, and as you're not otherwise engaged, I thought it was the first thing to tick off my wish list.'

Flynn swung himself easily up the steps and on to the foot plate of Queen Mab's cab. 'That sounds like a pretty cool plan. And if this is the first, what's the rest of the list like?'

'Oh, just daft stuff. You'd probably laugh.'

'I doubt it. Try me.'

Lola shook her head. She couldn't tell him. Couldn't risk today's tiny dreams being squashed. Flynn was a lovely man, but she hardly knew him. He seemed kind and happy-go-lucky, and he might well think her wish list was fun. But then again he might not.

He knew very little about her, either. They'd become friends and talked a lot, but only about superficial things really. Living a secret life, keeping her own counsel, rarely sharing emotions or hopes, meant that she found it difficult to tell anyone anything personal about her past, present or future. She simply couldn't share today's dreams with Flynn.

'It'll just have to wait until I get to know you better.' Goodness, had she really said that? 'That is, I mean . . .'

'It's fine. I understand.' His smile was kind, not mocking. He looked at her and laughed. 'And if you're sure you're ready for the guided tour, follow me.'

'Why are you laughing?'

'Because you're hardly properly dressed for this sort of thing.'

'I should have checked if there was a dress code, should I?'

'Sure. And kitten heels and tight skirts aren't it.'

'I'll manage,' Lola hauled herself on to the foot plate in the gloom and then taking Flynn's proffered hand, stepped up into the cab. 'Goodness, this is high up, and snug.'

Despite the size of the engine, there was only just room for two people – or three if they were on very friendly terms – in the cab. Flynn sat back on the coal tender, stretching his long legs out in front of him, leaving Lola with a massive steering wheel in front of her, a series of strange levers to her right, the firebox by her knees and the long cylindrical length of Queen Mab's boiler stretching away in front of her.

It was a peculiar feeling, standing with all that dark latent power just slumbering around her. Miles off the ground, with the canopy low over her head, and the rear wheel of the traction engine looking almost menacing in its size beside her, Lola felt almost claustrophobic.

It was, she admitted to herself, an amazing piece of engineering skill, and when Queen Mab had arrived at the pub and the coal had been roaring and the steam hissing and the flywheel slapping, it had been an awe-inspiring sight – but like this, cold, dark and silent, it did nothing for her at all.

Flynn was talking, pointing out pistons and valves and gearings, and mentioning things like heads of steam and dropping plugs, and ratios and pressures. She loved the sound of his voice, but the words meant little. It was exactly as she'd felt when taken on a school trip to the Science Museum. The technology and inventions had all been vaguely interesting, but not inspiring, and had left her with a guilty feeling that she really should feel more enthusiasm but knowing she couldn't.

'. . . and the three-speed gearing took a bit of getting used to,' Flynn was grinning. 'In the States they don't have multiple-speed transmission in their traction engines, so I was only used to playing with single-speeders . . .'

'Oh, sorry. What were you saying?'

He laughed. 'This really isn't your thing, is it? Would it be more interesting if you came on a road-run with me? You could steer while I drive. It's a two-man operation, you see.'

'Er, no, if you don't mind I think I'll pass on that. This –' She indicated Queen Mab with a dramatic sweep of her arms, 'is what I wanted to do. Be up here and see it from the working end and to be able to say I've done it. Thank you so much for showing me, and explaining it, and I think Queen Mab is totally amazing but the ins and outs of engineering really leave me cold, I'm afraid.'

'Yeah, you either love it or you hate it. No sweat. So, what's the next item on today's agenda?'

After stepping gingerly out of the cab, Lola paused in her slow backwards progress towards the ground and looked up at him. 'Oh, true female stuff. Including shopping. You either love it or you hate it.'

'Touché. And as I'm in the latter category, definitely not my area then,' Flynn hauled himself from the tender and stood in the cab and lovingly caressed the steering wheel. 'When are you going?'

'This afternoon. After closing time.'

'That won't give you much time for browsing, and retracing your steps, and trying on the same stuff over and over again. Oh, yeah, I've been there. Vanessa was one serious shopper.'

'You still miss her, don't you?'

'Sometimes. Her choice, though, not to come with me. We keep in touch . . .' He stared ahead for a moment, then smiled down at Lola. 'So, how about if I run the pub this lunch time and you get yourself off on your shopping marathon right now?'

'I couldn't . . .'

'Yes, you could.'

Yes, she could, she thought. Of course she could. Flynn had already proved that after the grounding in Opal Joe's and the Tralee bar he was a competent and friendly barman, and it would give her a whole day to enjoy herself.

'Yes, okay. Thank you so much.'

'No sweat. Have a good time.'

'Oh, believe me, I will.' Lola almost danced out of the shed on her kitten heels.

It was like skipping school, she thought as she click-clacked her way towards Sunny Dene. Not that she'd played truant very often, of course. Escaping from the confines of her exclusive high school would have taxed the ingenuity of Houdini. Anyway, she'd been a model pupil: diligent, biddable, and extremely law-abiding. The rules instilled then had stayed with her forever, all basically boiling down to the fact that hard work brings its own rewards. Which, of course, it had up to a point. But not much fun.

A blur of white van screamed passed her, throwing

up dust, then squealed to a halt.

'Hi!' Ellis yelled from the minibus's open window, his voice just audible over the 1910 Fruitgum Company. 'Are you skiving?'

'Actually, yes. I'm going into Reading for the day. You wouldn't happen to know when the next bus is, would you?'

'Well, if you'd like to change your destination it could be in about fifteen minutes. Posy's doing the post, I've got someone else on the school run, and I'm taking Gran and Tatty into Oxford. There's a New Age "do" on in the town hall that they're desperate to attend. You'd be more than welcome to join us.'

'It's really kind of you, but I was actually planning on going shopping.'

'Great, I love shopping,' Ellis beamed. 'And I'm not into crystals and hocus-pocus so I was only going to be mooching until they'd finished.'

Lola hesitated. She really didn't want Ellis trailing around the shops with her looking bored. She was pretty sure that his kind of shopping would involve electronics boutiques and hi-tech warehouses. He probably wasn't the least bit interested in Jaeger or Debenhams or Marks and Spencer – still, she could always lose him somewhere.

And, as today was meant to be a day for treating herself, and Oxford would be a very rare treat indeed, and one which first Flynn and now Ellis had made possible, it would be churlish to say no.

'That'd be lovely. Thanks so much. I'll just go and grab my jacket and bag.'

* * *

Twenty minutes later, the minibus was rocketing on to the A34 in the direction of Oxford. Lola sat in the front passenger seat beside Ellis. The Lemon Pipers were crooning nostalgically about their Green Tambourine. Tatty was wearing moon and stars dangly earrings and rustling through a huge sheaf of New Age literature, and Glad, looking very spring-like in a lime green two-piece and jaunty magenta hat, was puffing on a cigar.

Just a normal day out for Steeple Fritton.

Oxford, fabulous in pale mellow brick and burnished spires, was bustling with students and tourists and shoppers, all making the most of the mild March sunshine. Having escorted Glad and Tatty to the town hall with strict instructions to be back in the car park by five o'clock, Ellis looked at Lola. 'Right, I'm all yours.'

'Not what I'd heard.' Lola gazed in awe at the glorious sculpted skyline, then peered up and down the road. Deciding that the shops looked as though they were to the left, she set off in that direction with Ellis following close behind.

'So, Posy's told you about our little flare-up, has she?'

'She mentioned it, yes.' Lola crossed a rather strange cobbled junction and stared up at Carfax Tower. She knew it was Carfax Tower because it had a plaque that said so. She also allowed herself a momentary wallow over the high street's amazing Florentine architecture. 'She said, in the vernacular, you got snotty about her and Ritchie so she got snotty about you and Tatty. To be honest, I don't know why the two of you just don't admit you were made for one another and get together.'

'Me and Posy?' Ellis looked stunned. 'You're kidding. I wouldn't dare. Posy is far more hurt than anyone

234

realizes. It'll be ages before she trusts another man. She's like my little sister, even if she is older than me, and we just flirt a bit because it's good practice for her after being dumped, and I like to keep my hand in . . . Oh, are we going in here?'

Here was Marks and Spencer. 'Yes. Why?'

'Because my mum shops in M&S and you're nothing like my mum.'

Lola smiled. 'Don't try your charm on me, Ellis Blissit, because it simply won't work. M&S is full of surprises, you know. It's not just for ladies of a certain age. And if you don't want to venture into the hallowed portals you can always wait outside until I've finished.'

Unabashed, he followed her in. 'Are you buying underwear?'

Lola frowned. Wasn't this a touch too intimate an occupation to be sharing with the wild-child demon lover? 'Yes, actually. So, your waiting outside might be a good idea.'

'No way! I'm ace on underwear.' Ellis gave her a slow and very thorough appraisal. 'Size 12, hips sort of 34 to 36ish . . . bra size 34B . . . Close?'

'Far too close.' Lola shook her head. 'That's not normal.'

'Call it a gift,' Ellis was forging ahead towards the lingerie department. 'And years of study. Can I choose, then?'

'No you damn well can't.' She was laughing. 'A girl has to have some secrets.'

It was, she admitted to herself, not embarrassing at all; in fact, having Ellis dancing attendance, even if only from a discreet distance, shaking his head violently when she picked up sensible pastel-coloured cotton and nodding approval when she reached silver and navy lace, was extremely good for her ego.

He was the sort of man who would turn heads anywhere, and he was having a marked impact on the lingerie-buying ladies of Oxford. She smiled to herself, wondering what her girlfriends in Swansbury would say now if they could see her with Ellis – young, startlingly beautiful, wearing his black jeans and his faded cotton sweater, and at that moment indicating with his eyes that she should definitely buy the suspender belt that went with the silver and navy lace.

Oh, and if only bloody Barbara Marion, who probably thought that, as a mistress, Lola had spent all her time romping in thigh-high PVC, could see her, too. And Cousin Mimi. She smiled even more. Cousin Mimi would simply implode with outrage.

Nurturing these pleasant thoughts, Lola joined the snaking queue at the cash desk and fished for her credit card. The purse strings were still tight, but she'd budgeted enough money for today. Just a few treats . . .

Nigel had never accompanied her on underwear-buying trips – or on many other shopping expeditions, come to that. They'd had to be so discreet. But at the beginning of their relationship he had bought her underwear: proper mistresses' underwear – gorgeous lace and silk froth from La Perla and Janet Reger, all in pale boxes with ribbon bows and acres of pink or lilac tissue paper . . . All long gone.

Slowly, she moved towards the front of the queue.

Ellis was waiting at the check-out exit, still turning heads. 'I'm glad you bought all the glam stuff. Am I allowed to have a sneak preview when we get back to Sunny Dene?'

'Not a chance. But you can carry the bags.'

'Bugger, and you didn't get the suspenders. Boring of you. Where are we going next?'

They made their way back out into Queen Street. 'Promise you won't laugh.'

'Nope. But if I laugh it won't be at you. Will that do?'

'Probably. Okay then, I want to buy a pair of jeans.'

Ellis stopped walking. 'Why would I laugh at that?'

'Because I've never had a pair of jeans in my life.'

'Wow, really? Well, now you come to mention it, I suppose you do always look very Miss PA. Mind you, I like that. It's sort of authoritarian which reminds me of, er, well, no perhaps now's not the time. Come on, then, let's go shopping in some proper shops. No more mumsy stuff.'

They spent the next hour diving in and out of the sort of shops Lola had only ever scuttled past. Dark, intimate shops, with loud rock music, teenage customers and size six assistants. Ellis, naturally a jeans expert, advised on make and length and width and colour, and she eventually emerged with three pairs of Levis in various shades, all of which seemed to shrink her bum and make her legs look endless.

'You looked really cool in them. Dead sexy,' Ellis beamed at her as they forced their way through the crowds again. 'But they won't look right with buttoned-up blouses and court shoes. You need the right tops and some boots.'

'Do I?' Lola frowned, picturing Posy. Posy always

looked so gorgeous and pert and pretty in her jeans . . .
Sort of tumbled and casual. Not structured or strictured.
'Yes, you're probably right. After all, you're the expert
and I'm in your hands –'

'I wish,' Ellis grinned cheerfully.

Another hour, another clutch of shops filled with tiny
girls and body-pierced boys and thundering music, and
Lola was the proud owner of two pairs of boots – one
leather, one canvas – and half a dozen tops that Ellis
said would look unbelievably horny with tight jeans.

The words mutton and lamb were beginning to form
an unpleasant cliché in her head.

'Don't know about you,' Ellis said, as they wandered
pleasantly through the Westgate, 'but all this shopping
has given me a heck of an appetite. Shall we find
somewhere to eat?'

'Can you cope with carrying more bags?'

'Yeah, sure, but can't we eat first?'

'I had a bit of a whim,' Lola said, moving off at a
determined angle towards Sainsbury's, 'that we might
go al fresco. Buy some finger food. Have a picnic . . .'

Ellis, she found, was as enthusiastic about buying food
as he seemed to be about everything else in his life. By
the time they struggled back into the Westgate a mere
fifteen minutes later, they had bread, butter, cheese,
fruit, wine, salad, and a whole pack of disgustingly
glorious calorie-laden cream cakes.

'Does your whim involve eating out here on these
seats?' Ellis surveyed the benches' bedraggled incumbents with compassion. 'Because if so, I don't think
we've got anywhere near enough wine.'

'I thought we'd look at the city guide and find a park.'

'Sounds nice. But don't let's bother with the guide. Oxford has tons of parks, I've seen them on *Inspector Morse*. Let's just wander and see what we find.'

They wandered and found Christ Church Meadows.

Chapter Seventeen

Lola reckoned she had never, ever, seen anywhere quite so wonderful. In the warm spring sunshine, with the ancient golden-brick spread of Christ Church College on one side and the sparkle of the silent Isis as it undulated its way under rustic bridges and beneath willow fronds on the other, it was like something from another time.

The addition of wide gravelled pathways, huge expanses of meadows with grazing deer, and the blur of acid green and yellow as trees and flowers burgeoned into new life, made her want to turn cartwheels of sheer joy.

'Brilliant place,' Ellis agreed, sprawling on the clipped grass beside her and rummaging eagerly through the carrier bags. 'You'd never think we were only moments away from the city centre, would you? And I hate to get back to basics, but can I dish this food up now before I drop dead from starvation?'

'Yes, of course, but while we were clever enough to buy a corkscrew, we didn't remember paper cups, so we'll have to drink from the bottle.'

'Should have stayed with the old boys in the shopping

centre, then,' Ellis said happily. 'We'd have fitted in nicely. Mind you, you'll have to drink most of it as I'm driving. And now can I ask you a question that's been bugging me for ages?'

'As long as I can ask you one in return.'

'Yeah, course, anything you like. Me first, though – oh, could you pass that piece of Camembert? What I want to know is, why don't you have a car? You're so together, so professional. I can't believe you need to rely on public transport or my white van. Is it an ecology issue or can't you drive?'

Lola chewed slowly on a piece of cheese. If she told Ellis about what had happened to the car, then she'd have to tell him everything that had preceded it, wouldn't she? And how pathetic and tarty would that make her sound? She suddenly realized that she didn't want him to think her either pathetic or tarty. It truly mattered what he thought of her. She really didn't want him to react in the same way as Posy had.

Still, she'd confided in Flynn and he'd been fine. But then Flynn was different from Ellis. Very different indeed.

She swallowed the cheese and broke off a hunk of bread. 'Yes, I can drive. Until the day I arrived at Sunny Dene I'd had a car since I was seventeen, and it's one of my main aims to earn enough money to buy another, but . . .'

By the time she'd finished talking they'd eaten all the bread and cheese, most of the salad, some of the fruit, and had passed the bottle of wine backwards and forwards between them like merry inebriates with no inhibitions at all.

241

'Christ,' Ellis said eventually. 'How romantic.'

'Are you mocking me?'

'No way. I just think it's a beautiful story, and I'm so sorry that you're not still together and that his bitch of a wife had to screw things up for you after he'd died. And,' he reached for an apple, 'I'm amazed that you're as okay as you are. You must have felt so lonely, so bloody devastated. I mean, not only having to cope with the loss and the grief, but having to start everything all over again without any security. And having the car clamped and taken away must truly have seemed like the bottom of the pit. I really, really admire you for climbing out of it.'

She sat in silence for a moment, unwilling to speak in case she suddenly sobbed or did something equally crass. It was wonderfully liberating to have been able to tell the whole truth at last.

'Thank you. I mean, I'm sure you've heard some of the story from Posy, and maybe even bits from Flynn, but now you know as much as there is to tell.'

Ellis grinned. 'Posy gave me the expurgated girlie version, and Flynn is discreet to the point of boring when it comes to giving away secrets, either his own or other people's. I don't think Flynn is a kisser-and-teller, do you?'

'Probably not.' She smiled at him. 'And although it's possibly not the image you wish to portray, neither are you. In fact, you're not at all as I first imagined you would be.'

'Aren't I? Bugger.' Ellis smiled back. 'Have to work on the old sex-crazed, chauvinistic, good-time bloke stuff a bit more then, won't I? Can't have people thinking I'm halfway decent. Are we having the cakes now?'

'Yes, although we should have saved some of the wine to wash them down with. Still, help yourself. And can I ask my question?'

Ellis dug into the box and bit into layers of choux pastry and goo with relish. 'Yeah, sure, but if I offer to be packhorse, shall we walk and talk?'

Lola weighed up the dynamics of wandering along the riverbank with a fist full of squishy cake. 'I'd love to, if you think we can manage it without getting cream everywhere.'

'Well, if we do,' Ellis beamed, 'we can always lick it off one another, can't we?'

Quickly pushing away all manner of highly inappropriate mental pictures, Lola stood up, thrusting the last of the shopping bags into Ellis's arms the way she remembered Eamon Andrews doing on *Crackerjack*'s Double or Drop many moons ago.

He shoved his cream cake in his mouth while manoeuvring the shopping, then removed it again as they headed along the gravelled path towards the river. 'Okay, all set. Ask the question.'

'Why on earth are you burying yourself alive in Steeple Fritton?'

'Very Lynda Lee-Potter! Straight for the jugular. You missed your vocation. And I don't see it as being buried. I see it as a challenge. And now I've got the White Van Man stuff sussed I'm doing nicely, and I'm very happy in the village, thank you.'

'But your degree . . .'

'The reason I did mechanical engineering is the reason I'm in Steeple Fritton.'

Lola licked cream from her fingers and wondered if

243

the other riverside strollers were looking at them as a couple and imagining that they were mother and son. Just as people had looked at her and Nigel together, wondering if they were father and daughter. 'Don't be obscure.'

'Why not?'

She watched the college eights skimming along the river beneath Folly Bridge, their blades cutting V-shaped wavelets through the diamond-sprinkled surface. 'Because I was straight with you. And it intrigues me. You're so young, surely you want more out of life than being stuck in a Berkshire backwater?'

Ellis finished his cake. 'Okay, by the time I was fourteen I was a pub regular and hardened drinker. By sixteen I was into clubbing, raves and recreational drugs. By eighteen I'd backpacked around various bits of the world and lived at least three lifetimes. My A Levels took me years to obtain, my degree was a pain. I was old and jaded by the time I was twenty. What other people look forward to doing – all their letting off steam once they've got their education out of the way – I'd done and become bored with even before it was legal.'

Ouch. Lola winced. 'Well, that's certainly straight enough. Sorry, I wasn't prying. I had no idea. But surely –'

'When my parents finally found a school that would accept me back with my record of exclusion and absconding, I eventually did physics, maths and chemistry at A Level. I enjoyed the theory of engineering, but never wanted to become an engineer. I had a special crammer tutor who lectured in Mech-Eng at uni. He got me through A Levels and then taught me for the three years of my degree. I thanked him by having an affair with his wife for all that time.'

Lola looked at him. His eyes were fastened on the curve of the river, on the swans doing their stately glide, on the waggle-tailed ducks pestering people for food.

'I shouldn't have asked.'

'Why not?' He stopped staring at the river. His eyes were sad. 'If I hadn't wanted you to know I wouldn't have told you.'

'Did you love her?'

'Very much. It was first-time love and the real thing for me.'

'So, what happened? Did her husband find out?'

'Yeah. And she wouldn't leave him for me because she thought I wasn't old enough . . . that I wasn't serious . . . that the age difference would mean we had no future. It was a real kick in the teeth to discover that while I really loved her and was happy to spend the rest of my life with her, she just saw me as some sort of toyboy arm candy.'

'A bit of a role reversal, yes.' Lola pulled a sympathetic face. 'I'm so sorry.'

'That's why it suited me and my parents, not to mention my tutor and his reconciled wife, to take up Gran's offer of a retreat in Steeple Fritton. Out of harm's way to let the dust settle.'

'And you don't want to do anything else? Go anywhere else?'

'Not at the moment, no. Why should I? I've done it all already and I love the village, I like being my own boss, and I feel liberated for the first time in years.'

Lola sighed. They were all in the same boat. Well, not

Flynn so much, of course, because he'd left Vanessa, but she and Posy and Ellis. And of all unlikely places, Steeple Fritton was offering them sanctuary and the chance of a new life.

'So, the fling with Tatty . . . ?'

Ellis groaned. 'Oh, God – was supposed to be just that. The night I arrived in the village I felt so bloody lonely. Gran and the coven were off to the wedding reception at Colworth Manor, the pub then was like something out of the dark ages, and my heart was still fragile. I went along just to be with people and noise and music. Tatty was flirty and fun and it, well, just happened.'

'And it never occurred to you that she might be serious?'

They'd reached one of the rustic bridges over an opaque emerald Isis tributary. Ellis shook his head. 'Not for a moment. When Posy said last week that Tatty wanted forever and another baby it scared me to death, but I can't hurt her, can I? I know what it feels like.'

Lola leaned her back against the flaking wooden bridge. 'Poor you. And poor Tatty. But you'll have to tell her. If you don't you'll hurt her even more.'

'I know. But she's so lovely. Weird as hell, I mean, but a completely free spirit and totally barking. I really thought she was just up for a bit of fun. There should be some sort of code I reckon, for relationships. Like star ratings or something, to indicate who wants what out of it, and if your stars don't match then you should run like hell.' Ellis put the bags down by his feet, then looked at her. 'Do your stars match Flynn's?'

'You ask far too many questions.' Lola didn't meet his

eyes. 'And, um, from a woman's point of view I think you should ask Tatty what she wants from your, er, relationship. Could be Posy got hold of the wrong end of a bit of village gossip or something. You'll probably find that Tatty is only looking for fun, too.'

'You might be right. Hope so. There seems to have been more than enough unhappiness recently.' He leaned against the bridge beside her and stared across the meadows in companionable silence. 'You know, all that city of the dreaming spires stuff is pretty accurate, isn't it?'

Relieved to be back on neutral ground, Lola nodded. 'I was just thinking the same thing, seeing all the domes and steeples through the mist of the new leaves it's, it's just like Itchycoo Park.'

Ellis laughed. 'Christ, I never had you down as a closet Small Faces fan. Were you a teenage Mod? Is that why you don't share my love of Bubblegum? Why you simply fail to appreciate that Joey Levine and Art Resnick were the Rodgers and Hammerstein of the Sixties?'

Smiling, Lola shook her head. 'Not really. And I think Lennon and McCartney might have something to say about that. I suppose, if we're being honest, all that Levine and Resnick stuff that you play just reminds me of hearing it the first time round. You know, fizzing, happy music which accompanied miserable teenage parties, terrifying school exams, spots and puppy fat, and silly optimistic dreams that you knew would never come true.'

'You should have had my sort of teenage years,' Ellis grinned. 'If there was angst in there I sure as hell can't remember it. Mind you, I can't remember much of anything . . . Still, I can't believe that you were a teenager in the sixties. You can't be –'

'Don't say it. You don't mean it. It's very kind of you but – oh, look, can I tell you something? Something that I wasn't going to tell anyone. Something that I don't want you to breathe a word about but might explain things.'

'More guilty secrets?'

'Secrets, yes. Not guilty ones.'

Lola wondered for a moment about the wisdom of sharing anything more with Ellis. Would he rocket home to Steeple Fritton and tell the entire village? Would he laugh at her? Like Flynn, she hoped not, but she'd risk it. She simply had to tell someone.

'I did all this today, asking Flynn to show me Queen Mab, then the shopping, the jeans, the picnic . . . because it's my birthday. Today I'm fifty years old.'

Ellis didn't speak. Lola wanted the bridge to crumble away and the thick pea-green water to close over her head. He thought she was ancient, and of course he was right. Fifty! How could she be fifty? Dilys, round beach-ball Dilys, was probably fifty. Ellis's mother was probably fifty. *Old* people were fifty.

'Happy birthday then.' He eased himself away from the bridge and grinned. 'That's really cool. Although why you don't want anyone else to know, I have no idea.'

'I'm used to keeping things to myself. I spent very few birthdays with Nigel. He couldn't really get away that often without an inquisition. For years now my birthdays have been just another day.'

'Sad,' Ellis said. 'Very sad. Still, this has to be the start of the rest of your birthday life, then. From now on you'll have out-of-the-closet birthdays with cakes and ice cream and jelly and balloons . . . Hey, we could have a party in the pub tonight. We could –'

'No.' She shook her head fiercely. 'Seriously. I don't want anyone to know. I don't want any fuss. I don't want to be bloody fifty!'

'Why on earth not? I'd have thought being fifty was wonderful. Especially looking like you do. No, listen. I'm a connoisseur, I know about these things and I'd've said late thirties. You look like Jilly Johnson or Nina Carter. Blonde on Blonde. Elegant, toned, totally gorgeous, definite wow-factor.'

Immensely flattered, Lola laughed at him. 'That's really kind of you, but while I may be in their age group I certainly don't think I'm in their league.'

'Don't you believe it –' Ellis glanced at his watch. 'Shit, we really should be making tracks.'

'It's nowhere near five, is it?' Lola was suddenly reluctant to break the spell. The moment they walked away from Christ Church Meadows, her birthday would be over. As soon as they were back with Tatty and Glad, the magic would be gone. 'We've got ages before we were going to meet them in the car park.'

'Ah yes,' Ellis picked up the shopping bags, 'but that was before I knew that it was your birthday. Maybe you'll find yourself another present amongst all the joss sticks and stuff.'

Before she could protest, Ellis caught hold of her hand. Fleetingly hoping there was no sticky residue of cream cake left lurking, she hesitated for a moment as his fingers entwined with hers. This wasn't supposed to happen. Not the holding hands; not the togetherness; and especially not the tingle that had shot from the soles of her feet to the top of her head in less than a nanosecond.

As they retraced their steps away from the river and back towards Christ Church College, now bathed in the low-glow of the spring sunshine, Lola felt as though her feet were skimming across the gravelled pathway. Fifty? *Fifty?* She hadn't felt this way since she was fifteen.

She was vaguely aware of people looking at them as they left the Meadows and wandered back towards the town hall. Looking at them and smiling. Maybe they thought Ellis was some highly-successful student celebrating with his mother . . . maybe they thought she was a cradle-snatcher . . . maybe they thought . . .

But right then it truly didn't matter what they thought. People were smiling at them because they were smiling at one another. Their happiness at being together radiated waves of the same emotion and – Jesus Christ!

Lola yanked her hand away.

'What?' Ellis frowned at her. 'What's the matter?'

'We're the matter. Skippety-skippeting along here, grinning like idiots, in full view of everyone like damn lovestruck teenagers. I must be mad.'

'You're beautiful and it's your birthday and we're having fun. Sod what anyone else thinks.' Ellis grabbed her hand again. 'Stop being so buttoned up about everything. Tonight, when you get into your jeans and your boots and that black top thing you'll shed all your grown-up inhibitions. You'll feel as lovely as you really are. Stop putting yourself down.'

'But we aren't a couple, aren't together. This is crazy –'

'And fun, as I said. Enjoy it.'

Enjoying it was difficult. Far too difficult. Five minutes

earlier – when it had been a simple rush of emotion, a chemical reaction, purely instinctive – holding hands with Ellis and feeling on top of the world had been extremely easy. Now, realizing that she was enjoying it in a totally inappropriate way, was very difficult indeed.

She'd always liked being in Ellis's company, right from that first time weeks ago when he'd been so kind to her in the greasy spoon caff. The feeling then that she'd thought was mere gratitude, had grown into admiration for his love of life, and, as she got to know him better, into liking him for his friendship and honesty, and then into something really strange that made her smile when he was around.

It was sheer madness. She was more than twice his age, he flirted with happy indiscrimination, and he was already involved with Tatty Spry, to boot. Stifling a hysterical laugh at the preposterous thought that she, Lola Wentworth, fifty years old and allegedly in full control of her faculties, had had one lover who was old enough to be her father and was actually toying with the idea of taking a second young enough to be her child, she snorted with self-derision.

Ellis smiled as they reached the town hall steps. 'I'm so glad you've recovered your sense of humour. Hey, great, the hocus-pocus exhibition is still going strong. Let's go and see if Gran has stocked up with eye of bat and ear of toad or whatever it is that witches need for a nice goulash.'

Snatching her hand away for the second time and making sure that this time she was out of regrabbing reach, Lola followed him into the town hall. Expecting sitar music and wreaths of purple smoke at least, it was rather disappointing to find that the glorious split staircase – which should have had Scarlett and Rhett *in situ* – and elegantly panelled conference room were set out much the same as for any other trade exhibition.

True, the air was heavy with incense and there were a fair few New Agers drifting around looking otherworldly, but most of the people crowding round the crystal, feng shui, mystic water, and alternative therapy stands, appeared perfectly normal.

Ellis, exuberant as ever, instantly vanished through the crowd towards a section that promised magical metals, floral remedies and essential oils. Definitely Tatty territory.

'Garn!' Glad Blissit, looking like an enraged pixie in her lime green and magenta outfit, suddenly emerged through the melee beside Lola. 'Am I glad to see you. What a load of old bollocks this is.'

Lola laughed. 'I thought you were here as Tatty's henchman?'

'Not on your life. I only came along for the ride out. It's years since I've been to Oxford. Not that I've got to see much of it, only a glimpse through the windows, the rest of the day has been a lot of hippie mumbo jumbo. I should have come with you and young Ellis. Did you get all your shopping done?'

'Yes thanks. Ellis is carrying the bags. I think he's in that scrum over there looking for Tatty.'

'Oh, she ain't there. She's upstairs with the bigwigs. She's spent all afternoon stocking up on new paraphernalia for her shop. Damn daft idea of young Posy's to encourage her to offer massages and what-have-you, if you ask me. Tatty don't take much persuading to go way over the top with stuff. And of course, she was mighty miffed that Rose Lusty had snaffled young Malvina Finstock from the Cressbeds Estate and –'

'Malvina who?'

'Finstock. Funny little girl, lots of earrings in her tongue, shaven-head – oh, you must have seen her around the village. Any road, Malvina's been to college, see, does all the real trendy stuff in hairdressing and beauticiany things. And Rose has nicked her for the salon, because of Posy saying we should be offering everything to everyone like we're some sort of damn United Nations rescue mission. Tatty really wanted Malvina for her place, so she's gone right over the top this afternoon and got herself reregistered, which is why she's upstairs.'

Assuming that possibly Tatty would need to be registered as a masseuse, Lola nodded. 'Well, yes, good idea to keep it all legal. And it's a good idea that, um, Malvina can offer a more modern sort of hair styling. Not, of course, that there's anything wrong with Rose's, er, more traditional styles of course. And I think that a lot of people will enjoy Tatty's aromatherapy massages, and she'll build up a good client list.'

'It ain't the bloody aromatherapy she's signed up for,' Glad said, shoving her way into a particularly crowded corner. 'It's the bloody tattooing.'

Lola blinked. Okay, so maybe there wouldn't be a huge call for henna tattoos in Steeple Fritton, but as she and Posy and Ellis and Flynn were pulling out all the stops to get people into the village for all manner of things, and keep them coming back, it made sense . . .

'Wouldn't that be something that, um, Malvina would

be able to do though, in Rose Lusty's?' Lola asked when she finally ran Glad to earth in front of a table displaying what looked like desiccated dog turds. 'The henna tattoos?'

'Bless you, they ain't henna tattoos, duck. They're the real McCoy. All needles and blood and gore. It's what Tatty used to do, her trade, so to speak, before she went all airy-fairy alternative.'

Lola was speechless. There truly didn't seem to be anything she could say. Tatty was a tattooist. Of course, it made sense. She'd always assumed the name came from the way Tatty looked and dressed, or was maybe a diminutive of Tabitha or something . . .

It seemed she'd got so many things wrong today.

'And she's going to be doing it again? Running a tattoo parlour? In Steeple Fritton?'

'Ah,' Glad nodded her head, making the magenta hat leap up and down. 'We'll have the blame village filled with bikers and builders and squaddies and all manner of unsavoury blokes. Smashing!'

They'd moved on from the desiccated dog turds to a stand which apparently offered immediate spiritual enlightenment through the wearing of silver bells. Glad picked up a small selection and studied them carefully.

'Do you think these would suit me? No, don't answer that, duck. I reckon I'm a touch too old for dressing up like Mary, Mary, Quite Contrary. Oh, I wish Tatty'd get a move on, I wants to get home and catch *Star Trek*. Mind, if she's got her talons into young Ellis they're probably fornicating somewhere in a quiet corner.'

Lola tried not to look horrified. It was difficult. The

shaft of jealousy that had lasered through her almost took her breath away.

'Get away with you,' Glad cackled. 'I was only joking. Don't reckon even someone as flighty as Tatty'd manage to do it here. Mind you, can't say the same for our Ellis . . .'

Frantically wanting to change the subject, Lola rushed towards a stall that seemed to be full of small multicoloured pyramids.

'You won't be needing them,' Glad said helpfully over her shoulder. 'Not with that nice Yank bloke to keep you warm of a night at Sunny Dene.'

'Sorry?'

'Don't be sorry, duck. I wouldn't be, he's a looker all right. No, these here,' she motioned the magenta hat towards the small pyramids, 'these is all sex aids.'

Dear God. Lola backed away. Sex aids? *Sex aids?* How sheltered had she been? What on earth could anyone actually *do* with small Pyrex pyramids?

'They all contains stuff,' Glad, obviously an expert, continued. 'Frisky-making stuff. Like I said, you won't be needing that with that gorgeous Flynn geezer to keep you entertained under your eiderdown. Oh, look, here's Tatty!'

Lola had never been so glad to see Tatty Spry in her entire life.

'All sorted,' Tatty jangled her bangles and tinkled her necklaces and managed to get her spiral curls caught in her lace cuffs as she rearranged a mass of New Age parcels and bags. 'Not half as difficult as I'd imagined, being already qualified and registered, all they'll be doing is sending someone out to inspect the premises for

255

sterility and things, then I'll get my certificate and we'll be away. Can't wait.' She turned her huge beam towards Lola. 'Ellis says you've had a lovely day shopping, too. I'm so pleased.'

Lola nodded her head stiffly like an automaton. What on earth had she been thinking of? How could she have allowed herself to have even the faintest flicker of attraction towards Ellis? 'Er, yes, I've had a great day. Lovely, thanks. Um, where is he?'

'Oh, looking at something over there –' Tatty tossed her curls in the direction of the desiccated dog turd table. 'He said he'll be with us in a moment. Shall we wait for him outside? I can't wait to get home and tell the kiddies the wonderful news that their mummy is going to be a tattooist again . . .'

Chapter Eighteen

The Crooked Sixpence was packed. Lola, who had hardly had time to eat her Sunny Dene dinner and hurl herself into a bath before evening opening time, stood nervously in the doorway.

Self-conscious wasn't in it. The jeans and the boots and the black off-the-shoulder top may have looked the business in Oxford, with the dim lights and the loud frenetic music and Ellis's charming company. In the cold light of her bedroom, Lola thought she looked like a sad travesty.

There'd been no time to canvass opinion. When she'd arrived back from Oxford, Dilys and Norrie – doing the dinners with Dom, who was back from university for the Easter vacation, but without Posy who had apparently been at the shop and The Crooked Sixpence most of the day – told her they'd promised themselves a rare treat, a night out at the pub and kept winking and grinning like sly children. Mr D and Mr B were no better, behaving like real prima donnas and singing Vera Lynn songs in high falsettos. Flynn didn't even show up. So, throwing her long black coat over her new image, Lola had rushed to the pub and just hoped nobody laughed.

She closed the door behind her and nudged her way through the crowd to the bar. Flynn and Posy were serving three-deep customers, the Pinks were playing darts, there was a crowd round the fruit machine, and several young girls, including Posy's friends Nikki and Amanda, in very short, tight dresses, were trying to out-manoeuvre Glad who was hunched over the jukebox.

'Hi,' Posy grinned. 'Have a good day?'

'Great, thanks.' Lola didn't remove her coat. 'What about you?'

'Frantic. Dashing around doing the courier stuff for Ellis and then between here and the shop. Flynn helped me scrape the last of the flyposters off the windows and wash the paintwork, but I haven't got much further. No brilliant ideas of what to do with it yet.'

'We'll have to give it some thought,' Lola clasped her coat even more tightly round her. 'You're really busy in here tonight. What was it like at lunch time?'

'Hectic,' Flynn squeezed past Posy. 'We coped fine, though, didn't we? Apart from a bit of trouble with the cops . . .'

'*What?*'

'Just a bit of after hours drinking, what with us still not having all day opening,' Posy shrugged. 'We, er, forgot the time. But it's all right, honest. They were ever so nice about it.'

'Yeah,' Flynn grinned. 'They said they might have to keep an eye on us in future, but we told them once you were in charge there'd be no more of that sort of thing. Anyway, how did the shopping and the girlie stuff go?'

258

'Wonderful,' Lola still clung on to the coat. 'But are you sure the police were okay? I mean, I don't want anyone to think I can't run this place. And I certainly don't want the police checking up on me every half an hour.'

Flynn shrugged. 'Trust me. It'll be fine. Just a bit of teething trouble, that's all. Everyone gets things wrong when they first start in business.'

'I don't,' Lola frowned, knowing full well she shouldn't have been playing at teenagers-in-love with Ellis in Oxford and leaving the pub to Flynn and Posy. 'And has word got out? Do they all think we're having an after hours lock-in or something? I've never seen so many people in here, and on a week night. Is there something else I should know?'

Flynn and Posy exchanged grins, much as Dilys and Norrie had in the B&B. Lola frowned. Had she missed something? What on earth had happened here? She'd only been away for half a day.

'It was a little idea of Flynn's,' Posy said. 'I'm surprised you didn't see the poster outside.'

Poster? Lola had hurtled across The Crooked Sixpence's car park so fast she'd seen nothing at all. 'What poster?'

'For 'appy 'our!' Neddy Pink informed her gleefully, slamming down his Guinness tankard on the bar top. 'All drinks 'alf price!'

Appyower? Was this some sort of village tribal festival then? Like Harvest Home or Midsummer Solstice? Appy . . . ? The penny clunked into place. 'Oh! You mean Happy Hour! Right.'

'I didn't think you'd mind –' Flynn poured Neddy's

Guinness with his customary flair. 'It always went down a storm in Opal Joe's.'

Mind? It had filled the pub with new customers. Why on earth should she mind?

'No . . . no . . . it's a great idea. Wonderful. I've never seen so many people and – oh, my God! What the hell is that?'

'That's the other little surprise we've lined up for you,' Posy nudged past with two snowballs for the Pink twins. 'Flynn and I made a joint managerial decision in your absence.'

'The rep guy came in at lunch time and said we could have it on trial,' Flynn said, crashing Neddy's money into the till. 'We've got it for a month. The rental was next to nothing and should earn out real quick if it takes off.'

Lola gazed at the tiny raised dais in the corner, and the proliferation of audiovisual equipment and a whole serpent's nest of black wires. 'Um, yes, but what is it?'

'A karaoke machine,' Posy smiled. 'We thought you'd approve.'

'Karaoke? In here? Good Lord . . . I mean, well, yes, I can see that it may have its fans, but won't it be too loud?'

'Probably,' Flynn said, reaching across the top of Posy's head for the makings of a crème de menthe frappé for Rose Lusty, 'then mercifully it'll drown out that.'

'That', Lola guessed, was Glad's current Wurlitzer selection of Matt Monro on instant replay.

'And is this why your parents and Mr D and Mr B were all behaving like starlets backstage at The Palladium earlier, then?' Lola asked Posy. 'Limbering up for their big vocal experience tonight?'

'Probably,' Posy pulled a face. 'Mr D and Mr B reckon they can sing like the Beverley Sisters, but my mum is a different matter altogether. She makes everything sound like the National Anthem, all on the one note. Truly dire.'

'And Norrie? What about him?'

Posy shrugged. 'He sings in the bathroom a lot. Usually Kenneth McKellar.'

'Jesus,' Flynn winced. 'Was he a punk?'

'Not really, although he did wear funny clothes. Mind you, my real buzz will come when we get Ritchie and Sonia up there singing "I Got You, Babe" and I can wire their microphones directly to the mains.' Posy stopped pulling a pint and looked at Lola. 'Are you feeling cold? I mean, it's baking in here and you've still got your coat on.'

Lola took a deep breath, slowly undid the buttons and slid the coat off.

'Wow!' Flynn's eyes widened. 'Hot!'

'Cool, actually,' Posy grinned. 'You really must learn to use the language correctly if you want to be accepted by the natives. No, honestly, Lola, you look amazing. Is this what you bought today?'

'Some of it, yes.' Lola suddenly felt completely over-whelmed by emotion. She belonged here. Posy and Flynn and the others had become her friends. Real friends. They cared. On top of everything else that had happened today, it was almost too much. She blinked quickly. 'I thought it all might be a bit young, you know.'

Posy shook her head. 'Not at all. You look like a million dollars. Gorgeous. Ellis will be all over you, not to mention Flynn, and every other man in the village.'

'Just the unattached ones, of course.'

'Oh, of course.'

They looked at one another and laughed.

The karaoke news must have zipped round the Frittons like wildfire. By the time Flynn had handed out the song lists, and everyone had made their selections and handed them back, and the machine was wired for sound and vision, the pub was packed to the doors.

Lola had received so many compliments about her new appearance that she thought she'd burst with the smiling. And Ellis had been right, of course. Once over the initial mutton-dressed-as-lamb anxiety, she felt confident, felt attractive, felt okay inside and out.

Being fifty really wasn't too bad at all.

Dilys and Norrie had duly arrived and had bought drinks, had told her she was a bobby-dazzler, and that with Dom taking care of Sunny Dene – just in case anyone popped in – they were looking forward to a great night out. Mr D and Mr B, dressed in very tight beige trousers and very long lilac jackets and looking like a pair of geriatric Julian Clareys, were flirting heavily with Flynn. The pub was abuzz with laughter and excitement, and money was flowing joyously across the bar, and all the while Lola was aware she had one eye on the door.

Stupid, stupid, stupid . . .

With a very professional flourish, Flynn kicked off the proceedings, and Amanda and Nikki instantly became the Spice Girls. Well, almost. They were followed by Rose Lusty doing Alma Cogan frighteningly badly and a scrum of the local youths, tanked up on lager tops, who had a go at massacring Westlife with a certain amount of relish. Neddy Pink accompanied everyone throughout on the accordion, while Martha and Mary took over the Pan's People role just in front of the fireplace.

Mr D and Mr B then minced exaggeratedly towards the dais.

Flynn grinned at them. 'Shirley Bassey for you guys then, is it?'

Mr D and Mr B nodded perfectly groomed grey heads in sync.

'Bit underdressed aren't you?' Flynn was really at home with the microphone and at playing the crowd. 'Shouldn't you be in full flounce and slap?'

'Not today, dear,' Mr B grabbed the mike and fluttered his eyelashes. 'We're going for the natural look . . .'

The Crooked Sixpence erupted as the opening bars of 'Big Spender' trumpeted up to the rafters.

Most of the karaoke warblers were completely tone deaf, not that it seemed to matter, as they all received riotous rounds of applause. And clearly whether singing or clapping, it was thirsty work.

'With Flynn up there playing ace DJ and compere,' Posy panted, 'we need someone else behind this bar.'

Lola laughed. 'Well, if you like, I could ring Ritchie and ask him to come in.'

'No thanks. I'd rather die from exhaustion than be pummelled to death by Sonia's bump. We'll just have to manage . . . Oh, shit . . .'

'What?' Lola paused in spurting gin into a glass.

'I think my dad's going to sing.'

'Thank the Lord it isn't Dilys,' Lola said, deftly adding ice and a slice as though she'd done it all her life, then bit her lip. 'Oh, God, sorry. I didn't mean to be rude. I just mean, after what you said . . .'

'No, no, it's fine. Dad's definitely the better option. Fortunately Mum is so unused to going out and drinking that I don't think she could stand up if she wanted to. Oooh, no, he's going to do Meat Loaf. Why do your parents always have to embarrass you?'

'At least they're enjoying themselves.'

Posy smiled. 'They are, aren't they? They haven't been like this for ages. None of us have . . . isn't it strange? Still, no peace for the wicked. Yes, what can I get you? Right, two pints of Duck Pond and blackcurrant coming up, and they probably will be again later . . .'

Lola, busy, happy, and now knowing that Ellis was spending the evening with Tatty and hating herself for minding, stopped short in mixing a Bloody Mary, and listened to Norrie, a tingle creeping up her spine.

He was absolutely amazing. 'Bat Out Of Hell' had never sounded so good. She doubted if Marvin Lee Aday could have done it better himself.

It wasn't Norrie up there in his brown cords and his checked shirt and his lovat-green cardigan with sparse strands of hair plastered across his gleaming pate. It was a wild, roaring, raunchy rocker.

When the last notes died away, the pub was silent for a moment then everyone stood up and stamped and whistled and called for more. Norrie, perspiring happily, obliged with an equally wonderful rendition of 'Dead Ringer'.

'Wow!' Flynn yelled into the microphone. 'A star is born! What are we having next?'

As Norrie, to a standing ovation, went into a pitch-perfect 'You Took the Words Right Out of My Mouth', Posy, moist-eyed, shook her head. 'My God, he's brilliant. I never knew . . . It's like we're suddenly all discovering hidden talents, isn't it? Oh, and just in time, our extra barman has arrived.'

'Ritchie? I thought he wasn't –'

'He isn't,' Ellis grinned, squeezing in behind the bar. 'I am.'

Lola couldn't stop the smile stretching from ear to ear. It probably wasn't really melon-wide, but that's how it felt, and was totally beyond her control. 'I didn't expect to see you . . .'

'What? Tonight of all nights?' Ellis raised his eyebrows. 'I wouldn't have missed it for the world. And you look wonderful.'

'Thank you. I actually feel it, too.'

'Told you, didn't I?'

'You did. I should have listened. And you don't have to help out. You can stay the other side of the bar and be a customer, if you'd prefer. I mean, you're not on the payroll . . .'

'Call it a birthday present, then,' Ellis winked as he whisked off to serve the Westlife-killers.

By the end of the evening, the till had been emptied of notes three times, Lola, Posy and Ellis had sprinted up and downstairs to the cellar for restocks more time than they could remember, and everyone had eventually staggered off home, still singing.

Lola, who had been slightly concerned about whether Ellis would request a karaoke version of 'Happy Birthday', or one of the Lola songs which she'd always found so embarrassing, needn't have worried.

'Don't be silly.' He looked quite hurt when she voiced her fears as they clattered empty glasses together and cleaned ashtrays. 'You asked me to keep it a secret and I will.'

'Sorry. Thanks. And is Tatty –?'

'Full of ideas for advertising the new tattoo parlour, and busy sending off for all the up-to-date regulations and design catalogues and everything.'

Lola nodded. Ellis was kind. He wouldn't prick Tatty's bubble. Not today. Not when she was so happy. Probably not ever.

The pub was wreathed in cigarette smoke hanging in a blue haze across the emptiness. The echoes of the silent music still throbbed. It had been, as everyone said, the best night anyone could remember in The Crooked Sixpence.

Lola looked across at Flynn and Posy, who were unplugging the karaoke machine and coiling the wires. 'Ellis has offered to finish the clearing up with me. You've both worked your socks off today, and I really appreciate all you've done, so go home and get some rest.'

Home . . . she'd said home again. Sunny Dene *was* home.

'Cheers,' Posy grinned, swiping her curls from her eyes. 'I'm almost asleep on my feet. So, is the karaoke staying, then?'

'Absolutely,' Lola said, as she emptied the beer dregs from the drip trays into the slop bucket. 'It's been brilliant, especially discovering Norrie.'

Posy laughed. 'He'll be signing autographs as he dishes up the full English's now. Flynn was just saying that we should incorporate the karaoke into the carnival, have a sort of *Stars In Their Eyes* show.'

'Oh, yes, that'd be great. Wonderful. When's the next parish council meeting? You'll have to suggest it.'

'A couple of weeks' time. I'll definitely put it forward. Then we could have Queen Mab outside in the car park on carnival night, and the soundalike show in here, and –'

'The carnival queen bestowing her favours anywhere she wants to,' Ellis added happily.

Lola and Posy gave him matching mock glares.

'Okay, sorry. Just a thought.'

Within half an hour everything was tidied, Flynn and Posy had left, yawning, for Sunny Dene, and Lola slumped into one of the hearthside chairs. It had been a truly lovely day. Her best birthday ever.

'Fancy a nightcap?' Ellis was still behind the bar. 'Something different for your birthday? I'll have whatever you choose.'

Why not? 'I'd love a Cointreau and bitter lemon.'

'Is that a recognized drink?' Ellis pulled a face. 'Sounds more like a punishment.'

'It was a very fashionable drink when I was growing up.'

Ellis clattered amongst the bottles. 'Oh, right. In the Dark Ages, you mean. Like mead or wassail. Oh, well, I'll try anything once.'

She laughed at him, watching him as he poured liqueurs into two glasses and flipped the top from the bitter lemon. It seemed as though she'd always known him. Sitting here, happily tired, after a day packed with surprises, he was simply becoming part of her life.

Dangerous thoughts . . . Stupid . . . She shrugged. It didn't matter. Not tonight.

She'd done exactly this with Flynn, of course. Sat here, by the fire, sharing a drink in the empty pub. And they'd drunk a toast to friendship. Which is what they had. She and Flynn would always be friends.

Ellis placed the drinks on the table and sprawled opposite her, his long black-jeaned legs taking up most of the hearth. 'Happy birthday.'

'Thank you. You've made it very special.'

He grinned and fished in the pocket of his jeans. 'It's not over yet. Here . . .'

She looked down at the tiny purple and silver striped box. 'I can't . . . I mean . . .'

'Yes, you can,' he pushed the box into her hands. 'It's nothing much. You didn't give me a lot of warning, and yes, I did buy it at the town hall, and no, it isn't a desiccated dog turd.'

Laughing, she lifted the lid on the box. Three slender silver chains coiled against purple tissue paper. Lola picked them up, each one with a different link formation, delicate and exquisite.

'Ellis, they're gorgeous. Thank you so much. Really . . . oh, God, now I think I'm going to cry . . .'

'Don't do that,' he leaned forward. 'I'm just pleased you like them. They all have different properties: these three are for health, happiness and love. They had wealth and prosperity and stuff like that too, but as a child of the sixties I thought you may find them slightly materialistic.'

She smiled at him again. 'Health, happiness and love sounds like the perfect package to me. Hang on, I'll unfasten them.'

'You might need a hand putting them on,' Ellis leaned forward, his spiky hair brushing her face. 'Shove your foot up on the table, only mind the Cointreau.'

'Uh? What has my foot go to do with anything?'

'They're ankle bracelets,' Ellis grinned. 'Dead sexy.'

'I'm not wearing ankle bracelets! Tarts wear ankle bracelets!'

Ellis sat back slightly, looking puzzled. 'I thought that particular premise went out around the same time as the ones about only tarts have pierced ears or wear red nail varnish? And as you've already got both of those, you might as well go for the set. Now, put your left foot up on the table, and don't kick the drinks over.'

Keeping both feet firmly on the floor, Lola shook her head. 'I'm not wearing ankle bracelets.'

'Now you really are showing your age. Even my Gran doesn't think someone's a floozy just because her ears are pierced,' Ellis picked up his drink and knocked it back in one, pulling a face. 'Ugh, it's like Benylin! And let me tell you that ankle bracelets are discreet, pretty, and very, very alluring against smooth skin. Trust me. It'll be like the jeans. You'll feel incredibly sassy once you're wearing them.'

Slowly sipping her drink, Lola sighed. It was churlish of her to refuse his present and she could always take them off later, and anyway, wasn't today supposed to be about all things new? Different experiences? 'Look, I'm sorry –'

'No –' Ellis held out his hands. 'I should apologize. I've insulted you. I didn't think –'

She laughed. 'You haven't insulted me at all. You've just given me a glorious present which I was insensitive enough to be rude about because of some preconceived

269

notion probably drummed into me by my mother. I was being stupid, and it highlights the difference in our ages only too well. We're an entire generation apart.'

Ellis's eyes gleamed. 'I know. Wonderful, isn't it? I can't believe you were lucky enough to enjoy Joey Levine and Art Resnick in real time. So, are you going to let me turn you into an ancient floozy?'

'Everyone thinks I'm that already.'

'There you go then. Now, stick your foot up on the table.'

She did, and watched as Ellis carefully pulled up the leg of her jeans and rolled down the top of the canvas ankle boot. Thank heavens she'd shaved her legs. In her Nigel days, of course, she'd had her legs waxed regularly. Maybe Tatty offered leg-waxing, and maybe that wasn't such a good idea . . .

Ellis's fingers gently brushing her skin as he fastened each of the three clasps made her shiver. Madness. Total madness . . .

'There.' He sat back. 'Don't they look the business? You have such slim ankles, and still tanned. You must have had a great holiday last year.'

'Solarium. Gym. Sauna. Beauty salon.' Lola admired the three tiny chains slipping silkily against her ankle bone, twinkling in the lamplight. 'All the trappings of the bored and regularly-neglected mistress. And these look wonderful. You're right, again, you smug so-and-so. They look gorgeous and feel superb, and thank you.'

She thought that he might lean forward and kiss her. He didn't.

'My pleasure.' He pulled the boot and jeans into position, and stood up. 'And has it been a great birthday?'

270

'Wonderful. Thanks to you.' She finished her drink and stood up too. 'And I'm totally exhausted.'

'That's because you're an ancient floozy,' Ellis said cheerfully. 'I'll help you to lock up then I'll walk home with you.'

'There's really no need. Steeple Fritton always seems fairly thug-free.'

Ellis waited nonetheless while Lola put on her coat, then checked the windows and doors, the fire and the ashtrays, as she switched off lights and finally locked The Crooked Sixpence's front door.

The night was dark and cold. She shivered and Ellis put his arm round her shoulders. He was much taller than she was, and she fitted against him. It didn't seem odd at all. It seemed scarily right. She and Nigel had never walked like this: in twenty-eight years they'd rarely walked anywhere together. This was like being a teenager all over again. Heady stuff.

'The ankle bracelets feel lovely. And no one knows they're there. Like a secret.'

'Glad you like them. It seems sad though, only having one present on your birthday. Did, um, whatshisname buy you loads?'

'Nigel. Oh, yes . . . but rarely on the actual day. And then only through the company accounts. Marionette Biscuits paid for all my presents. He'd never risk Barbara finding anything untoward on the personal credit card statements.'

'If I'd been him, I'd have dumped her and made you official. I'd have been so proud to be with you.'

'He couldn't. He didn't want to upset Barbara, or the children, and then there was the business . . .'

She stopped, listening to herself. Wasn't that exactly what every 'other woman' was told? She'd never doubted that Nigel would one day leave his family and be with her, but now . . . She shook her head in the darkness. He was dead and it was over and if they hadn't shared the life she'd imagined it was far too late to mourn it now.

'Someone's still up,' Ellis said as they arrived far too quickly outside Sunny Dene. 'All the lights are on.'

'Probably Norrie taking Trevor and Kenneth out for their last walk and singing Meatloaf's greatest hits.'

Ellis smiled down at her. 'Probably. Good night, then. And happy birthday . . .'

He slid his hands inside her coat, round her waist, pulling her towards him. Then he bent his head and kissed her. Lola remained immobile for a moment, then kissed him back. No one but Nigel had kissed her for twenty-eight years, and very few men before that . . .

Ellis made her float . . . made her feel like she'd never felt before . . . Ellis was a very experienced kisser, she thought hazily, sliding her hands up into his hair. Gentle . . . arousing . . . waking so many buried emotions . . .

Eventually he moved away from her, smiling. 'Sorry.'

She opened her eyes. 'Don't be. It was wonderful . . . the best present.'

'Better than the ankle bracelets?'

'Not better, different . . . And completely mad.' Trying hard to sound controlled, she touched his cheek. 'Tatty certainly knows what she's doing. Good night, Ellis, and thank you for today.'

He kissed her again, very gently, then watched until she'd closed Sunny Dene's door behind her.

Dom was just vanishing into the kitchen and grinned

at her. 'Can I have some of whatever you've had? You look like you're illuminated. I've heard all about the karaoke – God, I wish I could have been there.'

Still floating, Lola beamed at Posy's gangling bespectacled brother. 'It's going to be a permanent fixture so you'll have plenty of time to have a go. You're up late, you weren't waiting for me, were you? I have got a key.'

'No, no, we've got another guest in. She arrived out of the blue this evening, so I've had to make up the bedroom and prepare a hopefully okay dinner.'

'Never mind, you'll get your reward in heaven as your mother is so fond of saying. Is she staying long? It'll be great for your mum and dad if she is.'

'She said she had some business in the area so she was just booking on a day-to-day basis, but hopefully she'll be here for the week. Mind you, she was a bit sour-faced.'

Lola giggled. 'I'm sure that's what everyone said about me when I arrived, too. Well, good night then . . .'

'Night.'

Lola swung across the stone-flagged hall towards the skewwhiff stairs. She couldn't remember when she'd last felt so happy. So alive. She touched her lips gently with her fingers, reliving the kiss, and wanted to laugh out loud.

As she passed the desk at the foot of the stairs, the register was open. Against the day's date was one entry. The new visitor to Sunny Dene. The name printed out by Dominic and signed in a strong black scrawl.

Barbara Marion.

Chapter Nineteen

The next morning, Posy hitched herself up on to one of the shop counters and surveyed her empire. She and Flynn had spent many mornings in the empty shop – try as she might, she'd forever think of it as The Stuffed-Ferret Emporium – scraping years of grime from the windows, sweeping the floors, washing down walls, and now, thanks to a thoroughly disturbed night, she knew exactly what she was going to do with it.

The surge of entrepreneurial inspiration had come somewhere in the small hours, while unable to sleep because of a lot of door slamming, and feet running up and down Sunny Dene's skewwhiff stairs, and prolonged loo flushing.

The shop was going to be called Gear Change, and she was going to hurl it open to the cash-rich dowagers of Steeple Fritton. The idea had germinated from Ellis's schemes to make money from the weekenders and the Fritton landed gentry, and Lola's suggestion for a fancy dress store.

Now, well, since last night, the ferret emporium was going to be a second-hand clothes shop, opening three days a week – where people could cash in on their last-season's designer labels, or chain store mistakes. The owners of the clothes put their own price tag on their garments, and when the clothes were sold, half the price would be returned to them and Posy and Gear Change would keep the rest.

Since first light, Posy had been belting around the village on the BMW, letting everyone know what she'd planned to do and begging for their cast-offs. Within two hours she had her first pile of black sacks and boxes of clothes stacked in the doorway.

'What the heck was going on at the B&B this morning?' Flynn asked, leaning on his broom. 'I heard Lola walking the floor most of the night, and then she stormed out dead early.'

'No idea,' Posy shrugged. 'But I know she kept me awake most of the night and nearly took the door off its hinges when she went out. And I couldn't get any sense out of Mum and Dad when I asked them. Mum's got her first hangover for more than twenty years, and Dad thinks he's about to become rich and famous and kept offering me his autograph.'

Flynn laughed. 'Yeah, well, Norrie deserves his moment of glory. He was amazing. And Mr D and Mr B made ace divas, too. It was an all-round great night.'

'Which makes Lola's behaviour even more weird. I mean, after last night's roaring success I'd have thought she would be on Cloud Nine.'

'Thunder Cloud Nine by the look of things. I reckoned she'd be back for breakfast but she wasn't, and she wasn't in The Crooked Sixpence just now when I checked to see how Queen Mab was doing.'

Posy tried not to smile at the tenderness in his voice. She was pretty sure that the cadence change was for Queen Mab – not Lola. At least, she hoped so. Still, she, better than most people, understood how Flynn felt about his twenty-ton baby. After all, she loved the BMW like a child.

'Maybe she had something important to do in Reading or Newbury or somewhere. Something boring that she'd forgotten about. Like the books for The Crooked Sixpence or VAT returns or something. She's bound to be back in the pub for lunch-time opening.'

Flynn didn't look convinced. 'Yeah, maybe so. Although I think Ellis might have something to do with it.'

'Ellis? Why?'

'Well, look, I don't want this to upset you, but Dom told me that Ellis kissed Lola last night. Seems he watched them through the window.'

'Sneaky little pervert,' Posy giggled. 'And why on earth would it upset me? There's nothing between me and Ellis, and he kisses everyone. He even kissed me once. He was probably only being friendly and Lola certainly wouldn't have let him kiss her if she didn't want him too . . . God, do *you* mind?'

'Nope.' Flynn grinned at her. 'Lola isn't my type. I like her very much, and we're good friends, but she doesn't push my buttons.'

'So, your Vanessa in Boston isn't an elegant blonde, then?'

'Far from it. Wild and red haired, with a temperament to match.' Flynn stared across the empty shop for a moment, then shrugged, 'And history. Say, who was that severe-looking woman in the dining room this morning?'

'No idea. She nearly bit my head off when I was serving breakfast, though. Ignorant old trout. Dom says she booked in last night. I know we need all the money we can get, but I hope she doesn't stay long. Now, what are we going to do next?'

Flynn twirled the broom. 'Unpack the bags and boxes? Now you've had the idea and got some stock, I guess it'd make sense to try getting the rails and shelves filled and sell some of it.'

'When Ritchie and I had talked about taking this shop over, I'd always imagined we'd run it as a sort of bric-a-brac place. Junk shop – don't know what you'd call it – but somehow that doesn't seem such a good idea now. Not when everyone else in this row seems to be working flat out to up their profiles and become competitive with Harrods. I think Gear Change strikes about the right balance and certainly corners about the last gap in the market.'

'Junk doesn't seem to be a great money-spinner,' Flynn agreed. 'You'd just get lumbered with everyone's dust-gatherers. And I'd guess that the car boot sales on the common have probably cornered the market in selling second-hand rubbish.'

'I'm not going to be selling second-hand rubbish!'

Flynn laughed. 'A rose by any other name . . .'

Before she could further defend her entrepreneurial dream, the door flew open.

'Hi, Flynn –' Ritchie stood in the doorway. 'Seems like I missed a great night last night with the karaoke. I wish I'd been working, but – oh, hello, Pose.'

'Hi . . .' Posy tried to appear disinterested. It was difficult. Ritchie was looking at his most attractive:

not all ironed and pristine Mr Upholstery Department Manager, but jeans and a sweatshirt, sort of rumpled looking. 'Why are you scooting round the village on a weekday morning? Have you been sacked?'

He shook his head, looking discomfited. 'It's Sonia's last but one hospital visit before the baby's due. She's along at Bickeridges buying more supplies of jelly. She eats it by the kilo. Straight from the packet. Doesn't even break it into cubes. Turns my stomach to be honest. I thought I'd just pop in and see if Flynn was here and find out about the karaoke –'

'Crap,' Posy said, swinging her legs idly from the counter and hoping that she looked cool. 'You knew I'd be here and you just couldn't resist it.'

Flynn laughed, turning it into a cough as Ritchie looked at him.

'Well, you've seen me now.' Posy slid from the counter. 'So don't let us hold you up, then. No doubt you're absolutely gagging to get up to the Royal Berks and run through the pushing and heaving and blood and gore.'

Ritchie winced. 'We're having the birthing pool and Marti Pellow.'

'Bet Marti's looking forward to that.'

This time Flynn didn't even attempt to disguise his snort of laughter.

'I can't believe you're going to open this place up as a clothes shop,' Ritchie ignored Flynn and glared at Posy instead. 'Not when we were going to make it into a real nice antique shop.'

'Ah, yes . . . I vaguely remember. That was before you couldn't resist the charms of Miss Shagability, wasn't it? Somewhere in the dim and distant past when I trusted you with my life and you lied your socks off to me?'

Ritchie went red. 'Yeah, okay, but it just seems really funny that you're doing things without me.'

'Oh, I know. I felt much the same about being at your wedding, only sitting in the audience instead of being up front in the co-starring role.'

They stared at one another. Flynn, still clutching his broom, beat a tactical retreat into the storeroom. Ritchie looked embarrassed and scuffed his trainers across the clinically clean floor, and Posy took a deep breath. It was getting better. Just a bit. She didn't hurt anywhere near as much as she had. The thought of him with Sonia no longer kept her awake at night, although the baby was still a bit of a bugger.

'Can you tell me something? Something I never felt brave enough to ask before. Was it just Sonia that you cheated with, or were there hordes of them during the years we were, well, us?'

'Only Sonia,' Ritchie raised his head and met her eyes. 'Just Sonia. And I wish to God it hadn't been.'

'Oh, you mean you wish there'd been an entire harem?' Posy felt very relieved. She believed him. It was nice to know she hadn't been a serial-cuckold. It was also satisfying to know that Ritchie and Sonia weren't blissfully happy. Mean, yes, but she was only human.

'You know what I mean,' Ritchie frowned.

'Yes, of course I do. Oh, and one more thing. Was it the thongs? Should I have worn thongs instead of just knickers? Would thongs have saved our relationship?'

'Not the thongs. Honest. I didn't know about the

thongs until, er, until, well, later . . . It was just this stupid feeling that there'd never been anyone else but you, and after we were married there'd never be anyone else, and I just sometimes wondered what it would be like. And Sonia was always there, always hanging around, and I knew she fancied me and I was flattered. Then one night I was out with my mates from work and Sonia was in this pub and we were both drunk and I thought, well, I thought just once. It was only supposed to be just once. But we got a bit involved and –'

'Spare me the dot-to-dot.' Posy turned away from him. He'd never told her how it actually happened. She wasn't sure she really wanted to know. 'I get the picture.'

'I'm so sorry.'

'For me, yourself, or Sonia?'

'All of us. It's a mess.'

She looked at him. 'It's life, Ritchie. It's happened, and we've all got to get on with it. Especially you. Especially for the baby's sake.'

Christ! She sounded almost grown-up and sensible. How scary.

'I wish I could turn the clock back. I wish –'

'Stop it, Ritchie. We've already said all this. Now run along, go and hold Sonia's hand and make the best of it.'

A blob appeared in the doorway, blocking out the sun. It was like the prelude to a horror film.

'What're you doing in here?' Sonia rumbled angrily through a massive mouthful of jelly cubes. Her teeth were disconcertingly scarlet. 'You're supposed to be with me.'

'Just what I was telling him,' Posy smiled sweetly. 'He seemed to have forgotten. Old habits and all that.'

'You're a right clever-mouth, Posy Nightingale! I'd like to remind you that I'm the one wearing the wedding ring! Look!'

Sonia thrust out her pudgy left hand and made an angry rocking movement forward. Posy groaned. She hoped she wasn't going to fall over. They'd never get her on her feet again without a block and tackle.

Ritchie grabbed Sonia's arm. 'Come on, babes. We're going to be late for the clinic.'

Babes? *Babes?* Oh, yuck!

Sonia wriggled herself away from him and pushed her bloated face towards Posy. 'I warned you once before and I'm warning you again, you keep away from him. See?'

'God, yes. Of course I see.' Posy tossed her curls and pulled her tight T-shirt down to the studded belt round her jeans. 'Don't worry, I'll stay well away from him. I mean, look what happened to you. You were size 8 once, weren't you? You'd be lucky to get into an 18 now, and of course it won't disappear once the baby arrives. God, no. There'll be cellulite and stretch marks and saggy bits and layers of fat for the rest of your life. So sad. The thongs will be but a dim and distant memory. You'll have to keep an eye on Ritchie then, won't you? I mean, once a cheater always a cheater. Bye.'

She stomped into the storeroom, listening gleefully as Sonia was dragged from the shop by Ritchie, still spouting vitriol.

'Ouch,' Flynn looked at her. 'That was mean.'

'I know,' Posy sighed. 'Not like me at all. Completely out of character. But it's made me feel a whole lot better.'

'Has it?'

'Yeah . . . well, sort of. Actually I was feeling better about it anyway. And I know it was cruel, but I hate her. I hated her before she screwed around with Ritchie. She's just really unpleasant. Always has been. It's sometimes nice to be able to let off steam, isn't it?'

Flynn grinned. 'I guess so. Me and Queen Mab think so anyway. Hey, would you fancy being steersman in the carnival procession?'

'Me? Wow. Yes, I'd love to have a go.'

'You declined the offer before, when we first fetched her from Fritton Magna.'

'I know,' Posy sighed. 'I was still being a misery guts then. Nothing suited me. Life's different now. Do you know, being here in the village and facing up to the problems was the only way to go. Persephone's owner was dead right.'

'Uh?' Flynn frowned.

'Long story. Okay, now what shall we do?'

'Get on your bike and deliver this.' On cue, Ellis stuck his head through the storeroom doorway. 'I've got a busload waiting to go to Newbury so I can't take it. It's a package for Fox Hollow. Urgent. It was wrongly delivered in Fritton Magna so I've done a deal with the regular courier. It's about the same size as the one you took to Mapleford, so it'll fit in the top box.'

'Okay, I'll go now,' Posy nodded. 'Oh, and have you got Lola tucked away somewhere? Good God, Ellis Blissit! Are you blushing?'

He shook his head. 'I don't do blushing. And I haven't seen Lola this morning. Why?'

'We heard all about your amorous exploits last night,'

282

Posy grinned. 'And Lola went missing from Sunny Dene early on. She's not in the pub so we just wondered if she'd found her way into your bedroom.'

Strangely, Ellis didn't laugh. 'I haven't seen her. Shit, I wish I hadn't got the coven all strapped into their seats otherwise I'd go and look for her. Have you tried her mobile?'

'Don't even know if she's got a mobile,' Posy said. 'Do you?'

Ellis shook his head. He did look worried, Posy thought. Maybe he'd tried to take it further than kissing and Lola had said no and Ellis had pushed his luck.

'You didn't try to, um, well, you know . . . last night?'

'No I bloody didn't!' Ellis's eyes flashed. 'Christ, Posy. You should know me better than that. Look, if Lola shows up, ask her ring me. You've got my mobile number. If she's unhappy about anything I'd like to try and help.'

'Yes, sure. Sorry. Look, leave the parcel by the door and I'll take it out to Fox Hollow straight away, then we could all meet up in the pub later and see what Lola's problem is.'

There was a fanfare of horns from outside. Ellis growled. 'Sodding hell! Sometimes I wish Tatty would act her age not her shoe size. I'll have to go. See you later.'

'He looks pretty concerned,' Flynn said, as Ellis stormed out of the shop. 'I guess he must really like Lola.'

Posy shrugged. 'I think they've always got on well. But Tatty would have something to say about it, I reckon, if

Ellis has any ideas of making it more than liking. Oh, well, I'll nip out to Fox Hollow and earn some money, then. What are you going to do?'

'Come with you.'

'What, in the jeep?'

'On the back of the bike, if that's okay with you. I haven't ridden pillion for years.'

'Okay,' Posy grinned. 'But I hope you're not a wuss.'

'A what?'

'Never mind. There's a spare crash helmet in the hall cupboard at Sunny Dene so at least your head'll be okay. I'm not going to make any promises about the rest of you.'

The journey from Steeple Fritton to Fox Hollow was a good one for the bike and a testing one for Posy. Lots of nice straight roads linked by tiny, winding, bendy ones. From Berkshire into the Oxfordshire countryside on a glorious day, riding the BMW with Flynn on the pillion was a bit of a dream come true. In the spring sunshine, with puffballs of white cloud flecking the sky, and very few people around, Posy and the bike both rose to the challenge, and swooped and soared happily.

Flynn, she was pleased to discover, knew exactly what he was doing, and leaned back against the top box, relaxed, trusting her. Not that she'd have complained if he'd clung on round her waist, she thought, with a grin into her scarf. She wouldn't have minded that at all.

And he'd been a real sport about wearing the spare crash helmet which was fondant pink.

Fox Hollow arrived all too quickly. She pulled the BMW into the forecourt of what looked like a warehouse standing alone at the end of a lane miles from anywhere, switched off the engine and removed her helmet. Flynn had already swung his legs from the bike, and having taken off his crash helmet was running his fingers through his hair.

'Pretty cool.' His eyes shone. 'I'd forgotten how much fun it was. You're one ace driver.'

'Thanks.' She was secretly delighted. Ritchie had always been such a namby-pamby about the bike. It was great to have the bike's performance, and yes, okay, her own prowess, appreciated. 'God, this place looks deserted.'

'Are you sure you have the right address?'

She nodded, tugging the thick oblong package from the BMW's top box. 'It's printed on here. Bradley-Morland. Honeysuckle Lane. Fox Hollow. This is it. Hey – wow!'

'What?'

'Look at that bike over there! A Norton 900 Roadster! Must be well over thirty years old. A real classic. Goes like stink! Someone here's got good taste.'

She stroked the black motorbike lovingly as she passed, then rang the bell in the huge double doors. There was no sign of life; no other vehicle except the Norton; no noise at all. It would be pretty galling to have to return the parcel undelivered to Ellis. She was only paid on completed deliveries and every penny counted towards the survival of Sunny Dene.

Flynn leaned across and took the parcel from her. 'Let me. It's pretty heavy, and no, I'm not insulting you by suggesting that it's *too* heavy, just being practical. Try ringing the bell again.'

She did. Still nothing.

'A bit of a wild goose chase,' she said. 'Sod it. We'll have to take it back to Ellis as undelivered. What a waste of time.'

'I wouldn't say that,' Flynn said cheerfully. 'It's been worth it just to ride shotgun with you.'

She beamed even more. He couldn't have said anything nicer. She rang the bell for a third time. There was still nothing but bird song and the distant swish of traffic on the bypass.

'Oh, let's give this up as a bad job. This place is so spooky, it's beginning to give me the heebie-jeebies. No, hang on, I think I can hear footsteps inside. Yes, I think someone's coming. Let's hope it's not some axe murderer or a drugs baron or a – oh!'

Chapter Twenty

Posy jumped as one of the double doors suddenly opened, and she found herself face to face with an extremely attractive man wearing paint-streaked black jeans and an unravelling cotton sweater.

'Hi,' he raised his eyebrows, both of which were also paint-streaked. 'Can I help you?'

'We've got a parcel for Bradley-Morland. Are you him?'

'I'm half of them, yes. Jack Morland.' He looked at the package in Flynn's hands. 'Oh, great. I think that must be the Crazy Gang medley. Would you mind bringing it inside, please? My hands are a bit, um . . .'

They all looked at his hands which were wet with streaks of cobalt and crimson lake.

'Sure. No sweat,' Flynn said, following Jack Morland through the doors. 'Are you an artist?'

'Sort of. Look, if you could put the parcel down there, would you mind if I just washed my hands before I sign for it.' He vanished into a tiny kitchen to the left of the doors.

Posy looked at Flynn in the gloom. 'Funny sort of factory. There's no one else here. Still, maybe if he's an artist, it's a studio.'

'It's pretty dark for a studio,' Flynn was peering into the cavernous recesses of the building. 'I thought artists needed oceans of natural light and stuff. And what's with the Crazy Gang?'

'Search me,' Posy shrugged. 'Wimbledon football team are called the Crazy Gang and there was an old music hall act years ago, but I don't think . . . oh, hi again . . .'

Jack Morland reappeared, wiping his hands in a piece of paint-soaked rag which Posy thought probably made the hand washing superfluous. 'You're a motorcycle courier, are you?'

Posy nodded. 'We spotted the Roadster outside. Nice bike.'

'Thanks. I love it. What've you got?'

'BMW 1200 Tourer.'

'Wow, shit off a shovel.'

'Something like that,' Posy laughed. 'And thank you.'

'What for?' Jack Morland raised his multicoloured eyebrows.

'For not assuming that the bike was Flynn's and that I was the pillion passenger.'

Jack laughed. 'Oh, I never make assumptions about gender roles. Not any more. Now, do you want me to check the parcel before I sign?'

'If you don't mind,' Posy said. 'It makes it easier if it's been damaged or isn't what you've ordered. I can take it back straight away.'

Inside its box, the package was securely wrapped in

thick paper and an awful lot of industrial brown tape, then bubble wrap, and still more tape.

'It's a bit like pass the parcel at kid's parties, isn't it?' Jack Morland grinned, ripping through the layers. 'Ah, I think we're getting somewhere. Oh, yeah. Look at this . . . Wonderful.'

Posy stared in total incomprehension as the contents of the package were revealed. A cardboard oblong, almost as thick as it was long, with two end covers in dark red card and concertina'd ochre-coloured heavy-duty paper in between, hardly seemed worth getting that excited about.

However, Jack was still looking at it as if it were the Holy Grail.

'Nell will be so pleased we've got this. We've wanted it for ages and had to have it cut in Belgium specially and flown over. It looks fine. Right, where do I sign?'

Posy produced the triplicate book, still having no idea what she'd delivered.

'Is it a music book?' Flynn asked.

'Don't be daft,' Posy grinned at him, then looked at Jack. 'Foreigners! What do they know?'

'Actually, yes it is,' Jack said, looking at Flynn with interest. 'If you recognized it, you must know about –'

'Just a bit . . . Have you got an organ?'

Posy frowned. It was all as clear as jabberwocky. And wasn't it all a bit personal to be discussing organs with a complete stranger? Americans were brash and upfront, of course, but even so . . .

Jack was nodding enthusiastically. 'Two. A Gavioli on our gallopers and we've just bought a Limonaire at auction.'

'No way! You've got a carousel?' Flynn's voice had taken on an awed tone. Like he was in church or in the presence of royalty. 'And two organs? Right here in this shed?'

'Yeah, most of our stuff is here. I'm doing a bit of renovation on the Gavioli before we go out for the season, hence the paint. The Limonaire is perfect. Didn't need anything except a bit of fine-tuning ... What about you?'

'I've got a showman's engine. A Fowler Super Lion. Queen Mab.'

Jack shook his head. 'You lucky bastard! My God! We've been on the hunt for one of those for the last three years.'

'I keep Queen Mab in Steeple Fritton, in Berkshire. I don't know if you'd know it.'

'Know it? I used to live in Newbury. Steeple Fritton is right on my old doorstep.'

'Great, then, you'll have to come over and visit. And so Bradley-Morland is a steam preservation company, is it?'

Jack laughed. 'Bradley-Morland is a funfair. A traditional fair, as they used to be, with rides that are all at least fifty years old. We're The Bradley-Morland Memory Lane Fair.'

'Holy shit!'

Posy decided this had gone on long enough. 'Could someone tell me what this mutual admiration society is all about? I got lost somewhere around "organ".'

Jack and Flynn, talking together, eventually managed to explain.

What she'd delivered, it transpired, was a specially cut

paper music book which, when the concertina'd card sheets fed through the keyframe of an organ, played tunes. This Crazy Gang one, as she'd suspected, was a selection of Flanagan and Allen's Greatest Hits. The organ, they explained, was the huge ornate music-maker in the middle of roundabouts, galloping horses, carousels? Get the picture? The Bradley-Morland Memory Lane Fair was a touring funfair offering nostalgia and feel-good entertainment. Flynn, he said, had just walked into Seventh Heaven.

'Phew . . .' Posy did a mock brow-wipe when they'd finished. 'Very comprehensive, and amazing. Do you mean, you've got a fairground in here?'

'Some of it.' Jack nodded. 'Not built up, naturally. These are our winter quarters. We're just about to hit the road for the season. Would you like to take a look?'

Flynn, matching strides with Jack, was away practically before the invitation had even been offered.

Posy, following more slowly behind them, was mulling over a fairly spectacular plan . . .

'Could we book you for our carnival?'

Jack stopped walking and looked over his shoulder. 'Yes, of course. As long as we're not already booked somewhere else. When is it? And where?'

'Steeple Fritton. June 10th. It'd be the cherry on top of the icing to have a proper old-time fair . . . I can just see it . . . On the biggest part of the common, all traditional, just what we need to bring the crowds in, and if it's a success we can do it every year.'

'I'll need to check with Nell,' Jack's eyes softened. 'My partner. She keeps all the dates. She's out scouting for new grounds at the moment. I'll give her a ring and go and check the diary in the kitchen at the same time. Hang on . . .'

Posy hung. Just. Now she'd had the idea her impatience to make it reality knew no bounds. A real old traditional fair for the carnival! On Steeple Fritton common! She almost jigged on the spot with ill-controlled eagerness.

As Jack wandered back towards the kitchen, punching out numbers on his mobile phone as he went, Flynn who had reluctantly stopped walking when Jack did, grinned at Posy.

'That'd be a really neat thing to do. An old-fashioned carnie, er, funfair would sure bring in the crowds. And you know what you said about me having Queen Mab outside The Crooked Sixpence at night, in full steam, and we said it needed music but –'

Posy almost clapped her hands and jumped up and down with excitement. 'Flynn! That was it!' Her words almost tripped over themselves in her enthusiasm. 'Remember, I said I knew what we needed but I didn't know where to find it? It was a fairground organ! That's what Googly Harris used to have at The Crooked Sixpence when he owned Queen Mab when I was a kid. It played all the old tunes, really belted them out, and everyone danced. Oh, and it was great, until of course Hogarth put a stop to it because it was fun.'

Flynn's eyes were gleaming with shared enthusiasm. 'And Jack says they've got a second organ here, so, if they have the fair on the common, we can have the traction engine and the other organ outside the pub and –'

Posy closed her eyes and prayed that Jack's partner, Nell, would say that The Memory Lane Fair was free for the carnival day. Oh, she could see it all: the colours, the roundabout horses going round and round and up and down, hordes of visitors pouring on and off the rides, the noise, the hullabaloo, everyone having the time of their lives letting off steam . . .

She opened her eyes. 'Ohmigod! Of course! The theme thing we needed to pull all this together and put Steeple Fritton well and truly on the map. We can call it Letting Off Steam!'

Flynn nodded slowly. 'Right, yeah, great idea. That'd tie in with everything we've got in place so far . . . Letting Off Steam . . .'

Posy clutched at his arm. 'Everyone will come to Steeple Fritton to do just that. It'll be Letting Off Steam Day, and the village can be advertised as the Letting Off Steam Village. With Queen Mab and the model railway, and Lola's karaoke in the pub, and all the stuff that Tatty and Rose and everyone has got lined up, it'll bring people in all the time. And those who want to stay over will use Sunny Dene, not just for the carnival day, which will be the culmination, of course, but –'

'All the time,' Flynn finished for her. 'We'll get posters and things done. Come to Steeple Fritton to Let Off Steam! Posy Nightingale you're a genius! I could kiss you.'

'Go on then.'

They stared at one another.

Posy's fingers were still embedded into the soft leather sleeve of Flynn's jacket. He covered her hand with his, moving his thumb slowly across the back of her fingers.

He exhaled. 'Are you sure about this? What about Ritchie?'

'Ritchie is married to Sonia.' Posy's voice was husky. She really couldn't tell Flynn that Ritchie had never, ever, in all their years together, made her feel like Flynn was making her feel now. 'Ritchie simply doesn't figure in my life any more. Unlike Vanessa . . .'

'History, as I said earlier.'

'Good news,' Jack reappeared from the kitchen carrying the Crazy Gang music book, and making them spring apart. 'Nell says most of the machines are free that day. We've got a booking at a fête in Witney, but they're only taking the smaller stuff. So that means you can have the gallopers, the helter-skelter, the big wheel, the ghost train, the speedway, the caterpillar, the swinging boats, most of the side stuff . . .'

Posy, still shivering from the touch of Flynn's fingers, nodded. It was all going to happen. It really was. 'Then we'll make that a definite booking. We'll sort out money and put it in writing and everything as soon as I get home.'

'Great. I've pencilled you into the diary here. Now, do you still want to have a look round?'

'Sure,' Flynn said. 'More than ever now. We were wondering if we could hire the Limonaire, too. Have her powered by Queen Mab outside the pub on carnival night?'

'Sounds wonderful. She's housed on a lorry, so transport won't be a problem. But I'll have to come and give your Fowler the once-over before then,' Jack said. 'And bring Nell. We might be able to come to some sort of mutual arrangement here. It's something we've wanted for ages. A proper showman's engine to drive the gallopers.'

They'd started to walk towards the back of the shed again. Flynn gave Posy a tiny secret smile. It was almost as erotic as the finger-stroking.

Great timing, Posy, she thought. Great bloody timing.

Four months ago she'd believed her heart was irreparably broken. Then the healing process had kicked in and she'd known she'd survive, alone, naturally, but she'd survive. Then it hadn't been long before she'd realized that she still had feelings for Ritchie, and Ellis's kiss in The Crooked Sixpence had sent tingles up her spine.

These had been welcome reactions. Nothing to worry about. If it meant she wasn't quite yet functioning on all reciprocal relationship cylinders, it had also meant that there was at least a spark.

That was okay. She'd live and die a spinster, but hey, there were worse things.

And now, out of the blue, Flynn Malone had made her go weak with lust simply by stroking her hand.

Oh, joy.

Flynn Malone, who'd be hightailing it back definitely to his homeland and probably to his girlfriend on the other side of the world before the year was out.

Great, great timing.

Flynn and Jack were happily comparing steam notes. Steam, it appeared, travelled the Atlantic well. It was a universal language. A bit like love.

Firmly reminding herself that they were there on business, in fact, on the very business that had aided her recovery from Dumped Fiancée to Normal Person, Posy wandered around the dismembered bits of The Memory Lane Fair. It was like a huge child's toy, ripped apart, each piece waiting to be lovingly slotted into the next to create magic.

Most of the intricate paintwork was jewel-bright and matched the splodges and streaks which decorated Jack Morland. What an amazing talent he had. And the ornate gold scrolled lettering was a work of art all on its own: Petronella Bradley's Golden Galloping Horses.

Petronella Bradley's Golden Galloping Horses seemed to take up most of the floor space. Petronella Bradley must be Nell, Jack's partner, and not just in the business judging by his body language when he mentioned her. Lucky Nell.

'. . . and this is the Limonaire . . .' Jack's voice rang high into the rafters. 'We're really lucky to have got it . . . and of course, if it was driven, as it should be, by a showman's engine, it'd look spectacular. Anyway, I'll just plug it into the mains now so that you get the picture.'

Flynn stood beside Posy and smiled down at her. 'Saved by the Crazy Gang, huh?'

'Yeah. I never liked them much before. Now I actively hate them.' She tried to sound flippant. 'Big mistake snogging one of your friends, anyway.'

'Snogging? Oh, right, you mean making out? Yeah, maybe.'

The Limonaire, a huge fairground organ, was set into the open side of a lorry, and a mass of glorious colours, pipes, drums, lights and carved figures started to creak and groan and flicker into life as Jack flicked the switch.

Entranced, Posy held her breath.

'Imagine this outside The Crooked Sixpence in the

darkness,' Flynn said softly. 'With Queen Mab all lit up too, and crowds of people.'

Jack, just visible up behind the pipes and drums, was feeding the concertina'd cardboard music book through the keyframe. With a wheeze and a drum roll, the lights flashed on, the figures started to move stiffly, and the shed was filled with loud, foot-tapping, happy music.

'My God!' Posy was awestruck. 'It's even better than I remembered it.'

Flynn said nothing. She looked up at him. He was miles away: probably with Queen Mab and glowing coals and hissing steam and the rocking motion, surrounded by the music of more than sixty years earlier.

The Crazy Gang book which had started all this, was flipping through the keyframe under Jack's expert guidance, filling the shed with classics such as 'Home Town' and 'Underneath the Arches' and 'Run Rabbit Run'. Posy, who was generally scathing about anything prior to the Backstreet Boys unless it was Adam Ant who she'd loved unashamedly through her youth, found her feet tapping and her head singing the words.

This was absolutely wonderful. It would bring the crowds into Steeple Fritton in droves and, more importantly, keep them coming back over and over again.

'What do you reckon?' Jack leaned out from behind the largest drum as soon as the music stopped. 'Are we in business?'

Posy, who could hear nothing but reverberations in her head, nodded wildly.

'Sure thing,' Flynn said. 'Let's exchange mobile numbers and get some dates worked out for you to come and take a look at Queen Mab.'

Jack leapt athletically out of the organ lorry and he and Flynn were immediately nose to nose.

Posy wandered across to where the galloping horses were stacked side by side after having been given their new livery for the travelling season. She stroked a stiff varnished golden mane. Petronella . . . the name was inscribed in a scroll along the horse's arched neck surrounded by tiny scarlet hearts. Posy smiled. What a declaration of love from Jack the painter to Nell the owner. There must be one heck of a story there somewhere.

'Posy,' Flynn's voice broke through the hearts and flowers. 'I know we could both stay here forever, but I guess we really should be going. I'm a bit concerned about Lola.'

'Yes, of course. Me too. And if she isn't back we'll have to open up The Crooked Sixpence.' She grinned at Jack. 'This has been absolutely brilliant. Thank you so much for agreeing to do the carnival and the pub, and no doubt we'll see you soon.'

'Count on it.'

Outside again, blinking in the sunlight, she grinned at Flynn. 'Sorted?'

He gave her a high-five, then hugged her. 'Sorted.'

Chapter Twenty-one

Nearly midnight. She'd have to make a move soon. The Mucky Duck's bar was practically empty and the very young barman was already growing restless. But where was she supposed to go? Not back to Steeple Fritton, that was for sure. Not yet. Not until Barbara bloody Marion was long gone.

Lola stood up slowly, and smiled as she approached the bar, knowing only too well how tired this boy must be. She'd already tipped him far more than she could afford out of solidarity. 'Another G&T, please. Could you make it a double? Thank you.'

'Are you a resident?' The barman stifled a yawn. 'I can only serve residents after half eleven.'

Lola sighed. At least it would solve one problem for tonight. She had no transport and nowhere else to go. 'Not at the moment, but I'll just go and book a room.'

The barman shrugged and started putting together another double G&T as Lola hurried out of the bar and into reception. As this was possibly the smallest hotel ever created, it only took five strides.

The woman who appeared inside the reception cubicle looked as though she was well used to strange females without luggage booking bedrooms in The Mucky Duck at the last minute.

'They're all doubles. All with facilities. Will that be with breakfast?'

'Oh, um, yes . . . I think so . . . thank you.'

'For one or two?'

'One of course.'

'No "of course" about it, love. Not in this game. Pay up front, sign here, there's yer key. Breakfast between seven thirty and nine. Not a minute earlier nor a second later. Good night.'

The drink was on the bar when she returned and the barman really looked as though he'd fallen asleep on his feet.

'Sorry,' Lola said quietly. 'I'm in Room 25. Could you put it on my tab?'

'Sure,' he raised a lethargic hand.

She resumed her seat. Two men, probably reps, watched her, half-smiled, and, getting no response, settled moodily back to their pints.

Lola sighed. She'd run away. She'd never run away from anything before, but now, just when life was wonderful again, she'd turned tail and run. While common sense told her that she should have stayed and faced up to Barbara, instinct had insisted that she should get out of Sunny Dene and Steeple Fritton, and quickly.

Barbara had no reason to hound her now. That part of her life was over. Barbara had everything: the money, the businesses, the properties, even, by now, the damn hatchback.

There was no reason at all why Barbara Marion should need to confront her. Was there?

She sipped the G&T. It was her fourth and she was still nowhere near the state of blissful oblivion she'd hoped for. If only she'd told someone. But there had simply been no one around to tell – not last night and certainly not this morning when she'd made her decision to flee. All day she'd wandered round shops and had cups of coffee she didn't want in noisy cafés, and all the time she'd promised herself that she'd go home and face Barbara – even if it meant washing a whole lifetime's worth of dirty linen in public.

But when it came to it, she simply couldn't do it. Cowardly, she knew. But facing Barbara Marion was like facing up to a suspect lump and thinking that given a day or two it may well disappear.

She should tell someone though . . . Anyone . . . They'd be worried about her . . .

The realization that there were people who might truly be concerned at her unexplained disappearance suddenly made her want to cry. No one had ever cared before. There had never been anyone to notice.

'Excuse me,' she signalled to the barman. 'Is there a phone I could use, please?'

'Here. Corner of the bar.' He didn't move; didn't look as though he could.

Lola walked over to the phone, and realized she knew no Steeple Fritton telephone numbers at all. As there was no sign of a directory, she'd have to throw herself on the mercy of the Dalek-voiced Directory Enquiries. So? Who to call? Not Sunny Dene. At this time of night everyone would be in bed. She couldn't disturb them.

The Crooked Sixpence? She doubted if the payphone in the entrance would even be listed and Flynn would be long gone.

Of course, there really was only one person she wanted to talk to. Only one person who may well be in bed at this hour but who would probably be awake . . .

She dialled 192 and asked for Glad Blissit's number. After a lot of clicking and whirring the nasal voice informed her that it was ex-directory. Lola could have screamed. Why the hell would Glad of all people want to be ex-directory? What did she have to be all secretive about? Anyway, Ellis probably wasn't there. He was bound to be with Tatty . . .

She dialled 192 again, and against her better judgement, asked for Tatty Spry's number. She couldn't not be listed, could she? She ran a business for heaven's sake.

The nasal voice sounded more optimistic this time as it intoned the number. Lola, not having a pen handy, grabbed at a cocktail stick and indented the figures into a beer mat.

The phone seemed to ring forever. Trying not to think of disturbing Tatty and Ellis in the middle of a sexual marathon, and pushing the awful vision of a slender and naked Tatty rushing to the phone wearing nothing but her waist-length curls and a lot of jangly necklaces and bangles while Ellis implored her to hurry back to bed, Lola almost gave up.

'Hiya. Tatty Spry. Alternative therapies. Massage. Oh, and tattooing. How may I help you?'

She'd never been so pleased to hear Tatty's voice. 'Tatty? It's Lola. So sorry to disturb you so late at night – oh, and I hope I haven't woken the children . . .'

'Not at all. They're all watching *The Blair Witch Project* on Sky. It's one of their favourites but they only enjoy it in darkness. Doesn't seem so scary in daylight, does it?'

'Er, no . . . um, Tatty, is Ellis there with you?'

'No, I haven't seen him tonight. He's probably at Glad's. He was looking for you earlier, though. All over the place. Getting in quite a state. He'll be pleased to see you. Why don't you pop round?'

'I'm not in Steeple Fritton. I'm, um, somewhere else. You wouldn't have Glad's number, would you?'

Tatty reeled it off. Of course she'd know it, Lola thought, as she scratched it on to the beer mat. Tatty and Glad were friends. It wasn't simply because of Ellis that the numbers tripped so readily from her tongue.

'Thanks. Really. Sorry to have bothered you.'

'No bother. Pleased that you're all right. Ellis thought something had happened to you. I think he's got quite a crush on you.'

'No!' Lola's emphatic denial jolted the barman from his torpor. 'I mean, no, we're just friends. I really wanted to let him know that I'm okay.'

'That's fine then,' Tatty's voice held a lazy smile. 'Oh, look, shall I give you his mobile number, too? Glad is probably asleep and she gets right nasty if she don't get her eight hours.'

Once again, Lola made stabbing hieroglyphics into the beer mat.

Tatty's voice smiled again. 'Got that? Good. Look, Lola, it's lovely to chat, but I'm in the middle of doing the new brochures for the tattoo parlour on my Apple Mac, and I want to catch the end of the film, too.'

'Right. Of course. Sorry. Thanks again. See you soon.'

'Yeah. See you.'

By now, the barman and the two reps were hanging on every word. Lola picked up the beer mat and squinted at the pinpricks. There were more scratches and holes than mat. Bugger. Feeding more money into the phone, she thumped out what she hoped was Ellis's mobile number.

Of course, she realized as she did so, she could have just given her message to Tatty, couldn't she? She could easily have left it to Tatty to pass on the glad tidings that she was alive and well and staying at The Mucky Duck. The Steeple Fritton bush telegraph was faster than any e-mail system. There was absolutely no need to speak to Ellis.

'Hi . . .'

Oh dear . . . Lola stared into the phone. No . . . Surely not? Not just at the sound of his voice? She whimpered at her own foolishness. 'Er, Ellis. It's me . . .'

'Lola! Where the hell are you? Are you okay? I've been frantic. Everyone's been frantic. What the hell is going on?'

'I'm sorry. I'm fine, honestly. I just had, er, had some stuff to do. Look, could you tell them at Sunny Dene that I'm safe, and I apologize for bothering people, oh, and ask Flynn to take care of the pub for a bit, and see if Posy will help out and –'

'Where are you?'

'It doesn't matter –'

'Yes, it does. Where are you?'

'Oh, some little place between Newbury and Andover. Micklesham.'

'Right. Where in Micklesham?'

304

'Ellis, it doesn't matter where I –'

'Where are you staying? Are you alone?'

'Of course I'm alone! I'm always bloody alone! No, sorry. Oh, it's a little inn-cum-hotel called The Mucky Duck, which I think is meant to be a joke, but –'

'Fine. I presume there's a bar?'

'Yes, I'm in it now.'

'Great. Get me a Jack Daniel's and a can of Coke in and I'll be with you in about half an hour.'

'Ellis! No!'

But the phone was dead. Impatiently she redialled. This time, Ellis's phone was switched off.

The barman and the reps had perked up considerably. The Mucky Duck probably hadn't seen this much action for years. Lola, ignoring the curious faces, ordered another G&T and the JD and Coke, and returned to her seat.

Ellis arrived twenty minutes later. The minibus, Lola thought, was probably smoking in the car park. He was wearing his faded black jeans and a big denim shirt over a white T-shirt. The barman woke up and preened himself. The reps didn't.

Deliberately trying not to look absolutely delighted to see him, she fixed a so-so smile as he walked across the bar towards her. 'This is so kind of you, but really there was no need . . .'

'There was every need,' Ellis pulled his chair closer to hers, and fizzed the Coke into the JD. 'I'm so bloody pleased to see you. Are you all right?'

'Perfectly. I didn't mean to drag you out.'

Ellis took a long drink, then leaned back in his chair.

305

'I've been worried sick. Everyone's been worried sick. We didn't know what had happened. I thought . . . I thought . . .'

'What?'

'That it was my fault, because of yesterday and the ankle bracelets and the kiss and everything.'

She shook her head. 'Nothing like that. Look –' she pulled up the leg of her jeans to show him the bracelets still sliding against her skin. 'They're still there. Yesterday was one of the best days of my life. And the kiss,' she smiled at him, 'didn't insult me at all. Far from it. As you well know. No, it was just something that happened after you'd left me, something that scared me, bothered me, oh, made me angry after such a perfect day.'

She told him about Barbara Marion booking into Sunny Dene.

'God, is that who she is? What an old witch! She's evil. She's been everywhere asking questions and demanding information. She's put everyone's backs up. The coven were going to run her out of town and Gran had to be prevented from decking her in the corner shop. And she was so rude to Dilys and Norrie at the B&B, Posy said Dilys had to be restrained from dumping a casserole on her head.'

Lola laughed. 'I wish she'd done it! No, seriously, I have no idea why Barbara is there, but I just don't want to see her. I suppose she knows I live there?'

'Guess so. She must have known that before she arrived, and if she asked for confirmation and pretended to be a friend, then Dom would have said yes, even if the others may have been a bit more wary. I wonder who told her where to find you?'

306

Lola had puzzled over the same question all day over the umpteen cups of coffee in the umpteen cafés. She'd been in touch with so few people since she'd arrived in Steeple Fritton. Sheila, Jenny and Mo, her girlfriends from Swansbury, would sooner die than reveal her whereabouts to Barbara. Which, sadly, left only one person.

'I think it was probably my cousin, Mimi. She really doesn't like me at all, thinks that by being Nigel's mistress I was going to somehow ensnare her husband. She'd feel it was striking a blow for cheated-on-wives everywhere by snitching. Although how on earth Barbara bloody Marion managed to get hold of her, I'll never know.'

'Maybe you should ask her.'

'Maybe . . .' Lola sighed. 'I know you'll think I'm a coward to have run away. I just didn't know what else to do. I really hoped I'd left the past behind me. I truly don't want it all raked up again. And Nigel's dead. There's no point . . .'

Ellis finished his drink. 'There doesn't seem to be, no. But honestly, until you face her and find out what she wants, you'll never know, will you? How did you get here, anyway?'

She told him briefly of catching the early morning bus from Steeple Fritton to Newbury, the day spent in the town, then catching the second bus to anywhere, which had terminated in Micklesham.

'Jesus! I've been in bloody Newbury today with Gran and the coven. I didn't even think of looking for you there.'

'Why would you? Anyway, I spent most of it hiding

307

in cafés, trying to summon up the courage to go back to Steeple Fritton.'

'You poor thing,' he leaned forward and took her hand. 'So, are you feeling brave enough now?'

She was suddenly feeling a lot of things. Brave wasn't top of the list.

'Maybe tomorrow. I've booked a room for the night and I'll get the bus back in the morning. Don't worry about me.'

'I'm closing the bar,' the barman announced, not even trying to disguise his yawning. 'Anyone want anything else?'

The reps belted up with their glasses.

Ellis looked at her. 'Do you want another?'

'No thanks. And you should be going. You won't be up for school otherwise.'

'Yes, Mum.' He grinned. 'Are you reminding me that as of yesterday I'm twenty-six years younger than you?'

'No, honestly. I meant for the school run . . .'

Ellis released her hand, pushed his chair back and stood up. Making a big deal of swirling melted ice over the withered bit of lemon in the bottom of her glass, Lola didn't look at him. She couldn't let him see that she was sorry he was leaving. She heard him walk away, and sighed. Well, why would he stay? He'd found her, knew she was all right, and he had loads of things to do in Steeple Fritton.

'Come on, then.' He was standing beside her, another JD and G&T on a tray. 'Lead me to your boudoir.'

Ridiculously pleased, embarrassed, and totally panic-stricken all at the same time, she shook her head. 'We can't . . . I mean, I can't . . .'

'Don't be silly,' he smiled. 'I'll sleep on the floor, or in a chair, or somewhere, and run you home in the morning. I'm not leaving you on your own when you're unhappy. And we can talk in your room. It's got to be better than here.'

Not knowing if Room 25 even had a chair, but assuming that it would have floor space, and not wishing to spend another minute under the scrutiny of the reps and the barman, Lola stood up. 'Yes, sure. Silly of me. I'm just not used to this sort of thing.'

Room 25, when they found it at the top of an ochre-coloured staircase, was slightly more depressing than the bar had been.

Very cold, with overhead lighting, 1970s furniture, a heart-rending print of a soaking-wet puppy, and an all-in-one colour scheme reminiscent of the filling of a mushroom vol-au-vent, it would hardly lift anyone's spirits.

'It's got a candlewick bedspread!' Ellis said delightedly, bouncing on the bed. 'I haven't seen one of those for years. Oh, and flannelette sheets in pastel stripes! It's brilliantly retro.'

'It's tacky and old-fashioned,' Lola smiled. His enthusiasm obviously knew no bounds. 'I don't think I even want to look at the bathroom.'

Ellis padded across the room and pulled open the adjoining door. 'Nope. You're right. You don't. Still, I'm sure we can still make it more cosy in here. You go and have a quick whatever in the bathroom with your eyes closed while I sort things out.'

'I, um, haven't got any clothes . . . no dressing gown, nothing . . .'

'Here,' Ellis peeled off the denim shirt and handed it to her. 'It should just about cover your modesty.'

Lola clutched it and fled into the bathroom. She looked at the shirt. It may well cover her modesty, but there was no way it would cover the sags, bags and wrinkles . . .

The bathroom was every bit as bad as she'd anticipated, and being very aware of Ellis happily singing 'Goody Goody Gumdrops' only an inch of plywood away, it meant that her ablutions were completed in record time.

She peered out of the door and laughed. The room had been transformed. Two pink-shaded lamps provided a soft-focus glow, the candlewick bedspread had been peeled back to reveal a rather faded rose-strewn eiderdown, and the sad puppy picture had disappeared.

'Oh, Laurence Llewelyn-Bowen eat your heart out! How did you manage this?'

'A bit of shifting around, digging out a couple of lamps that were in the bottom of the wardrobe. Makes all the difference.' Ellis stopped and looked at her. 'Wow!'

She pulled the denim shirt even closer. It hung from her shoulders and skimmed the tops of her thighs. Practically every fifty-year-old bit of her was on display.

'Er, I think I'd like to get into bed now. And don't say anything flippant, please. I'm embarrassed.'

'Don't be. You look amazing, and didn't I tell you that the ankle bracelets would give you a real edge?'

She looked down at her bare feet on the brown and orange floral carpet, at the three strands of silver looped above her ankle bone, and nodded. He was right. They looked very sassy and made her feel . . . well, suffice it to say that she didn't feel in the least like a fifty-year-old PA specializing in fancy biscuits.

'God, it's freezing in here, I need to get into bed – oh, damn, don't grin like that.'

'Me?' Ellis retreated to a far corner of the room and exaggeratedly squeezed his eyes shut. 'I'm doing nothing, seeing nothing, saying nothing. Just hurry up.'

Smiling to herself, Lola climbed into bed. It really was surprisingly comfortable, with soft pillows, and the heaviness of the blankets and eiderdown made her feel safe and snug – like she had as a child.

'Okay?' He opened one eye. 'Can I look now?'

'Thanks for not making it awkward. And thanks for being here tonight. I feel such a fool.'

Ellis carried the drinks tray to the bed, then sat on the end and handed her her glass. 'Here's to fools, then, because I've felt like a complete one all day.'

'You? Why?'

'Because I thought you'd gone for good and it was driving me crazy, not being able to do anything about it. And Posy and Flynn were being really vague and casual about it, like it was no big deal at all. And then I had to take the coven and their cronies into Newbury and all the time I wanted to find you and talk to you and I couldn't. I don't even have your mobile number.'

'Haven't got one.'

'You must have. Everyone has.'

'I haven't. Not any more. It wasn't mine, was it? Like everything else it belonged to bloody Marionette Biscuits.'

Ellis looked at her over the rim of his glass. 'Do you know, the more I hear about your set-up with the Biscuit King, the less I like it. And it's not just territorial jealousy. I think he behaved like a shit.'

Lola let the gin trickle down her throat and didn't answer. She couldn't bear to hear Nigel criticized, and yet . . . and yet . . . 'Do you mind if we don't talk about anything remotely connected to any of the Marions? Not tonight.'

'Of course.' He stared at her for a moment. 'Are you hungry?'

'I take it you are referring to food and not being euphemistic? Yes, then. A bit. I haven't eaten all day. Felt too sick. Why? Are you?'

'Yeah, but then I always am. It's my youth, you see. Shall I go and see what The Mucky Duck has to offer by way of room service?'

'This isn't Colworth Manor or some glitzy five-star establishment. Everything will be barred and bolted.'

'Maybe. Maybe not. Give me a couple of minutes.'

As soon as he'd gone the room seemed smaller, duller, emptier. Lola pulled the covers up to her neck and snuggled into the bed's growing warmth. It was wonderful to be here, safe, happy, drowsy . . . and with Ellis.

Nothing would come of the relationship, she knew that. The age difference was too huge. They were a lifetime apart. And she knew he'd sleep with her if she asked him to, because it was what they both wanted, and that they'd both enjoy it. But she couldn't because it wouldn't be forever. And this time, forever was what she had to have.

The door burst open again.

'*Voilà!*'

'That was quick. Don't tell me there were minions

just waiting downstairs to take orders from unregistered guests?'

Ellis dumped crackers, cheese, chocolate biscuits and a bottle of water on to the eiderdown. 'No such luck. But there was an unlocked kitchen cupboard or three. Don't look so worried. I left a fiver on the table.'

The picnic was almost as good as their previous one in Christ Church Meadows.

As they ate, Ellis chatted about Flynn and Lola taking the misrouted package to Fox Hollow and all the amazing events that had materialized from the meeting with Jack Morland. About how Letting Off Steam was going to be the theme for Steeple Fritton and the carnival, and how everything seemed to have fallen neatly into place – just so long as she gave the go-ahead for Queen Mab and the fairground organ to be outside the pub, and Posy's meeting with the parish council came up trumps.

'It all sounds fantastic,' Lola brushed biscuit crumbs from the eiderdown. 'And these people own a proper funfair as well, do they?'

Ellis nodded. 'Apparently it's called The Memory Lane Fair, all traditional rides, nothing new or white-knuckle. Flynn and Posy couldn't stop talking about it. Of course,' he grinned at her, 'they had to explain everything to me, me not remembering anything before scary, hydraulic, fibreglass fairground attractions. For you, being so ancient, it would probably be far more familiar.'

'Bastard!' Lola snatched at a pillow and aimed it at his head.

'Crone!'

'Toyboy!'

'Cradle-snatcher!'

She sat up indignantly, trying not to laugh. 'Oh, I'm far from that. My one and only lover was almost old enough to be my father, remember?'

'How could I forget?' Ellis stood up and replaced the pillow behind her head. 'Maybe it's time to alter that situation.'

He leaned down and kissed her. With the denim shirt sliding from her shoulders she kissed him back.

'You were going to sleep on the chair,' she said as he pulled back the covers.

'There isn't one.'

'Oh, no, there isn't is there? Oh, dear, what a pity . . .'

Chapter Twenty-two

'Breakfast for one, you said.' The woman from the reception cubicle glared accusingly across The Mucky Duck's over-flounced dining room the following morning. 'I distinctly remember. In fact, if I may remind you, your words were –'

Lola beamed. 'I know. And you were kind enough to point out that breakfast for one rarely happened here, and you were absolutely right, so, now it's breakfast for two.'

'*Bed* and breakfast for two?'

'Oh, yes . . .' Lola sighed. 'Oh, yes, definitely. Of course I'll pay the extra.'

'Is the young gentleman not paying, then?'

'God, no.' Ellis looked horrified across the regiment of sauce bottles. 'We teenage gigolos don't pay for *anything*.'

It was, Lola discovered, almost impossible to eat a Full English while holding hands across the table and laughing a lot, but they managed it.

Emerging from The Mucky Duck into a murky, close,

April morning, she couldn't remember when she'd last felt like this. Never, she thought. Absolutely never . . . And so what if it wouldn't last, couldn't last. She'd been wrong; forget forever: seize the moment was going to be her new motto.

Ellis pulled her towards him in the car park. 'Okay?'

'What? Your performance? Hmmm, I suppose so . . . Not bad.'

He kissed her. 'You could do with a bit of practice yourself.'

'We'll have to arrange something. And please don't kiss me again or I might just have to rush you back to the boudoir.'

'Insatiable,' Ellis said happily, sliding open the minibus's door for her. 'That's what I love about you older women.'

They drove back to Steeple Fritton holding hands on the steering wheel and singing 'Simon Says' very loudly.

The euphoria lasted until they arrived outside Sunny Dene.

'Don't worry,' Ellis hugged her. 'I've phoned ahead and arranged that Flynn and Posy will take over the school run, the courier drops, and the food parcels for the rich and famous. I'll be here in Sunny Dene cheering you on. I'm not going to leave you to face that old bag alone.'

'She'll probably say a lot of things you won't want to hear.'

'Lola,' Ellis took her face in his hands, 'she was your lover's wife. She's venomous by nature and she hates you. Of course she's going to say stuff neither of us likes, but none of it will be news to me, will it? Don't let it bother you. Just face up to her, listen to her, have your say, and walk away from her. Then it's over.'

Lola took a deep breath. It was the confrontation she'd dreaded, and yet now, because of last night and this morning and Ellis, she felt as though she could take on the world.

She nodded. 'Okay, but I have to see her on my own.'

'I understand that. But I'll only be in the hall. With Trevor and Kenneth primed and at the ready. Within screaming distance.'

'Her screams or mine?'

'Hers, definitely. I've got first-hand knowledge of what damage you can inflict with your fingernails.'

Lola was still smiling when she walked into Sunny Dene's flagged hall.

As Ellis had also had the foresight to phone Dilys and Norrie and tell them that Lola was fine and on her way back, there were no welcome parties in evidence. Barbara, they'd said, would be waiting in the visitors' lounge. With her heart thumping, and a dry mouth, Lola opened the lounge door.

Barbara Marion, dark and gaunt, was reading a newspaper. At least, Lola felt, as she was standing it gave her a slight advantage.

She cleared her throat. 'I understand you're looking for me?'

'Miss Wentworth, at last.' Without looking up, Barbara slowly folded the newspaper. 'And yes, you understand correctly.'

317

Lola shifted her feet. 'Well, I'm here, but I'm extremely busy and don't have long, so please say whatever it is you need to say and then leave.'

'All in good time. I'm here to tell you a few home truths, something I would have done earlier if you hadn't skedaddled so damn quickly. I went through everything in your tacky little love nest prior to selling it – appalling taste, by the way. Yours or my dear husband's?'

'Both . . .' Lola felt the lump growing in her throat. 'And?'

'And you'd covered your traces very well. Disappeared into thin air. You must have walked away with nothing, you poor fool. Toby Everton, my solicitor, helped with the inventory and –'

'What inventory?'

'The flat's inventory, you stupid woman.'

'But why would the flat have an inventory? It was my home, and Nigel bought it –'

'As an asset,' Barbara's hooded eyes flashed. 'A tax dodge. Officially a place to entertain customers. The flat, fixtures and fittings, belonged to the Marionette Biscuits empire. It was never meant to be anyone's permanent home.'

'Yes it was!' Lola blinked. 'It was Nigel's flat, our flat. He was going to live with me there after he'd retired –'

'No, he wasn't. He was never going to live with you. The flat was tied up with the business. It would have become the property of the new MD on Nigel's retirement. Only, of course, he died before retiring because he wouldn't hand over the reins at a sensible age and –'

Lola shook her head. No! Surely not! But that meant . . .

that meant that Nigel had *lied* about their future and about everything else. Absolutely everything.

She took a gulp of air. 'Toby Everton told me that the flat became your property as part of the estate, but he said nothing about it being a business asset. I'm sorry, but I don't believe you.'

Barbara pulled a face. 'Do you think I care if you believe me or not? I'm merely giving you the facts. Toby Everton is too soft-hearted for his own good. He told you to leave the flat because it was mine under the terms of the will. Because of the circumstances, he had no need to tell you that you'd have been out on your ear when Nigel retired, so he didn't. He will, of course, confirm this now if you wish to ask him.'

'But, but he, Toby Everton, said that Nigel adored me!'

Barbara laughed. 'Yes, I'm sure he did. I'm also sure Nigel was totally enamoured of you. Nigel always did have an eye for a pretty woman. But he would never have lived with you, and certainly not in your beloved apartment. That was never on the cards.'

'But why are you telling me all this now?'

'Because you thought that Nigel loved you more than anything or anyone.' Barbara's expression was still icy. 'I saw you at his funeral, completely distraught. But I wanted to take the happy memories away from you. I wanted you to be as miserable as sin for the rest of your life. Like I was for all the years I was married to him.'

'I don't want to hear any more,' Lola stood up. 'Whatever tax dodges Nigel pulled, he loved me. Really loved me. You'll never be able to take that away.'

'No?' Barbara stood up, too. Her voice was glacial.

319

'Then let me answer your first question and add a few facts of my own. Along with everything else relating to that flat, the phone bills, itemized, went to the Marionette accountant. I sat down and rang every bloody number that I didn't recognize.'

'But they were *my* phone calls!' Lola was appalled. 'You mean to say that you've checked on me via all my friends?'

'Yes, and it was your cousin, peculiar name, Mimi? Yes, your dear cousin Mimi who told me where to find you. I must say your other friends showed a great deal more loyalty than your family.'

Bloody Mimi! Lola groaned. She'd *known* it would be Mimi!

'However,' Barbara went on, 'it was during my phone-checking that I discovered one or two other pieces of information which I simply couldn't wait to share with you. Things which came as a shock to me, and even to Toby Everton. Nigel had more secrets than anyone ever knew.'

'I don't want to hear this. Nothing more. I'm honestly not interested in your petty, mean-minded schemes to get back at Nigel. Or me. There's no point –'

'There's every point, as I told you before. I want you to know what a complete bastard you threw the best part of your life away on. Like I did. I want you to despise him and to know what it's like to be made a fool of. Much as I hate to say this, Miss Wentworth, I think we're very much in the same boat.'

'Oh, please! Hardly.'

Barbara Marion straightened her severe cream suit. 'During the course of my, er, investigations I discovered that Nigel had two other homes and two other women in his life.'

Sunny Dene's lounge dipped and swayed. Lola clutched on to the armchair for support. 'You're lying. He couldn't. Wouldn't . . .'

Barbara smiled. The smile was mocking and cold. 'One in Bradford and one in Truro. Do those places mean anything to you?'

Lola took deep breaths, trying to steady herself. 'Well, yes, of course they do. I contacted them practically every day when I was at work. They're the towns where the other Marionette Biscuits factories are, I mean, were . . .'

'Exactly. And my dear husband, and your loyal lover, had a home and a mistress in each one. In fact, the woman in Truro even managed to produce a bastard by him. The child is fifteen now.'

Lola tried very hard not to laugh. If she laughed she'd become hysterical which really wouldn't help. This was all like something out of Catherine Cookson.

'I'm sorry, but Nigel wouldn't . . .'

'He would, could and did. And again, Toby Everton will confirm all this if you'd prefer to hear it from him. The only satisfaction I gained was discovering that, because of his sudden death, he'd made no provisions for these, these, tarts any more than he did for you.'

Lola had never really wanted to hit anyone in her life before. She had never felt roused to violence. Now she longed to fly at Barbara Marion and pummel her into the ground. She closed her eyes for a second and took deep gulping breaths until the feeling subsided slightly.

'I want you to leave now.'

'I'm going,' Barbara Marion smiled. 'I do so hope that I've managed to destroy your memories and ruin the rest of your life. Oh, and you may like to look at these . . .' She placed a pile of photographs and papers on the coffee table. 'Toby Everton has made copies. Evidence of Nigel's other women. Letters, property ownership, even photographs of him playing happy families in Bradford and Truro. Enjoy them. Goodbye, Miss Wentworth.'

Almost unaware that she was doing so, Lola held her breath until Barbara had left the room, then she released it in a huge juddering sigh. Feeling her way round the armchair, she lowered herself into it, averting her eyes from the pile of spite left by Barbara on the coffee table.

Too shocked to cry, she stared numbly out of the window. How could she have been so blind? How could she have been such a fool? Why had she not even thought that Nigel, cheating on Barbara, may well also be cheating on her? How could she have been naive enough to live a life that was a complete and utter lie?

Ellis, accompanied by a rather subdued Trevor and Kenneth, quietly opened the door and put a mug of tea on the table. 'Hot, strong, and three sugars. I know you don't take sugar but you need it, and a dash of brandy.' He slid his arm round her shoulders and kissed the top of her head. 'I expect you want to be left alone for a bit, but I'll still be here in the B&B somewhere. Okay?'

She looked up at him and nodded. 'Thank you. You heard?'

'Yes. All of it. I'm so sorry.'

'Me too. Especially as she was telling the truth.' She

tried to smile. 'Hell hath no fury and all that. Has she gone?'

'Oh, yes. Got Norrie to call a taxi to take her to Reading station. She's gone.'

'Good.' She looked into his eyes. 'I'd like to be on my own now. Just for a little while.'

'Of course. I'll be around when you need me. Okay?'

'Okay. And thank you. For all of it. And –' she motioned her head towards the pile of papers on the coffee table, 'could you take those away and lose them somewhere, please?'

'Sure.'

Ellis kissed her cheek and left the room. Trevor and Kenneth solemnly licked her hands, and settled down on either side of her. She picked up the steaming tea with one hand and fondled the dogs with the other. Then she started to cry.

It was nearly two o'clock when she emerged from her room. She'd sat in the lounge for hours, staring into space, remembering, crying. Now, having showered and changed, and given up on trying to get any make-up to make her bloated face look presentable, she walked slowly downstairs.

Ellis was in the garden with Dom, Norrie and Mr D and Mr B, playing with the model railway layout. She'd watched them from her window. Ellis would leave her now, she knew it. Even if last night hadn't been just a one-night stand, no man would want a woman who had been such a complete fool. And certainly not one more than twice his age. No fool like an old fool . . .

As she opened the French doors they all looked up

from shunting a goods train into some newly constructed sidings, and smiled kindly. Kindness, as Lola had discovered before, was far harder to take than censure. She blinked hard and smiled back.

Ellis moved away from the others. 'They know the gist of what's happened. Not the full details. No one will say anything. They're all your friends. They're on your side in this. How are you feeling?'

'Stupid. Confused. Hurt. Exhausted. Pretty awful, really.'

He nodded. 'Understandable. It must be like discovering you've been adopted or something. When everything you've believed in all your life turns out to be a big pretence. And everyone you've ever trusted is uncovered as a liar. It'll take a long time.'

'I know. It's also going to drive me crazy because I can't *ask* Nigel why he did it. Or how he really felt about me. Or anything. Barbara's done a good job.'

'She's a bitch. And a vindictive and hurt one. A dangerous combination. But, honestly, all you must cling on to is the thought that whatever else Nigel was doing in the time you were together, he made you happy. You made him happy. The time you were together was great, wasn't it? A lot of people don't ever have that.'

'I suppose not. It just all seems such a waste of my life.'

'Why? You spent it being happy. He may well have lived with you when he retired. It doesn't matter now. None of the "what if's" matter. He died. He's dead. You can't go back and change any of it. You had a wonderful time together, but now you've got to let go and move forward.'

Lola watched the dozens of tiny trains whizz round their intricate tracks, rattling through stations and halts, past miniature farms, over green rolling hills, and plunging into grey industrial towns. Sunny Dene's garden was springing into new life, perennial borders already plump with foliage, the lilac trees smelling sweet, the pollarded limes unfurling vivid leaves. Life beginning again.

She took a deep breath. 'Thanks for being here. And for understanding. And especially for the last couple of days. They were the best . . .'

'And for me.' Ellis stared at the trains, too. 'And we'll have plenty more. If you want to, that is. I mean, under the circumstances I'll understand if you don't want to see me.'

She scrubbed her fingers across her eyes. It didn't matter. There was no mascara to smudge. Without the mascara she knew she looked every one of her fifty years. 'Of course I want to see you. You've been . . . It's been . . .'

'Yeah,' Ellis smiled. 'It has, hasn't it? But you can call the shots. Just let me know when you're feeling okay . . . whatever.'

'And Tatty?'

'I'll tell Tatty. Tonight. I've never hurt anyone in my life, and Tatty doesn't deserve to be the first one.'

Lola sighed. 'No, she doesn't. But the age difference –'

'Doesn't matter to me. Or to you. And is no one else's concern. We'll be okay.'

She nodded. She thought they might be. Who could tell? Who could tell anything about relationships? No one could predict if they'd last or not – maybe the age difference would mean their odds were shorter than most. Maybe . . . And anyway, one thing was abundantly clear, nothing lasted forever. Why not grab a little transient happiness? It was better than the alternative, wasn't it?

'I suppose I ought to go into The Crooked Sixpence and start work.'

'Flynn and Posy have it all under control.' Ellis touched her cheek. 'They've been really worried about you and they send their love. I've told them the censored version and they'll do the evening shift as well. You just need to take care of yourself for a while. Go and have another brandy and go to bed for the rest of the afternoon.' He grinned. 'Alone. To sleep.'

She smiled at him. 'You're a very special man. Your tutor's wife must have been crazy to let you go.'

'I'm so pleased that she did, though. If she hadn't, I wouldn't have been here and I wouldn't have met you, and *that* would have been a tragedy, well, for me at least. Now go and get some sleep, and try not to think too much about Barbara fucking Marion and her evil spitefulness. She's gone and it's over. I'll call you later. Sleep well.'

Surprisingly, she did. A deep, exhausted, dreamless sleep that meant she woke feeling refreshed, if shaky and slightly sick. It was growing dark, and she switched on the bedside lamp. Nigel's face smiled at her from its frame.

'You old bastard.' She blinked away the threatening tears, and pushed the photograph into the top drawer of the cabinet. Maybe one day she'd throw it away. But not yet. Not just yet.

326

Not wanting to eat, and certainly not wanting to join in the happy frivolity echoing from Sunny Dene's dining room, Lola threw her black jacket over her jeans and sweater, and let herself out of the front door.

The Crooked Sixpence was early-evening busy. At least she hadn't interrupted Happy Hour or a karaoke night. As she walked in, everyone turned and looked at her. They knew. She held her breath. Everyone smiled. Kindly. She allowed her breath to escape in a sigh, and smiled back. It was going to be okay.

Glad, Rose Lusty and Vi Bickeridge were clustered round the jukebox and all waved cheerily. Of course, Lola thought, Tatty wouldn't be with them tonight. Tatty would be with Ellis. And probably crying.

'Nice to see you,' Vi shrilled. 'We've missed you, haven't we girls?'

The 'girls' nodded vigorously.

'Hope you gave that old witch a proper pasting,' Rose said. 'She was ever so rude about the facilities in my salon.'

'We don't want to be talking about her,' Glad frowned. 'Young Ellis says she's been sent packing. Poor Lola's been through enough. Anyhow, duck, it's got Gloria Gaynor on here. "I Will Survive". Reckon that ought to be our anthem, don't you?'

Lola nodded, unable to speak. No doubt Glad knew more than she was letting on about the previous night – Lola and her beloved grandson both missing from the village until after breakfast – but even so, the coven had accepted her into the sisterhood. It was all too much.

'Come and chuck a few arrers,' the Pink twins exhorted from the oche, as though they'd been playing darts all their lives. 'We're pretty nifty at 501 now, but we'll let you win seeing as Glad says you're going through a rough patch.'

'That's really kind of you. Maybe later.'

'And as we haven't got the old hokey-cokey machine going tonight, I'll play some really nice tunes to cheer us up, shall I?' Neddy waggled his accordion towards her. 'Nothing like a good old sing-along to "The Old Rugged Cross" to lift the spirits.'

'That'd be great. I'll, um, look forward to it.'

By the time she reached the bar, she was almost laughing.

Posy paused in pulling a pint and rushed out and hugged her. 'Oh, I'm so glad you're okay. Ellis told us. It must have been bloody awful.'

'It wasn't great,' Lola muttered into Posy's mass of curls. 'Thanks so much for all your help, and for being such a good friend.'

'Don't be daft. I owe you. I behaved like a real spoiled brat at the beginning. Too wrapped up in myself to have any time for anyone else. And you've changed my life too.'

'Okay,' Flynn moved Posy gently aside. 'That's enough girlie stuff or we'll all be in tears. Can you go and stop the Pinks wrecking the dartboard – again?' He waited until Posy was out of earshot, then looked down at Lola. 'It must have been hell. Is it all over now?'

Lola nodded.

'Great,' he kissed her cheek. 'I'm so glad. And you haven't come in here to work, I hope? Because tonight is your night off and we've got it under control here. So what would you like?'

'A G&T please, and thank you both so much. Oh, that's totally inadequate. I don't know what to say.'

'Don't say anything.' Flynn grinned at her. 'Go and sit by the fire. Ellis will be in later. I'll bring your drink over.'

He did, and squeezed her hand again. 'Be happy.'

'You know, don't you? About Ellis?'

'Sure. Boys talk too, you know. He's over the moon. I think it's really cool.'

'Do you?'

'Believe it. Hey, if someone as gorgeous, elegant, and sexy as you had come along when I was twenty-four I'd've *known* I'd died and gone to heaven.'

Lola was still smiling when the door flew open and Tatty, in her usual multicoloured layers and a lot of frills, squinted round the bar. Spotting Lola, she beamed, and pushed her way across to the fireplace.

'Hi, is everything okay now? Did you get hold of Ellis last night?'

Oh, yes . . . Lola thought. Oh, definitely yes, yes, yes. She pulled herself up quickly. 'Yes, thanks. Er, haven't you seen him today, then?'

Tatty shook her ringlets. A lot of her tinkled. 'I haven't set eyes on him. Which is why I'm here. His damn mobile's been switched off for hours. Mind you, I've been far too busy all day mugging up on the tattooing. Rose is lending me young Malvina as a trainee. We're going to share her, and we've been working out designs and practising. I want to be up and running with the tattoo parlour next week.'

'Great . . . great.' Managing to smile, Lola groaned inwardly. 'Um, actually I think Ellis'll be in here later.'

'I do hope so,' Tatty lifted her gypsy skirts and sank into the opposite chair. 'And I hope he won't be too long because I've left Clive Bickeridge baby-sitting the kiddies and between you and me he has no control over them at all.'

'Really? You surprise me.'

Tatty turned her head towards the bar. 'I really, really fancy a double brandy. I'm exhausted, but I think it'll just have to be a bitter lemon.' She smiled at Lola again. 'Actually I'm looking for Ellis because I've got some really, really good news and I want to share it with him.'

'About the tattooing?' Lola asked, feeling as guilty as sin. Tatty was so damn *nice*.

Tatty shook her ringlets and jewellery vehemently. 'No – oh, I'm just bursting to tell someone, and you're such a good friend, only promise you'll keep it to yourself for the time being?'

'Promise.'

'Well . . . there's something that I've known about for ages but hadn't done anything about properly because I'm usually okay dealing with it myself, you know how it is?'

'Yes,' said Lola, who didn't have a clue what Tatty was talking about. 'It must be good news though, the way you're smiling.'

'Oh, it is.' Tatty beamed. 'The best. You see, today I've been to the doctor, and she's confirmed that I'm pregnant again.'

Chapter Twenty-three

Posy thought that the parish council meeting had gone really well, all things considered. At least everyone had stayed awake and the vicar hadn't shouted too much and no one had raised the old chestnut of what was going to happen if it rained.

Fortunately they'd voted unanimously for the Letting Off Steam nametag, and had been visibly bowled over by the news about The Memory Lane Fair. The discussion about the Limonaire organ playing outside The Crooked Sixpence had caused slightly more uproar. Clive Bickeridge had been assigned to check out the bylaws. It also had been agreed that Queen Mab was to lead a procession of floats around the village, and the carnival queen competition was to take place at the end of May.

Posters and flyers were now being designed by the Townswomen's Guild. Proper posters this time, not the hand-written jobs of months earlier, which would be produced and laminated by the vicar's wife who had obtained the equipment 'ever so cheap, considering' from the shopping channel in the mistaken belief that it might make the hymn sheets last a little longer. Stalls had been allocated, and jobs allotted. Everything now seemed to be well in hand for making Steeple Fritton's Letting Off Steam one of the biggest events on the county's calendar.

And next week, Jack Morland and Nell Bradley were coming over to spend an evening with her and Flynn to talk about the fair and the traction engine, and to meet everyone else involved. Dom had returned to university, with Sunny Dene well and truly in the black for the first time in ages. The karaoke nights were bringing in punters from miles around, not to mention all the other Fritton-saving ventures they'd thought up really doing the business.

There were just a couple of niggling 'if onlys' blotting Posy's immediate horizon.

If only she hadn't been so damn boyish when Flynn had said he'd kiss her at Fox Hollow. If only, for once, she'd behaved properly and stood on tiptoe and fluttered her eyelashes and damn well done it. Now all she had was the memory of that slow, erotic finger-stroking, and the fact that she really, really, really liked him – and having turned him down once, he'd never give her a second opportunity to show him how she really felt.

Added to that, if only Lola wasn't behaving so strangely, life would be pretty near perfect.

Still, Posy thought, as she escaped from the village hall and headed for her evening shift in The Crooked Sixpence, Lola had been through a hell of a lot recently. She was entitled to be a bit withdrawn.

The news that Lola's Nigel had been a Love Rat hadn't

pleased Posy as she'd thought it would. So many things had changed in the last few months – not least her own intolerance. Lola's pain was tangible, and grossly unfair. And there was something really strange going on between her and Ellis, too. Try as she might, Posy couldn't get either of them to talk about it – although the news of Tatty's pregnancy didn't seem to have delighted anyone very much, except Tatty, of course.

The pregnancy had been the main topic of village conversation for two weeks now, eclipsing the reopening of the tattoo parlour, the initial success of Posy's Gear Change, the inception of Letting Off Steam, and even Barbara Marion's shattering disclosures. As she'd suspected, her own dumping-and-replacement-by-Sonia was now ancient history.

Ellis refused to be drawn but looked as though someone had given him a one-way ticket to Afghanistan. Glad was openly furious with Ellis. Dilys and Norrie and most of Steeple Fritton were crowing with 'I told you so' faces. Only Tatty was radiantly happy, grabbing anyone who stood still long enough, to ask their opinions on the chosen names, which sadly hadn't been Horatio and Hebe as Posy had forecast, but were currently Mercutio and Silva.

The April evening was closing in, but was still as warm as the day had been. Several people were drinking outside The Crooked Sixpence in the twilight, and they called greetings to her as she passed. Inside, Marc Bolan was boogieing from the jukebox and the place was about half full.

Still smiling, Posy was halfway across the pub before

she saw that Lola and Flynn were behind the bar – and in each other's arms.

No! The shaft of jealousy that shot through her took her breath away. Not Lola and Flynn! She suddenly realized that she didn't just like Flynn . . . It was more than that. Much, much more. And now – oh, God!

Aware that people were looking at her, she exhaled and fixed a smile. Lola wriggled away from Flynn, pulled an apologetic face at Posy, and fled towards the cellar steps.

'All okay?' Flynn asked as Posy squeezed in behind the bar. 'No one raise any objections?'

Determined to give them the benefit of the doubt, Posy upped her smile several degrees. 'None. They loved it all. We're definitely full steam ahead. The vicar and his henchmen are happily organizing it with all the precision and warm-heartedness of the Nuremberg Rally. Er, how's Lola?'

Flynn shrugged. 'How do you expect? Miserable. She's going to clean the pipes and reorganize the cellar again tonight rather than serving anyone. She still doesn't want to talk.'

'Poor thing,' Posy, praying that she'd leapt to entirely the wrong conclusion, began emptying the slop trays. 'It'll take a lot of getting over.'

'She'll never get over it,' Flynn levelled a glass under the Guinness pump.

'Oh, I think that's a bit over the top. It'll take time, but we'll all help her. Of course she's unhappy now and it's been a heck of a shock, but once she gets over the initial pain she'll be all right, you'll see. Look how she's blossomed recently, dropping all the starchy

334

power-dressing and looking sort of rumpled and sexy and really gorgeous.'

Flynn slid the Guinness towards Neddy Pink and looked at her pityingly.

Posy frowned. 'What? Why are you looking at me like I've missed something? I honestly feel dead sorry for Lola, but if I got over Ritchie doing the dirty on me, she'll be the same eventually, believe me. We women are pretty tough. She'll find someone else and –'

'She already has,' Flynn said.

'*What?*'

Posy clung on to the edge of the bar. So that was it . . . It was true. She'd always known that Lola and Flynn got on well together, of course, and the fact that Flynn had said Lola wasn't his type was typical male double-bluff stuff.

Oh, God – she couldn't bear it! Selfish or not, she simply couldn't spend the rest of her life living and working with Lola and Flynn as a couple when she . . . when she . . .

She looked at Flynn. 'Since when?'

'A couple of weeks ago. Listen, Posy, I shouldn't be saying anything. It's supposed to be a secret.'

'I bet it is. Goodness, you could have told *me*. I thought we were friends.'

'We are friends. Lola would have told you, I know she would, it's just that so much has happened since, and things have got complicated.'

Posy shrugged and assumed an air of disinterest. 'Oh, that's okay. I'm not that bothered to be honest.' She stomped along the bar and glared at a couple of lads from the Cressbeds Estate. 'Yes?'

They instantly recoiled. 'Christ, Pose. What's wrong with you?'

'Nothing. What do you want?'

'Two pints of lager and a bit of civility.'

'The first I can manage, the second's in short supply.'

'Bugger me, it's like being served by Hogarth all over again.'

For the next hour Posy served customers with grim determination, ignored Flynn, and cursed herself for being so stupid. If anyone was going to get Lola over Nigel's deception it would be Flynn, of course. She'd probably encouraged them to get together. It was all her fault. Oh, sod, sod, sod!

Lola eventually emerged from the cellar looking pale and gave Posy a wan smile. 'Did the carnival meeting go okay?'

'Fine.'

'Good. Can you and Flynn manage? Only I feel pretty awful not helping out, it's just that I don't seem to be able to smile much at the moment.'

'Flynn and I can manage perfectly, thank you. Oh, and now that Flynn's told me what's going on, I reckon if I was in your shoes I'd not only be grinning from ear-to-ear non-stop, but I'd also be whooping with joy and swinging from the chandeliers.'

Lola looked at her in amazement. 'You are very, very strange sometimes, do you know that? Why on earth could you imagine that I'd be feeling anything other than suicidal?'

'Christ! Where do you want me to start? You've got the most gorgeous, sexiest, kindest, funniest, nicest man in the world and –'

'Posy!!!' Flynn's yell brought The Crooked Sixpence to a standstill.

She shrugged at Lola. 'He gets very masterful, doesn't he?'

'Posy –' Flynn glared at her. 'Don't. Please.'

'Okay.' Smiling sweetly at him and Lola, she swept out into the bar to collect empty glasses from the tables. What did it matter, anyway? She'd survived Ritchie, she could surely survive this?

The Pinks, Vi and Rose, even Amanda and Nikki, all wanted to talk about Tatty's baby. Clearing the tables took ages. Every so often she glanced up. Flynn and Lola were always talking, heads together. Bugger it.

During a lull, while she was emptying ashtrays and half listening to Neddy Pink wheezing about playing the accordion during the carnival queen competition, the door crashed open. Sonia stood quivering on the threshold, the size of a small bungalow and nowhere near as attractive.

She glowered at Posy. 'Where's Ritchie?'

'How on earth should I know?' Posy was thrilled to notice that Sonia now had treble chins. 'We don't work the same shifts, as you're well aware, so he certainly isn't here.'

'Don't believe you.' Sonia wobbled. 'He didn't come home for his tea.'

The Crooked Sixpence was riveted.

Posy shrugged. 'Maybe he's got tired of your cooking. God, Sonia, he isn't here. I haven't seen him for ages. Maybe he's working late.'

'He isn't. I've phoned the shop. He left at his normal time. I think he's in here with you. You won't leave him alone, will you? You've enticed him! You're a cow! A bloody man-stealing cow! I'm going to –'

'Posy –' Lola called from behind the bar. 'Get her out of here.'

'Only too delighted.' Posy grabbed Sonia's podgy arm and wheeled her smartly out of the bar to rousing cheers from most of the customers, and whoops and yells from the Pinks.

Fortunately the evening had grown too chilly for the al fresco drinkers to be occupying the trestles, so there was no audience.

Posy let go of Sonia's arm. 'Right, now bugger off. Stop behaving like a mad woman and go home. Ritchie isn't here, understand? I haven't seen him, okay? Just get out of my face!'

Sonia took a deep breath and screwed her mouth up. Her forehead and chin rushed to meet each other. Posy winced. It was like Sigourney Weaver in *Alien* all over again. She truly didn't blame Ritchie for staying away. For a second there was silence, then Sonia let rip with a yowl that would have terrified a banshee.

'Shut up!' Posy snapped. 'For Christ's sake, have you no dignity? Oh, shit, what are you doing?'

Sonia had collapsed to the ground, clutching her stomach and still screaming.

'What?' Posy bent down. 'What – oooh, God!'

She took one last horrified look and flew back into the pub. 'Quick! Call an ambulance!'

'Good on yer, Pose! The Pinks stamped their feet and whistled. 'Way to go!'

They'd obviously spent far too much time with Flynn.

Posy yelled towards the bar. 'I mean it! Get an ambulance! She's having the baby!'

'What?' Lola looked confused. 'Where?'

'In the bloody car park! Just get an ambulance!'

Posy skidded outside again. Sonia was hunched and still screaming on the gravel. In less than thirty seconds the whole of The Crooked Sixpence were gathered round shouting encouragement.

'Do something!' Sonia roared. 'Get Ritchie! I want Ritchie!'

Posy, whose entire childbirth experience had been from sex education videos at school and soap operas since, patted her on the top of the head because it seemed like the only part that wouldn't cause damage.

'Piss off!' Sonia snarled. 'Get Ritchie, and get him away from me!'

At the business end of the action, Neddy Pink was just priming his accordion. Vi and Rose bundled him mercifully out of sight.

Amanda and Nikki looked at one another in total horror.

'Puts you right off sex, doesn't it?'

'God, yeah, if this is what it ends up like. Best contraceptive going if you ask me.'

Posy gazed helplessly at the crowd. The 'push, duck' and 'don't push for gawd's sake' factions appeared to be equally divided. All of them, without exception, were childless. None of them had a clue what they were supposed to be doing.

'We really need Tatty,' she said to Lola. 'She's the pregnancy expert after all.'

Lola gave a little shriek and ran back into the pub.

'Get Ritchie!' Sonia screamed. 'Get my mobile out of my pocket! I want Ritchie! Oooh!!!!'

Posy scrabbled through Sonia's pocket and shakily dialled Ritchie's mobile number.

'You still know it off by heart you bitch!' Sonia yelled.

Posy shrugged. 'Yeah, so I do. Christ! Where is he?'

She could hear Ritchie's phone ringing in her ear, and a strange echo as well. Bloody hell, gremlins on the line. That was all she needed.

The Pink twins stopped peering at Sonia, and tapped Posy on the shoulder. 'It's ringing in her 'andbag, Pose, duck.'

It was. Grabbing Sonia's handbag, Posy ferreted through heaps of junk and dragged out a second mobile phone. It was still ringing. She switched off Sonia's and it stopped.

'I took it off him,' Sonia gasped between bursts of pain. 'I forgot. I thought you'd ring him or he'd ring you, so I took it off him.'

Jesus Christ! 'You're completely mad! Now what are we supposed to do?'

'I don't knooooow!'

Flynn appeared amidst the mayhem. 'Ambulance will be here in about two minutes.'

Posy, if she hadn't hated him for loving Lola, could have kissed him.

She could also have kissed the paramedics when they arrived.

Sweet-looking, young, and totally in control, they muttered things like timed contractions and cervical dilation and administered something through a gas mask, and all the while calmed the screaming lump that was Sonia.

'Royal Berks it is then, love. If we step on it you'll get your baby delivered there in a nice clean bed. If not, it'll be the back of the ambulance. Either's preferable to this gravel, though, isn't it?'

Sonia gave another howl through clenched teeth as they shovelled her into the back of the ambulance.

Posy let out a sigh of relief, just as the youngest paramedic bundled her in, too.

'Best to have a friend with her,' he said cheerfully, slamming the doors. 'If her husband's not around.'

'She's not my fucking friend!' Sonia screamed, lunging towards Posy before collapsing again and pulling greedily on the gas and air.

'I'm not staying in here . . .' Posy started – but it was far too late.

With blue lights flashing and sirens wailing, the ambulance rocketed away from The Crooked Sixpence.

All the way on the bouncing, jolting, madcap journey, the paramedic timed Sonia's contractions, made her comfortable, attached various monitors, and kept up a string of unbelievably bad jokes as he asked questions and filled in pages on a clipboard. Posy huddled in the furthest corner of the ambulance, clung on to a strap and eyed the gas and air with envy.

It was hardly fair that Sonia should have all the relief.

Arriving at the Royal Berks was something like the end of the Wacky Races. Umpteen ambulances and cars seemed to be parked at odd angles, as trolleys and wheelchairs made collision course dashes for the doors.

'Um . . . I'll get a taxi back, then,' Posy said cheerfully to the paramedics. 'Now you've got her here okay.'

They must teach paramedics brute force as well as bad jokes, Posy reckoned, as they grabbed her and she found herself hurtling between them into the smell and noise and strange other-world atmosphere of the hospital.

'You stay with her,' the youngest one commanded as they whisked off towards Gynaecology and Obstetrics. 'She'll need a mate.'

'She's already had mine,' Posy muttered, but no one was listening.

By this time Sonia was so high on the gas and air it was like a girls' night out for one.

The handover was completed in record time, with incomprehensible words and figures being bandied between the green-suited paramedics and a very pretty nurse.

'Right, Mum,' the nurse smiled down at the writhing Sonia, 'let's get you sorted. You're not due in for a week or so, so we'll have to see what we can do. Lovely that you've got a friend with you.' She looked at Posy. 'Are you her birth partner?'

'No, I'm bloody not.'

'Whatever.' The nurse trundled Sonia away and indicated that Posy should try and keep up. 'We won't have very long to wait for baby to arrive. If you'd like to tell me what her choices were.'

'Her what?'

'Choices. For the birth.'

Oh, right. God . . . what had Ritchie said? Posy nodded. 'Oh, yes, she's having Marti Pellow and the birthing pool.'

There was a slight flicker of consternation on the nurse's face. 'Bit tricky right at this moment, what with this one being the teeniest bit early. Double booking so to speak. I wonder if Mum would mind Celine Dion?'

'She might not but I damn well would,' Posy said hotly. 'Haven't you got any Fat Boy Slim?'

'This is an emergency maternity unit, not bloody Radio One.'

Mercifully at this point, Sonia was wheeled out of sight. Posy collapsed on to an uncomfortable plastic chair alongside two very young boys and a grubby man with a beard, all wearing gowns and silly hats and with masks dangling on to their chests.

One of the boys looked at her. 'Are you with the one they've just wheeled in?'

'Sort of.'

'Wow. Are you lesbians, then?'

'No.'

The other boy sniggered a bit. 'You not going in, then?'

'Christ, no. I'll sit out here with the wimps.'

'We're not wimps,' the bearded man growled. 'We're on a break. We've all been in there for over twelve hours with our partners. We've been sent out to rest.'

Twelve hours? Dear God . . .

A plump man in grey combat trousers and matching baggy top appeared in the corridor. 'Who's with Mrs Dalgetty?'

Posy winced at the name. 'No one. We couldn't find Ritchie, er, her husband . . .'

The plump man twitched in agitation. 'So I've been

343

told. I was told she was with a friend. If you're her, could you come this way. Mum needs some support.'

'I'm not her friend and I've never been supportive. Don't look at me.'

'Come along! This is a time for solidarity. Not squeamish are we?'

'Yes.'

'Goodness, you wait until it's your turn. Come on.'

The boys and the bearded man looked distinctly envious as Posy slowly stood up and dragged her heels towards the delivery suite.

It wasn't a bit like they portrayed childbirth on television. There seemed to be an air of total disinterest. Monitors were beeping and Sonia was still gulping gas and air and there was a drip attached to bits of her hidden from view. The midwife and a nurse smiled happily at Posy and promptly disappeared.

The plump man in the fatigues beamed too. 'Mum seems to be doing okay. Pity Dad couldn't be on hand, but there you go. She's nicely sedated now and the contractions are under control. Push the button over the bed if you need anything.'

'I'm not staying in here alone,' Posy said stoutly. 'Supposing she has it?'

He laughed as he headed for the door. 'Well, that is the general idea, but actually I'd say we had a little while to wait yet. Hope so. I've got four more on the go along this corridor.'

He closed the door behind him. Celine Dion was screeching off key from an unseen source. Sonia wasn't making any noises at all but looked wet and lumpy and asleep so Posy ignored her.

Why the hell wasn't Ritchie here? He damn well should be here. He deserved to be here . . .

After she'd read all the labels on things, and not managed to silence Celine, and peered at Sonia a couple of times just to make sure she was still alive, boredom set in. Where was the excitement and the screaming and the heaving and shoving of earlier? Why had it all gone so quiet?

The door opened slowly and Flynn grinned at her. 'Is it safe to come in?'

Posy was so delighted to see him that she hurled her arms round his neck before remembering that he now belonged to Lola and she hated him. 'Oops, sorry . . .' She disentangled herself. 'Yes, all seems to be okay. Oh, you're such a star. Have you come to take me home?'

'Too right. I was dumbstruck when I realized what had happened. How on earth did you manage to stop yourself from killing her in the ambulance?'

'With difficulty. But who's looking after the pub?'

'Ellis arrived just as the ambulance left. I thought it would do Lola good to chat things over with him.'

'Brave of you, considering. Leaving her with the Lothario of Steeple Fritton, I mean. Oh well, shall we go?'

Flynn gave her a quizzical look then nodded. 'Sure. I've got the jeep outside and the parking seemed a bit odd and – Jeeze, what the heck is that noise?'

'Sonia in labour.'

'Not unless she's sharing her bed with a hundred piece orchestra.'

'Oh, that's Celine Dion on a bad tape. I can't find the

off switch. Marti Pellow and the birthing pool were a bit busy. Come on, let's get out of here.'

'Don't leave me!' Sonia snatched the mask off and yelled from the bed. 'You can't leave me on my own!'

Posy and Flynn looked at one another. Flynn shrugged. 'Do you reckon we should stay?'

Posy groaned. 'Christ, I suppose so, but this is just so farcical. I certainly don't want to be here, and I'm the last person on earth she wants with her. Still, at least she's stopped making a noise. They've given her something to take away the pain and apparently the contractions are gathering themselves up or something ready for the final push.'

'Oh, great. A little more information there than I needed, thanks.'

Sonia gave a sort of shuddering sigh and burst into tears. Posy stared at her with distaste, but knew they couldn't just walk away. They stood beside the bed looking at her. Sonia looked back with absolute loathing then clutched at Posy's hand and screamed.

On and on and on.

'Holy shit!' Flynn looked petrified. 'What's happening?'

'I think this is it –' Posy pushed the panic button and pulled an agonized face at Sonia. 'Er, hang on . . . we'll get someone . . . and bloody let go of my hand! You're breaking my damn fingers!'

The doors burst open again and the doctor and mid-wife and the pretty nurse all piled in. They took one look at Sonia writhing and screaming and elbowed Flynn and Posy out of the way.

The panic subsided in the blink of an eye. All was instantly calm and serene, with Sonia being hushed and praised and encouraged, and the midwife and doctor moving gracefully together with all the skill and finesse and grace of ice dancers.

'I must say,' the pretty nurse sidled up to Posy, 'if Baby Dalgetty is a boy and takes after his Dad, then he's going to be a right looker.'

'Um, I suppose so.' Posy shrugged. 'He's not bad.'

'*Not bad?*' The nurse looked across to the far side of the room and devoured Flynn with her eyes. 'He's the most bloody gorgeous thing I've ever seen.'

Posy shrieked with nervous laughter. 'Oh, *him*? God, yes he is, but he's not the father.'

'Sorry, I didn't realize he was yours. You are so lucky . . . Don't suppose you fancy part-exchanging him for a mechanic with a beer gut, do you?'

'Tough one,' Posy sighed, thinking that if only Lola hadn't come to Steeple Fritton then Flynn might really be hers and she could preen and primp and say so. 'But he's actually in love with my friend . . . oh, no, not the one in the bed. She's not a friend. I hate her. She's married to my ex-fiancé. He dumped me for her when he got her pregnant. No, this other friend is –'

The nurse blinked. 'Go on. This is even better than *EastEnders* – oh, damn, no more time for small talk. Here we go.'

Everyone had suddenly taken up playing positions round the bed. Sonia's language was atrocious. Posy and Flynn huddled in a corner, averting their eyes and closing their ears, then suddenly Sonia's staccato screams were overtaken by more lengthy high-pitched ones.

'It's a boy!'

Posy opened one eye and squinted across the room.

Sonia, all in disarray but beaming blissfully, was cuddling a blood-streaked bundle and cooing.

She tried to smile at Flynn and couldn't. She cleared her throat. 'Time to go?'

'Definitely.'

Taking one last look at Sonia snuggling up to Ritchie's son, Posy hurtled into the corridor. The young boys and the bearded man had gone. She swallowed the lump in her throat and brushed tears away with her fingers.

'Okay?' Flynn looked down at her.

She nodded.

'That must have been complete shit for you, under the circumstances.'

She nodded again. 'It was a bit weird and emotional, yes.'

'Come on, then.' He put his arm round her shoulders and pulled her against him. 'Let's go home.'

Chapter Twenty-Four

The unscheduled arrival of Baby Dalgetty five days earlier had gone straight into the Steeple Fritton Hot Gossip Chart at number one. Everyone had shown Posy the utmost sympathy, but she was also well aware that they kept peering at her on the sly to see if she really minded. She pretended she didn't. It wasn't that hard. Watching Ritchie's baby being born had been painful, and embarrassing, and definitely unreal, but she'd minded more – much, much more – about the way Lola had flown into Flynn's arms on their return to The Crooked Sixpence.

'Do you think this suits me?' Dilys swept out of the Gear Change fitting room and executed a neat twirl. 'I thought it would be nice for my "at homes".'

Posy nodded, clamping her lips together in case a stray snigger erupted. Her mother's afternoon 'at homes' were to start the following week – tying in nicely with the first guided tours of Norrie's model railway. Sunny Dene would be offering cream teas in the dining room. Dilys would be playing Lady of the B&B.

The dress she was wearing had been in a bundle deposited by a beanpole of a weekender. A fluid mass of rainbow handkerchief points in stretchy chiffon, it was definitely designer and possibly a size 10. On Dilys, who hovered just above five-foot-two and just below an 18, it lost a lot of its original pizzazz.

'It certainly looks, um, different.'

'Say if you don't like it, please.' Dilys surveyed her rear view in the strategically placed cheval mirrors. 'I don't want to be a laughing stock.'

'You won't be, Mum. It's gorgeous, if a little long.'

'Oh, I can ruck it up a bit, but the colours are lovely, aren't they?'

Posy had to agree that they were. Her mother, mollified, skipped off to the fitting room with another armful of designer frocks.

Gear Change was a bit like a jumble sale. No elegant casual browsing here. Most of the other Frittons, half the Cressbeds Estate, some strangers, and all of the coven, except Tatty who was working, were rootling through the stock with feverish frenzy.

It was, as all the enterprises were, going really well. It was all Steeple Fritton had needed to yank it out of the doldrums. A bit of ingenuity and a touch of inspiration. Posy wished there was some ingenious sprite hovering somewhere just waiting to sprinkle similar inspirational magic dust on her love life.

'What about this one?' Dilys emerged in something dark green and knitted, which set off her flame frizz of hair a treat.

'That's a blame tablecloth,' Glad stopped searching through a pile of cast-off DKNY T-shirts. 'Isn't it?'

'It's a Dawn French sweater dress,' Posy said.

'Oh, I like her!' Dilys galloped back to the fitting room. 'A girl with a proper body! I'll definitely take this one.'

Ellis pushed the door open. Gladys glared at him and turned her back.

Posy raised her eyebrows. 'Copybook still blotted, I see?'

'Well and truly,' Ellis groaned, leaning on the counter. 'Gran won't speak to me. Life is such a shit.'

'Tell me about it. Although I'd have thought you'd have to take some responsibility for adding to Tatty's brood. And you can't say I didn't warn you.'

'I know, I know. But, as I keep telling anyone who will listen, I was so bloody *careful*. Mr Safe Sex of the Century, that's me. I can't bloody believe it. It's ruined everything.'

'I suppose it has. Well, for you at least, and it's certainly curtailed your romping activities. Will you be getting married?'

'God knows. I suppose we'll have to if that's what Tatty wants. I haven't talked it over with her yet, she's still too overexcited about being pregnant to talk sense about anything. But I certainly won't let my child go fatherless. I do have principles. Christ, it's killing me. It's like your Ritchie and that Sonia all over again.'

Posy winced. 'Don't remind me.'

Ellis smiled. It was very half-hearted. 'Once, a few weeks ago, I'd have come belting in here to pretend to watch women try on clothes and you'd have nagged at me and we'd have laughed. I haven't laughed for ages . . .'

351

'Nor me.'

'Why not? I thought you were okay now, and over Ritchie and everything?'

'Oh, I am, but then I found out that Flynn . . . oh, yes!' Posy broke off to admire her mother who had sashayed out into the shop wearing a 1970s Zandra Rhodes strap dress in tangerine and pink. 'Lovely!'

Ellis watched Dilys posing in front of the Cressbeds faction, seeking approval. 'It's too small and she looks like a setting sun.'

'I know. But I like sunsets, and she likes bright colours, and we've all had enough misery so I'm not going to upset her or anyone else again – ever.'

'You're a very gentle girl under all that leather bikey rock chick stuff, aren't you?'

'I'm a fluffy mass of damn sugar candy.' Posy sighed heavily. 'All I ever wanted was to be in love and for someone to love me and to get married and have babies and be a wife and mother and do little things that bring in money and make life interesting and –'

'Whoa!' Ellis blinked. 'Don't tell me. Tell Flynn . . .'

'Oh yeah, right. He'd love that, just when he and Lola are being all kissy-kissy. Christ, now what's the matter?'

'Nothing,' Ellis shook his head. 'Just can't hang around here all day. I've got some courier work to do.'

Busy for the next hour, Posy didn't have time to dwell on Ellis's sudden disappearance. She felt sorry for him – even if, like Ritchie, it was his own damn fault. She was far too miserable thinking about Flynn and Lola to spend too much time on everyone's else's problems.

'This is going extremely well.' The vicar pushed his

way through the throng and strode up to the counter. 'Like all the other things which you young people have instigated in the village. Brought the whole place to life. People are pouring into the village and spending money, and, very importantly, coming back again. I'm most impressed.'

'Thank you,' Posy smiled warily. Why was the vicar in Gear Change? Was he going to admit to a cross-dressing secret? Did he hanker after a second-hand Coco Chanel or Alexander McQueen? 'Um, what can I do for you?'

'Well, I'm actually here for several reasons: first, to say that we have the go-ahead for Mr Malone's traction engine to power the fairground organ outside the pub on carnival night,' the vicar beamed. 'Wonderful news, no?'

Posy agreed. 'And good timing as The Memory Lane Fair people are coming over this evening to see Queen Mab so we can firm up all the details. And the second?'

'A little bit more tricky,' the vicar grinned roguishly. 'I've been sent to ask you a favour.'

Posy winced. Everyone in Steeple Fritton knew about the vicar's favours. They usually involved minding the paramilitary unit of the Brownies or making jam.

'It's about the carnival. Everyone seems to have their stall laid out, so to speak. But we're short of a fortune teller and well, everyone agrees that you absolutely look the part. All dark and mysterious and with those curls. And I'm sure you can find a lovely costume in here, and your mother has a wonderful selection of earrings and –'

'Don't try buttering me up,' Posy said. 'Anyway, Tatty would make a much better fortune teller than me. I mean, she doesn't just look right, she does it for a living, well, almost.'

'Exactly,' the vicar looked askance. 'Which is why I don't want someone who has a little dabble in the black arts – okay, maybe Ms Spry's dalliances with the occult are not quite akin to Satanism, but she's still a touch too close for the Diocesan Council's liking – being involved in what should be a light-hearted folderol.'

Posy sighed. There was going to be no point in arguing, and anyway it might be fun, and she hadn't been earmarked for anything else on the day, had she? 'Okay. Count me in.'

'Wonderful! Thank you so much.'

'And the third thing? Was there something else?'

'There was. I wanted to say how much I admired you for your actions the other evening. With young Mrs Dalgetty and the baby. It was supremely Christian of you, and can't have been easy. I think you were absolutely splendid.'

'I'll no doubt get my reward in heaven. And no, it wasn't easy, and it certainly wasn't by choice. I still dislike Sonia intensely and never want to see the baby or her, or Ritchie come to that, again. Does that lessen your opinion of me?'

'Not at all. The best deeds are those that are the most difficult to do . . .' The vicar stopped and looked longingly at a flimsy silver sequinned dress on the counter. 'I say, do you think my wife would like that? I bought her one similar to that some time ago, not that she ever has cause to wear it, but I think it's wonderful. Like a mermaid.'

'Maybe you should ask her opinion first,' Posy said diplomatically.

'Yes, yes . . . maybe you're right. I'll do that. Well, congratulations again on all your hard work, and I'm sure, if this is anything to go by, then the Letting Off Steam carnival will be a rip-roaring success.'

Posy exhaled loudly when he'd left the shop, relieved that she hadn't had to tell him that his wife had brought the silver sequinned dress in to sell that morning with a derisive snort of '. . . Goodness knows what he thought I'd look like in this! I never wear anything other than Damart! For goodness' sake find it a good home, Posy dear. Men have no *idea* what really pleases one, have they?'

Another busy hour later, just as Posy was locking Gear Change prior to sprinting across the road for her lunch-time waitressing shift in the pub, she noticed a small crowd outside Tatty's shop.

'Posy!' Norrie, with Trevor and Kenneth on their leads, appeared from the melee, waving excitedly. 'Come and see!'

'What's going on?'

'Tatty's opened up for business, and young Malvina is helping out and has just pinned up some designs. Come and have a look.'

Young Malvina was fast becoming a real Fritton asset. Posy had thought she might poach her too, to do odd shifts in Gear Change when the courier, B&B, and pub work all got too crowded. Young Malvina had recently been helping out in Rose Lusty's hairdresser's, and for the first time in living memory, customers were emerging through the bright pink doors with glossy fluid bobs and sleek highlighted layers, rather than Rose's perennial favourite – the High Court Judge Wig Effect.

Having reached Tatty's shop, Posy shook her head at Norrie as Trevor and Kenneth danced around her. 'Surely you're not going to have a tattoo, Dad? Not at your age? I mean, I know you've discovered a whole new lifestyle with the karaoke and Meatloaf and everything, but even so, I don't think –'

'Good God, no!' Norrie looked shocked. 'Not me. I get queasy at the mere thought. Mr D and Mr B are in there at the moment, though. Queuing. And look at some of these beauties. I rather like the look of the guillemot.'

There was a sort of Pick Your Own sheet of designs pinned up in the window. Posy squinted at them. 'I think that's an eagle, Dad . . . Blimey, that's not what Mr D and Mr B are having done, is it? Surely they're too old, I mean, won't their skin be a bit puckered?'

'Well, if it wasn't before, it will be afterwards,' Norrie laughed. 'No, seriously, I remember when Tatty used to do tattoos years ago, like her mother and her grandmother before her. Amazing artwork. Really smashing stuff . . . Oh, here comes the first of the walking wounded.'

Ritchie, looking pale, emerged from the shop. The sleeve of his shirt was rolled up to shoulder height, and a gauze pad held in place by sticky tape graced his bicep.

He and Posy stared awkwardly at one another.

Ritchie took a deep breath. 'I hoped I'd see you. I couldn't believe what happened . . . I thought Sonia was making it up when she told me and I've been meaning to come round and say thanks for what you did for her, and for the baby.'

'There was no need, and anyway, you could have phoned. Oh, no, you couldn't could you? You've had your mobile confiscated. Forget about it, I'm still trying. And take it from me, I definitely didn't want to be there, and obviously neither did you.'

'We'd had a row that morning. I just went for a drink after work instead of going straight home. It must have been the worst thing in the world for you to go through. I'm so sorry.'

'Ritchie Dalgetty! Listen to yourself! I coped because I had to. It was just fate. Not even someone as bloody-minded as Sonia could have cooked up that sort of stunt. Revenge of the Bride of the Upholstery Manager? I don't think so. And are you going to spend the rest of your life saying sorry for everything?'

'Probably . . .' He looked crestfallen. 'I've cocked up my life so spectacularly. Nothing's worked out how I planned.'

'Yes, well, I must admit that for twenty years I'd fondly imagined that being in on the birth of your baby would mean I'd played some part in the conception, too.'

'I'm so sorry –' Ritchie looked as though he was going to burst into tears. 'Shit, sorry for saying sorry, but I'm just so gutted that I wasn't there to see Bradfield being born –'

'Bradfield? *Bradfield?* You've called the poor little bugger, *Bradfield?*'

Ritchie looked hurt. 'It was Sonia's idea. Like Brooklyn Beckham.'

'Christ! You mean it was conceived in the back of your hatchback down a lane in Bradfield? Oh, I'm sorry, but that is so tacky! Still, I suppose it could have been worse, you could have found it impossible to stay faithful to me in a lay-by in Ufton Nervet –'

'Posy, don't –'

'Don't what? Say what I really feel? You may not believe this, but I've moved on now . . . yes, honestly. And I feel sorry for you, and I'd bet a million quid that you've just had bloody Bradfield tattooed on your arm.' She laughed at him. 'I knew you had. God, you and Sonia, the Posh and Becks of Steeple Fritton. Sad . . .'

She kissed Norrie on the cheek, and Trevor and Kenneth on the top of the head, and Ritchie not at all, and rushed across the road to The Crooked Sixpence.

Lola, still looking miserable, listened as Posy chattered about Gear Change and the tattooing and being a fortune teller and bloody Bradfield Dalgetty and Dilys's frock buying.

'And I'm going to have to pinch Flynn from you tonight because Jack and Nell are coming over to talk about their fairground stuff. I doubt if Ritchie will be allowed to abandon his paternal duties quite yet, so you might be able to persuade Ellis to give you a hand in here until we get back –'

'No,' Lola shook her head. 'I'll manage. Anyway, if you bring The Memory Lane Fair people in here I can scream if I need help.'

'Okay,' Posy wove her way through the tables with two shepherd's pies. She'd definitely missed something between Lola and Ellis. But what? Had they had some massive row? Or maybe Lola had been strident in her views on Tatty's pregnancy? There had definitely been some sort of split, though.

'Ellis was in the shop earlier. He's having a really rough time –'

'I'm sure he is, but if you don't mind I'd rather not talk about him.'

Posy juggled a cheesy pasta and two omelettes on a tray. 'But I thought you liked each other? And after all, he did go all the way out to Micklesham to find you when Barbara Marion was here, and –'

'Posy! Shut up!'

'That told you, duck.' One of the Pink twins cackled at Posy through an unfamiliar mouthful of tagliatelle as Lola hurtled into the kitchen, slamming the door behind her. 'Ellis has upset her good and proper. Mind, if you asks me, there's something mighty odd going on there. With her and your young Yankee bloke.'

'He's not mine, and there's nothing odd about it at all,' Posy snapped. 'They're just in love!'

The only bit of light relief for the rest of the shift came when Mr D and Mr B staggered in, shirtsleeves rolled up, gauze pads in place, to have double brandies and ginger ale. They both looked ashen-faced and shaky, and Posy hoped fervently that she wouldn't be called on again to make an emergency dash to hospital with one or both of them.

'We've had hearts and daggers done,' Mr D told her. 'Matching. Except mine says Wilfred and Wilfred's says Arthur.'

'Ah, sweet.' Posy smiled at them. 'Did it hurt?'

'A bit. She's very artistic though, young Tatty. She doesn't use transfers or anything, draws all the designs straight on to the skin by hand. And there wasn't much blood at all.'

Posy, who felt she'd had enough blood and gore in the maternity unit to last her a lifetime, shuddered. 'Oh, good. Another brandy each? Yes, I thought so . . .'

Chapter Twenty-Five

'They're late,' Flynn said, looking across the bar to the clock in the corner. 'It's gone half past seven.'

Posy sighed. 'No, it hasn't. That's fast. Lola put it forward to make sure the punters don't stay after hours. Stop worrying.'

She sat back in her seat and nursed her wine glass. She was pretending to be a grown-up. She could do this tonight with Flynn, like a proper business meeting, as a colleague and a friend. It really didn't matter that her heart gave a peculiar lurch every time he walked into the room, or that her lips wanted to curve into a smile when he spoke, or, well, any of that sort of stuff.

As promised, Jack Morland and Nell Bradley arrived at The Crooked Sixpence dead on time. Jack, obviously scrubbed-up, was even more delectable than she remembered, if still endearingly faintly paint-spattered. Nell, extremely tall with flowing red gold hair, was simply beautiful. And, by the way they shared glances and touched hands, they were clearly hopelessly in love.

It was almost too much for Posy to bear.

Still, bear it she had to. After everyone had been introduced and shaken hands and exchanged pleasantries, they set off along the track at the side of the pub towards Queen Mab's shed in the sweet-scented spring dusk.

Jack and Flynn, brothers in steam, were chatting together happily.

'He's gorgeous,' Nell said quietly to Posy. 'Exactly like John Cusack. And even if he wasn't, that accent alone is enough to make you go weak at the knees with lust, isn't it?'

Posy had to agree that it was.

'You're very lucky to have met one another,' Nell said as they ducked beneath green boughs of hawthorn and emerging willow. 'You're perfect together.'

Posy drew in her breath. 'We're not together as a couple. We're just good friends. He's in love with Lola, the landlady at the pub.'

'Really?' Nell raised a slender golden eyebrow. 'Then my sensory divining skills must be a bit awry.'

'Way off beam, I'm afraid. We're not destined to be another you and Jack, born to be together forever.'

Nell laughed. 'Believe me, we had some horrendous moments. Jack's a flattie, a non-fair person, and there was hell to pay on both sides when we got together.'

'No! You mean, sort of family rivalries, like Romeo and Juliet?'

'Far more complicated than that. Think tribal, racial, religious. Added to which, I was engaged to a traveller whom my parents considered the most eligible thing that wasn't Prince William, and Jack was living with a successful businesswoman who ran her own company and whom his parents adored.'

362

Posy mulled this over. 'And yet, you still got together, and it still worked out, and everyone's happy?'

'Eventually. We've been together for four years now and are still as besotted as the day we met. My family are fine about it, Jack's less so, but we're together and that's the main thing – oh, is this it? Wow!'

Flynn had pulled open the shed's massive doors and flicked on the lights. Queen Mab, in all her monstrous, gleaming glory, towered above them.

Nell and Jack were in raptures.

There was much talk of steam coal suppliers and pounds pressure per square inch and generating enough power and suitable water hydrants and connecting leads and AC/DC.

'This is going to be ace,' Flynn grinned as Jack and Nell stood high above them in the cab, oohing and aahing over Queen Mab. 'She's just what they've been looking for. Not simply for the carnival here, but to accompany them to various steam fairs to power the gallopers as she was built to do, or to do fund-raising events when they'll have the Limonaire organ playing in the street and again Queen Mab can provide the power. God, it'll be awesome.'

'So,' Posy said wistfully, 'you're planning to run away and join the circus, so to speak, are you?'

'Too right.'

Posy whimpered. She attempted to stretch her mouth into the sort of smile that everyone else was wearing. It just wouldn't go. How impossible it was to be pleased for him because he was so ecstatically happy and to know at the same time that this was the beginning of the end.

363

Not that there'd been a beginning of the beginning really. But Flynn and Queen Mab would be leaving Steeple Fritton and her, and yes, Lola, to travel with The Bradley-Morland Memory Lane Fair. Oh, God! Her and Lola. Sisters-in-Dump – again.

Reluctantly, after an hour of gazing and stroking and exchanging technical jargon, they closed the shed doors behind them and wandered back to the pub. Posy was delighted that The Memory Lane Fair would be such a draw at the Letting Off Steam carnival – but she wished with all her heart that they'd never delivered that package to Fox Hollow. If only Flynn had never met Jack. If only . . .

She pulled herself up. She was being ridiculous. Even if Jack and Nell and the fair hadn't come into their lives, Flynn would have still been in love with Lola. This was all of her own making. If she'd run away as she'd intended, she'd be living in Swindon now and probably be almost-happy with a computer techno nerd.

'Sod Persephone's owner!'

'Excuse me?' Flynn looked at her. 'Have I missed something?'

Embarrassed, Posy shook her head. 'Just, er, thinking aloud. Look, you entertain Jack and Nell. I'll help Lola out behind the bar for the rest of the night.'

The remainder of the evening came and went. Vi Bickeridge and Rose Lusty took advantage of Glad's absence and played a lot of Dickie Valentine, whom she loathed because of his overuse of Brylcreem, on the jukebox. Mr D and Mr B proudly displayed their gauze patches. The Pinks beat Jack and Nell at darts. Flynn grinned all the time and told everyone about The

Memory Lane Fair. Lola still looked like a thundercloud and Posy wanted to cry.

At half past eleven, Posy wandered back towards Sunny Dene. It was a still, mild night. Everywhere was velvet dark and the darkness was rich with the scent of grass and earth and mist.

Lola had stayed behind, as had Flynn, to make final arrangements with Jack and Nell. No doubt Flynn would tell her tonight that he was leaving the village, and Lola would be even more miserable. Or maybe she'd go with him. After all, Hogarth would be back at some time and would immediately return The Crooked Sixpence to its former doom and gloom. Lola would have nothing to stay for, and she and Flynn could ride off into the sunset together . . .

The sound of footsteps hurrying behind her prevented Posy from screaming out loud. If it was a mugger – which was unlikely given Steeple Fritton's tendency to be light years behind in things like that – she could scream anyway with good reason.

'Posy, slow down. We need to talk.'

Flynn's voice made her toes curl in delight. Then they uncurled as she remembered.

She stopped walking and looked over her shoulder. He was alone. 'Where's Lola?'

'Cashing up. And Nell and Jack have gone back to their current fairground. And that just leaves you and me.'

I wish, Posy thought. 'Is Lola upset?'

'Of course she is. That's why I need to talk to you. Can we go somewhere that isn't Sunny Dene for a while? I really don't want to be interrupted.'

365

'There's the bus shelter or the war memorial.'

During her teenage angst years, Posy had shed many tears in both locations.

'Bus shelter it is, then.'

Fortunately the bus shelter wasn't occupied by youthful lovers or anyone drunk enough to think there may be public transport to anywhere at this time of night. The seat was relatively intact and all-in-all it didn't smell too bad.

They sat down with room for another person between them.

'You don't need to say this,' Posy said, staring out across the road, a white silent curve in the moonlight. 'I know what's going on. I know that you're leaving, and that Lola will be going with you. It's okay.'

'Is it?' Flynn's voice was very low. 'Fine. Then let me put you straight on a few things. I have no intention of leaving Steeple Fritton. I'll join in on Jack and Nell's ventures as and when they need me and Queen Mab during their travelling season, but it will only be for a few days at a time. And only for about five months of the year. The rest of the time I'll be here.'

Posy's heart lifted a smidge, then subsided again. With Lola, of course. 'That's nice.'

'I'm glad you think so, because I think it sounds damn near perfect. Next, I am not in love with Lola. Nor is Lola in love with me.'

'But –'

He laughed softly in the darkness. 'I had no idea why those Pink women and Nell and everyone kept referring to Lola and me as a couple tonight. Eventually, after interrogation, they said that you'd told them –'

'No!' Posy shook her head violently. 'Well, okay, yes, but I saw you cuddling her –'

'When? Soon after the Nigel thing? Yeah, maybe. She was upset . . .'

'No, but you told me . . . you said Lola had someone else. That she'd fallen in love again and –'

'She has. With Ellis.'

'*Ellis?* But he's half her age and Tatty's having his baby and –' Posy groaned. 'Oh, my God! Poor Lola. *That's* why she's been so damn unhappy! And poor Ellis, too . . .'

'It's gruesome for them both. I guess they'd been falling in love for some time, and then when Ellis went to find Lola at that hotel she ran away to, they spent the night together and –'

'No!'

'Posy, do stop acting like some ancient dowager. I'm telling it like it is. So, they knew they were in love and they came home, and because of Ellis, Lola had the strength to face not only that Barbara woman, but the whole world. Damn the age difference, damn everything. Having one another was enough for them. They were ecstatic and then –'

'Tatty immediately announced she was pregnant,' Posy finished. 'Oh, shit-bloody-shit.'

'Eloquently put, as always,' Flynn grinned. 'And that's the reason why I've been taking good care of Lola. She's truly devastated, but because of Tatty, it's hardly something she can share, is it? Tatty's really happy to be having Ellis's baby. So, I've been the only shoulder Lola had to cry on.'

Posy let it all sink in. It certainly explained everything.

'Does Lola know that you're telling me?'

He nodded. 'She thought there'd been enough confusion and enough people unhappy. You will keep it to yourself, though, won't you? She'd die if anyone else knew.'

'Oh, God, yes, I won't tell a soul. But how on earth could Lola prefer Ellis to you?'

'It's a question I've asked myself many times.'

They sat in silence for a while. A middle-aged couple from the well-to-do houses strolled past with several elegant dogs. The couple were wearing matching Puffa coats and walking with matching strides. Posy eyed them enviously. Together so long that they dressed and moved as one person and probably weren't even aware of the fact.

The Puffas glanced nervously across at Flynn and Posy, in their jeans and leather jackets, hunched in the bus shelter and immediately called their expensive dogs to heel. As they disappeared across the common Posy could hear well-rounded vowels muttering 'thugs . . .', 'vandals . . .', 'probably doped to the eyeballs . . .', 'shouldn't be allowed . . .'

She giggled then clapped her hands to her mouth. 'Sorry. Bad timing.'

'Perfect timing if you ask me,' Flynn moved across the gap and sat closer to her. 'It's about time someone laughed around here.'

'But what can we do? To help Lola and Ellis, I mean?'

'Nothing,' Flynn slid his arm round her shoulder. 'There's damn all we can do to alter the situation. We'll just have to be supportive and be there for them when they need us.'

She looked at him. 'You know when we were at Fox Hollow and you said you could kiss me?'

'I vaguely remember, yes.'

'And I said it would be a mistake as we were friends.'

'I remember that, too.'

'Well, do you think you could forget it, please?'

'Sure thing. Consider it forgotten.' Flynn drew her gently towards him, stared into her eyes for a tantalizing moment, and then kissed her.

Posy simply melted away. No one on earth had the right to be able to kiss like that . . . No one on earth had the right to play havoc with every single nerve-ending . . . every single sensory receptor . . . every single pulse . . .

She clung on to him, reeling, kissing him back until the whole thing threatened to get very out of control.

Pulling away slightly, she smiled. Her voice, when she found it, was shaky. 'Um, right. Er, very moral things, leather jackets, aren't they? Impossible to get too close when you're both wearing one.'

'Simple solution,' Flynn shrugged his off and then slowly removed hers. 'There, now we'll have to cuddle up for warmth, won't we?'

'I suppose we will . . .' Posy wriggled against him, letting her fingers run through the silky layers of his hair, and knew that nothing had ever felt so blissful in her entire life.

Ages later, when the moon had shifted across the black sky, and even the homecoming Cressbeds youths were long gone, they still sat there. It hadn't all been kissing and touching. There had been a lot of talking and laughing, too: about misunderstandings and misconceptions and allowing past mistakes to get in the way of current emotions – and a lot of stuff that was nowhere near as cerebral as that.

And they'd also come to the conclusion that kissing a friend was a pretty good place to start a relationship. And now they had the rest of forever to be happy.

Flynn stood up and pulled her to her feet. He placed her leather jacket round her shoulders then slid his arms round her waist. 'You are wonderful, and I can't believe I've just been making out in a bus shelter at my age.'

'I don't even know how old you are, um, twenty-seven? Twenty-eight?'

'Thirty-two.'

'Blimey! Ancient! And I do love the phraseology. "Making out" sounds far more seductive than any equivalent we use.' She smiled at him. 'Do you think we'll be able to cope with the language barrier?'

Flynn kissed the tip of her nose. 'Well, if I get my way, we've got an awful long time to find out.'

They drifted back towards Sunny Dene, fingers entwined.

'Walking me home has its advantages, too, I suppose,' Posy murmured as they reached the drive. 'Seeing that you don't have to go on anywhere else either. Oh, and tell me that I'm being pessimistic here, but you're not going to spring anything nasty on me, are you? You're not going to do an Ellis and now tell me that you've seduced half the village and that they're all slapping paternity suits on you?'

'Not a chance.' Flynn unlocked the front door, managing to keep one arm round Posy's waist. 'I've been mad for only one woman since I arrived here.'

Posy swore that she crossed the flagged hall by floating. Trevor and Kenneth click-clacked out of their baskets in the kitchen, peered sleepily at her and Flynn, wagged their tails and click-clacked back again. Sunny Dene, it seemed, was slumbering sweetly.

'Shall we have a drink in the lounge?' She paused at the foot of the stairs, suddenly awkward. 'A, um, nightcap?'

'Yeah, good idea.' Flynn grinned at her as they switched on the lights in the floral flouncy multi-sofa'd room. 'And I'm no mind-reader, but I guess I know what you're thinking.'

Posy felt the heat rush into her face and reached for the bottles and glasses on the tiny bar. She mixed two rather haphazard drinks. 'Well, it's a strange situation . . .'

'Having rooms a few feet apart across a passageway is going to be a bit of a temptation, certainly. And saying "your room or mine" sounds pretty crass.' He took one of the glasses and smiled at her over the rim. 'So, shall we just let things take their own course?'

'Good idea. Then we can just blame Nature. Or too many JD and Cokes.'

'Yeah, blaming the alcohol seems to be a pretty good excuse both sides of the Atlantic – oh, hi, Norrie.'

Norrie, in pyjamas and dressing gown, and with his strands of hair awry, beamed into the lounge. 'Oh, it's you two. Heard voices, thought it might be Mr D and Mr B again. They've been in a bit of discomfort with their tattoos. I was going to suggest a nice glass of hot milk and whisky.'

'No, it's just us,' Posy wanted to giggle, and added, as

though it was very important to explain their behaviour, 'We were having a nightcap.'

Norrie stifled a yawn. 'So I see. Don't forget to switch the lights off when you come up to bed, oh, and don't put the chain on the door. Lola isn't home yet . . . Night, then.'

They chorused their goodnights, waiting for him to close the door, before moving into one another's arms.

The door opened again. 'Sorry, half-asleep, meant to tell you – oh, am I interrupting something?'

They didn't move apart. Posy beamed. 'Nothing at all. We're just sorting out a few misunderstandings . . . Dad? You don't look very pleased? I'd have thought –'

Norrie pushed the strands of hair into place, looking perplexed. 'To be honest, if this had happened yesterday I'd have been delighted. Never more pleased for you both. As it is . . . that's what I came down to tell you, we've got another guest in. I mean, we were thrilled because it's almost the last room booked and we haven't been this full up for ages but under the circumstances –'

There was a lot of clattering on the stairs, then over Norrie's shoulder, in the hall, Posy caught a glimpse of a mass of bright red hair and a very short vivid purple silk nightshirt.

This whirlwind of colour burst into the lounge like a meteor shower.

'I thought I heard voices! I was trying to stay awake to surprise you!'

The meteor shower hurled itself across the lounge and into Flynn's arms, dumping Posy unceremoniously to one side.

372

'Hi, honey,' she breathed ecstatically. 'Told you I'd make it one day, and surprise you, didn't I?'

Flynn looked in horror at Posy across the top of the scarlet aureole of hair.

'Yeah, you sure did. And you've done just that. Hi, Vanessa . . .'

Chapter Twenty-six

'You mean she's got an open-ended ticket? But how much longer does she intend staying?' Behind the bar of The Crooked Sixpence, Lola looked at Posy in disbelief. 'I mean, she's already been here forever.'

'She's been here for three weeks, two days and seventeen hours, not that I'm counting,' Posy said dolefully. 'It just seems like forever.'

'This can't happen to us, not both of us, not again.'

Posy shrugged as she heaped the lunch-time orders on to her tray. 'Yes it can. It has. I still think I'm not in quite the same desperate situation as you. At least Vanessa will go back to America eventually.'

'Will she?'

'Of course she will,' Posy said, with a complete lack of conviction.

'And how are you coping?'

'Okay, really. Flynn and I have agreed to put things on hold until she goes back. Neither of us want to upset her, and they were together for a long time, so at the moment he's not *with* either of us, if you get my drift.'

Lola did. She'd watched the sleeping arrangements at Sunny Dene very carefully. Flynn appeared to be sticking to his side of the bargain. But whether the voluptuous Vanessa undulated up and down the skewwhiff stairs in the middle of the night, was anyone's guess.

'He's not sleeping with her,' Posy said fiercely, snatching at a cauliflower cheese and a beans on toast. 'Honestly. He's not.'

'But he's not sleeping with you, either . . .'

'Well, no, but then he wasn't sleeping with me anyway. We'd hardly got that far, had we? I mean he *was* definitely sleeping with Vanessa back in Boston and he isn't now, so that's bonus points to me, isn't it?'

Lola gave a half-hearted smile. Why were even the most intelligent and feisty women so foolish when it came to being hopelessly in love?

'And how do you feel about her?'

'Oh, well I could cheerfully throttle her for being here, of course. But she's so damn *nice*. And Flynn says he doesn't feel anything for her at all any more except friendship.'

Well, he would say that, wouldn't he? 'So he's told her about you and him, has he?'

'No, not really, but –' Posy sighed heavily. 'I didn't want him to. She's only temporary. She's probably sussed something, but we, as a couple, hadn't really got off the ground, had we?'

'But she was his lover, and she knows all about traction engines, and she's crewed for him before on engines in the States. I know because she told Mr D and Mr B, and she knows exactly what makes Queen

Mab tick.' Lola shook her head. 'You want to be careful, Posy. Honestly . . .'

Posy sighed again. 'I'm not going to suddenly turn into Casey Jones meets George Stephenson just to prove that my knowledge of steam is greater than her knowledge of steam. Mind you, Dad's besotted. She's out in the garden showing all the model railway visitors round the layout like she was born to it. And Mum isn't the slightest bit jealous because Vanessa can turn her hand to helping out in the kitchen and the dining room when I'm busy with the courier run, or Gear Change or in here, so she thinks she's got a surrogate daughter.'

To be honest, Lola thought, Vanessa had cleverly delighted everyone in Steeple Fritton. She'd tried, early on, to ingratiate herself with Lola, telling her about her prowess at running Opal Joe's in Boston, but Lola was adamant that she didn't need any more bar staff. She'd already upset Posy enough by inadvertently employing Ritchie, she had absolutely no intention of making matters worse.

However, wearing clothes even brighter than Dilys's, and with her halo of red hair and her scampering exuberance to embrace English village life and love it to death, everyone adored Vanessa.

Flynn had sworn to all and sundry that he didn't. Lola wasn't sure she believed him.

'We ought to have a girls' night out to boost ourselves up,' she nodded towards the poster for the Letting Off Steam Carnival Queen contest beside the dartboard. 'Get ourselves down to the village hall tomorrow night, grab our free cocktails, hit the dance floor and cheer on the competing sisterhood.'

Posy pulled a face. 'I'd have thought that was the last place you'd want to be. One, we're both feeling suicidal, and two, it's not at all politically correct, and you've always been a stickler for –'

'And falling in love with a man young enough to be my son who is heavily involved with another woman who just happens to be having his baby, is completely PC, is it?'

'Well, if you put it like that . . .'

'I just think we should go out and enjoy ourselves. It should be amusing, and after all we're both free agents. We've both worked hard enough for this carnival, and anyway,' Lola studied her fingernails, 'I'm going to make the most of my last few weeks in the village.'

'What? You're leaving? You can't! What'll I do without you? You're my friend!'

'Nikki and Amanda are your friends,' Lola didn't look up. 'Ninety per cent of the village are your friends. You'll be fine.'

'No I won't! I don't want you to go.'

'Not what you said when I arrived here.'

'No, well, things were different then. Everything's changed. I've changed, and so have you. You can't leave.'

'I can't stay, either. What have I got to stay for?' Lola found a smeary bit on the bar counter to rub at. 'I can't stay around here watching Ellis and Tatty bringing up their baby . . .'

'It's what I've got to do with Ritchie and Sonia and dear, little Bradfield –'

'No,' Lola shook her head. 'It isn't. You'd known

377

about the baby and their marriage for some time. You'd accepted, more or less, that you and Ritchie were finished. You had months to get used to the idea, however awful it was. Ellis and I had only just begun our relationship, only had a few days of that pure heady rush of first love, then it was over . . .'

'Oh, God,' Posy sighed. 'But everyone loves you, and the pub is brilliant because of you and –'

'And Hogarth will be back sooner than he thought. In June. I've had a letter. Then there'll be nothing here for me. No Ellis, no pub . . . I don't have any choice but to move on again.'

'I don't want Hogarth to come back!' Posy practically pouted and stamped her foot. 'That's only a month away! I don't want things to change, to go back to the way they were. I love what we've done and achieved and turned ourselves and this village into –'

Lola could have wept at hearing her own thoughts spoken aloud. 'I know, Posy. I know. But at least this is your proper home. It'll never be mine now. I'll have to look for somewhere else to live, and start all over again.'

It wasn't merely the practicalities that made her need to leave Steeple Fritton though, Lola thought, as she locked the pub's doors after the lunch-time session. The emotions were far more painful. But with the continued presence of Vanessa at the B&B, Posy had enough troubles of her own to contend with. There seemed little point in burdening her with anything else.

Barbara Marion's revelations about Nigel had been a terrible shock, a complete body blow, but one she'd felt she could cope with because of Ellis. Ellis . . . Lola honestly couldn't think about Ellis any more. The pain was too great. She'd been so happy, so blissfully happy for what seemed like a blink in time, then it was gone . . . Like everything else.

To have lost both her past and her future in the same evening was almost too much to bear. But then she'd discovered that losing Ellis hurt far, far more than losing Nigel had done. And that's what scared her most.

It had all been an illusion. Nothing more. And to stay here in Steeple Fritton and see Ellis every day was more than her sanity could stand. And now, next month, Hogarth would be coming home to reclaim The Crooked Sixpence. There really was nothing left to stay for.

Lola sighed as she drifted towards Vi Bickeridge's corner shop for some shampoo and other vital supplies. She had no idea where she could run to next. But she'd soon have to decide.

'Lola!'

Tatty swept out through the rainbow beaded glass curtain, and smiled widely.

'Oh, er, hello.' Lola gazed bleakly at Tatty's radiant face, at the glossy curls, and at what she imagined was the swell of her belly, even though she couldn't see it, under the flowing gypsy layers.

'Have you got a moment?' Tatty continued to smile. 'Only there's something I'd like to show you.'

Oh, please God, Lola thought, not the first ultrasound scan or a set of newly-knitted baby booties. 'Um, well, I'm rather busy and –'

'This won't take a minute, promise,' Tatty linked her arm through Lola's in a chummy fashion, and practically dragged her through the curtain.

Tatty's shop was, as always, dark and pungent. Shadowy figures moved behind the voile curtains, and fat pastel candles danced and guttered on every surface.

'Through here,' Tatty motioned with her head, making various things tinkle. Lola followed her into a tiny cubicle with beanbags and mystic music and joss sticks.

'Meditation and relaxation,' Tatty explained. 'Stress therapy. We're just trying it out.'

In the gloom Lola could make out Glad, Rose Lusty and Vi Bickeridge sitting rather awkwardly on the beanbags and sipping something that smelled like warm disinfectant from tiny cups.

'They grizzled a bit about getting down there and they all say they won't get up again because of their rheumatics,' Tatty said cheerfully. 'But I've told them that a few minutes of inhalation and mind-clearing will take away all their aches and pains.'

'Want some herbal tea, duck?' Glad raised her cup to Lola. 'S'posed to be the dog's bollocks.'

'Er, no thanks.' Lola still felt awkward with Gladys. She had no idea how much Ellis had told his grandmother. She turned to Tatty. 'Is this what you wanted to show me? It's, um, very nice, but I don't think I need to be de-stressed.'

Glad snorted into her cup.

'No, no –' Tatty breezed on through another voile curtain, indicating that Lola should follow. 'That was just a detour, this is what I wanted you to see.'

Lola nearly passed out.

After weeks now of studiously avoiding Ellis, she certainly hadn't expected to see him reclining in a dentist's chair in Tatty's back room wearing nothing but a pair of black boxers.

Ellis, it had to be said, looked equally shell-shocked.

'I was just going to show Lola the tattooing,' Tatty squeezed passed Ellis. 'I thought if she could have a first-hand glimpse of what went on, she may put up one of my posters in the pub and have some of these natty little brochures on the bar, and be able to be an advocate for the business.'

Lola and Ellis simply stared at one another.

'What do you reckon? Lola? *Lola!!!*' Tatty laughed. 'Goodness me, is it the needles you don't like? I mean, I wasn't going to suggest you had a tattoo done yourself, although you'd be more than welcome. But Ellis has just agreed to let me try out something new.'

'I really ought to be going,' Lola muttered, staring at Ellis like a hypnotized rabbit. 'I'll certainly put up a poster in the pub and have as many of the brochures as you want, but I don't actually need to see it being done – oh!'

At that moment, young Malvina, all shaven-head, tattoos and body jewellery, swept through yet another beaded curtain. The rattle echoed inside Lola's head.

'Malvina is going to try out the Thermo Max on Ellis,' Tatty said, rather scarily pulling on a pair of surgical gloves. 'It steams the outline of my designs on to the skin like a huge transfer rather than me drawing them on, and saves a lot of time. It's the first time we've used it.'

Lola managed to stop staring at Ellis. 'Yes, I'm sure it's all very fascinating, but really I ought to go –'

'No, but look, this is what I wanted you to see.' Tatty unfurled a sheet of elaborate designs. 'I thought I'd offer local tattoos as well as the usual stuff. So, I've done this one for The Crooked Sixpence, and this one for the carnival, and this is a special I Love Steeple Fritton one, although there possibly won't be a lot of call for that. What do you think?'

'Very enterprising.'

Lola watched in fascinated horror as Malvina, also wearing disposable latex gloves, set to work on Ellis's thigh with swabs of surgical spirit and a disposable razor and then clamped the Thermo Max over his leg and steamed it into place.

'So, you'll advertise them in the pub then?' Tatty said, flicking her spiral curls over her shoulders and reaching for a machine with multi-headed needles like something out of an industrial embroidery factory. 'Lola? Will that be okay?'

'Um, yes . . . and now I'm leaving.'

'Don't.' Ellis beseeched her with his eyes. 'I'd like you to stay.'

'Why? Are you going to have the name of your beloved emblazoned on your thigh?'

'No.'

'That's a surprise.'

'He's chosen something quite unusual, actually,' Tatty beamed, switching on the machine and leaning towards Ellis. She raised her voice over the whine. 'The outline is always done like this, Malvina will keep wiping it down. There you see, it doesn't hurt. Does it Ellis, sweetie?'

Ellis had his eyes closed. Lola wanted to drag him out of the dentist's chair. She truly couldn't bear to see him mutilated, or to see him and Tatty in such close proximity. She could see very little except the beads of blood pinpricking Ellis's leg which Malvina deftly swept away.

Tatty looked up. 'There, outline nearly done. You won't be able to tell what it is yet, of course. Now, these are for the colours and for shading.' She reached for a further set of sterile needles and little cups of coloured inks and started fiddling with the machine. 'The needles go in and out of the skin so fast that there's virtually no pain at all, and –'

Lola wiped her hand over her face and took deep breaths. 'I don't actually feel very well.'

'Shame,' Tatty said, getting to work on Ellis's thigh with various brilliant colours. 'Malvina, be a love and take Lola outside and give her a cup of elderflower and rhubarb.'

'I'll be fine,' Lola said quickly, knowing that the elderflower and rhubarb would succeed where the blood and punctured skin had only just failed.

'Lola.' Ellis opened his eyes. 'I need to talk to you. I'll see you some time, okay?'

'You won't be able to show her the tattoo for a while yet,' Tatty trilled over the continual mechanical whine. 'It'll have to be bandaged until the scab forms. And of course, unless you're on very good terms, it's hardly in the sort of area you can show just anyone, is it?'

Lola lurched out through the voile curtains with Tatty's confident laugh growling huskily in her ears.

'Blimey,' Glad looked up from her beanbag. 'You looks proper pasty. What's going on in there?'

'Your grandson is having a tattoo.'

'Ah,' Glad sipped her warm disinfectant. 'I know. I suggested to Tatty that you might be keen to see it going on . . . for advertising the tattooing parlour in the pub, of course.'

Lola looked at Glad. She knew! She damn well knew! 'Um, and what did Ellis think about that plan?'

Glad cast a warning look towards Rose and Vi who were now sniffing lavender joss sticks. 'Ellis put the idea to me, actually, duck. But as you and him don't see too much of each other, he couldn't ask you outright, so I suggested it to Tatty and, well, here you both are . . .'

Lola smiled. 'Nice idea, but pointless.'

'That's as maybe,' Glad shrugged. 'But you should at least talk about things.'

'Talking won't change the situation.'

'No, bugger it, it won't.' Glad looked fierce. 'But it's a start.'

Rose and Vi were beginning to emerge from their lavender haze and blinked owlishly at Lola.

She smiled at Glad. 'So you didn't disapprove? The age difference and everything?'

'My duck, I couldn't have been more pleased. I know proper love when I sees it, and that's what there was there. That sort of love happens once in a lifetime if you're lucky, and it don't take no notice of age, sex, colour or creed. I could have killed him for making this current mess.'

'So could I.'

'You going to the Carnival Queen contest, Lola?' Rose Lusty, obviously confused by Glad's cryptic comments and a headful of aromatherapy, changed tack. 'We are.'

384

Lola nodded. 'Yes, I'm going with Posy. It should be fun. Although what sort of judge the vicar will make is anybody's guess.'

'It ain't the vicar,' Vi Bickeridge wriggled on her beanbag. 'It's a celebrity panel.'

'Oh, I know that's what it says on the poster, but it'll still be the vicar and a couple of people from the council.'

'Actually,' Glad took a final withering look at her half-finished cup, 'they've got famous people. From the weekenders. Vicar's done a grand job of rooting them out. There's a pop star and a model and a footballer.'

Lola smiled. The meditation and relaxation had clearly done the trick in finally addling Gladys's brain. 'So we're going to have Madonna and Kate Moss and David Beckham picking Miss Letting Off Steam, are we?'

'Don't you take the piss, my duck.' Gladys raised an eyebrow. 'Just make sure you're there if you knows what's good for you, if you gets my drift.'

Chapter Twenty-seven

Steeple Fritton's village hall was both decorated to the hilt and heaving at the seams. With The Crooked Sixpence closed for the evening in the certain knowledge that everyone capable of drinking would be at the hall for the free champagne cocktails, it meant that even those who had no interest in the choice of Miss Letting Off Steam were there simply for the alcohol.

The tables and chairs arranged on either side of the hall were already occupied by rival factions. The Pinks, the coven, everyone from Sunny Dene, and all the people from Cressbeds and Bunny Burrow were on one side; while on the other there was a smattering of weekenders, the well-to-do from the posh houses, the residents of the other Frittons, and total strangers who were either there to gawp at young flesh or have a free drink or both. Intermingled were those who had got the date wrong and had expected intermediate flower arranging for the over sixty-fives.

At the end of a rather imposing catwalk was a trestle table, presumably for the A-List celebs who were to do the judging, and the stage was set up with microphones and spotlights and balloons. Someone had even resurrected a glittering mirror ball which was suspended from the ceiling for use later when the catwalk would be cleared away for the dancing.

It was, all-in-all, very impressive.

Posy and Lola, done up to the nines and fortified by Posy's recommended going-out booster of several TJ Hookers – equal measures of Jack Daniel's and Tia Maria – were merry enough to forget Other Women and determinedly ready to party.

The entrants were all backstage, having paid their money and filled in their forms. Posy knew that Nikki and Amanda and most of her old school friends had entered. Also knowing her limitations, she'd declined the invitation to join them.

'Shall we get a drink and find somewhere to sit where we can get a good view and make caustic comments?' She glanced at Lola. 'After all, you did supply the booze, so it seems only fair that you should have a glass or two – oh, shit!'

'What?' Lola was a little unsteady on her feet, obviously not being quite as au fait with the TJ Hookers as Posy. 'Is there a problem?'

'Three problems. Who hired the bar staff?'

'The vicar said he'd organize it. Why?' She looked. 'Oh, bugger.'

'Precisely.' Posy glared at Flynn, Ritchie and Ellis, who were standing in a line behind the makeshift bar, and all playing the Tom Cruise role from the eponymous cocktail film by juggling shakers. 'Mind you, they're very attractive.'

'They are,' Lola conceded. 'For unfaithful, untrustworthy, lowlife scum.'

Posy shrieked with laughter. 'I think we've both overdone the TJ Hookers. You'd never use that language normally.'

'Probably not. But this isn't a normal occasion, and Glad, the old witch, knew damn well that Ellis would be here tonight, because she told me to make sure I was here, and, oh joy, Tatty isn't.'

'Er, she is now.' Posy motioned towards the door.

Tatty and the kiddies, all in their party best, which seemed to involve tassels and tinsel and a lot of net, trailed into the hall.

'Sod and damn and bugger – oh . . .' Lola clapped her hand to her mouth. 'Oh, goodness, don't let me anywhere near the vicar tonight, my inhibitions seem to have deserted me. But, well, really, why didn't she just stay at home?'

'I suppose she wanted to be here and there are no baby-sitters available, so what option did she have? Anyway, because she's late she'll have to sit at the back so at least you won't have to look at her.'

'It's okay for you to be smug, looks like you'll have Flynn to yourself for the evening. There's no sign of the pneumatic Vanessa.'

'No, there isn't, is there?' Posy shot a lingering glance towards the cocktail bar. 'And ooh, I really, really, really fancy Flynn.'

'There speaks a woman well tanked-up on a dubious mixture,' Lola broke off to glare across at Tatty again. 'Oh, damn it, let's grab a table as far away from Tatty and the brats as possible, and then one of us can get the drinks.'

'We can *both* get the drinks,' Posy insisted. 'Then we can both go for the kill.'

Stumbling amongst the tables, muttering apologies, Posy found two seats close to the stage. It meant they'd be sharing with the Pinks and on the next table to the coven, which was possibly why the chairs were still empty, but beggars and choosers and all that.

'You two looks lovely,' Neddy Pink grinned. 'You should be up there with the contenders.'

Lola shook her head. 'I don't think there's anyone over twenty-five entering –'

'And they all look like girlies,' Posy added, 'not biker babes. So, we're ruled out on all counts.'

'I dunno . . .' Neddy Pink eyed them speculatively. 'You both look like pretty tasty bits of stuff to me. I'd vote for the pair of you.'

'Thanks, Neddy,' Posy said happily, then looked at Lola. 'See, we can both still pull if we put our minds to it.'

The vicar, done up like Liberace, strode on to the stage to Ray Conniff's version of 'Standing On The Corner Watching All The Girls Go By' which oozed from the communal Dansette. Everyone clapped and stamped and whistled.

Lola groaned. Posy jabbed her in the ribs. 'I told you this was going to spectacularly non-PC. You can't grizzle.'

'Ladies and gentlemen,' the vicar screamed into the microphone. 'The first ever Steeple Fritton Carnival Queen contest is due to begin in about an hour's time, with a parade of all the entrants in evening wear. To those of you from the Townswomen's Guild who signed the protest petition, the swimwear section has been cancelled.'

There were a lot of jeers and boos. Especially, Posy noticed, from behind the cocktail bar. Bastards.

'However, in the meantime, do avail yourself of the champagne cocktails kindly supplied by The Crooked Sixpence, and the nibbles kindly provided by the Pinks.'

There was a sudden rash of spitting surreptitiously into hands.

'And now it is my great pleasure to introduce you to our famous faces. Our illustrious judging panel for this evening.'

Gladys shivered with expectation. Posy and Lola both smiled kindly at her. This was her dream come true. At last, celebrities in Steeple Fritton.

'First,' the vicar howled, 'straight from the Swinging Sixties when he topped the charts with his group, The Downtown Puggles – Florian Pickavance!'

The hall erupted with cheers and whistles and applause.

Posy leaned across to Lola. 'Who the hell is he? You must know, he's your era.'

'Thanks a lot. I've never heard of him or his damn Downbeat Puddles. I was hoping for Wayne Fontana.'

'Who?'

'Shut up.'

Florian Pickavance, all wrinkly in leather and lurex, waved at his besotted audience before making his way gingerly towards the judges table.

'Next,' the vicar yelled, 'our famous model girl, and I'm sure you'll all recognize her from the corsetry pages of the home-shopping catalogues – Valerie Smith!'

Valerie Smith, plump and mumsy, got almost as

rapturous a welcome as Florian. Posy could have sworn she'd once worked in the butcher's shop in Fritton Magna. Valerie's journey to her seat was slightly more steady than Florian's and earned her an extra clap.

'And finally, last but not least, champion goal scorer from the Ernest Hubble Berks, Bucks and Oxon Amateur Football League – Morton Titterton!'

The cheers rocked the rafters.

'Are you crying?' Posy looked accusingly at Lola.

Lola, chewing her lips, shook her head.

'Blame swizz!' Glad spat. 'Never 'eard of none of 'em!'

'Alcohol. I need alcohol,' Lola muttered. 'And quickly.'

Stumbling on feet all over again, they fought their way through the Fritton throng. Ray Conniff's Dansette music had changed to 'Girl From Ipanema', which was rather silly in such a crowded space as several people were attempting to Lambada.

Flynn, Ellis and Ritchie were very busy. Posy and Lola, with much eye contact, decided to split up and go for either end of the bar.

'Oh, hi, Pose, you look lovely . . .' Ritchie beamed at her. 'What can I get you?'

'Nothing. I want Flynn to serve me.'

'He's busy.'

'I'll wait.'

'Suit yourself.' He swivelled his smile to the other end of the bar. 'Hello, Lola. You look gorgeous. What can I get you?'

'Nothing, thanks. I'll wait for Ellis to serve me.'

'He's busy.'

'That's okay, I'll wait.'

Ritchie, looking mortified, shuffled back to his central position and served the coven instead. Posy had to admit, watching him and Flynn and Ellis in action, that they looked wonderful, and had got the art of squirting angostura bitters on to sugar cubes off to perfection.

'Hi,' Flynn eventually grinned at her. 'You look knockout. What would you like?'

'You,' Posy smiled. 'And a year's supply of champagne cocktails and a big feather bed.'

Flynn leaned over the bar and kissed her gently. 'Sounds ace to me.'

She touched his face. 'Where's Vanessa tonight? I wouldn't have thought she'd want to miss this.'

'Oh, she isn't.' He straightened up. 'She's up there on the stage behind the curtain with the vicar. She's entered the competition.'

Posy was outraged. 'She can't do that!'

'Sure she can. There was nothing in the rules to say you had to be a villager.'

'There weren't any rules at all, which is why there are some mighty odd contenders.'

'Exactly,' Flynn decanted champagne and brandy on to the soaked sugar cube. 'God, I wish it wasn't like this. She will go home, you know.'

'So she keeps saying.'

It was a rotten situation for Flynn, she understood that. He'd still been missing Vanessa so much when he'd first arrived in the village. They'd been together for so long. But her arrival could not have been more badly timed. How Flynn really felt about Vanessa now, though, was more of a mystery and one Posy wasn't too sure that she wanted to unravel.

She smiled at him. 'At least we're not in their shoes . . .'

They both looked along the bar at Ellis and Lola who were pretending like mad to be disinterested, but obviously wanted to leap on one another.

'Yeah,' Flynn nodded. 'That's tough stuff. Oh . . .' His eyes seemed to be fastened somewhere behind Posy's left ear. 'Jeeze!'

Posy turned round. Jeeze, indeed. Vanessa had slipped out from behind the curtain and was making her way down the steps towards them. With her red hair scraped into a spiky topknot and sprayed with pink and silver highlights, a pink stretchy dress which just covered her from nipple to crotch, and silver stilettos, she brought the village hall to a silent standstill as she teetered towards the bar.

'Hiya, guys,' she beamed. 'It's so hot under those lights and I'm so dry up there . . . Flynn, be an angel and pour me a drink. No, sorry, baby, make it two. Sonia wants one as well.'

Angel? Baby? Then, 'Sonia? *Sonia?*' Posy managed to find her voice. 'Sonia's entered the competition? Why the hell isn't she at home being a proper mother?'

'My parents are baby-sitting for little Bradfield,' Ritchie said cheerfully. 'Sonia was so proud to have regained her figure so quickly that she wanted to show it off and –'

Posy didn't wait to hear any more about the Dalgetty domestic arrangements or Sonia's figure. She hurtled past Vanessa and through the still open-mouthed villagers at the bar and grabbed Lola's arm. 'Come on! Quickly!'

Lola who looked as though she wanted to clamp herself to Ellis forever, put up a bit of a fight. 'Have you gone mad?'

'Probably. Just come on!'

After years of manhandling the BMW's gears and brakes, Posy's grip was too strong for Lola. She prised her away from the bar like a cork popping from a bottle.

'What on earth are you doing?' Lola frowned, then saw Vanessa. 'Christ!'

'Exactly. That's why I'm going to enter the contest. There's nothing in the rules that says people can't enter at the last minute and –'

'There aren't any rules,' Lola pointed out, 'but why –?'

'Because bloody Sonia's entered, too, and –'

'So have I . . .' Tatty trilled from behind them. 'Just this minute. The vicar's wife said she'd kindly mind the kiddies and as I'm dressed for the occasion,' she smoothed down the layers of frocks she was wearing – a sort of pale blue tutu over a navy blue silk nightie over a silver slip edged with beads and bells, 'I thought I'd stand as good a chance as anyone.'

Lola stared in disbelief. 'But you're pregnant!'

'Yes, I know, but without having to parade in the swimwear, it doesn't show, does it? There's nothing in the rules to say you can't be pregnant.'

'There are no bloody rules!' Posy and Lola howled together as they forced their way towards the stage.

The vicar, perspiring happily under his Liberace jacket and sparkling beneath the spotlights, seemed more than willing to pocket their money and sign them up.

'Be ready to parade in thirty minutes. Oh, and Ms Wentworth, you haven't put your age on the form here.'

'Guess,' Lola said unhelpfully. 'Can't stop.' She looked at Posy. 'Now where are we going?'

'To get dressed,' Posy panted, nodding towards the Pinks. 'Save our chairs, will you? We won't be long.'

'But we are dressed,' Lola protested as Posy dragged her out of the hall.

'Jeans and vest tops and fortunately a lot of slap, thank heavens. Nice clothes, but not drop-dead sexy or anywhere near glam enough. Gear Change will have everything we need.'

Five minutes later, it did. Still giggling from the TJ Hookers, Posy eventually managed to unlock the door and find the light switch.

'There! Cornucopia! Serendipity!! Pandora's Box, or God knows, choose your own epithet.'

'Not sure they're epithets, actually,' Lola said, rummaging through a pile of evening wear. 'And what are we searching for exactly?'

'Anything amazing that almost fits and that will knock spots off Sonia, Vanessa, and yes, even poor old Tatty.' She looked at Lola. 'Look, we started all this with absolutely nothing. From rock bottom. We've done it all on our own – the businesses, the survival, the carnival, everything. We didn't even need men to help us – well, not really, they just came as added extras. We owe it to ourselves to be upfront and brassy and brazen. Why should we be sitting there with all the oldies, while women who had sod all to do with any of it, take the spoils?'

'I'm one of the oldies.'

'What? Don't be daft. I mean properly old like my mum. You're drop-dead gorgeous – and you know it, so don't fish for compliments. Now, there's some Prada and some really groovy chick stuff from Stella McCartney here somewhere.'

'It's only a carnival queen contest –'

'No it isn't,' Posy snatched up a handful of lace. 'It's far more than that. This carnival is the public culmination of all our private triumphs, and if you're still insisting on leaving the village, at least you can do it with a bang. Now, grab this.'

Lola grabbed.

They made it back to the village hall with minutes to spare. Their progress had been slightly hampered by the two pairs of discarded Jimmy Choo mules which fitted neither of them but which Posy had claimed would make all the difference.

'Christ Almighty!' Ellis, who was dumping empty crates outside the door, stopped in his tracks. 'You can't go in there wearing that! You'll both be arrested!'

'If you've got it, flaunt it,' Posy smiled sweetly. 'And I'll be asking questions about the ankle bracelets later,' she grinned at Lola. 'They were from Ellis, I take it? Can't see it being Wrinkly Nigel's style somehow.'

'Bugger,' Lola groaned. 'I'd forgotten they'd be on show. I've worn jeans and boots ever since . . . ever since . . .'

Ellis looked as if he was going to cry. 'They were a birthday present.' He touched Lola's hand. 'I'm so pleased that you're still wearing them.'

'I'll be wearing them in my coffin,' Lola said fiercely.

She stared at Ellis for a moment, then leaned forward and kissed his mouth. 'I love you, Ellis Blissit. You've changed my life – well, the bits that were left that needed an overhaul. And although we'll never be together, I'll always be grateful and I'll always love you.'

'Jesus,' Posy sniffed. 'Don't do this. Not now. Our mascara'll run. Let's just get in there and knock 'em dead.'

Chapter Twenty-eight

It was very satisfying, Posy thought, as she sashayed into the village hall in Lola's wake, to notice that everyone stopped and stared. With the jeans and vests of half an hour earlier dumped in favour of filmy, flimsy designer frocks and the Jimmy Choos, albeit second-hand, she reckoned that Steeple Fritton had probably never seen such a rapid makeover.

'Hang on,' Posy caught up with Lola halfway across the hall and grabbed her hand. 'Are you all right? Really?'

Lola nodded. 'I'm not going to cry in public if that's what you're afraid of. I've perfected the art of private weeping over the years.'

'You poor thing,' Posy sighed. 'You really, really do love Ellis, don't you?'

'Really, really, yes. The age difference might have been a problem, but somehow I doubt it. I honestly think it would have worked out . . .' She shrugged. 'I'll never find out now though. It's probably my punishment, all the ill-wishing of every cheated-on wife in the world being heaped upon my head.'

'Crap. It's just a combination of bloody Tatty Spry and her sodding non-stop breeding agenda being added to blokes not being able to say no when it's offered on a G-string-garnished plate.'

'Maybe. For me and Ellis though, I think you can add extremely bad timing.'

Posy indicated the ankle bracelets. 'So Ellis gave you those before, before –'

'Before either of us knew about the new Tatty progeny, yes.'

'They are so cool. A really sexy present, and something no one else would have ever thought of. Oh, what a buggering mess all this is.'

'Tell me about it.'

Posy wrinkled her nose. 'But didn't Ellis just say the anklets were for your birthday? I didn't even know you'd had a birthday.'

'I've had fifty birthdays,' Lola hissed. 'The most recent one was a few weeks ago. The day of the first karaoke session, when I went into Oxford and did all my shopping and everything.'

'Aaah, sweet.' Posy smiled. 'And Ellis was with you and, and, that's when it happened? You and him? The falling in love?'

Lola started to walk towards the stage. 'It had probably been happening before then, but that's when I realized, yes. More fool me. He said he already knew.'

'Aaah,' Posy beamed again, then stopped. As the love affair was now over, it probably wasn't the best time to go starry-eyed. 'But – *fifty*? You've had *fifty* birthdays? You can't be fifty! That means you're older than my mum, and you look half her age. Blimey, maybe being a mistress has its advantages. I'll have to mention it to her as an alternative to HRT.'

Posy was relieved to notice that Lola was almost smiling as they climbed the steps at the side of the stage.

'Good God!' the vicar blinked as they struggled through the musty curtain. 'I mean, oh my goodness me. You two have pulled out all the stops, I must say.'

Lola and Posy grinned at one another in sisterly triumph.

There were thirty-three contestants backstage. Most of them, including Nikki and Amanda who greeted Posy with shrieks of welcome, were dressed for clubbing with a lot of lycra and body glitter and looked, Posy thought, a bit tarty. There was very little class on offer. Vanessa, of course, was in one of her own. And then there was Sonia . . .

Posy simply couldn't believe that the svelte, groomed, flat-stomached Sonia could have metamorphosed from the bloated, swearing, screaming lump she'd been on their last meeting. They pointedly ignored one another.

'No competition there,' Lola whispered. 'She looks like Jean Shrimpton.'

'Who?'

'She was a very famous model. Before your time. But she used to wear dead simple shift dresses and have her hair all flicked up like that.'

'Did she look all pouty and slender and glossy and doe-eyed, then, this Jean Shrimpton?'

'Mmm, yes, I suppose she did, now you come to mention it. Damn.'

'Right now, ladies,' the vicar clapped his hands. 'We're just about to start, so let's just run through our routine.

I'll announce you by name, you'll walk out on to the stage, straight down the catwalk, turn and smile at the judges, then return to me where we'll chat for thirty seconds. Understood?'

Everyone nodded dutifully. There was a lot of giggling and applying of last-minute lip gloss and hair spray. Posy was beginning to think maybe this was not such a good idea after all.

'It's a cattle market,' Lola muttered. 'I campaigned against this sort of thing in the seventies.'

'It's for the carnival and the village, and it's fun,' Posy knew her voice lacked conviction. 'You'll love it once you get started.'

The vicar pranced out from behind the curtains, silenced Ray Conniff, and made his introductions. As Ritchie and Flynn and Ellis had been more than generous with the champagne cocktails, his reception was pretty wild. Several people, including Neddy Pink, wolf-whistled him.

One by one, sadly to the tune of 'The Lady Is A Tramp', the contestants shimmied down the catwalk, bared their teeth at the judges, and shimmied back again, to be asked banal questions by the vicar.

Lola and Posy, still waiting in the wings, were stunned at the number of Fritton girls who wanted to travel to Third World countries and work with underprivileged children.

Tatty said dreamily that she just wanted love and peace, Sonia was keen to start a crèche in Steeple Fritton to help young mothers back to work, and Vanessa thought she might like to marry and settle down in a quaint English village.

'Over my dead body,' Posy growled.

'And contestant number thirty-two,' shouted the vicar. 'Lola Wentworth!'

As Lola seemed to be rooted to the spot, Posy gave her a little shove and she teetered forward on the sloppy Jimmy Choos. The audience roared their approval. Ray Conniff was on his umpteenth rendering of 'The Lady Is A Tramp', and whoever was in charge of the Dansette thought they'd be very clever and switched the track to 'Whatever Lola Wants (Lola Gets)'.

Unfortunately, Neddy Pink took the opportunity to whip out his accordion for the accompaniment. He was at least two bars behind Ray.

Peeping out from behind the curtains, Posy watched. Lola, wincing at the music and the audience participation, stared straight ahead at the bar. Ellis stared straight back. It was electric. The emotion was tangible. Lola smiled, but not for the judges; she posed and smiled some more, just for Ellis, then turned and glided back to the vicar.

Amid massive applause, the vicar shoved his microphone under his nose. 'Now, Lola, tell everyone what it is you hope for in your future.'

Posy held her breath.

Lola stared at Ellis again. 'I've enjoyed every minute of my time in Steeple Fritton and made some wonderful friends and had more fun than I've ever had in my life. Running The Crooked Sixpence has been a fascinating and rewarding experience. I intend to take both my new-found skills and the memories of my friendships with me when I move on to start my new life.'

Everyone clapped and cheered and whistled again.

They were long past listening to the words. Posy watched Ellis's face whiten and crumple. She watched him duck out from behind the bar, and Flynn grab his shoulder to stop him. She watched Ellis cry.

'And the final contestant, last but by no means least,' the vicar was getting hoarse. 'Posy Nightingale!'

Still trying to see if Ellis was okay, Posy skipped out on to the catwalk. It was highly embarrassing that Dilys and Norrie and Mr D and Mr B were all standing on their chairs and whistling through their fingers. The Pinks were chanting 'Po-sy! Po-sy!' the way the less restrained members of the Jerry Springer audience did.

The trip along the catwalk was one of the longest of her life; her feet hurt and in consequence she grimaced unpleasantly at the judges. Morton Titterton winked at her. She assumed he'd winked at all the contestants. She hoped he'd get stuck like it and have to explain it to his wife. The return journey to the stage was taken at almost a run. The Jimmy Choos were making her eyes water.

Once the applause had died down – and Posy had to admit, it was very heady stuff just strolling through the village hall and having everyone cheering – the vicar did his final microphone thrust.

'Oh, er, I've got two ambitions in life. I want to carry on with what we've been doing over the last few months, setting up small enterprises, expanding the potential of the village, enjoying it, and really putting Steeple Fritton on the map. I'd also like to get married and have loads of children. Well, not as many as Tatty, obviously, but some. Thank you.'

The cheering and foot-stamping was deafening. Posy didn't look at Ritchie, and certainly not at Flynn. What was the point?

'Right, ladies and gentlemen,' the vicar barked. 'You've seen all our lovely contestants, now the judges will need about fifteen minutes to confer. Clearly, their decision is going to be an extremely difficult one to make. The winner and her two runners-up will grace the main float on carnival day in two weeks' time. A huge honour. So, I suggest you refill your glasses and –'

Steeple Fritton needed no more encouragement than that. The lemming-like dash for the bar was awesome.

Backstage, the contestants huddled together, all tension gone for the time being. There were shrieks of laughter, and sneaky cigarettes being passed round, and a lot of reciprocal grooming. Keeping as far away from Tatty, Sonia and Vanessa as possible, Posy and Lola perched beside the Dansette in case anyone decided to resurrect Ray Conniff.

'You're not really leaving? You didn't mean it?'

Lola nodded. 'Yes. I thought I'd try applying for pub manager's jobs. I'll get accommodation that way, too.'

'You'll break Ellis's heart.'

'He's broken mine, so it seems a fair deal. And you're not really wanting to get married and have babies, are you?'

''Fraid so. Is marriage and motherhood very non-PC at the moment? Do you have to be running a global company and be at least forty-five before it becomes an option?'

'Well, it does seem the trendy thing to do. What does Flynn have to say about it?'

'Why would Flynn have anything to say about it at all, honey?' Vanessa towered over them. 'Flynn's coming back to the States with me.'

'Is he?' Posy tried to keep her smile from wobbling. 'He didn't mention anything to me. I thought he was going to keep Steeple Fritton as his base and chuck in his lot with The Memory Lane Fair on a part-time basis.'

'That was before I came along again.' Vanessa squatted beside them in a chummy way, displaying most of her underwear. 'We're going to take over his parents' house in Boston and he's going to help me as a bartender in Opal Joe's.'

Posy's mouth was definitely quivering. 'And Queen Mab?'

'Oh, he'll have her shipped over. It'll cost, of course, but then Flynn's okay for money. He'll see the carnie out, and then we're leaving.'

'Nice for you,' Posy shrugged. She didn't believe one word of it. Flynn would have told her if he'd changed his plans, she knew he would.

'Ladies, ladies!' the vicar reappeared. 'The judges have reached their decision. If you'd all like to line up on the stage . . .'

Everyone, it seemed, wanted to stand at the back. It took several minutes of frankly un-vicarish shoving and pulling to get them into line.

The curtains swept back to the strains of 'Dancing Queen', this clearly being the best Ray Conniff had to offer in his vinyl repertoire for such an auspicious occasion. The vicar stepped forward and Posy thought she was probably going to be sick. She very much hoped it would be over Vanessa.

'Ladies and gentlemen! The judges have reached their final decision! It was a very close run thing and I'm going to ask Florian Pickavance to present the lucky winners with their crowns. In time-honoured tradition, I'll announce the results in reverse order.'

There was a pause for the ritual hand-clapping and foot-stamping.

'The second Steeple Fritton Letting Off Steam Princess is – Posy Nightingale!!!!'

Posy now knew she was going to be sick. Several of the line-up swore nastily. Inching forward on the Jimmy Choos with the screams roaring in her ears, she allowed herself to be grabbed by a rather sweaty Florian. He kissed her damply on both cheeks and rammed a plastic tiara in amongst her Marc Bolan curls.

Stunned, she staggered back into place. Sonia and Vanessa glared at her. Amanda and Nikki kissed her. Lola just laughed.

The vicar revved up again. 'And now, first Steeple Fritton Letting Off Steam Princess, and runner-up to Miss Letting Off Steam is, Lola Wentworth!'

There was a great deal more swearing and several rather bitchy ageist comments as Lola tottered forward to be manhandled by Florian. Her tiara was lopsided. The village hall was in paroxysms of delight. Posy laughed, then saw Ellis's face and stopped.

Lola returned to the welcoming throng looking acutely embarrassed and stared at the floor.

'And finally, the moment you've all been waiting

for. The winner and Miss Letting Off Steam Carnival Queen is –'

The vicar paused for dramatic effect. Neddy Pink used the silence for an accordion fanfare.

'Sonia Dalgetty!!!'

'Noooo!'

Posy wasn't sure if the cry came from her or Sonia or Vanessa or all three.

Sonia, her hands clapped to her cheeks and making little moues with her pale, glossy lips, simpered forward. Florian, obviously a big Jean Shrimpton fan, groped as well as slobbered as he placed the crown on Sonia's head and spent an unnecessarily long time adjusting the sash across her chest.

Ritchie, Posy was pleased to notice, looked furious. Flynn and Ellis were nowhere to be seen. Sonia adjusted her full-blown crown, beamed at her subjects, and swaggered back into the line-up.

Congratulations were in short supply as everyone glared malevolently at Sonia. Then someone hiked up the volume on 'Dancing Queen' and the local paper took photographs, and they all smiled with hatred in their eyes.

'Ladies, ladies!' the vicar clapped his hands. 'Very well done. A wonderful turnout, and you're all winners in my eyes. Our very lovely queen and her equally lovely attendants will all look, er, lovely on the float and are a great credit to the village. And as soon as the band is ready, I'd like to ask our lovely Miss Letting Off Steam, Sonia Dalgetty, to take to the floor with the chairman of the judges, Florian Pickavance!'

There was a mad scramble as the catwalk was dragged

away and a bevy of paunchy men in tuxedos humped various musical instruments and amplifiers and reels of cable on to the stage.

'Shit,' Posy muttered. 'Florian's brought his Down and Outs.'

'Sadly not,' the vicar said. 'We couldn't afford them. We've got Ezra Samuels and his Caribbean Combo from Upton Poges.'

'Oh, goody.'

'And by the way, just in case either you or Ms Wentworth were disappointed at not having won, I did tip the wink, so to speak, to the judges. I felt that as you're to be our fortune teller, and Lola will be very much needed at The Crooked Sixpence for the Stars In Their Eyes karaoke, we couldn't afford to have either of you crowned as carnival queen and be therefore otherwise engaged for the entire day.'

'Fair enough,' Posy nodded. 'Not that either of us expected to win anyway. And did you also tip the judges the wink, so to speak, that Sonia would be the perfect choice?'

'Indeed not!' The vicar looked horrified. 'That would have been cheating. No, the final decision was the judges alone. She certainly wouldn't have been my selection. Between you and me, my money was on that gorgeous American girl.'

Posy snorted, straightened her tiara, kicked off her mules and marched down the steps.

After extricating herself from her parents and Mr D and Mr B, all of whom were moist-eyed with pride and insisted on a group hug, Posy searched the hall for Lola. She seemed to have vanished into thin air. So had

Ellis. Vanessa and Flynn were also missing, and Sonia and Ritchie were having a row. Tatty and her brood had joined the coven, and the younger Sprys were all tucking into heaped plates of nibbles that no one else would eat.

Warily, because of her bare feet, Posy headed for the bar.

Ritchie and Sonia didn't interrupt their row for a second. The gist, it seemed, was Ritchie being miffed at his beloved being the object of Florian's attention. Sonia didn't share his concern and was currently pointing out that it was the Carnival Queen's role to dance with all the judges, but she'd pass on Valerie Smith, and Ritchie would have to excuse her as her first official duty beckoned.

'Daft tart,' Ritchie muttered as Florian oozed through the crowd and clutched Sonia against his spindly leather and lurex body.

'Seconded,' Posy said cheerfully. 'Can I have a drink, please?'

'You should have won that. You look gorgeous.'

'Oh, shut up. Just pour me a drink.'

'No, I want to dance with you. Now.' Ritchie nipped out from the bar, and nodded towards Norrie who had arrived with a clutch of empty glasses. 'Would you mind taking over here for a moment, please? Ellis and Flynn have done a bunk and I really want to dance with Posy.'

Norrie looked perplexed. 'And does Posy really want to dance with you?'

'Course not,' Posy grinned at her father, 'but it's probably the best offer I'll get all night. You can make

409

champagne cocktails for five minutes, Dad, can't you?'

'I'm a quick learner.' Norrie squeezed in behind the bar. The customers were already three-deep. He still looked worried. 'If you hurt her again, I'll have your guts for garters, Ritchie. I mean it.'

'Don't worry. Apart from treading on my toes he can't hurt me at all. I'm now totally immune to the Dalgetty charm.' She wrinkled her nose at Ritchie. 'Come on, then. Let's see if you've lost your touch.'

Ezra Samuels and his boys struck up a rousing Glenn Miller medley and Steeple Fritton took to the floor. The mirror ball revolved on the ceiling, scattering rainbow prisms across the dancers, as Posy, leading Ritchie by the hand, picked her way between the jitterbugging couples. They'd danced together here all their lives: at youth club parties, their own subsequent 18ths and 21sts, and many and various celebrations before, after and in between. It seemed scarily normal to be back in his arms.

He laughed as her head fitted under his chin. 'Spooky. We always slow-danced to everything didn't we? It just seems so right.'

'No, it doesn't,' Posy muttered into his T-shirt. 'It's instinctive, that's all. And please be careful not to dislodge my tiara, I'm very proud of it. Oh, and I do know why you're doing this.'

'Do you?'

'Of course. To upset Sonia. A notion with which I wholeheartedly concur.'

They shuffled around a bit more. As everyone else was twirling and spinning, the shuffling occasionally had to stop altogether.

'There's more to it than that,' Ritchie muttered. 'I wanted to dance with you because it was the only way I could touch you again. I want to be with you, Pose. I still love you and, and I want you back.'

'Don't be so bloody stupid!'

Posy jerked her head up so quickly that her tiara slid round her neck. She wriggled out of his arms and replaced her crown. Honestly! Men!

'I thought you'd want me, too.' Ritchie's voice was almost a whine. 'I thought –'

'Oh, God! Listen to yourself!' Posy had to howl above one of Ezra Samuels' boys who was giving a trumpet solo. 'Yes, maybe I would have done. Once. Ages ago. Not any more. Everything's changed. Everyone's changed. You can't just walk away from your marriage and your child after a few weeks, Ritchie, and even if you did, I wouldn't take you back.'

The nearest couples eyed them with interest, but sadly Sonia and the wrinkly Florian were entwined like two melted candles and took no notice at all. It would probably take a crowbar to prise them apart at the end of the evening.

'So it's over?' Ritchie looked like a sad puppy. 'Really?'

'Of course it's over. It's been over for months. Good God –'

Ezra Samuels and his boys stopped playing at that moment. Sonia and Florian kept dancing. The band immediately struck up a sort of rumba, a signal for Steeple Fritton mayhem.

Posy shook her head. 'Go and get Sonia and carry her off to your Bunny Burrow love nest if you feel that

411

chest-thumping is called for here. Just don't try to score points by involving me.'

'I'm not, honest. I really, really miss you . . .'

'Tough.'

Making for the bar, Posy twirled away through the crowds being careful to keep her toes out of the way of the stomping feet. The Pink twins were dancing together and wearing wellingtons.

'Here I am,' she beamed at Norrie. 'Safe and sound and heart still intact. Have Ellis and Flynn not turned up?'

'Nope,' Norrie poured four champagne cocktails at the same time. 'Rose Lusty told your mother that they were outside necking.'

'Christ. With each other?'

'Apparently not. With Lola and Vanessa. Posy? Posy, where are you going?'

Outside in the warm, velvet darkness, Ellis and Lola seemed to have vanished but it wasn't difficult to spot Flynn and the glitteringly pink and silver Vanessa sitting side by side on the wall beneath the notice board. There didn't seem to be a lot of necking going on. Posy hoped that she'd missed it.

She hitched herself up on to the wall on the other side of Flynn.

'Hi,' Vanessa smiled guilelessly, 'we were just talking about you.'

'Really? Anything I should know?'

Flynn, who already had his arm round Vanessa's shoulders, leaned over and hugged Posy at the same time. 'Congratulations on being chosen as a pageant princess.'

412

'Carnival Queen attendant,' she corrected him, wanting to kiss him so badly. 'Thank you. And don't change the subject. Why were you talking about me?'

'Because of exactly that,' Vanessa leaned forward exposing her splendid cleavage. 'Flynn says you were going to crew on Queen Mab with him in the procession, but you won't be able to now, will you? Because you'll be on the float with Sonia and Lola as well as being the fortune teller, so I'm going to do it instead.'

Bugger. Posy shrugged. 'Okay, but you'll probably have to fight off my dad and Mr D and Mr B for that honour.'

'The more guys the merrier as far as I'm concerned,' Vanessa chuckled. 'Anyway, I'm probably a better choice than you. Flynn says you haven't ever been up in Queen Mab's cab on the road, whereas I'm used to it, steering steam engines, I mean. I helped Flynn out a lot in the Rough and Tumblers.'

Posy kept the smile fixed firmly in place. 'So everyone keeps telling me. It'll be nice for you to keep your hand in.' She looked at Flynn as a crowd of villagers tottered from the hall for a bit of a breather, and lit up cigarettes in the darkness. 'Um, have you seen Lola and Ellis?'

'They disappeared across the common about ten minutes ago,' Flynn said quietly. 'Not sure if it's a swan song or a long goodbye or they're eloping.'

'Ellis seems to be stuffed full of principles, so I don't think he'll be running out on Tatty,' Posy said sadly. 'My guess is that it's the long goodbye.'

'Mine too, honey.' Vanessa hitched her tiny pink skirt up to groin level. 'Mind you, it wouldn't have worked, would it? Not with an entire generation gap between

413

them. They'd have no shared history. Nothing to touch base on. It'd have all fizzled out in days.'

'Really?' Posy studied her bare feet; her toes were dusty and she thought the silver pearly nail polish looked out of place. Far too girlie. 'You think so, do you? You don't think that they'd have had as much chance of happiness and making it work as anyone else who enters into a relationship?'

'No way,' Vanessa continue to smile. 'Relationships are tricky at the best of times, far better if you both start on a level playing field. No differences to speak of.'

'Sounds pretty boring to me,' Posy straightened her tiara. 'So, you'd advocate no crossing of age, creed, colour or nationality, would you? All couples neatly sorted into matching ticky-tacky boxes, with no allowance at all for falling in love outside those confines?'

'Hey –' Flynn laughed. 'This is getting a bit heavy, isn't it?'

Posy shook her head. 'Not at all. But then you obviously agree with Vanessa, don't you? Each to his own. Otherwise, why would you and she be going back to Boston together as soon as the carnival is over?'

Chapter Twenty-nine

The morning of the carnival dawned as gloriously as anyone could have wished for. By nine o'clock the sky was cornflower blue, the sun spiralled across the village, and not a hint of wind ruffled the miles and miles of multicoloured flags and bunting.

Peering from the doorway of Sunny Dene, Posy blinked. Steeple Fritton had undergone an overnight transformation.

When had all this happened?

Last night, both the commons had been smothered by piles of tarpaulins, a few tents, heaps of unbuilt stalls, and an all-encompassing air of panicky excitement – but nothing else.

Now, the larger common outside the B&B, and the smaller one down the road by The Crooked Sixpence, had both metamorphosed into full-blown fairgrounds-cum-fête-cum-tented villages, with hordes of people swarming across the sun-burnished bleached grass, and a pot pourri of fragmented noises and exotic scents filling the warm air.

Trevor and Kenneth, anticipating their usual free-range romp, sniffed dubiously at the unfamiliar landscape with tucked-in tails. However, despite various misgivings, Posy couldn't help grinning. It was like being a child, going to sleep to rain and waking up to find everywhere blanketed by inches of unheralded snow.

'Oh, wow!' She shook her head. 'It's awesome.'

'And you,' Dilys, dressed from head to toe in her favourite tangerine, said as she passed across the hallway from the dining room towards the kitchen, 'sound exactly like Vanessa.'

Oh, ha-ha – Posy really didn't want to hear the V-word today. The owner of the V-word had left Sunny Dene at some ridiculously early hour with Flynn. To steam-up Queen Mab ready for the procession, she'd said. Posy had a sinking feeling that Queen Mab wouldn't be the only one getting hot and bothered. Bugger.

She shrugged. 'Actually, I caught all my Americanisms from Flynn, not her. But, Mum, you have really got to come and look at this. And tell Lola, too. She'll love it.'

'Lola went down to the pub before breakfast, and I've already looked, love. Your dad and I have been watching it going on from first light.' Dilys hugged the piled-high tray against her billowing chest. 'Amazing, isn't it? And have you noticed the other thing?'

'Which other thing?'

'There, at the end of the drive.'

Posy squinted then squealed with delight. 'Oh, fantastic! I've never ever seen it before. Well, not hung up, I mean.'

'Dad had to dig it out of the back of the shed.'

The 'No Vacancies' sign, slightly lopsided, swung on its rusty chains above the gate. It meant that Sunny Dene, for the first time in living memory, well, Posy's anyway, had every one of its bedrooms filled, and every one of its tables occupied by happy breakfasters.

'God, now you'll actually be able to turn people away and tell them they'll have to take second best at Colworth Manor.' Ignoring the loaded tray, Posy hugged her mother in delight. 'But seriously, it really is brilliant. It's all we ever wanted, isn't it?'

'I think that's how this all started out, yes,' Dilys nodded, straightening cereal bowls and cups and saucers. 'But it's become far more than bums on seats as far as the village is concerned. It's made a difference to everyone's life.'

'It's certainly changed mine . . .'

Posy stopped. Not the right route to travel. Not without mentioning the V-word again. Maybe today wasn't quite the right time to be introspective, anyway. Not with so many things still left unresolved. She pushed all the doubts out of her head. Plenty of time to think about them later.

She looked at Dilys. 'So, are you sure you'll be able to manage? With the extra work today? I mean, Dad is already tied up and –'

'Happy as a sandboy,' Dilys agreed. 'Bless him.'

Norrie, Posy knew, was out in Sunny Dene's back garden putting the finishing touches to the Letting Off Steam railway layout day. Dressed as an Edwardian station master, complete with stovepipe hat, frock coat, and green and red flags, he was anticipating an all-day rush from boys of all ages to play engine drivers.

'And don't worry about the bed-making or anything else,' Dilys continued. 'You've got enough on your plate. With Dom home for the weekend we'll soon see to the boarders. I don't intend to miss a minute of what's going on today.'

'Oh, good. I'd hate to think you wouldn't see me in all my regal glory, not to mention my Gypsy Rose Lee outfit . . . What? Why are you laughing?'

'I think she was a stripper, love, not a fortune teller,' Dilys grinned. 'And there's no chance of me missing any of it. Dom's got the camcorder primed so that one day you'll be able to prove to my grandchildren that you didn't always look like a boy. And, lovely as all this is, haven't you got to be somewhere pretty important?'

'Have I? Oh, yes, now you come to mention it . . .'

Half an hour later, astride the BMW, Posy chugged her way slowly along Steeple Fritton's lanes. There was too much going on to hurry, and there was far too much traffic anyway. Cars were approaching from every direction, and the parking areas were already filled with rows of vehicles shimmering beneath the heat of the sun.

Overhead, the roads were crisscrossed with flags and the trees hung with fairy lights; there was activity buzzing everywhere, and already dozens of people were scrambling across the bleached grass of the common. It was almost impossible to think that this had all come about from that cold and depressing Saturday night in The Crooked Sixpence with Ellis.

Oh, wow!

The Bradley-Morland Memory Lane Fair had built

up like magic, bringing Wonderland to Steeple Fritton. Posy felt another tingle of childlike excitement as the sun glinted in rainbow prisms from the maroon and gold paintwork of the old-fashioned living wagons, and the many ornate rides, and especially from the brass and mirrors sprinkled across the huge magnificence of Petronella Bradley's Golden Galloping Horses.

It was as spectacular as Nell and Jack had promised it would be. And it could have been Flynn's future if bloody Vanessa – oops, there was the V-word again – hadn't turned up and changed everything.

Still, there was no point in dwelling on it. Vanessa was definitely returning to Boston in August, and Flynn was supposed to be going with her. He'd said little to confirm or deny the rumour that night outside the village hall, and because she hadn't wanted to know the answer, Posy hadn't pressed him since. She was simply living for the moment, and if that meant flirting and teasing when Vanessa wasn't around rather than nothing at all, then that's what she'd take.

Did that make her weak and cheap? She wasn't sure, but didn't think so. She didn't really care. She was in love with Flynn, and as with Lola and Ellis, she still believed a miracle might just happen.

The village children were already scampering around between the silent fairground attractions with ill-concealed glee. There had never been a fair in Steeple Fritton before. There had never been anything like this in the village, ever.

Posy rode on, grinning at everyone who waved at her. It was impossible to feel any sadness today. Today seemed filled with magic – who knew what might happen. And if it didn't, well there'd be plenty of time for sadness later. Nothing – nothing at all – was going to spoil today.

Oh, wow – again.

Posy braked hard and slid her feet to the ground. Maybe she was sounding like damn Vanessa, but she didn't care. This was definitely an oh, wow moment.

Outside The Crooked Sixpence, taking up almost all of one side of the shingled car park, was a large dark red lorry. The side was lifted up to form a canopy, revealing a massive and amazing ornately decorated fairground organ. This must be the – oh, what had Jack called it? Funny name ... Lemonade? She peered closer at the curlicued golden lettering.

Limonaire! That was it.

It was set into the entire body of the lorry, surrounded by lights, and was a mass of drums and pipes and cymbals and amazingly carved Harlequin and Columbine figures.

Oh, wow – again.

Tonight, when the village was enveloped in musky darkness, this would come into its own – powered by the splendour of Queen Mab rocking and hissing alongside, blaring toe-tapping music into the sky, all ablaze with lights and colour ...

'Isn't it divine?' Tatty, full infant entourage in tow, stopped beside her. 'The kiddies are really looking forward to seeing it in action.'

The kiddies were clearly all ready for the fancy dress competition. To a sprog, they were kitted out as nursery rhyme characters and looked far better dressed than they did in their normal clothes.

Surprisingly, Tatty had pulled out all the party stops, too, and was wearing elegant billowing lilac lace layers to conceal her bump. Her ringlets cascaded over her shoulders and she appeared to be bedecked in the full contents of Claire's Accessories. She looked lovely, Posy thought, and immediately wished that Ellis hadn't thought so, too. It was going to be so awful in Steeple Fritton without Lola.

The Crooked Sixpence was closed and shuttered. Tonight, with the Stars In Their Eyes karaoke special and filled with the Letting Off Steam-goers, it would be thrumming with life and noise and laughter. But as soon as Hogarth returned then Lola would leave – and it would be back to giving Spit and Sawdust a bad name in the blinking of an eye.

Apparently the Ellis–Lola affair was really over and going to remain so. Lola had said that they'd walked and talked on the night of the Carnival Queen contest, but there had been no kissing and no pretence. Ellis had fathered Tatty's baby and because of that Lola would leave the village. It was a decision neither of them wanted to come to, but they had scruples and what other solution was there?

Posy glared at Tatty, and at the baby-bump under the lilac lace, and wished there was another answer.

The Crooked Sixpence would open at lunch time with Ellis and Ritchie doing the business until Lola escaped from her carnival princess duties. It had been decided to open the shops, too, to capitalize on all the visitors who may well have oodles of money to spend. Malvina, the shaven-headed treasure from the Cressbeds Estate, had produced three matching sisters, Imelda, Sancha and

Astrid, who were busily helping out wherever they were needed along the row.

'By the way, have you met Baz?' Tatty interrupted Posy's thoughts. 'I told him all about Letting Off Steam and he came over especially. He's staying at Colworth Manor, couldn't get in at Sunny Dene, and he's heard all about everyone and is dying to meet them.'

Baz? Posy shook her head. 'No, I don't think so. Is he a, um, friend of yours?'

'A supplier.'

'Oh, right. Christ, Tatty, you're not into serious drugs, are you? Not with the kiddies and being pregnant and everything? I mean, I know you were never averse to the odd spliff but even so –'

'Goodness! Nothing like that! Baz makes and blends oils.'

'What? Like a BP refinery?'

'Of course not!' Tatty jangled as she laughed. 'Aroma-therapy oils. He's been supplying me for several months.'

'Oh, yes. I vaguely remember you mentioning him. Baz from Basingstoke. Sounded like a *Blind Date* contestant.'

Tatty laughed again. 'He's over there somewhere with Zebedee and Orlando and Tallulah showing them how the organ works.'

Posy squinted against the growing intensity of the sun. Having assumed that Baz from Basingstoke would be a shiny-suited rep with a toupee, she grinned. A Jimi Hendrix lookalike was hunkered down beneath the Limonaire, pointing up at the intricate musical instru-ments to the obvious delight of Humpty Dumpty, Wee Willie Winkie and Little Bo Peep.

'He looks, um, nice . . .' Posy said quickly. After all, what else could you say about someone skinny and swarthy and wispy-bearded, and wearing a leather waistcoat and trilby and obscenely tight trousers?

'Oh, he is,' Tatty beamed. 'And he's going to be wonderful at the karaoke tonight.'

Posy nodded. 'Red hot on Voodoo Chile and Foxy Lady, is he?'

'Tommy Steele, actually. He's older than he looks.'

'Oh, right, I'll look forward to it.' She glanced at her watch. 'Crikey, I must be going. The vicar will be having a fit. See you later . . .'

The vicar was, as predicted, pacing up and down the vicarage's drive.

'Where on earth have you been? We've got less than an hour!'

'Sorry, got delayed.' Posy eased the BMW on to its stand and shook her curls free from the crash helmet. 'Heavens!'

Mainly because the vicar and his wife had spearheaded the carnival committee, the vicarage garden was the designated meeting place for floats, and the spot from where the procession would start. Hoping that from chaos would come calm, Posy blinked at the mayhem. It looked like there had been a multiple pile-up on the M25.

Every lorry, tractor and van known to Steeple Fritton was pulled up under the vicarage windows. Flatbed farm trailers, unrecognizable with their various themed scenes in luminescent polystyrene and plastic and paper, were hooked up behind each vehicle. Balloons, streamers, banners, and yet more flags, adorned headlights, rear lights, mirrors, bumpers and radiators.

'Crikey, is that a shrine? And what's that supposed to be? Is it a beehive? Oh, I know that one! It's –'

'There's no time to stop and stare,' the vicar said testily. 'Ms Wentworth is in the changing room, er, the orangery, with my wife, waiting for you. You're the last to arrive. Have you got the frocks?'

'Mine and Lola's, yes. And my fortune-telling outfit.' Posy scrabbled in the motorbike's top box and produced two Tesco carriers. 'Here they are. Mum finished them last night. God, I wasn't supposed to provide bloody Sonia with one as well, was I?'

The vicar shook his head. 'Your language, Posy, leaves much to be desired. And no, as our Letting Off Steam Carnival Queen, Sonia has provided her own.'

'Christ! Er, sorry, I mean, oh!' Posy gawped as Sonia undulated out from the vicarage's spectacular orangery. 'So she has. Bugger me!'

It was really, really, really unfair. How come Sonia Thongs Dalgetty could look that good – again?

Sonia's dress was strapless, white, and silk. It curved round her breasts, clung to her minuscule waist, then fell straight down to her ankles in a simple sheath looking exactly as if it had been made for Jennifer Aniston. Come to think of it, Sonia had changed from Jean Shrimpton into Jennifer Aniston pretty damn well. The hair beneath the golden crown was sleek and glossy, the smile still pale and pouty, and her eyes sparkled.

Was all this glamour for Ritchie's benefit or the wrinkly Florian Pickavance who was allegedly going to open the carnival? Loyally, Posy hoped it was the former.

Ignoring Sonia, she grabbed her Tesco carrier bags and sprinted into the orangery.

The vicar's wife was dresser-in-chief. Having got the Brownies transformed into what looked like miniature Goths and Vandals, the WI into a lot of Abba, the Young Farmers into something that was possibly *EastEnders* but more probably *The League of Gentlemen*, the choir into a mixture of elderly and overweight Teletubbies and Tweenies, and the youth club, obviously reluctantly, into that perennial favourite, St Trinian's, she swooped on Posy with glee.

'Super! You've got the frocks and the tiaras? Good, good. Malvina's going to do your hair and make-up. What about shoes?'

'Jimmy Choos. In the bag,' Posy gasped, as the vicar's wife attempted to snatch at them. 'And I can take my own clothes off, thank you.'

Fifteen minutes later, her curls teased into glossy profusion by the multitalented Malvina, and wearing more make-up than Ivana Trump, Posy staggered through the fancy-dressed crowds in the orangery looking for Lola.

She eventually found her standing in front of a collection of decorative wattle-and-daub screens, wide-eyed and trying to sip a gin and tonic through solidly thrusting lips.

'Good Lord, what on earth happened to you?'

'Malvina,' Lola muttered through clenched teeth. 'I told her I didn't want false eyelashes or the industrial strength lip gloss. I feel like a waxwork.'

'You look gorgeous,' Posy said, 'if a little rigid. I've got the dresses and tiaras and things. Here . . .'

She passed Lola's dress across and unfurled her own.

They were identical in style, strappy, low-cut, full-length, in layers of chiffon. Posy's was pink, Lola's pale blue. 'We're going to look like the bloody Beverley Sisters.'

'No we're not. There were three of them – oh, but you wouldn't know that, would you? They were aeons before your time. God, I wish we weren't doing this.' Lola eased her lips and eyes open and looked at her dress. 'Thanks. Oh, it's really pretty. Dilys has done a wonderful job considering she had so little time and we weren't exactly helpful about what we wanted.'

'Dad did the sequins and the ribbons,' Posy admitted, 'but he'd rather we didn't tell anyone. Are you okay?'

'No,' Lola shook her head as she unzipped her jeans and wriggled them down to her hips. 'After weeks of trying to behave like a grown-up, intelligent, late-middle-aged woman, I handed the pub keys over to Ellis earlier –'

'And?' Posy paused in tugging off her T-shirt.

'And he said he loved me.'

'Bastard.' Posy struggled her own jeans down to her knees. 'And what did you say?'

Lola pulled her vest top over her head. 'That I loved him, too.'

'Oh, very grown-up. About fourteen and a half, I'd say.'

'Ladies! *Ladies! Please!*'

The vicar's wife's anguished screech halted them both in their tracks. They paused. All the Teletubbies, most of the Tweenies, and a whole crowd of St Trinians, were goggle-eyed.

'*Behind* the screens for changing! *Behind!*'

Chapter Thirty

The floats were in position. Fortunately the vicarage had a canopy of sycamore trees to shield the waiting procession from the worst of the heat. The dappled light sprinkled huge doubloons of gold across the extravaganza making it look like one of Disneyland's most lavish productions.

Carefully gathering her drifty dress up to her knees, Posy scrunched along the vicarage's gravel in the soaring temperature, gazing in stupefaction. Not all the float-occupants had been in the orangery. In addition, The Leonora Leggett School of Dance from Upton Poges were 42nd Street; the coven – excluding Tatty and including Neddy Pink – were, as Conquest, War, Famine and Death, the Four Horsemen of the Apocalypse; the Townswomen's Guild were Swan Lake; and unidentified motley crews made up Circus Days, Bonnie and Clyde, Toyland, and The Swinging Sixties.

The vicar, once more sweltering in his Liberace jacket, clapped his hands. 'All ready? All in position? Let's just go through the running order again, then.'

The Townswomen's Guild, who, being at the end of the queue, were in the full glare of the sun and of course covered in feathers, swore loudly.

'First, the Newbury Brass Band –' the vicar indicated the group of perspiring but very elegant navy and gold clad figures huddling in a small patch of shade. 'Followed by Flynn Malone on his traction engine, Queen Mab. Then our Carnival Queen float, then the others in numerical sequence. You all have your numbers, don't you?'

There was an obedient nodding of heads.

'Good, good, then, as it's nearly midday, let's get the show on the road!'

The bassoon player from the brass band gave a short and rather rude solo.

'Excuse me,' Posy clutched her tiara and waved at the vicar. 'We seem to be one missing. Where's the traction engine?'

'Jesus Christ!' The vicar looked at his wife as though it were her fault. 'I thought you had him?'

'I wish, I mean, I have no idea where he is, darling.' The vicar's wife shook her head. 'Weren't we supposed to meet him at the Lesser Fritton crossroads?'

'Were we? Yes, yes, of course. Just testing,' the vicar nodded, frowning at Posy. 'Right now, all take positions. Hold on tightly, and we'll be away.'

Posy scrambled up on the back of Les Bailey's coal lorry which had been mercifully sandblasted for the occasion. Sonia was already on her golden throne – a 1970s peacock rattan chair recently hand-sprayed. The princesses' thrones, on either side, were nowhere near as spectacular but at least they were dry.

Sitting down, arranging her frock, clinging on, and wondering if the over-ballooned, lily-strewn, dove-covered, rose-arched, hearts and flowers float would make it safely out of the drive, never mind the miles of twisting lanes round the Frittons, Posy grinned at Lola.

'It could be worse. We could be dressed as Teletubbies. They'll probably faint before we get to the common.'

'Fainting seems like a pretty good option to me,' Lola said, fanning her face. 'And I do hope we're not supposed to wave.'

'Of course we're supposed to wave,' Sonia glared at them both. 'Smile and wave. Haven't you been practising?'

Les Bailey roared his engine into life at that moment, making the rickety rose arches wobble alarmingly. One of the doves fell off.

Posy clung on even tighter to the arms of her throne and leaned towards Sonia. 'You wave all you like, but don't speak to me, okay? Smiling and waving is fine. Speaking to me will get you chucked off this bloody float faster than you can whip off your thongs for other people's fiancés. Okay?'

The Newbury Brass Band struck up 'The King Cotton March', and with Neddy Pink as Famine joining in on the accordion from somewhere towards the back, the carnival procession moved slowly away.

Once she'd got used to the motion and the fact that the temperature was at boiling point, Posy found it all enthralling. They'd hardly started and yet she'd never seen so many people in her life. Crowds lined the lanes, people hung over gates, children and dogs scurried excitedly alongside, and everyone was shouting and cheering.

As they wound their way away from Steeple Fritton and towards the Lesser Fritton crossroads, there had been few mishaps. The Brownies weren't Goths and Vandals as Posy had imagined, but The Sound of Music. An easy mistake to make, she felt. There had been a rather nasty altercation between two Liesls and a Kurt, and one of the Friedrichs had been head-butted by a wailing Brigitta. Brown Owl, who was Maria, was perched on a lopsided cardboard mountain, swigging from a hip flask, loudly singing 'The Hills Are Alive' off key and appeared not to have noticed.

'Shit!' Posy blinked as the band stopped playing and the convoy shuddered to a halt.

Lola leaned across the lilies and doves. 'You can do this . . . Smile.'

Posy couldn't smile. She could only stare at Queen Mab, waiting to take up her place in the cavalcade.

A fat bowser lorry was parked beside the engine and two fat bowser men were attempting to insert a hose into one of the engine's orifices. Steaming, glinting in the sun, rocking with unleashed power, the traction engine looked astounding.

Flynn looked even more so.

Dressed in very faded jeans and a black T-shirt, he grinned down from the cab as the vicar bustled along the line towards him. Mr D and Mr B, wearing matching overalls, were perched on the coal tender at the back, and Vanessa was shoulder to shoulder with Flynn behind the steering wheel.

'Ohmigod!' Posy blinked. 'Look at her!'

Lola looked. 'Oh, dear . . .'

It was like Ginger Spice before the reinvention. Wearing

Daisy Duke denim shorts, thigh-high boots, a shocking pink bra top, and with a peaked engine driver's cap on top of the bright red hair, Vanessa looked simply sensational.

'You can quite see why he prefers her to you, can't you?' Sonia said. 'After all, she looks like a woman. Which is exactly what Ritchie said to me when he –'

Posy jabbed the heel of her Jimmy Choo into Sonia's exposed toes.

There was a short agonized squeal, and Sonia toppled forward. Most of her white silk dress stayed on the throne owing to the wet paint.

'Oh, dear . . .' Lola said again, averting her eyes.

'Clumsy of you,' Posy beamed as Sonia resumed her throne and made little yelping noises over the state of her regal frock. 'No, no –' she smiled happily at the vicar who had nipped smartly back along the row, 'No problems. Sonia just felt a little faint. All okay now, though.'

'Good.' The vicar looked, for a man of the cloth, somewhat disbelieving. 'We're just waiting for the water tender to finish topping up Queen Mab's boiler, then we'll be away . . . Which doesn't mean anyone may leave the floats for any reason whatsoever. Posy, where are you going?'

'Just need to stretch my legs for a moment. Cramp. Only a second. Honestly.'

Gathering her dress up round her thighs, and ramming her tiara more firmly into her curls, Posy scrambled from the back of the coal lorry.

The misfit of the Jimmy Choos made hobbling towards Queen Mab slightly less elegant than she would have liked, but hey . . .

Mr D and Mr B waved down at her camply. She waved back.

Vanessa widened her eyes. 'Hi, Posy. Isn't this all *darling*? And oh, my, don't you look just stunning?'

Posy whimpered. How could you hate someone who was so bloody cheerful and so unremittingly nice?

'Wow!' Flynn grinned down at her. 'You seriously look a million dollars. Hardly dressed for engine crew though, are you?'

'Not yet, but I will be later,' Posy smiled. 'I've seen the Limonaire outside the pub and it's awesome.'

Vanessa giggled.

'Yeah, I know.' Flynn nodded. 'And the carnie, er, fair is everything that Jack and Nell promised. This truly is going to be one of the most amazing days of my life.'

Posy felt suddenly hopeful. Was there a wistful note in his voice? Did he really want to send Vanessa back to Boston alone and throw in his lot with The Bradley-Morland Fair and spend the rest of his time in Steeple Fritton? Was he maybe having second thoughts about going home?

'Mine too.'

'All done, mate,' one of the bowser men yanked the water hose away from Queen Mab with a flourish. His eyes flickered hungrily between Vanessa and Posy. 'That'll see you through most of today, but we'll be on stand-by tonight if you need a top-up.'

'Great,' Flynn said happily. 'I'll buy you a beer or three.'

'Posy! Float! Now!' The vicar had come over all dictatorial. 'We're ready to move!'

With Mr D and Mr B merrily shovelling more coal

432

into the firebox, and Vanessa expertly pushing and pulling levers, Queen Mab started to get up steam. After a series of hisses and a belch that would have done credit to Neddy Pink, the gearing started to clank into place, smoke rose in staccato puffs from the chimney, and Flynn gave an ear-splitting shrill on the whistle.

'See you later,' he yelled down to Posy above the chugging roar. 'I want you to tell my fortune.'

'Posy!!!!' The vicar was turning purple.

'Count on it.'

Posy grinned at Flynn, then blowing him a kiss, skipped back to her float as fast as the Jimmy Choos would allow.

'Well?' Lola raised a painted eyebrow as Posy scrambled back on to her throne.

'Oh, yes,' Posy sighed happily. 'Oh, yes, yes, yes! I'm definitely, stupidly, madly in love, and it's crazy and will break my heart, and I don't bloody care.'

She sat back on her throne, bracing herself for the lorry's jerk forward as the band started to play the 'Radetsky March', and Queen Mab rolled and rumbled majestically ahead of them. Oh, this was absolute heaven . . .

If she sat sideways for the entire procession she could watch Flynn's shoulder muscles move beneath the T-shirt as he drove the engine, with an equally blissful non-stop back view of his toned waist and lean hips and denim-clad bum.

Not even Sonia's glowering presence could spoil her joy.

After winding through the narrow streets of Lesser Fritton and Fritton Magna and gathering more and more people as they went, the cavalcade had completed its circuit and trundled into Steeple Fritton village for the first time.

The roar of delight as they came into view sent shivers of delight down Posy's spine.

The carnival was now in full swing: an undulating mass of colour and noise and motion. The fairground was a dizzy maroon and gold musical centrifuge, packed with people; all the tried-and-tested stalls were surrounded by jostling throngs; the commons were so crowded that it was impossible to see a blade of grass; and still cars queued out towards the bypass.

Steeple Fritton was on the map at last.

Once Florian Pickavance had declared the carnival open – with a lot of giggling from Sonia as they crammed together on the makeshift stage – the vicar's welcome speech had made it clear – well, almost clear then – that the crowds on the commons were witnessing the birth of a new cultural heritage.

That every year from now on, Steeple Fritton's Letting Off Steam day would become bigger and better. That they would be forever providing the traditional entertainment and nostalgia missing from today's fast-fix society.

Posy felt he'd credited himself with a touch too much of the glory, but it really didn't matter. Not today. And he had remembered to plug all the village enterprises too, and point out that details of these could be found in the carnival programme. Saatchi & Saatchi couldn't have done it better.

Now sneakily holding hands, Florian and Sonia were

called upon to judge the floats and the kiddies' fancy dress. There were the usual cries of outrage as the respective spoils went to the Townswomen's Guild and an under-fives Posh'n'Becks.

The clamour for liquid refreshment was phenomenal as the temperature continued to hover in the 80s, so Lola, having ripped off the tiara and the false eyelashes and unpeeled the lip gloss, had returned to The Crooked Sixpence. Posy hoped that this would mean Ritchie could be spared to join in the celebrations and watch his beloved Sonia schmoozing with the Wrinkly Rocker.

Not that she really wished any lasting unhappiness on Ritchie, but a little teeny bit would surely be fair . . .

Queen Mab had taken up her position outside the pub, and was now steaming quietly under the watchful eyes of Mr D and Mr B until she'd be called upon to provide the evening's entertainment. Which meant, of course, that Flynn was free – apart from the V-word.

Posy, having met up with Amanda and Nikki and most of her other village friends, bumped and barged her way round the common, having a go on everything, leaping on and off all The Bradley-Morland Fair rides, smiling at everyone, stopping to chat, and knowing that she was constantly searching for a glimpse of Flynn's dark hair and broad shoulders, or the sound of his lust-making husky accent.

'Aren't you going to get changed, love?' Dilys's voice made her jump. 'There's quite a crowd already for the fortune teller.'

'Damn, is there?' Posy grinned at her mother. 'I'd got a bit sidetracked. How are you doing?'

'Oh, better than we ever thought possible.' Dilys's

tangerine earrings bobbled with delight. 'All my home-made cakes have sold out, and Dad and Dom have got a queue right round the block for the railway, and the local paper has taken photos. And, the best news, one of the weekenders says he's going to get a chum of his who works on the lifestyle section of one of the Sundays to come down and do a piece on the whole village.'

'That'd be amazing.' Posy swallowed the lump in her throat. 'I never thought, I mean, well, all this . . .'

'It just shows that dreams can come true,' Dilys said, 'with a bit of a shove in the right direction and a lot of damned hard work. And, fantastic as this all is, if you don't want the vicar screaming at you again, I think you'd better turn into Madame Za-Za pretty bloody quickly.'

Posy did.

Crawling in under the back of the tarpaulin so as not to be spotted by the punters and getting changed in the tent had been difficult, but she'd managed it. Now smoothing down her moon and stars black chiffon skirt and red pentagon vest top, tying a black and silver scarf round her curls and fastening in Dilys's biggest gold hoop earrings, she felt she was ready for business.

The crystal ball, tarot cards and palmistry kit – all loaned by Tatty and arrayed on a green baize bridge table – meant absolutely nothing to her, but it didn't matter, did it? It was only a bit of fun after all.

Crossing the gypsy's palm with silver seemed to be adding to the Letting Off Steam coffers very nicely indeed. Dozens and dozens of people passed through the darkened tent during the afternoon. Peering into the crystal ball or turning over tarot cards or reading gnarled and grubby hands, Posy made it all up as she went along.

After telling everyone, over and over again, exactly what they wanted to hear – lottery wins, marriage to tall, dark and handsomes, astounding career successes – she was very hot and completely exhausted.

Just as she was wondering if she could sneak off for a pint of shandy before dehydration took a serious grip, the tent flap opened again.

Ellis grinned at her. 'Just thought I'd give you a try. After all, you never know what the fates have in store, do you?'

Posy narrowed her eyes. 'Sit down.'

Ellis sat.

Posy moved her hands mystically over the crystal. 'Okay, I see a rushed wedding in the near future. And a baby. And a stonking success at many, many business ventures. And total, total lifelong misery, you bastard.'

'Hey –' Ellis blinked. 'Steady on, Pose. That's a bit harsh, isn't it?'

'Because of you, Lola's leaving Steeple Fritton with a broken heart. What the hell did you expect me to predict?'

'Oh, Christ . . . Okay. But you know how I feel, don't you? I love her so much. If I could change things I would, like a shot.' He ran his fingers through his spiky hair. 'I'm so bloody unhappy. Can't you tell me something nice?'

'I'm not real, you know. This is only pretend.' Posy's heart softened. 'Oh, okay . . . after all if it hadn't been for you nagging me, none of today would have happened and we'd all still be in the doldrums. I owe you something. Give me your hand.'

She peered into Ellis's palm. It looked much the same as any other palm, only cleaner than most she'd seen today. The meaning of the lines and whorls was a complete mystery.

'I see an unexpected solution to all your worries. You will be released from the burden you've been carrying. You will be free to follow your heart. You'll briefly travel over water, but return to the village where you'll make your home. You'll live a long, happy, healthy and successful life, and marry the woman of your dreams.'

She sat back. Ellis blinked and said nothing.

'Oh, come on,' Posy sighed. 'That's the best I can do.'

Ellis stood up. He looked as though he was going to burst into tears. 'Thanks. I couldn't have put it better myself.'

He barged out through the tent flap just as Flynn walked in.

'Jeeze –' he looked at Posy, 'what the hell did you tell him?'

'The truth, and then what I thought he'd like to hear.' She grinned. 'So, which do you want?'

'Well not the truth,' Flynn sat down, stretching his long legs under the table, 'not if it's going to make me cry.'

'Crystal, cards or palm?'

'Palm, definitely.' He reached across and closed his fingers round hers. 'Sorry they're a bit dirty. Engine stuff.'

'Engine stuff is fine by me.' Posy shivered with delight as Flynn did the sensual finger stroking again. 'Um, let me see. Oh, yes, well, you're going to live until you're a hundred and three, and you're going to have fourteen children, and you'll be amazingly happy all your life because you'll have followed your heart and – what?'

Flynn leaned closer across the card table. His hair feathered towards his slanting eyes. There were faint smudges of coal dust on his cheeks. He smelled of heat and engine oil and smoke and lemons. It was the most erotic cocktail in the world.

'Do an Ellis on me. Tell me what you think I'd want to hear.'

Posy sucked in her breath. 'Dangerous territory. What I think you want to hear, and what you think you want to hear, might just be poles apart . . . Are you sure?'

'Absolutely.'

'Okay, then. You're going to make a major life-change. You'll spend the rest of your life in a country other than the one of your birth. You'll follow your heart – sorry, that bit crept in again. It did that with Ellis, too. Must be one of Madam Za-Za's strong points, following hearts. Er, sorry, where was I? Oh, yes, you'll make your living doing the things you enjoy most and will always be happy.'

'And –' Flynn was smiling. 'What about the marriage and the fourteen children?'

'Um, well, the marriage will come as something of a surprise to many, being not what is currently on the cards. That's a mystic reference there, in case you missed it. Your heart will be captured by a foreign love. It will be a love that lasts forever. And will be blissfully happy. A true partnership. And, um, there will be four children and –'

'What happened to the other ten?'

'Unless you're Tatty Spry, four seems more than enough to me.' Posy smiled back at him. She couldn't help it. She adored him. 'How does that sound?'

'Perfect.' Flynn leaned across the table and brushed his lips gently against hers. 'Just perfect. Exactly what I'd have predicted for me, too. Such a shame you're not a real fortune teller. If you had been, I might just have believed it could all come true.'

Chapter Thirty-one

By nine o'clock the evening was dissolving into a warm navy and lilac dusk. Bats swooped and dived, catching unsuspecting moths on their downward trajectory, and the air was filled with the scents of crushed grass and fried onions and hot oil. The Memory Lane Fair was blaring its triumphal noise across the common, an aurora of lights arching across the darkening sky, with snakes of people still waiting to scramble on to the rides.

It had been the best day Steeple Fritton had ever known.

The pub was packed; the entire population of the Frittons and beyond were squeezing in and out of The Crooked Sixpence's doors, and hordes of drinkers had also spilled out into the car park waiting for the Limonaire to start playing.

'Going to be a bit of commotion,' Posy yelled at Lola behind the bar, 'what with Stars In Their Eyes in here and the organ out there.'

'We're going to take it half an hour at a time,' Lola

poured four lager tops in one go. 'Mind you, to be honest, with this many people making so much noise, two lots of music probably wouldn't make any difference.'

Ritchie and Ellis and Vanessa were also working flat out behind the bar. Flynn was busy getting Queen Mab ready for her evening stint. Sonia, still wearing her full regalia and with apparently no regard for Ritchie's feelings, was nose-to-nose with Florian Pickavance by the jukebox. Baby Bradfield, snug in a Mothercare carry-basket, was asleep under the table.

'Three Guinness when you've got a moment, Pose!' Neddy Pink bellowed across the heads. 'I know it's not your strong suit, duck, but yon Yankee bloke is busy outside. Give it a whirl, gel!'

Posy whirled. She'd learned to pour a reasonable Guinness at last, thanks to Flynn. Thanks to Flynn, she'd learned an awful lot.

Neddy Pink and the coven were still in their Four Horsemen guise, but then few people had bothered to change. She was still Madam Za-Za, Lola was still a carnival princess and Vanessa was still Ginger Spice. For strangers, wandering into the pub in search of rural refreshment, it must have looked very parallel universe.

The vicar, also still dressed as Liberace, was hosting Stars In Their Eyes. Posy felt he was muscling in on stuff that didn't concern him, but as Flynn was usually in charge of the pub's karaoke nights and obviously couldn't be tonight, she hadn't raised too many objections.

There was a general murmur circulating that the diocesan council were going to have the devil's own job getting the vicar back to sermons and flower arranging rotas.

The nonparticipating members of the audience had been given score cards. This was serious stuff. Tonight there was going to be a prize winner. The prize was to be presented by Florian, of course.

The vicar tapped the microphone. 'Welcome to Stars In Their Eyes! Our first few plucky soundalikes are just getting ready in the lavatories, and in a very short time I'm going to be introducing . . .' he peered at his notes. 'Er, Meat Loaf, Cleo Laine, The Seekers, The Village People, Adam Ant, Tommy Steele, Dusty Springfield and many, many more!'

There was the customary Steeple Fritton stamping and clapping.

'Dominic Nightingale is going to be videoing the entire show for village posterity. And also –' the vicar put on his Jonathan Ross smirk, 'to make the voting a lot less biased, we're not going to tell you who's being who!'

'Oooooh!' Steeple Fritton was impressed.

'Shame no one's taking bets,' Posy muttered as she concocted six snowballs. 'I'd have a thousand quid double on my dad being Meat Loaf and Malvina being in the lavs as we speak doing the make-up.'

Lola grinned. 'Hope she goes easy on the lip gloss then, otherwise it's going to be a pretty silent sing-along. And, I know we're still frantically busy, but do you want to sneak off outside for ten minutes or so, while, um, the V-word is otherwise engaged in here?'

'You're a star,' Posy ducked out from beneath the counter hatch. 'And I'll do the same for you and Ellis one day.'

Lola gave a lingering glance along the bar to where Ellis was morosely mixing martinis, and then across the packed pub to the fireplace where Tatty and the kiddies were sitting with the coven.

She sighed. 'Nice thought, Posy. But somehow I doubt we'll ever need it.'

Outside, in the darkness, Posy caught her breath. Queen Mab was ablaze with lights: hundreds of bulbs round the canopy and over the cab illumined the twisted brass and the deep red gloss of the paintwork. Thrusting through the bodies and squeezing close to the hedge, Posy made her way slowly towards the engine.

Alongside and towering above her, the Limonaire was also lit up, the pipes and drums and cymbals gleaming, and Harlequin and Columbine poised ready to dance. It was all so wonderful. Better than they could have ever imagined it would be. If only . . .

She shook herself. Tonight was definitely not the time for if onlys.

The crowds beside the engine were five or six deep, scrambling everywhere, pressing dangerously close to the shimmering boiler, ignoring the hissing steam and the red-hot glow of the coals. Mr D, Mr B and Flynn were keeping them clear as best they could.

'This is completely mad . . .' Nell Bradley leaned down from the stage in front of the Limonaire and gave Posy a huge grin of delight. 'I haven't seen anything like this for years, not since our first outing with the gallopers. Queen Mab is going to be one heck of an asset to our outfit.'

So Flynn hadn't told Nell and Jack that he was going back to Boston, then. It didn't mean he wasn't,

444

of course, but it might just mean that he hadn't yet decided.

'Who's in charge of your, um, roundabout, er, gallopers, tonight?' Posy raised her voice. 'Has Jack got it to himself?'

Nell shook her head. 'No way. Jack'll be along to help me out in a moment. He wouldn't miss this bit with the engine for the world. Sam and Claudia, my brother and sister-in-law, are being left in full galloper-charge. We travellers are all pretty versatile, as you'll probably find out . . .'

'I wish, but you know I said that Flynn and I aren't –'

'I know exactly what you said,' Nell pushed her shaggy red-gold fringe out of her eyes. 'And I still don't believe you. You were made to be together, and if the appearance of his long-term girlfriend makes that a bit tricky, then –' she shrugged expressively. 'Well, like I said before, no one could have had more stumbling blocks than me and Jack.'

Posy sighed. If she and Flynn could be together and half as happy as Nell and Jack it would be total bliss. But, despite Madam Za-Za's cleverly tailored predictions, she knew it simply wasn't going to happen.

Nell pulled a sympathetic face. 'All you need is a bit of faith, and a lot of luck. Oh, and if you're just on your way to visit Flynn, which I guess you are, can you pass this to him, he's going to need it if we're going to have any music tonight. Tell him it's connected my end, so I'm ready when he is.'

'Oh, yes, right.' Posy took the end of the huge coil of grey cable from Nell. It weighed a ton. 'Will he know what to do with it?'

'I'd put money on it,' Nell laughed.

So would I, Posy thought hotly, as she managed to burrow underneath a couple of dozen armpits and an equal number of fists clutching beer mugs, feeding the cable out as she went and not garrotting anyone.

Eventually she pulled herself and the snaking cable up Queen Mab's steps.

'Bloody hell! It's boiling up here! It's like a –'

'Furnace?' Flynn raised his eyebrows, stepping away from the blazing firebox. 'Nice on cold mornings though. Great to see you up here at last – oh, and is that for me?'

'Nell said you'd know what to do with it.'

Flynn obviously did. As Posy sat back on the heap of coal in the tender and watched, he slithered out of the cab, dropped easily to the ground, unhooked a stepladder, and with Mr D and Mr B as assistants and a lot of less than helpful suggestions from the dense crowd, fastened the ends of the cable to two connections at the front of Queen Mab.

'Okay,' he grinned, clambering back into the cab. 'We're connected to the Limonaire. Now the electricity generated by Queen Mab will drive the mechanics of the organ. Simple, huh?'

'As astrophysics,' Posy said, impressed. 'And on a slightly larger scale than what I've been used to, with the model railway, I mean. So, go on then. What happens now?'

'We have to keep the fire going to heat the water in the boiler which turns into steam which builds into pressure. Okay?'

'Okay. Steam train stuff. And?'

'The pressure drives the piston and the crank shaft. Once we've reached the right steam pressure, which shows on this meter here, then we have to maintain it at constant, so that the belt there will be driven evenly by the flywheel and become an electrical generator and we'll have power. Still making sense?'

'Oh, absolutely.'

Flynn poked out his tongue. 'As soon as the organ bellows have enough air electrically pumped into them, then the pressure will open the pipes, and as Nell feeds the music books through the keyframe, like Jack did for us at Fox Hollow, we'll have lights, music, action!'

'So simple and so perfectly explained.'

'I thought so.'

His enthusiasm was infectious, and even if she didn't totally grasp all the principles of making electricity, it was a heck of a buzz to be up here, high above the ground, being stared at enviously by so many people. She'd been stared at enviously a lot today, she thought. It was heady stuff. She could become used to it.

What was even more of a buzz, and what she could become even more dangerously used to, was being with Flynn.

'Will you teach me to do all this?'

'Sure thing. Hang on while I just –'

Posy watched as Flynn pushed Queen Mab's levers and the huge belt slapped and flapped, and the massive circle of the flywheel whirled so quickly that the colours blended into transparency, and the engine hissed and rocked and roared, and the glorious evocative smell of steam and coal smoke filled the air.

Nell leaned out of the front of the Limonaire and gave them the thumbs up.

Posy held her breath. With a wheeze and a thunderous drumroll, the Limonaire burst into 'The Can-Can'.

It was an ideal tune to start with. The blare of noise and the blaze of lights was absolutely electrifying. Instantly, everyone in the massive crowd was dancing, high-kicking their way round the car park. People were running from both the commons to look. Children were being shoved to the front or hoisted on to shoulders for the best vantage points.

Flynn turned and curled his arms round Posy's waist. 'God, this is dream come true stuff, huh?'

She snuggled against his chest, aching to kiss him. 'Just what I was thinking earlier. It's wonderful . . . Flynn, are you crying?'

'No way. Are you?'

'Course not.'

They grinned at one another. This part of the evening was theirs. Posy looked up at him. 'And what happens next?'

'With us or Queen Mab?'

'I'm not that naive. Queen Mab, of course.'

He kissed the top of her curls. 'All I have to do now is make sure the pressure doesn't drop. Nell and Jack will be doing the hard work playing the organ and I'll be out here taking the glory.'

'And you have to stay up here all the time? No sneaking off?'

'Why? Did you want to sneak off with me into the bushes during your break?'

'You know bloody well that I do.'

'Me, too . . .' He traced the outline of her mouth with his forefinger. 'Trust me, Posy. Please. I know what I'm doing.'

'Oh, goody . . .' She gently bit the end of his finger. 'I wish I did. So, you're up here for the whole evening are you?'

'Mr D and Mr B have volunteered to take over – will take over – when I need a break, which is kind of them as it means they've had to forgo their Judy Garland bit on the karaoke, and no doubt Norrie will be up here faster 'n greased lightning once he's finished being Meat Loaf again.'

Posy sighed happily. 'Oh, good. So there'll be plenty of time to teach me everything that you've already taught Vanessa.'

'I think you're way ahead of Vanessa on all counts.' He looked into her eyes. 'This is killing me. You know it is, don't you?'

She nodded. The Limonaire was playing 'Liberty Bell'. Everyone was still dancing.

'Don't spoil tonight by talking about it,' she swallowed. 'Whatever you've decided to do will hurt someone and I really, really don't want it to be me tonight. Okay?'

'Sure,' he nodded. 'When I was leaving the States I thought I'd never get over Vanessa not caring enough to come with me. I missed her when I was in Tralee, but it got better. When I came here . . .' He stared out into the navy sky. 'Well, when I came here I was actually glad that she'd stayed behind. You know? And then –'

The organ burst into 'Sabre Dance'. Everyone danced playing air guitars.

449

Posy placed her fingers across his lips. 'Don't. Vanessa is great. She loves you and she's playing this just right. We've got to do the same . . . and don't look at me like that because I might just have to –'

'Pose!' Dom appeared at the bottom of Queen Mab's steps. The lights reflected a trillion times in his rimless specs. 'Sorry to interrupt, but Dad's first on in Stars In Their Eyes. He's being Meat Loaf, although we're not supposed to know it's him, and you've got to come and cheer him on.'

'Yes, of course I have.' She reluctantly wriggled out of Flynn's arms. 'See you later.'

'You bet.'

Inside the pub, Norrie had been totally transformed by Malvina. Up on the karaoke dais he *was* Meat Loaf. He had a long flowing straggly wig, and a leather waistcoat and motorcycling boots over his jeans. As soon as he started singing 'Bat out of Hell', with all the right movements, The Crooked Sixpence erupted.

'God, he's good,' Lola mouthed as Posy slid behind the bar again. 'Everything okay out there?'

'So-so,' Posy mouthed back, staring at her father with awed pride.

Norrie was simply astounding again. He'd lost none of his oomph and certainly deserved the double standing ovation. As he came off stage Dilys and Dom hugged him and everyone tried to shake his hand. Posy flung her arms round his neck and told him he was a superstar.

'Thanks, love . . .' he beamed. 'This has been the best day of my life.'

Funny, Posy thought as she fought her way back to the bar, everyone had said that. It must be true, then.

There was a rush for drinks as the vicar waited for the pub to calm down and then announced the Village People.

'Who are they?' Vanessa mimed as she undulated past Posy with a clutch of G&Ts.

Posy shook her head. 'No idea – oh, but look at them!'

The Village People – cowboy, cop, Indian, construction worker, biker and GI – were absolutely authentic. Malvina, Posy reckoned, was a genius. The costumes and the make-up were one hundred per cent right.

The pub roared and screamed in delight as the music kicked in and The Village People stomped, hands on hips, on to the stage and proceeded to perform a raucous version of 'YMCA' with all the arm movements, and even managed the perfectly coordinated macho dance routine.

Lola was wiping tears of laughter from her eyes. 'Stupendous!' she yelled at Posy. 'And the only way we'll know who they are is to see who's missing!'

Posy glanced round the pub . . . Crikey! Surely not?

The only familiar faces no longer visible were the three Pinks, Glad, Rose and Vi.

'Er, I think it's the Pinks and the coven.'

'No way!' Lola shook her head. 'Dear God, they must all be over seventy-five! They'll all need mouth-to-mouth . . . Oh, this is brilliant.'

Steeple Fritton evidently thought so too. The applause as The Village People left the stage was absolutely deafening.

Posy's face ached from smiling, her arms ached from

pulling pints, and her feet just ached. She wasn't even thinking about her heart.

'And now,' the vicar was growing hoarse, 'you may think there's no way we can follow them! Well, I believe our next act will be able to do just that! Ladies and gentlemen – Adam Ant!'

'Oh, wow, I always rated him!' Vanessa clashed two bottles of Bacardi Breezer together in her excitement.

'So did I,' Posy admitted. 'Although I was far too young to really appreciate him at the time, I loved the music when I was a kid, and he was definitely the most drop-dead sexy bloke around in the eighties. This should be good.'

Instantly, the sensual rhythmic throb of Ant double-drumming rocked the pub's floorboards, and then, with a yell, the Adam lookalike leapt on to the stage.

Dressed in skintight leather trousers, thigh-high boots, a white shirt slashed to the waist and a fancy highway-man's coat, Adam preened and posed. His black hair was tied back, with just a few tendrils falling into his eyes, and adorned with odd bits of coloured beads and feathers. One long exotic earring hung to his shoulder and the elaborate make-up was perfect.

Malvina had got it absolutely spot-on again.

'Holy crap!' Vanessa breathed. 'Look at him!'

Posy was looking. So was Lola. And every other woman in the pub. Sonia had even eased herself away from the Wrinkly Rocker.

The pulsing staccato drumming was joined by a throb-bing guitar bass line, then by a loud and jaunty brass section. Adam, all flawless made-up skin, heavily kohled eyes, pouty pale mouth, and with the trademark white slash across his cheeks, moved like he was making love.

As one, Vanessa, Lola and Posy stopped serving and stared open-mouthed.

'I think I'm being unfaithful . . .' Lola gulped.

'Me too, honey.' Vanessa didn't blink.

Posy chewed her thumbnail in excitement. The hairs on her arms were on end. Her stomach had dissolved with lust. Everything inside shivered.

The insistent intro halted for a split second, then Adam launched into the raunchy, toe-tapping 'Goody Two Shoes'. Not only could he dance like a dream, his voice sent shudders of delight through Posy's body.

Amanda and Nikki and dozens of other girls were stampeding towards the stage.

'Maybe he's one of the guys from the Cressbeds,' Posy muttered, not taking her eyes from him. 'Amanda and Nikki have some gorgeous blokes living in their road.'

'Not that gorgeous,' Lola whispered. 'We'd have noticed.'

'Isn't anyone else serving?' Ritchie looked at them in disgust.

'Shut up!!!' Vanessa, Lola and Posy all yelled together.

Hypnotized, Posy watched every sensual movement, listened to every perfectly executed erotic word. He was the most beautiful boy in the world and his performance was like a slow, perfect seduction.

When the last note died away, Adam made a theatrical bow, leapt off the stage as easily as he'd leapt on, and disappeared through the wall-to-wall throng. The pub, as one, stood on their chairs and clapped and screamed; roared and whistled.

Amanda and Nikki and the other Fritton maidens galloped off in hopeful hot pursuit towards the lavatorial changing rooms.

'He'll be lucky to get outta there alive,' Vanessa said, squirming away to join them. 'Jeeze! What a guy!'

'If I wasn't a responsible, sensible, grown-up landlady I think I'd be in there with them,' Lola groaned. 'Mind you, I'm not sure he went that way. Posy, I said . . .'

But Posy wasn't listening. Ducking under the counter flap, she shoved her way through the erupting, applauding crowd and out of the pub.

Nell and Jack were taking their break, sitting, arms round each other, on the front of the Limonaire. Queen Mab, still surrounded by hundreds of people, rocked slowly backwards and forwards in the illuminated darkness. Mr D and Mr B, grinning broadly and humming a duet of 'Goody Two Shoes', were just climbing down the steps, gingerly clutching empty Malibu glasses.

Posy ignored everyone and hurtled through the crowds. She pulled herself on to Queen Mab's foot plate, up the steps, jumped into the cab and stared at Flynn, very out of breath, and still dressed as Adam Ant.

'Sussed.' He held his arms open and grinned at her. 'How did you know? I thought the full make-up and this –' he flicked at the ornate hair braids, 'were a great disguise.'

'Not for a connoisseur like me. I've spent months looking at your face, watching you move. Sadly, I've also memorized every inch of your body, but I still wasn't absolutely one hundred per cent sure . . .' Posy stepped into his arms, took his beautiful face between her hands, and kissed him. 'That was the most seriously sexy thing I have ever seen.'

Flynn kissed her back, passionately, making love to her with his lips.

Eventually, Posy looked up at him. 'It's really funny kissing someone wearing more mascara than me and loads of lipstick.'

'But not unpleasant?'

'Nah . . . A huge turn on, actually. You'll have to give me a private performance sometime.' She smiled shakily into his dark, smudgy eyes and kissed him again. 'Flynn Malone, I love you.'

'Me – or Adam?'

'You definitely, but Adam comes a pretty close second. You were phenomenal, how, I mean, when . . . ?'

'That was down to split-second timing. I knew I had to be outta here and getting ready as soon as Meat Loaf went on – oh, you mean when did I learn the Adam Ant stuff?' Flynn ran his fingers tantalizingly slowly underneath the Madam Za-Za vest top. 'Well, I was heavily into Insect Nation stuff in the eighties when I was a kid. I loved the New Romantics. And I was in all the musicals at high school. Adam always seemed to get the girls going, so I thought it'd be right for tonight. I did it for you.'

Oh, wow. 'So why didn't you tell me?'

'I wanted it to be a surprise, and I wasn't sure if I could pull it off –' he looked down into her eyes. 'I love you, too. You know that, don't you?'

She nodded. She knew. And it still wouldn't be enough to keep him in England if Vanessa had her way.

Flynn pulled her against him. She could feel his heart

455

beating beneath the ruffled shirt, feel the warmth of his body through the leather. She'd recovered from Ritchie marrying Sonia. She'd never recover from Flynn taking Vanessa back to Boston.

'Oi!'

A raucous growl echoed up from the car park and made her peer down into the ever-growing crowd underneath Queen Mab. A huge lumbering figure was forcing his way through the jostling crowds.

He paused in bewilderment, and for a moment his shadow fell across the spilled light from The Crooked Sixpence's open door. Posy blinked. Ignoring the noise surrounding the engine and organ and the roar from the pub, she looked up at Flynn in horror.

'Holy shit! It's Hogarth!'

Chapter Thirty-two

'What the bloody hell is going on in here!!!?'

Hogarth lumbered into the pub just as the Dusty Springfield-alike was reaching the poignant bit in 'Son of a Preacher-Man'. Despite his voice being at its usual decibel level, no one heard him.

Looking round as though he'd stumbled into Sodom and Gomorrah on a bad day, he tried again. 'Have you all gone bloody mad!!!?'

Still no response. All eyes and ears were on Dusty.

Watching him, Lola froze behind the bar. For weeks she'd been rehearsing all the things she'd say to Hogarth when he came back to the village: the trouble was, all the imaginary scenarios had been played out in peace and quiet and relative sanity.

Improvisation seemed to be the only answer.

'Oh, hello,' she shouted cheerily across the heads as Dusty got into her stride again. 'How lovely to see you. This is a nice surprise. Can I get you a drink?'

'No you bloody can't,' Hogarth growled, shoving people aside. 'I wants to talk to you. Now!'

'Now is not the best time, actually. As you can see we're right in the middle of the busiest night of the year. Look, go and sit down and I'll bring you a pint across.'

'Cheeky wench! This is my damn pub!'

'You left me in charge. As manager. I still am. I'll get you a drink and we can talk later. But definitely not now, I'm far too busy. Who's next?'

Grizzling and grouching, blinking at the goings-on around him as though he'd suddenly emerged from a Tardis time-travel trip, Hogarth staggered away looking for a vacant seat.

'Nicely done,' Ellis said, passing Lola a couple of Newcastle Browns.

'Thanks. I'm shaking, though.'

'I usually have that effect on women.'

Lola shook her head. 'Don't. Please. I can't bear it. It's much easier if we just ignore one another.' She looked across at Tatty and the kiddies. 'What else can we do?'

'Christ knows,' Ellis slammed away to serve Amanda and Nikki in their skimpy dresses and didn't even try to look as though he was enjoying it.

Lola watched him with a lump in her throat. She knew he was hurting as much as she was. The sooner she left Steeple Fritton the better for both of them. Or so she kept telling herself. Still, now Hogarth was back she probably wasn't even going to have a choice. It was definitely going to be sooner rather than later.

Dusty Springfield vibrato'd her final notes to tumultuous applause, and the vicar hopped up on to the karaoke podium announcing a half an hour break before the next session of Stars In Their Eyes.

458

Ellis reached across her for the Tia Maria. 'Hogarth seems to have found a seat. Do you want me to – oh, hi, Posy. Decided to join us again, have you?'

'I've got to tell you!' Posy, looking strangely dishevelled and wild-eyed, elbowed her way towards Lola. 'Hogarth's here! I've just seen him outside! I thought I'd better warn you in case –'

'Too late,' Lola motioned with her head towards the far corner beneath the grandmother clock where Hogarth now sat blinking like a large perplexed bear. 'Thanks for the thought though, and, um, what on earth have you got all over your face and neck and chest and hands and –?'

'Oh, er . . .' Posy scrubbed at her cheeks and mouth and looked at the pan-stick smeared across her fingers. 'Um . . .'

Ellis grinned. 'You found him then?'

'Who? No! Not *Adam Ant*?' Lola's eyes widened. 'You fast cat! You've been snogging Adam Ant in the car park? You'll be lynched by every other woman in here. They're still baying for him outside the lavs. Come on then, who was he, and more importantly, *how* was he?'

'Simply stupendously, wondrously, fantastically out of this world.'

'Fairly okay, then?'

Ellis winked at Posy. 'Oh, come on. Are you going to tell her or shall I?'

'You *knew*?' Posy stared at him. 'And you didn't tell anyone?'

'We men like to keep some things secret. Who do you think put him through his paces night after night in the cottage after Gran had gone to sleep? And we had to scour every bloody fetish shop in Berkshire to get the costume together. He did it all for you, seemed to think you'd enjoy it. The bloke's as smitten as hell, even though I've told him he must be mad.' Ellis beamed proudly. 'Pretty bloody good though, wasn't he?'

'Sensational.'

'Will one of you tell me what's happening here?' Lola interrupted. 'I'm beginning to feel as dazed and confused as Hogarth.'

'It was Flynn,' Posy said, clearly trying not to smile.

'Flynn? *Our Flynn?*' Lola leaned across the bar. 'Flynn? No! Really? Wow! Dear God. Okay, now let me give you a word of advice, Posy. You hang on to that boy. He is amazing. No one has the right to be that damn sexy, and fully dressed and in a crowd. Just think what he'd be like in, I mean . . . Well, don't you let that get away.'

'No, Mum,' Posy grinned. 'Oh, and has Hogarth said anything, you know, about this place?'

'Not yet, I didn't give him the chance. But we're going to talk later when this is all over. Now, are you capable of working, or has the devastating Mr Malone robbed you of all your senses?'

'Pretty much . . .' Posy smirked as she ducked under the counter. 'By the way, does Vanessa know about, um, Adam Ant's alter ego?'

Lola shook her head. 'Not an inkling. She's still trying to break down the lav doors to get at him.'

'Shame,' Posy giggled, 'because all she's likely to get in there is Baz from Basingstoke turning into Tommy Steele. Right, who's next?'

The evening roared on. With the karaoke inside and the Limonaire out, all conversations were held at Concorde-thrust level. Lola, helped by a dreamy Posy and a sulking Vanessa, a sad Ellis and a bad-tempered Ritchie, served drinks, exchanged mimed banter, took money, and knew that when she closed The Crooked Sixpence's doors at the end of the night, it may well be for the last time.

When the Cressbeds Estate Seekers, last up on the karaoke dais, were mournfully informing everyone in harmony that 'The Carnival Is Over', Lola was sure she wasn't the only one with tears in her eyes.

'Ladies and gentlemen!' The vicar squawked excitedly, his voice growing louder and louder. 'We've come to the end of Stars In Their Eyes! I didn't know we had so much talent in our village! I'm sure you'll all agree that each and every one of our acts should be packing them in nightly at the Palladium! Well done to everyone who took part! And I'm also sure you'll agree with me that it has been a huge and spectacular success, and something we should add to all the regular Steeple Fritton events!'

There was a roar of approval. Lola didn't dare look across at Hogarth.

'The voting papers have been collected and we'll be announcing the winner and presenting the prize in about fifteen minutes, so there's just time for you to replenish your glasses.'

There was the usual stampede to the bar.

Vanessa, who had returned from the lavatories looking very disappointed, shrugged at Lola. 'It's got to be Adam Ant, hasn't it? Whooo! What a *babe*.'

461

Lola didn't meet Posy's eyes and tried to keep a straight face. 'Um, well, they were all very good.'

'It won't be Adam Ant,' the vicar's wife paused in collecting three sweet sherries. 'I know that for a fact. Too many complaints from the cricket team and the bowls club. The old boys didn't like their wives coming over all frisky over some ponce in make-up.' She blushed. 'I'm quoting there, you understand. Actually, if it were down to me I'd have given him the prize there and then and whisked him off to a four-poster bed for a fortnight. I voted for him six times, but I don't think it'll help.'

Lola and Posy were in helpless giggles.

Florian Pickavance stepped up on to the stage and held his arms Messiah-like in the air. Everyone clapped dutifully. Sonia was beaming and clapping louder than most.

'It is my proud privilege to announce the winner of tonight's Stars In Their Eyes competition. But before I do, I'd just like to say –'

'Bloody get on with it!' Steeple Fritton roared impatiently.

The vicar was making little 'hurry-up' motions with his hands.

Florian looked miffed. 'Oh, okay. The winner, and it was a very close run thing, and after a recount, and there were a lot of spoiled papers for one particular participant and you actually spell the word P-H-W-O-A-R, ladies, and some of the suggestions I think you'll find are anatomically impossible –'

'Get on with it!!!'

Florian frowned. 'Oh, all right . . . The winner, with no offers of Tantric sex sessions as far as I can see, is Meat Loaf!!! Well done, Norrie Nightingale!!!'

462

Lola hugged Posy as the pub erupted once more. Dilys was in tears and Dom trailed his father with the camcorder. Norrie, still in costume, leapt on to the stage, shook Florian's hand, graciously accepted his prize of a free makeover at Rose Lusty's and a massage at Tatty Spry's, then roared into a reprise of 'Bat Out Of Hell'.

Neddy Pink joined in on the accordion as Martha and Mary hurled themselves into yet another improvised dance routine.

'Brilliant,' Posy said to Lola, her lips wobbling. 'Couldn't be better. How wonderful for Dad. Bless him. What a lovely end to a totally, totally amazing day.'

Lola nodded. Well, it had been incredible. So far. But it wasn't over yet, and as far as she was concerned, the worst was still to come.

''ere!' Hogarth lumbered up to the bar. 'I've had just about enough of this. Seeing as you've got half the bloody village working in this pub, I thinks you and me should have that chat. Now.'

'Fine. Come through . . .'

Taking a deep breath, Lola led Hogarth into the back room.

'What the hell's gone on in here?' He gawped at the microwave and the toaster and the juicer and the cleanliness and order. 'You've changed everything.'

Lola nodded. 'You didn't say I couldn't. You didn't say anything at all. You gave me a free hand and –'

'But all of it, all that malarkey out there, all this noncey stuff in here, it must have cost a bloody fortune.'

'It's paid for itself about ten thousand times over,' Lola reached for the ledgers. 'I've kept the accounts.

The books are up to date, and you can check with the accountants if you want to.'

Hogarth flicked through the books, his eyes popping from beneath his heavy lids. 'You made this much? And this is all profit? Since I've been gone?'

Lola shook her head. 'Those figures there are only for one month. The first. It gets better. There, and there and there.' She sat back. 'What I've done is turn this place into a gold mine for you and a focal point for the village. I hope you won't change it back again, the village needs it so much.'

Hogarth made a sort of harrumphing noise, still staring at the neat rows of figures and the double underlined profits at the bottom of each page. Eventually he looked up and nodded slowly. 'You've done well, my duck. Very well indeed. The old pub isn't how I want to see it of course, but I bows to your managerial skills.'

'Thank you. I did wonder if maybe you'd be angry because I'd made so many changes.'

'Mebbe I would have been, if I'd been intending to come back here and take up the reins. But I'm not.' Hogarth fumbled in one of his stained and raggedy pockets and held out a photograph. 'Here. What do you reckon?'

Lola looked at the picture of a young, brown-skinned, pretty girl with her black hair in plaits. Was Hogarth intending to branch out into some sort of escort agency? Or maybe she was a niece? Or a young pop or film star he'd taken a fancy to in his sad and lonely middle-age?

'Um, yes, she's very pretty.'

'Patricia,' Hogarth took the photo back and gazed upon it lovingly. 'My wife.'

'Jesus Christ!' Lola clapped her hands to her mouth. 'Oh, Lord, I'm sorry. I mean, your wife? Heavens . . .'

Of course! Hogarth's 'business trip' had been a visit to one of the more far-flung regions to purchase a mail order bride. Poor Patricia. She must have drawn the short straw.

'Um, and is Patricia with you tonight?'

Hogarth shook his head. His jowls moved in time. 'She's saying goodbye to her family.'

Oh, how heart-rending. All those thousands and thousands of miles away. 'In Indonesia or the Philippines?'

'West Bromwich.' Hogarth looked at Lola as though she were insane. 'Patricia is the daughter of one of my business colleagues in the Midlands. We've been seeing each other for some time. She runs a couple of my shops up there. But now we've tied the knot, we've decided we're going to sell up everything else and have just one little foodie enterprise going. And my share of these,' he tapped The Crooked Sixpence profits with a black-rimmed nail, 'will help nicely.'

Lola tried to assimilate all this information and failed. Still, she wouldn't make the same mistake twice. 'So, you and Patricia are going to open a fast-food caff in Walsall are you?'

'No we're bloody not. We're buying a beach bar in Barbados. Which is why,' Hogarth leaned forward, 'I wants to give you first refusal on this place.'

Lola whimpered. It wasn't fair. It really wasn't fair.

Hogarth frowned. 'There's a nice little flat upstairs. It'll need a bit of doing up, mind. And I'm not going to be ripping you off, duck. I'll only ask a titty little deposit what you'll be well able to afford out of these figures here. The rest you can get as a loan which they'll chuck at yer with what you've done to this place, and then it'll only be a matter of going to the magistrates and changing the name on the licence in a few weeks' time, and away you goes!'

Oh, if only. If only . . .

Lola shook her head. 'Hogarth, thank you. It's a wonderful and generous offer and I'd love to. I love the pub, love the village, it's changed my life. But I'm not stopping. I'm going to be moving on, too.'

'Bugger me!' Hogarth massaged his jowls. 'I'd have thought you'd have snatched me hand off. Look, duck, I'm going to be around for a couple of days until Patricia joins me. Let me know if you changes your mind. If you don't, I'll just put it on the market.'

He held out a rather greasy hand. Lola shook it. She wanted to cry.

Back out in the bar, the evening's entertainment was winding down. Through the open door, the lights of The Memory Lane Fair still zigzagged across the sky, and the noise and shrieks and screams echoed distantly from the common, but the music from the Limonaire had stopped, and Queen Mab was no longer rocking and hissing. Lola could see the frantic packing-up activity going on in the car park.

Inside, the karaoke had been cleared away too, but no one seemed in any hurry to leave. Steeple Fritton was still clustered in the pub, anxious to make the most of the late licence.

Posy was beaming and humming to herself as she mixed Bloody Marys for the coven.

'You've been with Flynn again, haven't you?' Lola said.

'No, not really. Well a bit . . . He's helping Nell and Jack clear up outside.' Posy squirted Worcestershire sauce with relish. 'He thought it might be a good idea to get out of the Adam Ant stuff before Vanessa spotted him. I helped. It was amazing. He's soooo . . .' She stopped, completely starry-eyed, and looked guiltily at Lola. 'Sorry, not what you want to hear right now. So, what did Hogarth say to you?'

'Not a lot. He offered me this place permanently.'

'Oh, wow! That's ace. That means – oh, no it doesn't, does it?' Posy's face crumpled. 'Oh, shit and bloody corruption!'

'Exactly,' Lola said. 'Couldn't have expressed it more succinctly myself. Appalling timing, as with everything else in my life.'

Ellis was pushing his way round the pub, collecting glasses, and Lola allowed herself a moment's delightful staring. She loved him. Stupid, wrong, idiot chemistry, but there it was. He was smiling, as she was, but not with his eyes. Life played such damn cruel tricks . . .

He shoved his way towards the fireplace and was talking to his grandmother. Lola watched as Glad whispered something in his ear that made him laugh. She loved it when he laughed. She didn't want him to stop laughing just because of her . . .

Now he was leaning across Glad and talking to Tatty. Bastard. The kiddies were all blissfully asleep in the

467

empty hearth, curled round one another like puppies. Tatty really was a feckless mother . . .

Ellis was laughing again now. This time with Tatty. Properly. And hugging her. And kissing her.

Lola's eyes misted with tears. It was too much. Really far too much. How could he be so bloody insensitive and cruel? How could he do this?

Posy, also watching, put her arm round Lola's shoulder. 'Git! What the hell does he think he's doing? Oh, holy shit! Now Tatty's coming over here.'

'Can you serve her, please?' Lola said. 'I really don't think I can bear it.'

Tatty flicked her spiral curls and jangled her beads. Her smile was ear-to-ear. 'No, thank you very much, Posy, but I don't want a drink. I want to say something. To everyone.'

Lola leaned back against the optics and held her breath.

Tatty clapped her hands several times, then getting no response, thumped a tankard up and down on the counter top. Eventually the pub stopped yelling at one another and looked at her.

'Hiya!' Tatty beamed. 'I just wanted to make an announcement.'

Lola and Posy exchanged horrified glances.

'I just want to say that as this has been the best day anyone can ever remember, I've decided to make it my special day, too!'

The pub stared at her. Lola stared at the floor.

Tatty beamed even more widely. 'I want to tell everyone that I'm getting married! A week on Saturday! And you're all invited!'

There were a lot of yells of congratulations, more clapping and foot-stamping, a few whistles, and a great deal of bawdy comments.

Lola clung on to the bar and still stared at the floor. It was dipping away from her.

Tatty clapped her hands for silence. 'Baz and I would like you all to be our guests at the registry office and then afterwards here for the reception.'

Bitch, Lola thought viciously. Imagining she's going to have the reception here.

'Lola!' Posy hissed. 'Lola! Are you okay?'

'Yes, yes, of course . . .' She blinked back the tears.

'Lola, she's marrying Baz. Baz from Basingstoke. Tommy Steele. Jimi Hendrix. The massage oil bloke. She's not marrying Ellis – oh, God, don't cry.'

'I'm not crying,' Lola said, as the tears poured down her cheeks. She sniffed and reached for a bar towel to mop at them. 'There. See.'

Tatty smiled beatifically at Lola. 'Weddings make me cry, too. Still, it'll be yours and Ellis's next, won't it? He's so madly crazy about you.'

'But the baby . . .' Lola could hear herself saying the words but had no idea she was actually speaking. 'Ellis's baby?'

'It's not Ellis's baby,' Tatty stroked her bump and looked a bit discomfited. 'I never said it was. I told him I was pregnant, but I never said he was the father. Actually,' she smiled sheepishly, 'I was already pregnant when I met Ellis. But I'd thought Baz would be like the others and just clear off, so I, er, carried on . . .'

Lola couldn't speak. Neither, it appeared, could Posy.

Tatty jingled and rattled a bit more. 'Ellis is gorgeous,

but he never loved me. It was just a bit of fun with me. Not with you, though. He fell in love with you straight away. I knew that, but I also knew that he'd marry me if he thought the baby was his. It would have been lovely, but in the end I couldn't do that to him, or you. It was just so lovely being with him, and I just kept putting it off until I had the courage to tell Baz and see if he'd be willing to accept his child. If not,' she shrugged and artlessly flicked back her ringlets, 'I'd have brought the baby up alone. After all, another one wouldn't have made that much difference, would it?'

Lola still couldn't trust herself to speak.

'But Baz came up trumps?' Posy said, grinning almost as broadly as Tatty.

'Absolutely.' Tatty shot a glance towards the wispy bearded one who was now sitting cross-legged amongst the kiddies in the hearth. 'He's thrilled about the baby and he's the first man who has ever wanted to marry me, and I'm the happiest woman in the world.'

'No you're bloody not,' Lola and Posy spoke together, and laughed.

Lola reached across the bar. 'Congratulations, Tatty.' She kissed the much-blushered cheek. 'I hope you and Baz will be very happy. The champagne's on the house. Posy will see to it. Now if you'll excuse me, there's someone I've got to talk to. Someone who should be told that I've changed my mind about the rest of my life before it's too late.'

'Ellis?' Posy grinned towards the beaming crowd round the fireplace.

'No, not Ellis.' Lola flicked him a lingering smile, then

opened the bar hatch and ducked beneath it. 'At least, not yet. First, I must speak to Hogarth . . .'

Two hours later, Lola wriggled luxuriously on top of her floral duvet and stretched one naked leg out towards the pink-shaded bedside lamp. The muted light played on the three strands of the ankle bracelets. Downstairs, Sunny Dene was still partying, the French doors open to the warm night. The music and laughter floated up into the bedroom.

'Do you want to go and join them?' Ellis asked, lazily tracing the outline of her ribs with his tongue.

'What do you think?' She stroked his black spiky hair.

'Probably that the best parties are for two people who have an awful lot of catching up to do.'

'Exactly,' she smiled contentedly, moving her hand down until it rested on his thigh.

'You do like it, don't you?'

'I love it.' Her fingers traced the outline of the intricate tattoo. 'You know I love it.'

Tatty was a real artist. The tiny heart surrounded by roses and delicately shaded was like a perfect miniature watercolour.

Underneath it, in black scrolled letters, it read 'Goody Goody Gumdrops'.

Ellis eased himself back up the bed and leaned on one elbow looking down at her. 'I knew that when you saw it, when you ran through the words of the song in your head, that you'd know . . .'

And, of course, she had. Eat your heart out, Stephen Sondheim.

'It's the most amazing thing that anyone has ever done for me.' Lola smiled at him. 'But there's something I have to tell you. Lovely as it was of you to ask me, I can't marry you.'

Ellis sat up quickly, looking poleaxed. 'What? Why ever not? And don't you dare give me all that old guff about age difference. We're in love. We'll always be in love.'

'Oh, yes. I know that. I'm as convinced as you are that this will last forever, even if my forever might not have quite as many years left to run as your forever.'

'Then why –?'

Lola laughed and pulled him on top of her. 'Because of your name,' she giggled in his ear. 'I can't be known as Lola Blissit. It sounds just like a stripper.'

'So it does,' Ellis murmured, kissing her, and glancing at the pale blue carnival princess dress draped across the dressing table where it had landed, and then at the navy and silver knickers and bra hanging recklessly from each of the bed knobs. 'How very, very wonderfully appropriate . . .'

Chapter Thirty-three

It was three weeks since the carnival. The beginning of July and still scorchingly hot. Tatty had married Baz from Basingstoke. Lola was the landlady of The Crooked Sixpence. Ellis was temporarily sharing Lola's room at Sunny Dene while they did up the flat above the pub. Hogarth and Patricia had left for Barbados, and Hogarth had given Posy the deeds to the Gear Change shop as a leaving present. And Vanessa still hadn't gone back to Boston.

'But what I don't see,' Posy wrinkled her nose in total non-comprehension, 'is why we need to be doing it like this?'

'Because I want to see London,' Flynn paused in hurling bags and cases into the back of the jeep and grinned at her. 'Because it's a nice gesture to run Ellis and Lola to the railroad station. Because they're our friends and it'll be great to see them off on holiday. Because –'

'Oh, I know all that.' Posy scuffed at Sunny Dene's gravelled drive with the toe of her sandal. 'I agree with all that. What I don't see is why we have to get so dressed up to do it.'

'I'd prefer to be undressed too, but on Victoria station we'd probably be arrested. Not that I know exactly how your indecency laws work over here, of course, but back home they frown upon nudity in public places. And my dad was a cop so I know what I'm talking about, okay?'

She laughed. After all the emotional upheaval, Lola and Ellis were taking a much-needed and well-deserved holiday, and Flynn had volunteered to drive them to the station.

'I'd still be happier in jeans.' Posy looked down in disgust at her short, strappy, swirly dress and the high-heeled sandals. 'It's okay for men. Look at you, drop-dead gorgeous in anything, and black trousers and a white shirt looks perfectly smart-casual. I'm just not a dressy person.'

'You look wonderful. Beautiful. As always.' Flynn slammed the jeep's tail door shut and scrunched round to her side. 'Okay, you want the truth? I thought we might treat ourselves as we'll be in London. Go to a show and then on to dinner, if you'd like to, that is . . .'

'If I'd *like* to?' She stared at him. 'Really? Really, truly? Oh, wow! I've never done that before. That's definitely worth getting tarted up for. In that case . . .' She stood on tiptoe and kissed his cheek. 'I'll forgive you. D'you know, I think I could eventually get to like you.'

'And,' Flynn muttered, running his fingers slowly down her bare shoulder, making love to her with his eyes, 'if we ever had any time alone, I'm sure I could get to like you quite a lot as well.'

They stared at one another. If the looking-and-not-touching had been frustrating before, since the night of the carnival it had been absolute hell.

There had been a few snatched moments and some lust-stirring kisses and a lot of 'I want you, now' eye contact. But there was always, always someone else around. And then, of course, there was still Vanessa.

'Flynn, honey!' On cue, Vanessa stomped out of the B&B's front door. 'Are we ready to go?'

We? Posy frowned at Vanessa. *We?*

'Almost ready.' Flynn peeled himself away from the jeep and didn't look at Posy. 'I'll just go and give Lola and Ellis a yell.'

As soon as he'd ducked through the front door, Posy glared at Vanessa. 'Are you coming with us, too?'

'Sure thing. I've never been to London. I couldn't go home and walk into Opal Joe's and tell everyone I'd been in England and never seen London, could I?'

Well, no . . . Posy supposed she had a point. But that meant there'd be three of them for dinner and a show. Three of them in the jeep on the way home. Three of them. As always.

And Vanessa wasn't even dressed up. In fact Vanessa, in her shorts and cutoff top, was hardly dressed at all.

'Isn't this exciting?' Lola bounced out of the front door, all glossy blonde hair and brown limbs, and looking stunning in a short grey linen shift dress and spiky-heeled grey sandals.

'For you, yes,' Posy nodded. Then she smiled. 'Sorry to be such a grouch. No, it's brilliant and you look amazing, and the ankle bracelets still look pretty perky, too.'

'Thanks. I can't believe any of this has happened.

And I still haven't got a clue where we're going. Ellis won't say anything except we're catching the train at Victoria and going through into France, which sounds wonderful enough, but what happens after that I have no idea.'

'Just enjoy it. You really deserve this. Both of you.'

'Oh, we intend to make the most of every blissful moment, but you don't look exactly on top of the world.' Lola raised her eyebrows. 'Do I gather all is not well on the Vanessa front?'

'Flynn said we're staying on in London after we've seen you off. Dinner and a show, which will be amazing – but she's coming as well . . .'

'God, she's worse than a damn limpet. Do you want me to say something to her? Suggest she stays at home?'

'No. Thanks for offering, but what's the point? Vanessa is determined to hang on to Flynn. He's going back to Boston with her, I know that. I'm just his English flirtation, as she keeps telling me. Nothing serious, apparently.'

'Oh dear.' Lola squeezed Posy's hand. 'Still, look on the bright side. Miss Pump-Up Bra has never made out, as she puts it, with Adam Ant, has she?'

Posy snorted with laughter. 'No, you're right, she hasn't, and if I get my way she never bloody will.'

Flynn and Ellis, grinning and surprisingly smartly dressed too, appeared at that moment, accompanied by Dilys, Norrie, Dom, Mr D and Mr B – and, naturally, Trevor and Kenneth. There was a lot of hugging and 'see you soon' and 'have a good time' and 'send us a postcard'.

Posy kissed and hugged everyone as well even though she'd be back in a few hours. She hugged Trevor and Kenneth twice because they looked so miserable at the sight of the luggage.

'Posy, you sit in the front along with Flynn,' Vanessa said bossily, 'and I'll squeeze up in the back with Lola next to Ellis, which won't be any hardship at all.'

Not sure if Vanessa had been magnanimous because she really was a nice girl, or because she knew it would be sheer bloody frustrating torture for Posy to have Flynn's body so close and so untouchable for the entire journey, she clambered into the jeep's front seat.

They sailed out of Steeple Fritton, with all the coven and everyone else waving them goodbye along the lanes. The shops were busy, and there were cars and people everywhere. Since Letting Off Steam, the village had sprung to life, like the monochrome-to-technicolour bit in *The Wizard of Oz*.

Malvina and her sisters had promised to keep Ellis's various ventures ticking over, and Ritchie and Sonia were unbelievably running The Crooked Sixpence during Lola's absence. There had apparently been a scuffle in the car park late on carnival night, and if Florian Pickavance had a nose bleed and Ritchie had bruised knuckles afterwards, nothing more was ever said.

Glancing in the driving mirror, Posy could see Lola and Ellis sort of glued together, touching all the time, laughing, kissing, talking, hopelessly in love. She was so happy for them. They deserved this bliss. She looked down at Flynn's lean thigh brushing against her bare leg and shivered. If only. Oh, if only . . .

Vanessa, on the other side of Ellis, caught her eye in

the mirror and winked. Posy looked quickly away and wished that the journey was already over.

Having parked the jeep at Victoria and unloaded an unbelievable amount of luggage on to a trolley, they set off into the cavernous station in convoy looking for the right platform.

'This is it,' Ellis said, checking the tickets and suddenly pushing the trolley with Schumacher speed, 'down here. Betcha I get there first.'

He disappeared round a corner, with everyone in hot pursuit.

'Holy shit!' Posy turned on to the platform and skidded to a halt. 'Is that what I think it is?'

Beside her, Lola had gone white.

They stared speechlessly at the train. At the snake of gleaming 1930s carriages adorned in umber and cream livery. At the cream curtained windows tied back with gold tassels. At the lace-clothed tables just visible, with gorgeous softly glowing brass lamps, and vases of orchids and rosebuds.

'Welcome to the Orient Express –' Ellis held out his hand to Lola.

Lola shook her head. 'I'm dreaming . . .'

'No, you're not.' Ellis closed his hand round hers. 'I'd give you the world if I could. I'll spend the rest of my life making you happy, and this is just the start.'

An elegant steward in a white and gold jacket, black tuxedo trousers and white gloves, was walking towards them, ushering them on board. Their luggage had disappeared as if by magic.

The platform was filled with well-dressed people all

behaving impeccably and being welcomed by a rank of stewards. Some of the women were wearing hats and gloves. It was like a scene from *Brief Encounter*.

'Oh my God,' Posy looked at Flynn with tears in her eyes. 'It's totally awesome, oh, sorry, you are such a bad influence on my grammar.'

'But a good influence in other areas?'

'Suppose so . . .'

'That's all right then.' Flynn smiled at her, then motioned his head towards the Orient Express. 'She truly is a beauty. I mean, I knew what Ellis had planned, of course, but I've obviously never seen the train, only pictures. Would you like to have a closer look?'

'Will we be allowed on board?' Posy whispered. She felt she had to whisper. 'Won't they chuck us off?'

'It's not due to leave just yet. I'm sure no one will mind if we explain that we're seeing friends off.'

'He must love her so much. Oh, what a present to give someone.'

'He reckons she's pretty special, yeah. And this was his way of proving it, just in case she had any doubts left,' Flynn said, taking Posy's hand and helping her up the step.

'What about Vanessa? Isn't she going to have a look round, too?'

'Hardly dressed for it, am I, honey?' Vanessa shrugged, looking as stunned as everyone else. 'I'll just have to do my admiring from down here on the platform.'

Once aboard the train, trying not to stare at the other passengers who all looked like *Vogue* models, Posy tiptoed into one of the Pullman carriages and caught her breath. The floors were mosaic, the gleaming walls all intricate inlaid wooden marquetry, the deep upholstered chairs in rich jewel colours. There were Art Deco lamps everywhere, and mirrors, and brass fittings, and fresh flowers. It was truly like stepping back into a different age.

The Orient Express was absolutely the last word in seductive opulence.

Oh, lucky, lucky Lola.

'And they're going to be eating and sleeping on here?' She still kept her voice low. 'All through England into France?'

Flynn nodded. 'And then into Switzerland, across the Austrian Alps, and on to Venice for four days, and, of course, back again . . .'

Posy exhaled. She had never been truly envious of anyone in her life before. But right now she envied Lola with every fibre of her being.

'Hey, wow,' Flynn nodded to her, 'just take a look at the dining car.'

Posy looked. Starched white linen tablecloths, rows of dazzling silver cutlery, sparkling crystal glasses, and yet more softly-shaded brass lamps, and even more fresh orchids. And the menu . . . and the wine list . . .

There was no sign at all of Ellis and Lola.

'Excuse me, sir.' One of the white-coated stewards was beckoning to Flynn. 'A word, if I may?'

Posy froze in horror. They were going to be asked to leave. How embarrassing was that?

'I'll just go and explain to him. Say we're looking for someone,' Flynn touched her face gently. 'Don't look so upset. It'll be fine.'

There was a brief, gentlemanly, low-key conversation and Flynn came back, smiling.

'He was cool about it. Understood. Shall we go and have a quick look at the cabins?'

'Bedrooms?'

'Yeah, I guess . . .'

'Okay. Knowing Ellis, they're bound to be in their bedroom, aren't they? If we're really quick they might still be dressed and we'll be able to look round, and at least we can say goodbye properly.'

With Flynn leading the way, they walked along the glorious, deep-carpeted corridors towards the rear of the train, smiling at other people who were doing the same thing, almost as though they belonged there. Posy's heart was still thudding with the fear of discovery and being asked to leave.

Flynn stopped walking and listened at one of the doors.

He laughed. 'This must be theirs, they're playing bubblegum music – "Goody Goody Gumdrops" – weird stuff. Still whatever turns you on, I guess. I reckon they don't want to be disturbed, so let's have a look along here . . .' Flynn paused outside the next cabin door, slowly pushed it open and peered inside. 'Okay, this one's empty.'

Posy glanced in through the half-open door. There may have been no people, but there was a pile of luggage on the floor. They'd have to be quick. She stepped inside.

Oh, God. To sleep in here would be like heaven.

More glowing inlaid wood on the walls and wardrobes, golden lamps, more flowers, mirrors, a perfectly gorgeous Art Deco bathroom, and the biggest double bed with white linen sheets and a golden eiderdown.

Flynn looked around, then smiled at her. 'What can I say? How perfect is this, huh?'

'Just perfect,' Posy whispered. 'More than a dream. It's a fantasy. A real fantasy.'

'Yeah, well, maybe one day it won't be just Ellis and Lola.' He sighed. 'Say, would you do me a favour?'

'Of course. Anything.'

'Go back out into the corridor and give these to Vanessa through the window. She'll be right outside on the platform.'

'Okay, but –' Posy looked at the keys to the jeep in his hand. 'What is she going to do? Go shopping or something? Come back for us later?'

'Yeah, it's not fair to make her hang around when she wants to do some sightseeing, is it?'

'No, I suppose not.'

Posy stepped into the corridor, leaned through the nearest open window and motioned to Vanessa who was standing a little way along the platform.

Vanessa caught the keys and grinned up at her. 'Pretty cool, is it?'

'You wouldn't believe. God, Lola is so lucky.'

'And not just Lola, honey.'

'No, well, Ellis as well, of course, but this was his surprise for her . . .'

'And Flynn's for you.' Vanessa continued to grin broadly.

Posy shook her head. 'No. We're just looking round. We're not travelling or anything.'

'Oh, yes you are, hon. To Venice on the Orient

Express with the sexiest damn man on the planet.' She clutched the jeep keys in her clenched fist. 'I'll be back to collect you when you return, then I'm off to Boston. Alone. Opal Joe's needs me. Flynn Malone sure as shit doesn't. No hard feelings. Have the best ever time. See ya . . .'

Posy, totally speechless, made a sort of gurgling sound, but Vanessa bounced away down the platform towards the car park, waving as she went.

In a complete daze, she managed to find her way back to the cabin. Flynn was sitting on the bed, grinning at her.

She stared at him. 'I don't believe it.'

'Start believing. It's for real.'

She gave a little scream of delight. 'Really, really?'

'Really, really.'

'And Vanessa . . . ?'

'Vanessa and I talked things through soon after she arrived. She'd changed, but I'd changed even more. We'd been together for a long time, and I owed it to her not to hurt her. Or you. I think she hoped I'd give up on you and go back to Boston with her, but I knew I couldn't even contemplate it. Eventually she realized that and wished me well.'

'So, she doesn't mind?'

'She helped set this up and keep you from finding out, so I guess she approves of my choice.' Flynn pushed his hair away from his eyes. 'She's a tough cookie, and anyway she's got a huge family in Boston and she was very homesick. She wanted to go home. Whereas, all I want for the rest of my life is right here.'

Posy let the words sink in. 'Honestly? Truthfully?'

'Would I lie to you?'

'You lied about the show and dinner.'

His slanting green eyes narrowed. 'Oh, yeah. So I did. Well, we can still abandon this and do the theatre and a restaurant if you'd rather.'

Posy shook her head. 'Tricky one. How soon do you want my answer?'

'Right now.' He pulled her on to his lap, stroking her fingers. 'You know, I still can't believe that we all actually managed to keep this a secret from you, and Lola.'

'Neither can I.' She curled her body into his. 'So, you and Ellis . . . ?'

'Have been planning this for ages. We had to let other people in on it, of course, and I was damn sure someone would let the cat out of the bag. So, this will make up for you missing a night out in London, will it?'

'Oh, yes. Oh, God. Oh, thank you so, so, so much.' Posy slid her arms round Flynn's neck and kissed him gently. Then kissed him again. Because she could. And she wanted to. Desperately. For ever and ever.

He kissed her back, a lot less gently, setting her body on fire.

Shakily, she looked down at his fingers now seductively stroking her thigh. 'And you're not going back to Boston?'

'Oh, one day. For a visit. With you. But otherwise Madam Za-Za got it dead on target.' Smiling, he tipped her gently from his lap into the downy luxury of the bed. 'And I guess I really ought to thank her for that.'

'We can't, not here. This isn't our cabin. All that luggage . . .'

'Is ours. All packed by me and your ma, and Vanessa who actually likes you very much. I think between them they've packed your passport, clothes, make-up and everything else a girl could need for a week of sheer self-indulgence.'

'You're everything I need,' Posy wriggled herself beneath him and started to tug his polo shirt away from his chinos. 'Everything.'

'So, this was worth getting dressed up for, was it?' Flynn said huskily, sliding the straps of her dress over her shoulders. 'And, um, even more worth getting undressed for?'

'Oh, yes, yes, yes. And – oh, thank God for Persephone's owner.'

'Uh?' Flynn paused. 'Persephone? Why do you keep mentioning Persephone?'

'Persephone is a dog. Without Persephone's owner I wouldn't be here. We'd never have met. It's a long story. I'll tell you later. Right now there are far more important things to do . . .'

Flynn kissed her, pulling the strappy dress over her head. 'Oh, yeah, too right, but if our first baby is a girl, Persephone is a pretty neat name.'

'Fine.' Posy wriggled her nakedness against his spectacular body. 'As long as if it's a boy we can call it Adam.'

'Funny you should mention that,' Flynn murmured, shedding the last of his clothes and slowly moving his fingers teasingly and tantalizingly across her skin. 'Because I've packed the Adam Ant outfit, the music and the make-up – just in case you fancied that private performance you requested . . .'